# PRAISE FOR
## *THE TAKEOVER*

"Fast-moving."                    —James Patterson

"Great . . . wonderfully exciting."
                    —*San Jose Mercury News*

"Resembles Robert Ludlum when Ludlum was
fresh. A grand first novel."
                    —*St. Petersburg Times*

"A fast-paced roller coaster of love and lust,
murder and betrayal, politics and business."
                    —*USA Today*

"Offers insider's knowledge of the high-stakes
world of investment banking."
                    —*Wall Street Journal*

"Entertaining and energetic. Superbly taut."
                    —*Financial Times*

"Money, sex, secrecy, conspiracy, killings . . .
exciting."                    —*Mystery News*

"Fast-paced and convincing."    —*Chicago Tribune*

"Enormous wealth, murder, dirty tricks, political
intrigue, colorful villains, relentless pacing.
Enjoy!"                    —*Publishers Weekly*

# Stephen Frey

# THE INNER SANCTUM

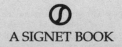

A SIGNET BOOK

SIGNET
Published by New American Library, a division of
Penguin Putnam Inc., 375 Hudson Street,
New York, New York 10014, U.S.A.
Penguin Books Ltd, 80 Strand,
London WC2R 0RL, England
Penguin Books Australia Ltd, Ringwood,
Victoria, Australia
Penguin Books Canada Ltd, 10 Alcorn Avenue,
Toronto, Ontario, Canada M4V 3B2
Penguin Books (N.Z.) Ltd, 182–190 Wairau Road,
Auckland 10, New Zealand

Penguin Books Ltd, Registered Offices:
Harmondsworth, Middlesex, England

Published by Signet, an imprint of New American Library,
a division of Penguin Putnam Inc.
Previously published in a Dutton edition.

First Printing, July 1998
20  19  18  17  16  15  14  13  12

*For Lil*

# Acknowledgments

Special thanks to:

Elaine Koster, Dutton publisher, for her continuing support.

Lori Lipsky, my editor, for her outstanding contributions.

Michael Pocalyko for his tireless assistance with this project.

Cynthia Manson, my literary agent, for all her work.

Stephen Watson for his counsel.

Others I'd like to thank:

Gordon Eadon, Russell DaSilva, Jim Wilson,
Kathy Thornton, Tom Lynch, Barbara Pocalyko,
Arnold Dolin, Laurie Parkin, Mary Ann Palumbo,
Leigh Butler, Kevin Haas, Denise Cronin, Aline Akelis,
Lisa Johnson, Tracey Guest, Alicia Brooks,
Robert Wieczorek, Jr., Barbara Fertig, Betty Saif,
Jim and Anmarie Galowski, Brooke McDonald,
Chris Tesoriero, Jim McPartlan, Pat and Terry Lynch,
Mike Lynch, John Paul Garber, Rick Slocum,
Rick Stoddard, Walter Frey, Kathleen Halligan,
Dileep Bhattacharya and Nita Mathur, Howard Sanders,
Richard Green, Kevin Erdman, Gerry Barton,
Liz Eodice, Marie Patton, Julie Plaza, Brian LaLonde,
Jim O'Connor, Kevin Kops, Louis Frey,
Georgette Gruen, Kiran Sondhi, Mark Rothleitner,
Bob Carpenter, Dennis Hedgepeth, and Tom Gates.

# Prologue

The man sat calmly in a large leather chair at the edge of the lamp's faint arc of light. He inhaled deeply, held his breath for several moments, then slowly tilted his head back and blew thick, pungent smoke toward the ceiling. He was in no rush. He had negotiated many times before and was acutely aware of the value gained from projecting indifference in these situations.

David Mitchell peered through the gloom at the figure in the leather chair, but could distinguish little except the indistinct outline of the man's body and the glow of a cigar tip as it moved. David wanted to push the meeting forward but said nothing for fear he might give away his impatience—and in the process, the deal.

"So what is my incentive?" the man finally asked, his gravelly voice filtering through the smoke-laden air.

"Two million dollars," David answered. "A million when the contract is signed and another million when full production begins."

"Two million dollars." The man chewed on the words

for a moment, then spat them out. "You've asked a great deal of me. I don't think two million is enough." He tapped the cigar gently on the side of a crystal bowl and a perfectly symmetrical inch-long ash fell into it.

"How much *is* enough?"

"More than two million."

David drew in a long breath. He was annoyed at the lack of progress but tried not to make it obvious. "Can you really deliver?" It was a bold question, and despite the dim light he noticed the man's relaxed posture suddenly stiffen.

"Of course I can." The voice was still steady but now conveyed a repressed anger at the younger man's audacity.

"How can I be certain?" David asked quickly, sensing that he had struck a nerve.

"You can't be certain. You just have to trust me."

"I'm giving you two million dollars. I need more than trust, I need guarantees."

"Impossible. There can be no guarantees."

A few moments of uncomfortable silence ensued.

"Perhaps I've made a mistake in coming here." Instantly, David wished he could have taken back the words.

The man reclined into the chair. "Fine," he said confidently. "Then leave."

David felt a drop of perspiration trickle from the end of his eyebrow slowly down the right side of his face. He couldn't enter into a transaction on such fragile terms. But he couldn't walk away from it either.

The man saw David's indecision and made his

move. "What you get for your money, Mr. Mitchell, is my ability to act alone. And don't underestimate how important that is. It's what makes this situation attractive to you. There will be no time wasted on fact-finding missions and no committees adding years to the process." His tone intensified. "Don't think for a minute I'm being greedy requiring more than two million dollars for my participation. If I decide to accept your proposal, what you pay me will be nothing more than a rounding error on your profit statement."

A rush of anticipation surged through David. That was true. The payoff would be immense. "Then how much *do* you require?" He asked the critical question once more.

The man shook his head. "Come back to me with a revised proposal. Work through our mutual acquaintance."

"But time is of the essence. I want to know what you require *now*." David felt the protective wall around his emotions crumbling, and his left eye blinked once—involuntarily.

If the face hadn't been cloaked in shadows, David would have noticed the trace of a smile turn the corners of the man's mouth up. The blink of the eye—the crack in Mitchell's countenance—had not gone unnoticed. "I won't suggest a number. I never do." He pointed the smoldering cigar tip at David. "But I'm becoming impatient. Make certain your next offer is your best offer."

David nodded, realizing there would be no end to the negotiation tonight. "All right, I will."

Mitchell had scored higher on the psychiatric exam

than anyone in the firm's history. Now the man saw why. Despite excruciating pressure, Mitchell was maintaining his demeanor admirably. There had only been that drop of perspiration and tic of his eye. Most of his predecessors had fallen apart by now. "You're doing the right thing, Mr. Mitchell," the man said gently. He didn't give a damn about Mitchell, but spoke the words compassionately to manipulate the younger man's emotions. It was business, that was all. They wanted Mitchell for the long term. They wanted him locked in now, not getting cold feet later and accidentally saving himself. "You're definitely doing the right thing."

"I know," David said, trying to exude confidence.

"Without a big hit like this one they'd crucify you. They'd let you bleed up there on the cross until you expired, then they'd burn you. And believe me, you wouldn't rise from the ashes. There would be no phoenix story here."

"I know," David said again, this time through clenched teeth. The man was absolutely right. The pressure was intense. Without a strong performance, much stronger than he had shown so far, he would be terminated, and there wouldn't be another job—not like this one anyway.

The man puffed on his cigar. Someday, if Mitchell proved worthy, they might allow him insight into the bigger picture. They might let him see why one had to win and the other lose. And they might let him understand how they could make that happen.

David rose from his chair. It seemed obvious the meeting was over.

"Mr. Mitchell."

David turned back as he reached the door. "Yes?"

"I want you to understand two things before you leave."

"And they are?"

"First, I've never used my position this way before. I am entirely ethical. I am not corrupt."

David's silence spoke volumes.

The man's eyes narrowed as he sensed skepticism. "Second, I'm considering your proposal because I believe it is in the country's best interest. Money is not the driving force in this situation, not my primary motivation."

For an instant David thought he saw the face, but then it faded into darkness again. "What are you talking about?"

"My paramount concern is national security. And I'm willing to use any means necessary to achieve that end. That is why I'm willing to consider your proposal. The money is secondary. Do you understand?"

"Yes." David stared at the dark figure, marveling at the man's ability to rationalize. At his ability to avow with sincerity that $2 million—or whatever the number turned out to be—wasn't the real issue. "I'll be back to you tomorrow through our mutual acquaintance."

"Good."

David stepped into the deserted corridor and closed the door. Cool fresh air rushed to his face, and for a few moments he stood there cleansing his lungs of cigar smoke, allowing his heart rate to slow down. It had taken immense courage to proceed with this meeting. Christ, the whole thing could have been a setup.

Finally he began walking away, the sound of his hard soles on marble echoing into the far recesses of the corridor. But it hadn't been a setup, and now the final piece was almost in place. By tomorrow night all the hard work, planning, and payoffs would begin returning dividends.

# Chapter 1

"That's quite a caseload you're lugging home tonight, Jesse." Neil Robinson, branch chief of the city's Office of Internal Revenue, nodded at the young woman's overloaded bag as the two of them threaded their way through the after-work crowd spilling onto Baltimore's downtown sidewalks.

"Oh, I just threw a bunch of old files in there before we left to impress you," Jesse laughed, as they dodged several men in suits coming around a corner. "I want you to think I'm working hard so you'll get me a new grade and I can get a raise."

"You've got to be kidding. I just got you your new grade two months ago. And you got your raise then." Robinson tried to sound annoyed but turned his head so she wouldn't see him smile. He knew full well the files in her bag were active. Jesse Hayes and her friend Sara Adams were the hardest working revenue agents at the branch. But somehow Jesse consistently combined her amazing efficiency with a contagious smile and a positive attitude—something Sara couldn't always manage.

"Pull a few strings for me, Neil," Jesse said, yanking the bag's strap higher on her shoulder. "Aren't I worth it?"

"Of course you are, but that isn't how the government works. They don't care what you're worth, just how long you've been around."

"That doesn't sound very encouraging." Jesse grinned. "How am I going to feed my four children?"

Robinson raised an eyebrow. "Jesse, when did you have children?"

"When I decided this would be a good time to go for another raise."

Robinson shook his head and laughed, then checked his watch. Five after six. He was five minutes late for his meeting with Gordon Roth. Robinson prided himself on being punctual, but tonight he was consciously late. Hopefully, Roth wouldn't wait around. "Where are you headed, Jesse?"

"Class."

"Oh, right, business school," Robinson reminded himself. They stopped at a corner waiting for the light to change. "A master's degree in business." He looked at her proudly. "Sounds pretty good, doesn't it?"

"It'll sound a whole lot better when I'm finished."

The light changed and they moved ahead with the crowd.

"How's school going?" Robinson sensed her frustration.

"Fine, I guess. I shouldn't complain, but sometimes it isn't easy to sit in class for three hours after a day at the office." She sighed. "I hope having an M.B.A. will be worth all of this."

"Have patience," he said paternally. "It will be worth it in the long run."

Jesse recognized the delicate admonishment. "I know I shouldn't sound so frustrated, Neil. It's just a lot of pressure."

"Sure it is, but you have a way of finishing things you start. And nothing worth anything in life comes easily." He pulled a handkerchief from his suit pocket and wiped perspiration from around his mouth. Perhaps he should just skip the meeting with Roth altogether.

Jesse smiled at Robinson as they hurried up the street. They didn't have the typical supervisor-subordinate relationship. He was her boss, but a true friend as well. "You know I'll always be grateful to you for writing that recommendation, Neil. I think it made the difference in my being accepted at the Maryland Business School."

"No, you got yourself in, Jesse."

"Well, it was extremely important. A woman in the admissions office told me the recommendation had a big impact." Jesse paused. "And it's nice of you to let me leave early one day a week to attend the municipal finance course."

Robinson held up a hand. "Not a problem. Hell, you do more by noon than most of the others do in a full day. And that's not a criticism of them. They work hard too." For a moment Robinson and Jesse were separated as they made their way through a large tour group milling about in front of a hotel entrance.

"When do you graduate?" he asked, as they came back together.

"Next June."

"Then it's off to New York, right? To work for one of the investment banks up there."

Jesse hesitated. Going to New York would mean leaving the IRS, and she didn't feel entirely comfortable about her boss knowing that her ultimate goal was to resign. But they had talked about the matter several times and he had steadfastly encouraged her to pursue the new career. "That's my hope. But there's so much competition for those jobs."

"Don't worry. I know people in New York who can help. I'll make a few calls at the appropriate time. It's amazing how many friends I've developed in the financial community since becoming a senior official at the IRS."

They exchanged knowing glances. Everyone wanted a friend at the IRS.

"I couldn't ask you to help me again, Neil," she said loudly as a commuter bus roared past. "You've already done so much."

"Stop. I'm glad to help. I respect how hard you've had to work to get where you are. I had to do the same thing. I had people help me, and I promised myself to do the same thing for others when I got to this level, at least for people who deserve it."

"I really appreciate that, Neil."

Robinson slowed down as they came to the next corner. "Light Street." He nodded at the street sign as he wiped his mouth with the handkerchief once more.

"This is where I get off. I've got a meeting at the Hyatt Hotel in a few minutes."

"Are you all right, Neil?" Jesse had noticed the perspiration above his upper lip even as they were leaving the office. It was a sure sign he was nervous about something.

"What do you mean?"

Robinson had seemed distracted all day, now that she thought about it. "Is anything bothering you?"

"No, everything's fine." He touched her elbow gently, as if to reassure her. "I hope class goes well. And keep your chin up. It'll all work out."

Jesse smiled. "Thanks." Neil Robinson was a wonderful man. There was no way she could ever repay him for all his kindness. "See you tomorrow." She began to walk away.

"Oh, Jesse!"

She stopped and turned back. "Yes?"

He began to reach into an inside pocket of his suit jacket, then slowly let his hand fall to his side. For a few moments he gazed at her intently as pedestrians flashed between them.

"What is it, Neil?" she asked.

"Nothing," he said finally. "I'll see you tomorrow at the office." Then he waved and walked away.

Jesse shrugged, shifted the bag to the other side of her body, and headed for her car.

Five minutes later, Robinson was standing in the Hyatt's third-floor lobby, scanning the crowd.

"Mr. Robinson?"

Robinson felt a tap on his shoulder. "Yes?"

"I'm Gordon Roth."

"Oh, hello." Disappointment overtook Robinson as they shook hands. He had been so close to walking out. "Please call me Neil." Roth was not what Robinson had anticipated. Sandy blond hair fell to the bottom of Roth's suit collar in the back, and he wore a neatly trimmed beard and mustache. "You aren't exactly what I expected. I thought you guys all had crew cuts and no facial hair."

A thin smile crossed Roth's face, as if he found irony in Robinson's remark. "Why don't we find a place where we can have some measure of privacy?" Roth pointed toward a small table in a secluded corner of the lobby. "How about over there?"

"Okay."

The two men threaded their way through the couches, tables, and chairs of the hotel lobby, now packed with business types. Finally they reached the table in the corner, where the hum of conversation was not so loud.

"Is this all right?" Roth asked.

"Sure."

Here they enjoyed a panoramic view of Baltimore's inner harbor. It should have been a popular spot, and as Robinson sat down he wondered how this table could still be available with the room so crowded. "We certainly have a nice look at the USS *Constellation*," Robinson observed, pointing down at the Revolutionary War ship—now a maritime museum—moored in the harbor.

"Mmm." Roth had no interest in the history floating beneath him. "Waitress?" He motioned to a young woman.

The woman finished taking another table's order and moved toward Roth. "What can I get for you, sir?"

"I'll have a scotch and water, Glenlivet if you have it." Roth nodded at Robinson. "What would you like?"

"A beer. A long-neck National Premium would be perfect. Nothing tastes better than a cold beer at the end of a hot, humid Baltimore day, Gordon."

"Right." Roth smiled insincerely as he turned to the waitress. "You'll bring a nice chilled glass for my friend, won't you?"

"Of course." The waitress scribbled on her order pad and moved quickly toward the bar.

Robinson admired the *Constellation* again, then shook his head. He shouldn't be here. He had piles of paperwork in need of attention. Being branch chief was no bargain—not even in September, five months after the April rush. But Gordon Roth had been extremely persistent over the phone the last few days, and Robinson wanted to keep this thing quiet.

Roth crossed his legs and relaxed into his chair. "Tell me, Mr. Robinson, why are you so interested in Elbridge Coleman?"

Robinson felt his pulse accelerate instantly. Roth was picking up exactly where he had left off on the phone.

"Why have you pulled all of Coleman's personal tax returns for the last seven years? Why have you pulled the corporate tax returns for Coleman Technology?" Roth launched the questions rapid-fire.

A strange, almost inaudible alarm triggered deep

within Robinson's brain. Roth was pushing too hard, too fast. "I need to see your identification," he said firmly.

Roth reached inside his suit coat, removed a large black leather wallet, and flipped it open so Robinson could see the heavy gold badge and photograph inside. "As I said over the phone, I am special detail to the Assistant Attorney General." Roth flipped the wallet closed and replaced it inside his suit pocket.

For a moment Robinson considered asking for another look at the identification. He was suspicious because Roth had snapped the wallet shut so quickly. But the badge had seemed official enough, and how in the hell was he going to tell if it was authentic, even if he did get another look? The second request would only irritate Roth, and Robinson wanted no part of that. Within the federal government the Justice Department had the reputation of being hard-nosed and vindictive.

"Let me ask *you* something, Gordon," he said. "Why are you so interested that I've pulled a few tax returns?"

Roth nodded. "That's a fair question." He tapped the arm of the chair with his fingers before answering, as if carefully considering how much to reveal. "As you know, Elbridge Coleman is running as the Republican Senate candidate against the incumbent Democrat, Malcolm Walker, in the upcoming November election." Roth automatically lowered his voice as he noticed the waitress returning with their drinks. "We think we may have uncovered some irregularities with Coleman's campaign. Therefore, we want to know what, if anything, you have. We assume you aren't pulling those tax returns just for something to do."

Robinson sat up in his chair. "Irregularities?" That sounded interesting. Perhaps this was going to confirm what he had found.

The waitress finished pouring beer into Robinson's chilled glass and walked away to take another table's order.

"Yes, irregularities," Roth said, after the woman had gone.

"The nature of your suspicion does interest me, I have to admit." Robinson tried to contain his enthusiasm. "What do you have?"

Roth deflected the question for a moment by raising his glass. "To cooperation by different units of government." He took a long drink of scotch.

"Right." Robinson took a sip from his beer as well. "But what do you have on Elbridge Coleman?" He was becoming impatient.

"No." Roth shook his head. "First I want to know why you are pulling Coleman's tax returns."

The alarm intensified. Listen to it, Robinson told himself. "So much for cooperation within the government, I guess." He grimaced and took another swallow of beer.

For a moment Roth said nothing, just stroked his beard. Finally, he pointed a finger at Robinson. "You've done very well for yourself. IRS branch chief—that's a nice position for a man who grew up in the projects of Jefferson Heights."

Robinson nodded warily. He had pulled himself out

of the predominantly black ghetto with a great deal of hard work. But why did Roth know so much?

"And from what my superior tells me, they have bigger and better things planned for you. I wouldn't think you'd want to jeopardize all of that."

"How am I jeopardizing anything?" Robinson was annoyed by the other man's arrogance.

Roth rolled his eyes, as if the risk should be clear. "Mr. Robinson, I didn't know it was standard procedure for an IRS branch chief to perform an audit completely on his own, especially an audit of a man running for the United States Senate. I thought that duty fell to the revenue agents. From what we understand, you haven't assigned this audit to any of the agents reporting to you. You have requested the returns very quietly. You haven't told anyone else about it at all."

Robinson felt his temper rising. Roth probably had the office bugged and the phone tapped—it was the only way he could be so well informed. And Justice could put those things in place very easily. "That's correct. I haven't told anyone." Robinson was angry, but uneasy too. It *was* far from common practice for a branch chief to pull tax records on his own. Revenue agents were supposed to initiate audits, and only with justifiable cause—unless the audit was part of an authorized random program. The senior people were constantly worried that the ACLU would uncover an example of an IRS employee using the tax code to carry out a personal vendetta.

"I doubt you'd want your senior people in Washington to know you were initiating audits of Senate candidates without their prior approval." Roth launched another missile. "That could become a political nightmare for you if anyone just happened to find out." The insinuation was clear.

Robinson had met only a few Justice people, but they were all the same—arrogant and full of information. Unfortunately, in this case, the information was accurate. If his superiors in Washington were to find out what he had done, it *would* become a political nightmare. One that could damage the solid reputation he had worked for many years to build.

The missile had found its mark, and the effect was etched into Robinson's face. "So why have you pulled the returns?" Roth asked triumphantly, as if there was no doubt the question would finally be answered.

The alarm was screaming at Robinson now. Tell Roth nothing. "I had a gut feeling."

"What do you mean?"

"Elbridge Coleman came from nowhere. He showed up back in the spring, started burning a whole lot of money on ads, and walked all over the other Republican candidates in the primary. Some of them were seasoned politicians with name recognition, and he crushed them. Now Coleman is running strongly against Malcolm Walker in the general election because he continues to buy advertising and, in my opinion, votes. Malcolm Walker is a popular man in Maryland. Coleman must be spending a lot of dollars to do as well in the polls as he is. Maybe there's something else going on."

"There's nothing wrong with spending one's cash, Mr. Robinson. Coleman made a great deal of money when he took his software company public. If he wants to spend it on a Senate campaign, I think he's allowed to do that. It was a free country last I heard."

"Coleman started that company less than four years ago knowing absolutely nothing about software. Now he's sold sixty percent of it to the public for fifty million dollars and suddenly he wants to move Malcolm Walker out of the Senate. Walker is an outspoken critic of the Defense Department, and I've ascertained that Coleman Technology quietly does a great deal of business with several large defense firms. It doesn't take a rocket scientist to figure out that the Pentagon brass and the senior executives at the big defense firms wouldn't mind seeing Walker defeated and Coleman take his place." Robinson showed his cards. The alarm went eerily silent.

Roth leaned forward. "So you think Coleman is the tip of some sort of conspiracy."

"It's possible." Robinson paused. "And I intend to find out."

"Sure it's possible." Roth laughed sarcastically. "Seriously, if people were going to go to so much trouble to get Walker out of the Senate, why wouldn't they just kill him? It would be much easier and cost a lot less money."

"Maybe they will."

"You thought this up yourself, did you?"

"Yes, I did." Robinson glanced around uncomfortably.

Roth lowered his voice. "Does your interest in Coleman have anything to do with the fact that you are black and so is Malcolm Walker? That you want to see Walker beat a man like Elbridge Coleman who represents the establishment?"

"What?" Robinson almost spilled his beer.

"Malcolm Walker is a respected man in Maryland, a man blacks hold up as a role model. Maybe you just want to do your part to see him stay in the Senate. To see him remain a role model for your people." Roth hesitated. "Or maybe it runs even deeper than that."

"Look, I've had just about enough—"

Robinson was interrupted by a scream from the bar. He turned quickly in his chair to see what had happened.

"You're an ass!" a young woman yelled at a man wearing a charcoal suit and red tie. "You aren't going to talk to me like that and get away with it!"

The man shrugged nervously as the lobby went silent and he became the focus of the crowd's attention. Suddenly the woman reached toward the bar, picked up her glass and splashed its contents in his face, then ran for the exit.

Robinson watched the commotion a moment longer, then turned back to face Roth, who seemed to have found the incident amusing. Robinson picked up his glass. He was irritated and took a long swallow. "Gordon, I don't appreciate your accusation that I would use my position at the IRS to investigate Elbridge Coleman because he is white and Malcolm Walker is black." Justice Department or not, Robinson wasn't going to put up with a comment like that.

Roth waved a hand. "I'm sorry. It was an inappropriate remark. You have every right to be angry. Look, the truth is that we suspect there might be something strange going on in Coleman's campaign. I don't think we at Justice would go as far as to suspect conspiracy, but we want to do some more digging." Roth placed his glass down on the table. "Are you all right, Mr. Robinson?"

Robinson felt his pulse suddenly racing out of control, his heart beating as if it would burst. "I don't know. I'm feeling a little light-headed." He loosened his tie and undid the top button of his shirt. "God, my tongue!"

"What's wrong?"

"It's so dry I can barely feel it." He slurred his words as his tongue stuck to the roof of his mouth.

"Maybe I should call a doctor."

"No, I . . . God!"

Roth stood, deliberately knocking over Robinson's beer glass. "What is it?"

Robinson grabbed his chest. "My heart," he gasped. "Jesus Christ, it feels like somebody's stabbing me with a knife!" He stood up, wavered for a moment, then stumbled forward and fell to the carpet.

Roth turned to the crowd. "Help us here!" he yelled. "Is anyone a doctor?"

A man from a nearby table jumped up and raced toward them, dropping to his knees as he reached the stricken Robinson. A waitress ran to call 911. People stood, pushing forward to see what was going on. And without attracting attention, Gordon Roth slipped through the onlookers to the outer edge of the crowd, then walked calmly to the escalators.

Robinson gazed up at the young man about to administer CPR. The table in the corner of the lobby had been available because Roth wanted a secluded place in which to operate. Roth had made certain the waitress brought a glass for Robinson's beer because it was easier to drop poison in a wide-mouth glass than a thin bottle. And the woman throwing the drink in the man's face had been the diversion. It had given Roth the opportunity to slip the drug into the glass undetected. Everything made so much sense now. If only Robinson had listened to his instincts, to that alarm screaming at him from within.

The young man bent over to breathe oxygen into Robinson's lungs. It wouldn't make any difference, Robinson knew. They were too efficient, too careful. There would be no second chances. Then his eyelids fluttered shut, and he was gone.

A few moments later, Gordon Roth climbed into the passenger side of the white Explorer parked on a side street near the hotel.

"So, how'd I do?" The young woman who had thrown the drink in the bar smiled at Roth from the driver's seat.

"An incredible performance." He leaned across the seat and kissed her, pausing to stroke the pearl necklace he had purchased for her earlier in the day. "Oscar potential."

"Really?"

"Really."

The young woman giggled. "Now what?"

"Let's have some dinner."

The police officer moved slowly toward the Explorer, parked beneath a light near the loading dock of a deserted warehouse. His senses were on alert, but he wasn't overly concerned. It was probably nothing more than a drunk couple fooling around. It happened here in the Fell's Point area all the time. Probably just a man and woman who had met at a nearby bar and couldn't go home because they were both married and were too cheap to rent a hotel room. The policeman shook his head. What a wonderful world.

He flashed his light inside the truck and instantly realized the situation was much more serious than he had anticipated. A young woman sat behind the wheel, hands at her sides, head back, eyes wide open but unseeing, her throat slashed from ear to ear.

Gordon Roth watched the officer from the darkened window of an abandoned building overlooking the loading dock. As the officer trotted back to his squad car to radio for assistance, Roth removed the wig, beard, and mustache, stuffed them into a bag already containing the bloodied clothes he had worn to kill the woman, and headed toward the stairs.

# Chapter 2

One day was much like another to an IRS revenue agent. There were audits, reviews, and paperwork today, just as there had been yesterday, just as there would be tomorrow. Jesse sighed as she surveyed the mess covering the top of her desk. It never got any better. No matter how hard she worked there was always more to do.

She leaned back in her chair and scanned the front page of the *Wall Street Journal*. A short article about the initial public offering of a high-tech company caught her eye. The company had raised $400 million dollars yesterday by selling 40 percent of its stock to public investors. The entrepreneur who had started the firm ten years before could retire forever if she so desired. And the investment banking firms managing the transaction—Goldman Sachs and Merrill Lynch—had earned almost $25 million in underwriting fees.

Jesse shook her head as she surveyed her small, drab office. Investment banking in New York City. Now that would be exciting. Her $28,000-a-year government salary would be a drop in the bucket to those people.

It wasn't that she was greedy. It was simply that she knew what it meant to go without, and it wasn't any fun. She had grown up in Glyndon—a rural town north of Baltimore—with her nine brothers and sisters. While her classmates had spent weekends buying clothes, records and tapes, she had worked at a local stable making money to help put food on the family table. Her father—a lineman for the phone company—worked hard, but with so many mouths to feed a lineman's pay didn't go far, even with the overtime. And her mother had stayed home to care for the children and pursue her lifelong dedication to the Catholic Church.

Jesse reread the article. What would it be like to earn several hundred thousand dollars a year? Was it such a bad thing to want that?

"Jesse?" Sara Adams leaned into the office and knocked on the open door.

"Hi, Sara. Come in." Jesse put the paper down. She disliked being interrupted during her morning perusal of the *Journal*, but her expression gave away no hint of irritation. She made it a practice to be as polite as possible. Treat others as you would have them treat you, her mother had always said. Jesse had always followed that advice.

"Reading about investment bankers again?" Sara pointed at the *Journal* as she sat down in a chair before the desk.

"How'd you know?"

"I saw the article on Goldman and Merrill taking that high-tech firm public. I know how much you want to do that." There was distaste in Sara's tone.

"Is that so wrong?" Jesse sensed the resentment.

"From what I've heard, the people working at those investment firms in New York are driven by nothing but money. It's a dog-eat-dog world in a dog-eat-dog city."

"So you don't think I'd survive?"

"Forget about survival, I'm talking about quality of life. All they ever do is work. Fourteen hours a day, seven days a week. They're miserable, even if they don't realize it. Just as you would be if you got a job up there." Sara adjusted an earring. "And any free time you had would be spent in that cement jungle called the Big Apple. You were raised in the country, for crying out loud. In Glyndon, Maryland. You'd hate New York City."

"I could do it," Jesse said quietly.

"You're one of the nicest, most genuine people I've ever met. Why would you compromise yourself? Just for the money?"

"Is it so bad to want comfort? To want a few nice things? I'd like to be able to help my mother out, too. She's getting old, and it's hard for her to stay in the house now that she's alone. She needs to be in a retirement community, but she doesn't have the money. God knows I can't provide that for her on twenty-eight thousand a year and take care of myself too." Jesse's frustrations rose to the surface.

"How are you paying for school?" Sara was relentless. "It's got to be costing a lot of money."

"Loans."

"So you might be making more money when you graduate, but you'll have all those loans to pay off."

"It'll be worth it in the long run." Neil's words from last night.

"Be happy where you are with what you have. Take the time to live a little." Sara's face brightened. "Speaking of which, I want you to come with me tonight to the Mount Washington Tavern. This new guy I've been dating has a cute friend. I told him all about you, and he wants to get together. He's a banker, Jesse. You know, stable with money. The type you ought to be dating these days." Her tone grew maternal.

"I'm sorry, Sara. I'd like to come out with you, but on short notice we're having a guest lecturer tomorrow night in one of my classes. The woman is a legend in the financial community, and I need to prepare. I don't want to look foolish in front of her if I'm asked a question."

"That's exactly what I'm talking about. You never have time for yourself. It's rush, rush, constantly. You're going to drive yourself crazy going to business school three nights a week just to make it to New York. It can't be worth all the stress."

"I think it is."

"Well, it doesn't matter anyway. You couldn't leave the branch."

"What's that supposed to mean?"

"You wouldn't be able to tell Neil Robinson you were resigning. You're his golden girl."

"He respects your work just as much as he does mine, Sara."

"He wouldn't want to hear you were leaving," Sara said firmly.

"I think he'd be happy for me." She didn't want to tell Sara the extent of Robinson's support. Sara might get the wrong idea. "He'd encourage me to go to New York."

"I wouldn't be so sure." Sara hesitated. "Look, I know I sound negative. I'm sorry about that. I know you're working really hard with the job and school, and I admire your drive and determination." The hard edge in her voice faded away. "Come out with us tonight," Sara urged. "We'll have fun. Besides, you need to get back into the dating scene. We're both going to be thirty pretty soon, and it won't be easy to find a husband after that. Look at the statistics."

Jesse wadded up the napkin and tossed it at Sara. "God, you are a perfect revenue agent, aren't you? So caught up in statistics and probabilities."

"Good morning, ladies." Helga Ketzer's thick German accent preceded her through the doorway. "Here is the file you wanted, Jesse," she said loudly, moving into the office. Helga, the secretary Jesse shared with several other revenue agents, was short, stout, and opinionated. She placed the heavy file on the desk and turned to go.

"Wait a minute, Helga," Sara called. "We need your opinion on something."

Helga turned back around. "Yes?"

"Don't do this, Sara," Jesse implored. She hated being the center of attention, even with people she knew well.

Sara ignored the plea. "We were just talking about Jesse's love life, Helga."

"Please don't," Jesse begged.

"And I was saying how she needed to start dating again," Sara continued. "How she needs to find someone."

Helga put her hands on her hips and looked at Jesse. "Yes, child, you must find a husband soon. It's such a waste for you to be alone. You are so nice, and beautiful. Well, you could be beautiful." The older woman brought her hands to her mouth and laughed. "Did I say that?"

"Excuse me?" Jesse managed a smile through her embarrassment.

Helga moved close to Jesse. "You have natural beauty. Blond hair, blue eyes, high cheekbones, and beautiful skin. But you need to pay more attention to yourself." Her voice became more forceful. "You always wear your hair up in a bun. Let it down once in a while. Use some makeup. And these clothes you wear, they are so loose and baggy. Let men see what you have. A little cling on a curve never hurt. You know that's what they see first. It's a shame but it's true."

"Helga!" Color rose to Jesse's cheeks.

Helga pointed at Sara. "Jesse, you should do as Sara does. Wear makeup and fix your hair." A sly smile crossed the older woman's face. "Of course, if you fixed yourself up, you would have the men's undivided attention, so perhaps Sara wouldn't want you to do that."

"What?" It was Sara's turn to be embarrassed.

Jesse laughed quietly. Helga was a piece of work.

"Sorry, Sara, I call things as I see them." And Helga was gone, humming to herself as she walked away.

Sara stood up, as if to follow Helga. "Sometimes that woman makes me so mad."

"Hey, you invited her into the conversation," Jesse pointed out. "Besides, she just likes to talk. You know it doesn't mean anything."

"That's easy for you to say. She said you would have the men's undivided attention." Sara made a face as she moved toward the door. "Hey, how about a little clothes-shopping at lunch? I heard about a great new boutique in the Galleria."

"Sounds fun." Sara was always shopping. She had inherited $20,000 from her grandmother last winter and was burning through it quickly.

"Well, I guess I'd better get back to work." Sara sighed. "We'll talk more about tonight at lunch. We haven't gone out at night together in a long time." She hesitated. "I miss that."

"I'll tr—" Jesse's computer interrupted her, beeping three times in rapid succession, indicating that she had a new E-mail. She tapped on the keyboard and retrieved the message.

"What does it say?" Sara paused at the door. "Is this evidence of an office romance I don't know about? Are you exchanging secret E-mails with someone?"

"No, it's about a meeting I have to attend later today."

"Well, that's not very interesting. See you at lunch," she called as she walked out.

"Right." Jesse made certain Sara was gone, then her eyes raced back to the screen.

If you are reading this, something has happened to me. You must pick up where I've left off.

Go to the Greyhound bus station in downtown Baltimore. Find locker 73. The combination is 22-31-7. Inside is a key to my house on the Severn River near Annapolis. The address is 6 Gull Road. In the lower left-hand drawer of the desk in the den is a file of information I have obtained regarding a U.S. Senate race. There is a cover memo on top of the file outlining certain suspicions I have about the race. It's being manipulated by outside interests. The supporting documentation will explain.

Get there as fast as you can. I've never told anyone about my house on the river, but they will still find out about it quickly enough because they can find out anything about anyone. They are that powerful. I'm sure they've already been through my home in Baltimore. Be careful. Trust no one.

Neil

For several moments Jesse didn't blink as she read the message over and over. Finally the words blurred on the screen. And then she smiled. Of course. The day after tomorrow was her birthday. Her coworkers were setting her up. They were going to have a wonderful time watching her run out of here and surprise her at Neil's river house, or maybe at the bus station.

Suddenly Jesse heard a sharp cry from the hallway, then Helga appeared in the office doorway, hands over her mouth.

"My God." Helga's cheeks were wet with tears.

"What is it?" Jesse flipped off the computer screen.

Helga sobbed, unable to speak.

Jesse rose from her chair. "What is it, Helga?" she asked more firmly, moving out from behind the desk to comfort the older woman.

Helga dropped her hands from her face. "I have terrible news," she said hoarsely. "It's Neil Robinson. He died of a heart attack last night in the lobby of the Hyatt Hotel."

# Chapter 3

The Hughes Building—a modern, glass-encased edifice—rose fifteen stories above the heart of Towson, an upper-middle-class Baltimore suburb located just north of the city limits. On a clear day David Mitchell could see Baltimore's skyscrapers rising out of the downtown area twenty miles from his ornate top-floor office. He could see Glen Owens too—the poverty-stricken east Baltimore row-house neighborhood where he'd grown up.

When David had first joined Sagamore Investment Management Group four years ago, he'd brought his widowed mother up to his tastefully decorated office to see its dark wood paneling, antiques, and rich Oriental rug. The blue bloods had enjoyed the apple-pie gesture—and his mother's polyester pantsuit—but David paid no attention to their snobbish smirks as she turned away after shaking their hands. She wanted to see what her youngest son had made of himself, and he wanted to show her.

David had kissed her good-bye in the lobby after her short visit. She had been so proud. He shut his eyes tightly. What would she think of him now if she knew? He hated to think about it.

Sagamore managed almost $200 billion and would have ranked as one of the country's largest investment funds, except that the firm shunned publicity and didn't publish the figure. In their endless search for financial information, *Forbes* and *Fortune* used every means available to determine the number, but only a few people at the firm knew, and they would not divulge it during the infrequent interviews they gave the press.

Sagamore did not accept money from just anyone, and so it didn't have to make the public filings required of Fidelity, Vanguard, and the other huge money managers. Sagamore took cash exclusively from wealthy individuals and corporate pension plans in private transactions, and only after the executive committee deemed the investor worthy. The investor list was a closely guarded secret too, known only by the same short list of people who knew the amount of money the firm managed.

Investors had to pass an extensive application process before Sagamore would accept their money, but it was worth enduring such unusual treatment because of the firm's extraordinary success. Begun in 1979, the firm had struggled initially. But in the last fifteen years it had beaten the return on the Dow Jones Industrial Average every year, and usually by a wide margin. A million dollars invested with Sagamore in 1984, its first year of stellar results, would have been worth almost $100 million today.

David had joined Sagamore at twenty-eight, upon

earning his M.B.A. from the University of Virginia. After two grueling years of the case method he had graduated number three in his class. Numbers one and two had hurried to Wall Street, but Sagamore had enticed David home to Baltimore with a generous compensation package, the important attraction of avoiding the hardships of a New York City lifestyle, and the implicit guarantee that the pressure to perform at Sagamore would be nothing compared to what was required by the Street. David particularly liked that aspect. It wasn't that he couldn't take the pressure, he simply had no desire to devote every waking hour to his job.

As was customary at Sagamore, he had spent a year as a portfolio assistant, then become one of fifteen full portfolio managers, initially responsible for $5 billion dollars of the firm's money, then, six months later, $10 billion. The work was stimulating, exciting, and, though the senior people had advertised differently during the recruiting process, every bit as pressure-packed as a Wall Street position.

Every portfolio manager's performance—no matter how senior the individual—was reviewed monthly and rated on an absolute basis against the Dow Jones index and on a relative basis against other Sagamore portfolio managers. On the first day of each month the firm sent an E-mail message to all employees ranking the portfolio managers from first to last based on their previous month's performance. Too many months on the bottom half of the list meant intense scrutiny from the executive committee and the very real possibility of being fired from the high-paying job.

This acute pressure led to a variety of consequences. Ulcers were commonplace. At least five of the portfolio managers regularly visited psychiatrists. And since David had joined Sagamore, two men in their early fifties had committed suicide—one with a closed garage door and a running car motor, the other by leaping from the Chesapeake Bay Bridge.

The bottom half of the monthly E-mail list was a nasty place for a Sagamore portfolio manager. David had found himself mired there shortly after becoming a manager and had been unable to escape since. He gazed at the skyscrapers in the distance. He would be out of the lowly position soon—as long as tomorrow went well.

"David?"

David continued staring out the window, lost in thought.

"Little brother, I apologize for rushing you, but I've got to get back to the garage."

David turned away from the window and sat down in the desk chair. "Sorry, Will. I've just got a few things on my mind."

"I understand. You've got a lot of pressure on you here." Will was the oldest of the four Mitchell brothers. Will had never gone to college and was now a mechanic, as were the other two brothers. David was the only one who had made it to college—and out of Glen Owens. "You know I hate asking you for this."

"I know." This was difficult for both of them. "How much do you need?"

Will picked at the grease lodged beneath his fingernails. Finally he glanced up at his brother, then looked away. "It's just so stupid. I should have had insurance on the damn car. But I'm trying to save money, what with the twins and—"

"How much do you need to fix it, Will?" David interrupted. He didn't have time for this.

"Five thousand dollars."

"Okay." Being constantly strapped for cash could break a person's spirit more effectively than a physical beating. David had seen it break his father. Now the same thing was happening to his older brother.

"Hello, Mr. Mitchell."

David recognized Art Mohler's tight-jawed, upper-crust voice immediately. Mohler was Sagamore's senior portfolio manager and one of three members of the executive committee—the delegation that ran the firm and kept its important secrets. He was the man to whom David and the other portfolio managers reported. The bane of their existence.

Mohler didn't actually run his own portfolio, but presided over everyone else's. No portfolio manager could enter any stock position worth over $20 million without Mohler's prior approval, which David had originally thought would be a good thing. If a stock lost value, there would be someone else to share the blame, he reasoned. But it didn't work that way at Sagamore. If a stock performed well, Mohler took a large share of the credit. If a stock tanked, he blamed it on you. And the other members of the executive committee allowed Mohler that privilege.

"Good afternoon." David forced himself to be polite even though Mohler constantly rode him about his lowly standing in the monthly rankings.

"It's only a good afternoon if we're making money." Mohler was in his late fifties but appeared younger. He was short and thin, wore half-lens tortoiseshell glasses, and dressed as though he were about to film a Brooks Brothers commercial.

"Art, this is my older brother, Will," David said as he stood up. "Will, this is Art Mohler. Art is one of our senior executives."

Will rose quickly from the office couch and extended his hand. "How do you do, sir?"

Mohler grimaced at Will's grimy fingernails. When they had finished shaking hands, Mohler wiped his palm on his dark suit pants. The subtle snub was not lost on Will—or David.

"I better get going." Will picked up his jacket off the couch.

"I'll make the arrangements for what we talked about," David mumbled.

"Thanks, little brother." Will nodded deferentially at Mohler. "Nice to meet you, sir."

"Mmm."

"See you, Will," David called after his brother.

Mohler watched Will move toward the reception area, then turned and scowled at David. David Mitchell was tall and dark, a definite distraction to the women in the office, and from the wrong side of Baltimore's tracks—something Mohler disliked intensely. David's presence interrupted the old-money consistency that had ruled the firm since its inception. Mohler had voted against offering David a job but the other two committee members had overruled Mohler. He had never forgiven David for that. "David, I don't think it's a good idea to let your brother come up to our offices anymore."

"Excuse me?" David had been about to sit back down but stopped.

"We often entertain high-powered clients here at Sagamore. We want them to leave with a good impression. I think you understand what I'm driving at."

"He's my brother. He's a good man," David said evenly, easing into his chair. "That's the only impression people would leave with."

Mohler smiled condescendingly. "Your fifth anniversary with Sagamore is only a year away now. I would think you'd want to act in the most circumspect manner possible." Mohler sat down on the couch. "That would include taking a direct order from a member of the executive committee."

David shifted uncomfortably in his chair at the mention of the five-year anniversary. If you had been in the bottom half of the monthly list a majority of your time with Sagamore, the executive committee quietly requested your presence on your fifth anniversary and terminated you. David had been in the bottom half most of his four years with the firm.

"I'll be fine," David said calmly.

"Don't be so sure."

"So why did you come to my office, Art?" David ignored the warning.

"I want to talk about General Engineering & Aerospace." Mohler removed his half-lens glasses, chewed on one of the stems for a moment, then replaced them on the bridge of his patrician nose. "Two and a half years ago, against my better judgment, you convinced me to put a billion dollars of Sagamore's money into GEA common stock. A *billion* dollars. Into a new issue of common stock that amounted to buying almost thirty percent of the company. And it's looking like one of the worst large investments this firm has ever made." Mohler opened a notebook on his lap, extracted several papers, and reviewed them. "When you bought the GEA stock, it was trading at twenty-five dollars a share. Now it's at twenty-two. In two and a half years it's gone down three points. In case you didn't realize, that's the wrong way, son," he sneered. "Remember, we want it to go up."

A wave of resentment coursed through David, but he managed to keep his temper in check.

Mohler removed another piece of paper from his notebook. "I have a graph here you gave me when you presented the GEA investment idea. It shows that you believed GEA stock would be at fifty dollars a share by now. That we'd *make* a billion dollars and double our money. Instead we've *lost* a hundred and twenty million. At least on paper. What's going on?" Mohler was quickly becoming angry.

Once a month they went through this over the GEA investment, and every month Mohler's criticism grew sharper. "You know, Art, I think—"

"GEA is going nowhere." Mohler didn't allow David to finish. "The defense industry continues to shrink, and the company hasn't won a major Pentagon contract in three years. It's time to jettison this position. Call the investment banks. Call our people at Alex Brown and Goldman Sachs. See what they can do for us. It's a big position, but maybe they can arrange a couple of private trades."

"What?" It was the first time Mohler had instructed David to actually sell the stock. And the directive couldn't have come at a worse time. "We can't get out now."

Mohler rose from the couch. "What if GEA's stock price drops further? We'll totally blow this year's earnings. Do you think this is funny money or something? Because it isn't. This is real money we're losing," he yelled. "Big money."

"I don't think it's funny money at all. I remember very well what I predicted for GEA when I pitched this idea to you two and a half years ago, and I know it hasn't happened yet," David said, standing up. "And I'm telling you, there's no one more upset about it at this firm than me." He leaned over the desk. "But I don't need you coming in here once a month reminding me that the stock keeps going down. I'd like to be out of the position too, but we'd slit our own throats getting out at this point. I don't know about you, but I don't want to take a hundred-and-twenty-million-dollar loss."

"Well, you'd better do something!" Mohler's eyes bulged.

"Gentlemen, gentlemen." Elizabeth Gilman's cotton-soft voice floated into the office.

Instinctively both men stepped back. Elizabeth was the firm's senior, managing, and founding partner. Among the three individuals on the executive committee, her vote on matters of importance counted much more than that of either Mohler or its third member, Martin Broadbent. She did not approve of heated conversations, as she called them, on the premises. It wasn't how privileged people ought to act, she would say.

"Hello, Elizabeth." Mohler was suddenly reserved.

"Good afternoon, Ms. Gilman," David said politely.

Elizabeth smiled. "David, you've been here four years. I appreciate the respect, but you need to start calling me by my first name. Otherwise you're going to give me a complex and make me start feeling my age. And that wouldn't be a good thing."

"All right . . . Elizabeth."

She smiled again. "Wonderful. Now let's all try to get along. It's a big sandbox and there's plenty of room to play in it without getting in each other's way. If we do happen to have a little disagreement, let's settle it in a more civilized fashion."

Both men nodded.

Elizabeth turned to leave, then leaned back into the office. "How is your mother, David?"

"Fine, thank you, Elizabeth."

"Please tell her I said hello."

"I will."

"Very good." She walked from the office.

David watched her go. She was a lovely lady. The only senior executive at Sagamore who didn't get caught up in the pressure and take out frustrations on others.

Mohler made certain Elizabeth was out of earshot, then pointed at the younger man. "Remember what I told you, David. Get us out of the GEA position. Hawk it on the street corner if you have to, but get us out," he said, then stalked from the office.

David put his hands on the desk and let his chin drop slowly. Tomorrow had to go well.

"Head up, kid. Just play the game."

David glanced up. Nash Sollers, one of the older portfolio managers, stood in the doorway. "What?"

"It's all part of the game, son. Just do what they want. You'll be okay."

"What do you mean by that?"

"Nothing specific, everything in general. Be smart and all will be fine." Sollers walked away.

David was tempted to follow and press Sollers for answers. But there wouldn't be any. There never were.

# Chapter 4

The house, a quaint brick abode surrounded by tall oak trees, was set atop a gentle rise overlooking the Severn River. Fifteen miles to the south, the Severn met the Chesapeake Bay at Annapolis, site of the United States Naval Academy. In the summer, even at this late hour, the river would still be a buzz of activity there, clogged with pleasure crafts, fishing boats, and Navy vessels. But here the river was quiet.

Moonlight played across the Severn's glassy surface. Ospreys peered silently down from the treetops searching for prey. And the only sounds were the rustle of leaves as a gentle breeze made its way upriver and the occasional crash of talons through salt water as one of the ospreys found its mark, then shrieked hauntingly as it lifted away from the surface with the fish snared in its viselike grip.

Jesse stood on the darkened porch, shivering despite the heat of the summer night. It was all exactly as the E-mail had explained. Neil Robinson was dead. The combination to locker 73 at the Greyhound bus station in downtown Baltimore had been 22-31-7. Inside the locker had been a small key. And the key had opened the front door to the house at 6 Gull Road.

Neil had been a wonderful manager, and a good friend. A man who had given her confidence that she was as capable as anyone. Now he was gone and she would miss him terribly.

He had sent the message to her through the local network, Jesse assumed, via the option in the branch's central computer that allowed supervisors to transmit electronic mail on a delayed basis. A message from the grave requesting her aid. He had helped her many times. Now, as frightened as she was to be here, she would help him.

Jesse stepped toward the door, then hesitated. She glanced around. The lights of the closest house, a quarter of a mile away, glowed eerily through the trees. Another shiver raced up her spine.

Get hold of yourself, she thought. She took a deep breath, pushed the door open, and moved into the house, clicking on the flashlight she had brought with her from the car. She felt dampness between her fingers as she pushed the plastic switch. The fur-lined leather gloves encasing her fingers were causing her hands to perspire heavily.

Jesse was wearing gloves so as not to leave fingerprints, she was using a flashlight so no one would know she was in the house, and she had parked in a small grove of pine trees in a secluded area a half mile down Gull Road from Neil's house so no one would see the car—and its license plate. All of this she had done just in case there was something to the ominous tone of Robinson's message.

A heavy scent of cedar reached her as she moved into the house. She pointed the flashlight straight ahead. Cedar walls. She played the light about the place quickly. The room was cozy, and tastefully furnished. Sadness overwhelmed her again at the thought of Neil's body lying cold in the morgue. Stop it, she told herself. Grieve later. Get in and get out of here as fast as you can.

There was a desk in the den just as Robinson's E-mail had described. She moved to it quickly. She had to get out of here. She had a strange feeling that something was wrong. That danger lurked.

The desk's lower left-hand drawer slid back easily on its rollers. She pointed the soft light down into the drawer. As the message had indicated, there was a file inside. She picked up the manila folder quickly, opened it, and glanced at the first two words. "Dear Jesse." She read no further. This was clearly the right file, and she would finish it later in a safer place.

Gordon Roth moved through the open front door of 6 Gull Road, the .44 caliber Magnum drawn before him. His night vision goggles made navigation easy, and he headed immediately toward the back of the small house. It was there that he had detected the faint glow of a flashlight through the window during his reconnaissance of the property. Somehow, someone had beaten him to this place. Someone who was trying to hide his or her presence, and therefore must be searching for the same thing he was after. But it didn't matter. The person wouldn't be alive much longer.

Adrenaline coursed through Roth's body, but not at

a fever pitch. He had learned over the years to control the flow. He could regulate it, like fuel to an engine, as needed. He had the element of surprise on his side, so he did not need to be in attack mode. He did not require the high-octane pulse—not yet, anyway. With a moderate flow he was better able to assess the situation and calculate the attack. Only at the last instant would he unleash his full fury.

He licked his lips as he pressed his back against the wall just outside the den's doorway. Death. It fascinated him. He had made a practice of staring into the victims' dying eyes. To try to comprehend what they were enduring as the last breath rushed from their lungs and their eyes rolled back. Roth killed because that was what they required of him—and because he liked it.

He closed his eyes and allowed the adrenaline to flow more freely. The target was close now. Like a predator, he sensed the prey in the night without actually seeing it.

Calmly Roth held the gun up before his face, both hands clasped around the handle so the barrel pointed vertically, toward the ceiling. Adrenaline began to pour into his system now. It was over. The victim was helpless.

In one motion he pushed off the wall, brought the Magnum down, turned the corner, and moved smoothly through the doorway of the den.

# Chapter 5

Carter Webb—Georgia Republican, senior member of the powerful Senate Appropriations Committee and chairman of its Armed Services Subcommittee—rose stiffly from the uncomfortable wooden chair. A new welfare bill sponsored by the Democrats had become entangled in a Republican-led tax-cut proposal, and the wrangling and backroom negotiating had just begun. It was going to be a long night.

Webb walked across the thick carpet toward the door to the right of the podium. He didn't have far to go to reach the exit, because after twenty-nine years in the Senate he sat in the front row. That was the tradition in this hallowed room. The longer your tenure, the closer you sat to the Vice President and Senate Majority Leader. There had been only one major exception to that rule in the past three decades. Ted Kennedy had remained in the back row despite his decades as a member of the Senate. As a tribute to his brother, he had taken the same seat Jack had occupied as a freshman senator from Massachusetts in 1953, and he had remained in it ever since.

Webb turned right after exiting the Senate floor and moved slowly down the short hallway to the large double doors. With a shove of his shoulder, he opened the right-hand door and moved into a large waiting room, then took an immediate right into a smaller room. There he relaxed against the polished wood wall and rubbed his aching neck, enjoying the solitude.

It was quiet here, away from the melee. Away from the fighting between the damned bleeding hearts, who wanted to make it easier for the inner-city poor to receive food stamps, and his money-grubbing brethren, who wanted to make poor people pay more taxes. Ten years ago, even five, he would have been in the middle of the fray, waging war on the tax-and-spend do-gooders. But now, in the twilight of his career, he was more conscious of conserving energy and picking his battles carefully.

"Good evening, Senator."

Webb glanced to his left through the dim light. The speaker was Phil Rhodes, a small man who struck Webb as too boorish to handle his high-profile job. But there was no arguing Rhodes's success. Over the years he had become one of the most recognized defense-industry lobbyists in Washington. General Dynamics, Lockheed Martin, and McDonnell Douglas constantly called on his services to help them land big Defense Department contracts.

"How the hell did you get in here?" Webb asked. "I thought the Capitol Police had closed this area off for the night."

Rhodes shook the senator's hand as an underboss would the hand of a Mafia don—gently, with his head bowed slightly forward. The senator—a member of the Armed Services Appropriations Subcommittee for twenty-six years and its chairman for the last fifteen—could make or break the fortunes of a defense contractor. Those defense contractors kept Rhodes in Armani suits and Gucci shoes, so he would kiss Webb's ring if it would help win business.

"I think they did close it off, but I'm on a first-name basis with most members of the Capitol Police. I'm going to be putting a lot of their kids through college, so they cut me a little slack." Rhodes spoke in a high-pitched Brooklyn accent.

Webb smiled for a moment. The sad thing was that the crack about paying for college probably held some truth—not that Rhodes would personally foot the bill. That tab would be picked up by the defense firms for which he lobbied.

"How's it going in there tonight, Senator?"

"A pain in the ass, as usual."

"I see. It's too bad you can't head back to Georgia to do some campaigning as a means of getting away from all of that." Rhodes motioned toward the doorway and the Senate floor beyond. "But I guess campaigning isn't really necessary." Webb's reelection was a foregone conclusion. He was an institution in the Senate.

Webb laughed cynically. "Yes, I doubt too many of my colleagues would believe I really needed to take any time off to gather votes."

Rhodes nodded, then fell silent for a moment as he watched the senator stretch. Webb was tall, broad, and silver-haired, with a jutting jaw; an imposing man who was often described by the press as presidential-looking. But Webb would never be President, Rhodes knew. He had made too many enemies in both parties.

"The grapevine is talking," Rhodes finally said.

Webb exhibited no outward reaction to the news. So Rhodes was here tonight to *give* information. Which was, of course, why the little man was so successful. Rhodes viewed his job as a two-way street. His primary objective was to help his defense industry clients obtain business, but if he had information he knew was important to the other side, to those who could dole out the money from the Defense Department budget, he would relay it as quickly as possible. Most of the other lobbyists didn't understand the goodwill this approach generated.

"And what exactly is the grapevine saying?" Webb asked calmly.

"It's saying that a very important top-secret project is under way in Nevada, out at Area 51. And that if the project passes prototype stage, it could be the most significant program to come out of the black budget in years." Rhodes was certain Webb would be interested. "I know that officially there isn't a black budget, but I thought you'd want to hear the talk anyway."

Webb said nothing for a moment. It was the first time the information had come back to him from a source outside the circle. It could be just someone's lucky guess, or a shot in the dark by one of Rhodes's clients. But Rhodes didn't work that way. He took a much longer, relationship-oriented view. So the only conclusion was that Rhodes was telling the truth. And unfortunately, the little man with the Brooklyn accent was almost always accurate when he cited the "grapevine" as his source.

"Where did you hear this?" he asked.

It was a tacit acknowledgment that the lobbyist's information was at least partially accurate, and Rhodes was elated. He had probably just earned a favor, perhaps a contract for one of his clients. "This is off the record, sir."

"Of course."

"I have a mole in Senator Malcolm Walker's office."

"You son of a bitch." Webb slapped the smaller man on the back and smiled approvingly. "Good for you." Then his smile faded. Here was an opportunity, one he wasn't going to let slip away.

"I think it's always a good idea to be as close to your enemies as possible," Rhodes remarked, proud of himself for eliciting such a strong reaction from the normally reserved Senator Webb.

"I couldn't agree more, Phil. That prick Malcolm Walker is trying to put the entire defense industry out of business."

"That's absolutely right." Rhodes checked the waiting area for anyone who might have wandered in through one of the dark entrances. "Anyway, my mole says that Senator Walker has infiltrated Area 51. Apparently he has an informant out there feeding him information on this big black-budget program. Walker is going to blow the cover on the project once he's gotten enough data from his informant. Supposedly this informant has the access to figure out what's going on."

"Really?" Webb was suddenly animated.

"Yes, sir. If my mole's information is accurate. And she's been very accurate so far." His eyes darted to Webb's. He suddenly wished he hadn't slipped and revealed the sex of his mole. But the senator didn't seem to have noticed, and Rhodes breathed a small sigh of relief. He didn't want Webb pushing too hard. "It's not exactly good news, I know," he continued. "But I thought you'd want to hear about all this as soon as possible."

Webb slammed the polished wood wall with his large hand. "Some of the idiots in this city just don't understand how difficult it is to protect a nation." He was seething. "That bastard Walker is going to screw up everything."

"I agree, sir."

Webb turned to face Rhodes. "Do you have a name, Phil? The name of Walker's informant at Area 51?"

Rhodes shook his head. "My mole in Walker's office will give me general information, but that's all. No names."

"What is your mole's incentive?"

"I provided money. There was a need. I'm sure my mole has rationalized that money can be accepted because there isn't anything specific being given in return. Such as the name of Walker's informant at Area 51." Rhodes didn't like where the conversation was headed. "Senator, it's been nice talking with you, but I really should get going."

"Phil." The senator blocked the lobbyist's departure.

"Yes?" Rhodes asked hesitantly.

"I'd like to meet that contact of yours sometime. Your mole in Senator Walker's office, I mean." Webb tightened the screws.

"Um, well . . ." Rhodes coughed uncomfortably. He had not anticipated this. "I'd like to accommodate you, Senator, I'm just not certain the person will agree to meet."

"Make her agree," Webb countered forcefully. Rhodes could become an extremely valuable asset, if cultivated correctly. "You have more power than you realize, Phil. You are in the intelligence industry. Use your access to people who can lay bare a person's entire life. Use your access to people who can find a smoking gun, or that one skeleton in the closet that will allow you to manipulate the person in question any way you want." Webb smiled wickedly. "I could find the skeleton in your closet," he said casually, as if he were relaying the score of a ball game or greeting someone for the first time.

The image of his girlfriend's heavenly body drifted through his mind. A girlfriend his pudgy wife knew nothing about. "I'll arrange the meeting," Rhodes said softly. Suddenly he was in deep with the good senator from Georgia.

"Good. And call me as soon as you have the name of Walker's Area 51 informant. That is very important."

"Yes, sir." Rhodes shook Webb's hand, then melted into the gloom.

Webb stared into the darkness long after Rhodes had disappeared. He needed to make a phone call before returning to the Senate floor.

# Chapter 6

Malcolm Walker had had an advantaged upbringing as the only child of two physicians who had clawed their way out of poverty-stricken inner-city childhoods, then met and married as medical students. They had attended Johns Hopkins on grants from the United Negro College Fund and ultimately settled in Homeland—an upscale north Baltimore neighborhood. Walker had matriculated at Macon Academy, an exclusive Massachussetts prep school, starring in football and track from sophmore year on. He'd graduated summa cum laude from Harvard undergraduate and Harvard Law in only five years, and afterward accepted a position at the high-profile Washington firm of Baker & Stroud, handling civil rights cases.

Six years after coming to Baker & Stroud, Walker ran a grassroots campaign for, and was elected to, the Maryland state senate. Four years later, at the tender age of thirty-three, he became a United States senator. In campaign speeches he cited lessons learned as the son of parents who had lifted themselves from the ghetto through hard work and determination. He spoke of the times when, as children, his parents did not eat because there was no money. He talked about the dilapidated homes in which they were raised. And he discussed the dreams they had achieved. He was articulate, attractive and a sworn enemy of Washington insiders and behind-the-scenes money deals between politicians and big business. And despite all the advantages of his youth, he related naturally to the plight of the working class—and they to him.

Establishment opponents constantly attempted to undermine the loyalty of Walker's constituents by depicting him as a fraud, as himself a member of the elite, focusing on his list of degrees from privileged schools and his sizable, publicly disclosed investment portfolio. However, Walker had managed to deflect the criticism and maintain the allegiance of his followers—until Elbridge Coleman had appeared on the political horizon and began burning millions on advertising that subtly appealed to white voters who had supported Walker in the last election. The ads consistently misrepresented Walker's record as only voting for legislation favorable to black communities and ignoring others, which in fact was not the case. His record indicated no bias whatsoever; however, he lacked the financial wherewithal to fight the onslaught, and the spin was having a major effect on his white constituency. A constituency he *had* to have to win reelection.

Walker smiled pleasantly at the talk show host sitting across the studio.

"We're back from commercial break here at WBCC radio Baltimore. This is *Night Speak* and I'm Cynthia Jones." Her creamy voice drifted through the microphone and out onto the airways. "Our guest tonight has been United States Senator Malcolm Walker, first-term Democrat from Maryland." The woman kept her lips close to the mike as she turned her head slightly to make eye contact with Walker. "I want to thank you so much for taking the time to come on our program tonight, Senator. I know you have a hectic schedule."

"Not at all, Cynthia," Walker said in his deep voice. "It's been my pleasure."

"Good. Well we have just several moments left so only time for a few more questions and one very important phone call."

Walker gave the host and the producer a curious look but neither responded to his silent question about the phone call. A call no one had mentioned during the prep session just before air time.

"Senator," the woman continued, "tell us why your appeal and voter support is so broad. You're black, but in the last election you received more than fifty-five percent of the white vote."

Walker launched into his prepared impromptu remarks. "Cynthia, it's because I talk common sense and people appreciate that kind of thing no matter what race they are." He'd said these things so many times he could recite them in his sleep. But he was a polished politician and could project enthusiasm no matter how many times he crusaded. "As we've discussed tonight, in my first term I've gone out of my way to focus on cutting the Defense Department's budget and that's certainly irritated some people in Washington. But it only makes good sense and voters know that. The DOD spends over three hundred billion dollars a year. *Three hundred billion.* And much of that is appropriated for weapons we just don't need. Take aircraft carriers for instance. Do we really need to sink, no pun intended, another five billion dollars into a floating target? I don't think so. Many of these contracts are simply directed to firms to enrich the entrenched military establishment. I believe the DOD budget could be half of what it is now, and the United States would easily remain the world's only military superpower.

"Cynthia, imagine what we could do with another hundred and fifty billion dollars a year if we really did cut the budget by fifty percent. Think of the opportunities. We could train inner-city youth to become part of a skilled labor pool. We could increase the number and quality of police officers. We could vastly improve our school systems. You see, race becomes irrelevant when you talk about these things because everyone benefits. I'm all about making this country a better place for everyone."

"Senator Walker, do you really believe we could cut the military budget in half and remain strong?"

"I know we could. And so do those in power in Congress and at the Pentagon."

"Then why isn't anything done?"

"Because many people are getting rich off that fat DOD budget. It's a gravy train."

"That's a powerful accusation."

"One I intend to prove."

"Tough words," the host crooned. "One more question before we take the phone call, Senator."

"Certainly, Cynthia."

"This is difficult, but as a reporter I need to ask. Why has the November Senate election for your seat suddenly become a race? Why has Elbridge Coleman, the Republican candidate, been able to close the gap in the polls lately, if you talk so much common sense?"

Walker had hoped to get through the interview without fielding that one. He wanted to tell the host about the establishment machine he felt certain was doing all it could to defeat him. But he didn't have names or money trails or anything else that would prove his suspicions. And if he blamed Coleman's recent success on some faceless group, it would sound like the rantings of a loser. "It's just a blip. Come November we'll still be in Washington."

"I'm glad you're confident." The host raised an eyebrow as if she wasn't certain Walker should feel so secure. "Now for the phone call." The host looked away. She knew Walker wasn't going to be happy about this development, but *Night Speak* needed ratings and this was sweeps week. "On the line we have the Reverend Elijah Pitts, leader of the Maryland-based Liberation for African-Americans."

Walker rolled his eyes and grimaced. In only a few years LFA had risen to prominence by spearheading initiatives designed to assist economically depressed areas. Bringing more government money to poor neighborhoods, bringing jobs to those same neighborhoods and monitoring fair hiring practices were just a few of Reverend Pitts's favorite causes. In fact, he and LFA had assisted blacks *and* whites. But Walker's research showed that many suburban whites mistakenly viewed LFA as militant. So he and his staff had decided to maintain as much distance as possible from Reverend Pitts for fear of losing the white bloc Walker so desperately needed to defeat Coleman and win reelection. Walker gave the host an icy stare, but she simply smiled back.

"Good evening, Reverend Pitts. Thanks for being on with us tonight."

"It's always a pleasure, Cynthia." The Reverend had been a guest on *Night Speak* several times. He paused. "Hello, Malcolm."

"Hello, Reverend." Walker forced himself to be polite. They knew each other well, having attended many public functions together. Walker tapped his chair nervously. Pitts was always trying to corner Walker into publicly endorsing LFA. But that, the pollsters had determined, would spell disaster. "How are you this evening?"

"Fine, Senator," Pitts said in an equally cordial, equally forced tone. "I've enjoyed listening to your words of grandeur this evening." Sarcasm seeped into Pitts's voice.

"Mmm."

The host smiled. Things were becoming interesting.

"But, Malcolm," the Reverend's tone became paternal, "you need to pay more attention to your core constituency. You need to build a bridge to LFA. Together we could really accomplish some of your grand design."

"I think you and LFA have done some very postitive things for Maryland." Walker glanced at the clock on the wall. Only one more minute and the host would have to sign off. But the second hand seemed to be going backward. "Some very positive things."

"You are skillfully avoiding the issue. Of course, you're a skillful politician so what should I expect? Embrace LFA, Senator Walker. Together we can be even stronger. Right now! On the air tonight!" Pitts thundered.

Walker cleared his throat. Thirty seconds.

"Malcolm."

"Reverend, we should get together and discuss our views. Perhaps you should come to Washington."

"Malcolm!"

"I'm afraid that's all the time we have, gentlemen," the host cut in. "Thank you, Senator Malcolm Walker, for being our guest on *Night Speak*."

Walker's shoulders slumped as the woman signed off. He'd be more careful about doing these call-in shows in the future.

# Chapter 7

Roth cased the room quickly, sweeping the gun from left to right, left eye closed, right eye staring down the sleek barrel to the small sight, and then beyond to the gray and green shapes perfectly defined by the night-vision goggles he wore.

Bookcase to the left. A desk beneath a bay window in the center with the chair pulled out and no one in the crawl space between the drawers. A large leather chair in the far corner next to the desk and a closet to the right, door closed. But nothing human. He checked the crawl space again just to make certain. There was no way the person could have left here in the short time it had taken him to move inside the house.

His eyes shifted to the closet. That had to be the answer. Somehow the prey had sensed his presence and in a pathetic effort to escape death had hidden in the most obvious location. As if it wouldn't be the first place he would check. But it was the only place to hide, and as Roth well knew, survival was the most powerful human instinct.

He trained the Magnum on the closet door, not

taking his eyes from the knob as he moved silently to the wall beside the door. He was ready for the prey to burst from within in an attempt to gain the advantage of surprise.

Roth reached for the knob, then pulled his hand back from the brass as if he'd received a shock. He wanted to take the person alive, then perform the execution at a remote location and leave no trace of his presence here for the investigation that would inevitably follow. But this mission was too important to risk any possibility of failure. If he tried to take the prey from the house alive, there was that slim chance it might escape. He had to kill it here. There was no alternative.

With the left side of his body pressed against the wall next to the closet, Roth reached out with the gun in just his right hand—exposing only his arm as a target in case the prey had a weapon—and pointed the barrel at the door, then fired three times into the door exactly four feet above the floor in a neat pattern across the wood. In rapid succession the bullets smacked angrily through the door just a few inches apart.

Instantly something behind the door fell heavily to the floor. Roth ripped at the knob and hurled the door open. On the floor lay a laundry bag. It had dropped from a hook on the back of the door, its string neatly cut by one of the bullets. Roth cursed softly. The prey had not been so stupid after all.

He whipped around, eyes flashing about the room, a small seed of concern suddenly taking root at the base of his brain. The prey was escaping.

The shrill sound of insect calls humming in the night filled his ears. A slight, almost imperceptible breeze of salt air caressed his face. Insect calls louder than they should have been. A salt-air breeze. His eyes shot to the bay window. He moved quickly to the desk, leaned over it, and put his hand against the window. It was unlocked and slightly ajar.

A large porcelain mug spilled its contents of pens and pencils as Roth jumped onto the desktop and yanked open one side of the window. The banker's lamp toppled over as he put one foot on the sill, but Roth took little notice as it smashed to the floor. He wasn't concerned about disturbing the house now. The bullet holes, the mug, and the lamp could be taken care of later. The only concern now must be to track down the prey as quickly as possible. Roth squeezed through the window and jumped six feet to the ground.

Jesse sprinted through the gauntlet of trees and shrubs, guided only by moonlight, spurred on by the sound of gunshots from the house. The foliage tore at her face, arms, and clothing as she stumbled through the blackness, avoiding the sharp branches as best she could. She had sensed the predator as he had peered through the window, though she was still not certain exactly how. Perhaps her ears had picked up a foreign sound or her nose an unfamiliar scent. Whatever it was, she had known instantly she must leave and that the front door was not an option.

Her shoulder suddenly clipped a thin sapling obscured by the darkness and she fell heavily to the leaf-covered ground. The file from Robinson's desk slipped from her hand and its contents spilled to the ground. A sharp pain shot from her shoulder to her fingertips, and she bit her lip to keep from crying out. She lay on the ground for a moment rubbing the shoulder, then picked herself up, took off her gloves and stuffed them in her pants pocket, retrieved the papers lying strewn about the dry leaves and kept going. She had to keep going. The predator was back there in the darkness. She could feel him.

Her plan was to move quickly through the forest forty yards in from the road, using the trees as cover, until she reached a spot close to where she had parked her car. Then she would cross the road, find the car in the grove of trees, and escape. It would have been much easier to simply race down the asphalt, but her instincts told her she would have been too obvious on the road, too vulnerable. There was a strong possibility the intruder wasn't working alone, and she was much safer in the cover of the woods even though it was slower going.

*Be careful.* God, if she had only known how serious Robinson's message had been. And in the next instant the ground fell suddenly away, and she tumbled down a ravine, screaming as the darkness enveloped her.

Roth's head snapped to the right. A scream, a terrified scream, human not animal. Female, judging by the pitch, and it was close. Closer than he could have hoped. Relief rushed through his body as he bolted toward the line of trees at the edge of the neatly trimmed lawn. The odds were suddenly back in his favor.

Jesse stood up, water dripping from her clothes, and

moved out of the stream. She picked up the file, which had fallen on the bank. She checked it. It hadn't been damaged. Then she heard the footsteps crashing over dry oak leaves.

For a moment Jesse stood still, uncertain of whether to run or hide. Finally she turned, waded through the water, and began struggling up the other side of the ravine. But the moist ground gave way maddeningly in her fingers, and after climbing only a few feet she slid back to the bottom.

Leaning on the bank, she hesitated for a moment to listen, trying to discern sounds other than the pounding of her heart. The footsteps were still coming fast. She glanced quickly to the left and right, then headed upstream, toward Gull Road.

She tried to stay on the bank, out of the water, but the stream took a sudden curve, and in the darkness she stumbled into a shallow pool and splashed into the icy, spring-fed water again.

Roth heard the splash and altered his path toward it as he dodged trees. The prey was close. He gripped the Magnum tightly and pressed forward. Then suddenly he too slipped down the steep ravine, tumbling over and over until finally he fell into the stream at the bottom. But he was up quickly, shaking himself, listening for sounds that would lead him to the quarry. He was disoriented from the fall and uncertain whether the splash he had heard was up-stream or down from his position. Seconds were passing. The prey was moving away. He had to make a decision.

Jesse heard Roth fall, and against every instinct she didn't run wildly away. Instead she moved more slowly than she had before, careful not to tumble into the water again. Careful to be as quiet as possible. Careful not to give away her position, because there was no longer any question that the predator was close.

Terror and the urge to scream suddenly overwhelmed her, but she managed to control the fear, realizing the odds were small anyone would hear her—except the pursuer. She stopped, leaned against the face of a large rock for a moment to suck in warm humid air, then pushed on.

Through the darkness and a break in the treetops the moon appeared, and then a bridge beneath the moon. It was the same bridge she had crossed on foot twenty minutes ago to get to the house after hiding the car. Only twenty minutes ago, but it seemed like hours now. She glanced up at the overpass, just a dark shape against a dark sky. The car was close, only a few hundred feet from the bridge.

She gripped the file tightly and jogged ahead. The bank was clear of foliage close to the bridge, and she was able to make progress more easily. She pressed her hand against her wet pants pocket and felt the car keys. Starting the engine might give away her position, but she would be gone before the pursuer could take advantage of it. And once she began driving, not even the fires of hell were going to stop her.

The air became cooler and slightly stale as she moved beneath the bridge. Moonlight shimmered off the water's surface, casting eerie, pale shadows on the cement. And just the slight sound of her footsteps on the rocks seemed to echo loudly inside the bridge.

Once out from under the bridge, she waded the stream and climbed the embankment. It was gently sloped on this side of Gull Road, and in seconds she had reached the top. She sprinted across a field of clover and slipped into the pine grove, then quickly located her Camaro. Frantically she pulled the keys from her pocket, inserted them into the lock, opened the door, and slipped behind the wheel. She patted the car's dashboard once gently, like an old friend, before thrusting the keys into the ignition.

The Camaro roared to life. She slammed the stick shift into first gear, let out the clutch, and punched the accelerator. The car leaped forward as she flicked on the lights. A sense of satisfaction gripped her as she yanked the stick back into second and hurtled down the rutted dirt path toward Gull Road. She could handle a performance vehicle as well as anyone. Her older brothers had seen to that.

As she guided the car between the pine rows, she reached for the leather gloves she had stuffed into her back pocket. She dug deeply and pulled one out, throwing it onto the seat beside her. Then she dug her hand in again searching for the other, but the pocket was empty. "Dammit!"

Gull Road rushed up to meet the dirt path. With both hands she jerked the steering wheel right, aiming the car away from Robinson's home—and the predator. The Camaro fishtailed slightly as dusty tires met asphalt, but she easily controlled the spin.

She flicked on the high beams and suddenly came face to face with her pursuer. He stood in the middle of the road, cap brim pulled down to his eyes, pointing a gun directly at her. Without hesitation Jesse thrust the stick forward into third gear and jammed the accelerator to the floor. But the figure didn't move, and she screamed as the Camaro hurtled toward him.

Sixty feet, fifty feet, forty. Roth waited until the last moment before pumping the clip's six remaining shells into the Camaro. The bullets ripped through the windshield, spraying shattered glass throughout the car's interior, then exploded out the back window.

As he fired the last bullet, Roth dove for the reeds at the side of the road, but he was an instant late and the Camaro's front left fender grazed his lower leg. The impact spun him through the air, separating the shoe from his foot. He landed heavily on his face and knee on the loose gravel at the edge of the asphalt. Despite the pain shooting through his cheek and up his leg, he lifted his head to check the license plate. But as the Camaro raced past, the lights suddenly dimmed.

Jesse rose up quickly from the passenger seat onto which she had ducked only an instant before the figure standing in the road had begun firing. She was covered with glass but ignored the sharp slivers and the tiny cuts on her forearms. She gripped the steering wheel hard with her left hand as the wind whipped through her hair and reached down with her right to turn the lights back on. As her head sank back she suddenly realized the headrest was gone. One of the bullets had blown it out through the shattered back window.

Roth spat out the dust and dirt in his mouth, then sat up and rubbed his throbbing leg. Blood from a cut over his left eye trickled down the side of his face, but for some moments he remained oblivious to it. He stared through the darkness at the sound of the fleeing car, then nodded his head as the lights came on too far away for him to discern the numbers and letters of the license plate. Whoever was driving that car was a formidable enemy, someone he had to seek out and destroy if the mission was going to remain on track. But the trail was quickly growing cold as the car raced away.

Roth reached inside his windbreaker and pulled out the leather glove he had found on the leaves. This would be all he needed to pick up the trail again.

"What do you have?" The man's voice was calm.

"A leather glove. Judging by the small size and design, I'd say the glove was worn by a female." Roth's leg was still killing him, but his expression gave away no hint of pain. He had endured much worse. "Inside the glove was a hair. A long hair. Again, I'd say female. Maybe the person ran her fingers through her hair before putting on the glove."

"So at least we have something."

"Yes."

"What is your plan?" the man asked.

"We were lucky. The hair had a follicle, and we can pull a DNA sample from the cells in the follicle. We know the person I chased tonight is one of twenty-two people in the department. If I can collect hair samples from those people, say from their brushes or coat collars, we might be able to get a match using DNA analysis."

"It will take time to collect the samples," the man pointed out.

"I'm fast," Roth assured the man.

"But even if you could get the samples quickly, it's still a long process in the laboratory using a hair follicle. Two to three weeks, probably. Using blood would be different, but that's out of the question. And we don't have two or three weeks." The man was becoming anxious.

"So we come at it another way."

"What do you mean?"

"In this case we have a limited pool of twenty-two people. We're almost certain our target is one of them."

"Yes."

"The lab can eliminate people from suspicion by examining the samples I collect and comparing them to the hair in the glove in terms of color and texture. Plus, if the lab finds certain chemicals on the hair from the glove, say chemicals found in specific dyes or shampoos, and the *same* chemicals on just one of the samples I collect, we can be reasonably sure we've got the right person. I think 'reasonably sure' isn't a bad thing in this case."

"I couldn't agree more."

"There's still another way to come at this thing," Roth offered.

"What's that?"

"The glove has a tag sewn on the inside. The name of the store from which it was purchased, I assume. It's an exclusive leather goods shop in the Galleria in downtown Baltimore. Maybe people at the store could give me information. With the scanners and automatic reorder entry systems retail stores employ these days, they should be able to give me a list of names of those who purchased this exact type of glove from the store in the past year or so. At least those who purchased by credit card. If that list contains a name from the department, I think we should move on that person immediately."

"Absolutely." Suddenly the man was feeling much better.

"Is it all right if I use the Justice Department badge for that? I'd probably get results faster."

"Use anything you have to. Just find the person who took that file from Robinson's house."

# Chapter 8

Jesse moved quickly down the long corridor, a thick envelope from the records room under her arm. She had decided against contacting the police about being chased at Neil Robinson's house last night. Police complaints were a matter of public record, and they would probably be the first thing the person who had chased her would check.

Turning the corner into her office doorway, she almost ran into a man coming out. She didn't recognize him and was instantly suspicious, still on edge from the experience last night.

"Excuse me," he said softly.

The man had long blond hair and a beard and mustache. She noticed him pushing a cellophane bag into his pants pocket. "Can I help you?"

"Yeah, I'm looking for Sara Adams."

Jesse eyed the visitor badge clipped to his shirt pocket. Sara must be expecting him. The people at the front desk wouldn't have given him the badge without calling her first. "Go left at the next hallway." She motioned down the corridor. "Her office is the fourth door on the right."

"Thanks." The man moved past her without another word.

Jesse watched him walk away, limping slightly. Perhaps she should call Sara just to make sure. Then she shook her head and brushed off the odd feeling. She was just imagining things.

Jesse felt the tap on her shoulder and jumped, emitting a muffled shriek as she whirled about, hands over her mouth. She had been far away, replaying last night's chase through the woods and this morning's run-in with the bearded man coming out of her office. Wondering if she should have contacted the police. Wondering if the man was looking for her. Knowing he was.

"Sorry to startle you, Jesse, but I have someone I'd like you to meet." The professor nodded toward the woman standing next to him.

"Yes, of course." Jesse took several short breaths to calm herself.

"Elizabeth Gilman, meet Jesse Hayes," the professor said quietly. He didn't want anyone at the cocktail party to hear this, lest he be accused of favoritism. "Jesse is my best student."

"I think that was rather obvious, given the class discussion." Elizabeth smiled warmly at Jesse. "Honestly, I thought your comments were excellent. Best of the bunch."

"That's very nice of you to say, Ms. Gilman." Jesse's voice shook slightly, and with good reason, she thought to herself. Elizabeth Gilman was a legend in the financial world. She had organized Sagamore as a small life insurance company in the late seventies and expanded it into one of the best-performing, most highly respected investment funds in the country.

"Please call me Elizabeth." The older woman laughed. "Do I really look that old?" She pointed at the professor. "Don't answer that. Not if you want me to come back again."

Jesse saw Elizabeth's eyes sparkle as the professor laughed. Despite her age she was dynamic and beautiful. Stark gray hair swept back away from her classic, thin face—a face practically devoid of wrinkles or age spots, a face still full of energy and enthusiasm. Jesse glanced down at the floor. Her throat was suddenly dry, and she could think of nothing to say that might interest such an important person.

The professor sensed Jesse's unease and pushed the conversation forward. "Elizabeth, I can't tell you how much we appreciate your taking time out of your busy schedule to come down here and teach a class," he said. "It's terribly important for the students to see and hear from people in the real world, not just the academicians. And for us to have someone of your stature come here, well, it's—"

"Thank you." Elizabeth didn't take her eyes from the young woman as she politely interrupted the professor. "Jesse, I was impressed with your observations about the stock market." Elizabeth's diamond earrings shimmered in the chandelier light.

"Thank you."

Elizabeth leaned forward so the professor couldn't hear. "There's no reason to be nervous, Jesse. I eat and sleep just like you. I've just been a little lucky with a few investments." The older woman leaned back again.

"It isn't luck," Jesse replied. "Your success is a function of putting yourself in the best position more often than anyone else does. It's a function of playing the odds."

"True." Elizabeth nodded approvingly. "Say, why don't you come out to Sagamore and visit us? I'm always looking for young talent."

"That would be wonderful!" Wall Street suddenly seemed much less important.

"In fact, there's someone I want you to meet right away," Elizabeth continued. She motioned to a young man who was talking with several of Jesse's classmates.

David acknowledged the wave subtly, excused himself from the group at an appropriate point in the conversation, and moved toward Elizabeth.

"Jesse, this is David Mitchell." Elizabeth patted David's broad back as he took Jesse's hand and smiled. "David is one of our portfolio managers at Sagamore. I asked him to come down from Baltimore tonight with me for exactly this reason—in case I identified someone in class who might fit in at Sagamore."

"Hi, Jesse." David let go of her hand gently. Blond, blue-eyed, and sweet. Unlike the others he had been forced to converse with for the last hour, this one was worth writing home about.

"Jesse, I think you might enjoy talking to David for a few minutes about Sagamore." Elizabeth had barely finished speaking when she began to cough deeply.

"Are you all right?" the professor asked, startled at the intensity of the attack.

"Yes," she gasped. "I'll be fine. I just need a drink of water."

"Of course, Elizabeth. Come with me and we'll get whatever you need." The professor took her by the arm.

Elizabeth coughed again several times, then turned to Jesse. "It was wonderful meeting you. I look forward to seeing you at Sagamore when you visit."

"Thank you. I hope you feel better."

"I'll be fine." She stepped over and patted Jesse's hand. "Good-bye."

"Bye."

David hesitated for a moment as Elizabeth and the professor moved away. "So what can I tell you about Sagamore?" He looked past Jesse as he took a sip from his glass, trying to seem distant, not wanting her to detect his immediate interest.

Jesse gave David a quick once-over. He was handsome—jet-black hair, effortless smile, a dimple in his left cheek, and a healthy glow indicating that he took care of his body. But everything about him screamed establishment. From the dark three-button suit with inch-and-a-half cuffs on the pants to his expensive tie and short haircut, he seemed a model conservative. She laughed to herself. Given her meager upbringing, she ought to be drawn to this man like a bee to nectar. Men with money promised financial security, something she had never known. But she usually found these types so boring. They loved sports, their possessions, and themselves, and she needed much more than that. She needed excitement, a man who would share life with her and show her the world.

But maybe she should listen to Sara's advice about dating men who offered financial stability and not worry so much about intangibles. She glanced at David again. He certainly emitted that conservative air. But there was a hint of mischief in the glint of his eye. And now that she looked at his haircut carefully, she noticed that it bordered on punk. The sides and back were cut a bit too short and the top a bit too long. She liked that. "How much money does Sagamore have under management?" she asked innocently, knowing how closely guarded a secret that was.

David shook his head. "I can't tell you," he said pretentiously, then broke into a wide grin. "Because I don't know. They don't tell the rank and file like me important things like that. They just tell us to make money."

Jesse covered her mouth and laughed. So he didn't take himself too seriously. She liked that too.

Two hours later, as they moved through the double doors of the reception room toward the waiting limousine, Elizabeth put a hand on David's forearm. "I noticed you and Jesse Hayes had quite a discussion after I left."

"That's what you wanted, right?"

"Yes. My first impression is that she would fit in well at Sagamore when she graduates. What do you think, David?"

"I think she's bright and aggressive."

"Exactly." Elizabeth waved good-bye to the professor one more time as the driver opened the limousine door. "David, I want you to get to know her. Take her out for dinner a few times, on the firm of course. Find out if she's really for us." She winked at him. "There aren't enough female portfolio managers at Sagamore."

David smiled and tilted his head to one side. This wasn't going to be a bad assignment.

# Chapter 9

The room, utilitarian and plain, was buried deep within the building. And for good reason. The people who met in this inner sanctum required absolute secrecy and isolation in order to plan their strategies. Enemy listening devices could be anywhere, even hidden in vulnerable areas close to the chamber. And if those devices picked up anything, it could prove disastrous.

Members accessed the massive building through public entrances under the veil of ethical designs, but typically their intentions were far less noble. On the occasion of a meeting, each individual was quickly led from unrestricted areas into obscure corridors and secluded stairways by escorts who themselves were not fully aware of the true purpose of the individual's presence.

The room was fortified by subtle but effective defenses. There were no windows because high-technology audio-detection equipment could sense the minute vibrations of glass panes produced by even muted conversations and translate the vibrations into words. Tiny speakers placed at uniform intervals within the walls of the room produced white noise to negate bugs that adversaries might have managed to plant in the hallways and rooms just outside the chamber. Before each assembly, an intelligence expert swept the room's interior for listening devices. Those in attendance were electronically frisked before they were allowed entrance. And during meetings, members sat close together at a small table, spoke in low voices, and listened to an opera or symphony as they strategized. The preventive measures seemed extreme, but, as yet, there had never been a security leak.

The chairman acknowledged each of the other members, then turned toward the individual who sought membership and said in a low voice, "Please give us an update."

Elbridge Coleman, Republican candidate for the United States Senate, nodded. "The latest CNN/*Time* magazine poll will be released tomorrow morning. Our campaign people have already obtained the results through our friend at CNN. The results show that I'm now two points *ahead* of Malcolm Walker. Specifically, if the election were held today, I would receive forty-six percent of the vote while Walker would take forty-four."

"That leaves ten percent undecided," the chairman noted.

"Yes, that's right." As Coleman responded, he heard someone else in the room make a comment but could not discern specific words. The room's acoustics were terrible. It was another built-in defense mechanism.

"Excuse me?" Through the low light he made eye contact with the individual he believed had spoken.

"What is the poll's statistical margin of error?" The voice was only slightly louder this time.

"Plus or minus four points," Coleman replied calmly.

"So we can't yet be certain of a lock on the seat."

Coleman smiled politely despite his irritation at so obvious an analysis as well as use of the word "we." He could not argue the fact that they had a large stake in what was going on, but it was his sweat staining the campaign trail. "No, we can't." Coleman tugged at the sleeves of his suit coat. He was tall and thin, with a trustworthy face and a strong natural presence. Handsome, but not obnoxiously so. "I think it's important to remember that just a month and a half ago, at the end of July, we trailed Walker by five points. We've gained nine points in only forty-five days." Coleman was careful not to allow irritation to leak into his tone. This was a beauty contest, and they could kick him out of the show at any time, so he would mind his manners. Swallowing his pride was a small price to pay for admission into this circle. "The trend is excellent. We have significant momentum. I believe by this time next month, for all intents and purposes, Walker's Senate seat will be mine. His campaign will be dead in the water. The November election will be only a formality."

"You and your campaign staff have performed admirably, Elbridge." The chairman sensed Coleman's slight vexation. "We do have momentum. We simply want to make certain it is maintained at its current level. We must finish strong. We all have a great deal riding on this."

"Of course." Coleman nodded deferentially to the chairman. He appreciated the compliment regarding his and his staff's performance. He hesitated, looking at each of the members in turn before speaking again. "We are running very strong and Malcolm Walker is running scared. That's the bottom line."

"Fine, fine." The chairman was obviously pleased. "And you have plenty of money left, Elbridge?"

"My campaign treasurer assures me that the after-tax proceeds from the initial public offering of Coleman Technology will be more than sufficient to fund the remainder of the campaign. And, of course, forty percent of the stock remains in my name. We could liquidate some of that in a private sale at any time if we need more money for the campaign."

"Very good," the chairman said. Everything was proceeding as planned. "That will be all."

Coleman recognized his cue to exit. He stood up, nodded respectfully at each of the members, and walked toward the door.

"Elbridge," the chairman called quietly.

"Yes?" Coleman hesitated for a moment.

"Please tell your guide to use the Potomac exit."

"All right." He turned, moved through the door, and was gone.

The chairman swiveled around to face the others. "I think we should feel very good about Mr. Coleman's campaign. As we all know, there are never any sure things in life, but this would appear to be as close to a lock as possible. We have two other campaigns in preliminary stages out West, but I don't think we'll ultimately need them."

"We should turn up the heat on the other front too," a voice broke in quickly. "We need to make absolutely certain we win this election. We've set this thing up and spent a great deal of money on it—let's use it."

The chairman nodded. "I agree. I've waited on that because it's our ace in the hole and I didn't want to use it too early. But I think you're right. It's time. We're close enough to the election now that Walker wouldn't be able to mount an effective counteroffensive. I'll take care of it myself."

"Thank you," said the member who had made the suggestion, acknowledging the chairman's assistance.

"There is something you need to know." The chairman's voice became serious. The others recognized the tone and were instantly uneasy. "We've had a small security leak." All eyes were suddenly riveted to the chairman's. "As you are aware, two nights ago we took care of our problem at the IRS. Gordon Roth silenced Neil Robinson. Permanently. As it turns out, Robinson's suspicions about Elbridge Coleman's campaign were even more accurate than we had originally believed. We should be elated that Robinson is now out of the picture." The chairman paused. "Unfortunately, Robinson was more resourceful than we had anticipated." The man knew this little missile was going to cause a nuclear explosion. "I think Robinson was actually able to pass his suspicions about Coleman on to someone after Roth killed him."

"What the hell is that supposed to mean?" one of

the others asked. "How could Robinson pass on suspicions *after* he was killed?"

"A few days ago, perhaps in response to Mr. Roth's repeated telephone contact, Robinson prepared a short memorandum briefly referencing his suspicions about an unidentified U.S. Senate race. It was stored on his hard drive."

"But I thought we had gotten to his office before anyone else did. I thought we had confiscated his computer's hard drive and all his disks."

The chairman nodded. "We were there the morning after his death. Unfortunately it didn't matter. Robinson used an option in the IRS branch's local area network system to send the memo from his computer to another one on a delayed basis. If he didn't disengage the option within a specific number of hours of logging off his computer, the memo would be sent automatically. Until yesterday when he arrived in the morning he shut off the time delay release simply by logging on. Obviously, yesterday morning he didn't log on, so the memorandum was automatically sent out to its predetermined destination. We got there, but too late to stop the memo from going out."

"So then we should be able to follow the electronic path, shouldn't we? We'll simply determine the memo's destination and take appropriate action immediately."

"It isn't that simple," the chairman cautioned. "Robinson had arranged for the memo to be sent to an IRS central processing unit in Florida first, then had the CPU send it back to Baltimore."

"Why did he do that?"

"To hide the identity of the receiving party, I

assume. If he had sent the memo directly through the branch's local system, it would have been easy to pinpoint which personal computer it went to. But by sending the memo to the CPU in Florida first and then back to Baltimore, he was able to cover his tracks. We were able to determine which cell the memo was sent to, thanks to a systems person at the IRS who is on our payroll. However, the CPU erased the link from the cell to the specific receiving computer."

"What's a cell?"

"A group of personal computers, a department."

"So which department was it sent to?"

"The revenue agents."

"How many of them are there?"

"Twenty-two."

"Then we need to check each of their computers."

"We already have. No results. Whoever received the memo was smart enough to erase it from his or her computer memory and not make a copy. We checked the printer logs as well."

"How do we know that what Robinson sent by computer had anything to do with the Coleman campaign?"

"We don't," the chairman responded. "I'm guessing, but it's a damn good guess. We found a hard copy of an unaddressed memo among Robinson's possessions stating that if the party to whom it was sent was reading it, something had happened to him. It asked for the person's help, then gave directions to a small house he owned on the Severn River. In the house there was to be a file of detailed information about a Senate race he believed was being manipulated. And thanks to the conversation Roth had with Robinson at the Hyatt, we all know which campaign Robinson was referring to. I strongly believe it was this same memo that was sent electronically the morning after his death."

"Where was the hard copy of the memo found?"

"In the suit Robinson was wearing when he died."

"What?" The members' anxiety was instantly heightened.

"Yes. It was as if Robinson was thinking of giving the memo to someone before he met Gordon Roth at the Hyatt. A coroner at the city morgue found the memo in Robinson's coat pocket. Fortunately we were able to get to the hard copy before anyone else did. We got to the coroner too. Just to be careful." It was a damn good thing Roth was so efficient.

"Have we retrieved the file from the Severn house?"

"We tried, but someone beat us to it. Almost certainly the same person who received the delayed computer correspondence from Robinson."

"So what the hell are we going to do?"

The chairman brought his hands together. "Systematically figure out which of the twenty-two revenue agents received the correspondence from Robinson, then take the appropriate action. And pray to God we find that person before that person finds us." His expression brightened. "Fortunately, we have the means to do so. Whoever beat us to the file at the Severn house inadvertently left us a trail. One we can follow quickly. And I assure you we will."

The others nodded their assent.

The chairman glanced up. "As you've no doubt noticed we are missing a few members this evening. They are at Area 51. Keep your fingers crossed that all goes well tonight with the A-100."

# Chapter 10

The A-100 prototype climbed sharply from Area 51 into the darkness just settling over Nevada. The plane was commencing its fourth and final scheduled test flight. Contingent upon successful completion of this last mission, the defense firm that had secretly been awarded the huge contract could begin full-scale production of the new Navy fighter-bomber immediately. It was a contract worth almost $150 billion over the next seven years and would make the firm one of the biggest in the defense industry.

The landing gear retracted into the jet's fuselage as tires lost contact with pavement, creating the perfect attack profile—low and practically devoid of right angles. Sleek configuration, combined with the unique composite skin of the craft and the jamming devices on board, made the A-100 almost immune to enemy radar detection.

As he felt the familiar thud of doors closing over landing gear, the aviator relaxed into his seat and began his first in-flight safety and security check. It would be a constant process until he had touched down at the target two hundred miles to the north.

Commander Richard Pierce enjoyed a reputation as one of the most experienced fixed-wing pilots in the entire United States Navy. He was as calm and cool under pressure as they came. But despite his glittering combat record and many test-flight hours at the controls of this and other prototypes, he had been anxious all day. This particular plane was worth almost $500 million, and, more important, represented the Navy's attempt to reestablish itself as an equal and indispensable member of the armed services triumvirate.

Without the "black wing"—as Pierce had nicknamed the A-100—the Navy might ultimately be forced to cede deep-strike missions to stealth bombers of the Air Force, an action that could make $5 billion aircraft carriers vulnerable to reelection-minded politicians searching for ways to cut federal spending and earn points with their constituents—ways that could have a domino effect in terms of new destroyers, new cruisers, and, most important, budget dollars.

The Navy is comprised of three parts, subsurface, surface, and aviation—in which carriers are included. Air Force and Army brass constantly questioned the need for the surface and aviation components of the Navy given the high-tech abilities of guided missiles. They argued that surface vessels and aircraft carriers were easy targets and therefore obsolete, hoping to claim a huge piece of the $90 billion Navy budget for themselves if it became available as a result of their backroom maneuvers. Without the A-100 the Navy might become only a bit player in the $300-billion-a-year defense game. With it, the Navy could justify its surface and aviation operations and would be back on equal footing with the Air Force and the Army.

Pierce guided the A-100 into a gentle five-degree turn to north. It was such an important flight, but only a few people in the world even knew of the plane's existence. Of course, that was always the way with black programs. Everything was top-secret. The contractor's civilian employees flew into and out of Area 51—the isolated Nevada government installation—on planes with windows covered black so passengers couldn't see out. Everyone was searched entering and exiting the installation's massive hangar housing the five prototypes. And people with knowledge of the A-100 black project faced ten years of solitary confinement at Leavenworth if convicted of simply acknowledging the project's existence to an individual without A-100 clearance.

It was that way for everyone involved. Pierce's wife had no idea where he was. And if today's flight ended in disaster, which was always a possibility given the nature of the business, the coffin his wife buried would be empty—though she would never know that. There was always the possibility that a piece of the plane's top-secret composite skin could become lodged in Pierce's remains for an international grave robber to discover and take back to his government.

But the personal sacrifices didn't bother Pierce at all. He was totally committed to the A-100, to its place in naval history, and to the leaders managing the project. And he would do anything they asked to make certain the plane was brought to full-scale production as quickly as possible. Anything.

Thirty-seven feet long with a seventy-foot wingspan, the A-100 was really nothing but a giant wing, an aerodynamic marvel. Upon design and test completion it was to replace the thirty-five-year-old A-6 Intruder as the Navy's carrier-based workhorse fighter-bomber. The A-6 had been in service since Vietnam, but political wrangling and tight budgets had inhibited the Navy brass from replacing it.

Pierce glanced out the left window at the wing sweeping back away from him. It was a beautiful plane. Responsive, powerful, and practically invisible, it was the finest machine he had ever flown.

He scanned the computer-generated topographical map on which was superimposed an outline of the aircraft, then demagnified the image on the screen several times—decreasing the size of the plane's outline and increasing the scope of the map—and located the runway from which he had just taken off. Four minutes into the flight and he was already fifty miles out.

Pierce increased the scope of the map again and searched for the target—a "carrier box" located on a remote runway in the middle of the Nevada desert where the Navy simulated at-sea landings and takeoffs. The carrier box was a rectangle of white lights positioned on the runway to match the dimensions of an aircraft carrier deck. The box was complete with arresting cables and a catapult.

Pierce located the carrier box quickly. It was slightly over 150 miles out to the north.

The objective of this last mission was simple: to simulate an at-sea landing and takeoff, two of the most dangerous maneuvers Navy pilots had to execute on a regular basis. Land the A-100 within the white lights, then take off via catapult. If he could do so, the contractor could begin production of the plane immediately. And the admirals could kiss his ass from now to eternity.

He glanced at the box on the screen once more, then checked in with Carrier Air Traffic Control for the first time. "Approach, Tiger six two three." In order to limit the number of eyes watching the flight, the CATC would act as Strike, Marshal, and Air Boss—the progression of controllers typically responsible for guiding a jet home after its cycle of operations. Black programs required this kind of job economy to ensure secrecy. "How copy?"

"Loud and clear, Tiger six two three." The CATC's response was terse.

Pierce heard tension in the CATC's voice. Christ, the higher-ups were probably crowded around the poor bastard, making him nervous as hell. Admiral Cowen, Chief of Naval Operations, William Harcourt, Secretary of the Navy, and Jack Finnerty, president of GEA—the defense firm responsible for manufacturing the A-100. All sweating bullets at the command center overlooking the carrier box as they waited for Pierce to guide their little $500 million piece of hardware safely onto the runway in the middle of nowhere.

"Request permission to land."

"Tiger six two three, cleared to land. But could you do me a favor first and turn on your beacon? With all that radar avoidance equipment on board, your damn plane's a bitch to find, and there are people here who'd really like to know where you are right now."

"Roger." Commander Pierce flipped on the beacon. The A-100 would now emit a clear, constant pulse, enabling the CATC's radar to locate him easily. He chuckled to himself. The radar-avoidance equipment on this plane was a thing of beauty. Pilots would be able to fly into downtown enemy cities, drop payloads, and be gone before anyone knew what had happened. "My ETA"—he paused to check the computer—"is eleven minutes and twenty-two seconds."

"Report, see you at ten." The CATC was requesting another check at ten miles out.

"Wilco," Pierce replied. It was the standard naval aviation response, short for "will comply."

At ten miles out, Pierce checked in again, as the CATC had requested. Through the cockpit glass, Pierce eyed the carrier box, now plainly visible through the darkness, the tiny white landing lights perfectly replicating the dimensions of a carrier deck. At this point the box was five thousand feet below him and ten miles to the north.

"Cleared to land."

Pierce descended quickly to a thousand feet, leveled off briefly as he "let down" into pattern, and lined up into a course that would take him due north to the box. After a few moments he throttled back to 350 knots and descended to eight hundred feet.

Two miles south of the carrier box, Pierce slowed to gear down speed—250 knots—then dropped the landing gear. Instantly the cockpit rocked against the air turbulence generated by the now less than aerodynamically efficient shape of the plane.

At a mile south of the carrier box and six hundred feet above the sand, Pierce adjusted the A-100's course one more time and rolled into long final. Now the plane was perfectly aligned with the runway lights running down the center of the box.

Pierce gripped the stick tightly. Landings were nothing but controlled crashes. And no matter how many times you executed them, they were still nerve-racking experiences, especially with the fate of the entire Navy in your hands.

Moments later he was a half mile south of the carrier box. Now he had descended to three hundred feet and slowed to 150 knots. Much slower than just seconds ago, but still incredibly fast to try to stop forty thousand pounds of aircraft in such a short space.

"Call the ball," the lone landing safety officer shouted into Pierce's ear through the radio.

Pierce checked the datum lights—three green lights to the left, three to the right, and a yellow meatball in the middle. These lights indicated to the pilot whether his angle of approach was acceptable for landing.

"Ball!" the LSO shouted again.

Pierce smiled. The LSO was feeling the same stress as the CATC. Usually he wasn't so anxious. "Tiger six two three, A-100 ball, six point five," he intoned calmly, his last phrase a reference to the plane's fuel weight.

"Roger ball, Tiger." The LSO was relieved. "Looking good."

A quarter of a mile. An eighth of a mile. In the glow

of the lights Pierce could barely make out the four arresting cables stretched tightly across the runway. A sixteenth. It was always strange when you landed, when you came close to earth, to realize how fast you were traveling. There was no way to truly appreciate the speed at thirty thousand feet, even during the day when you flew through clouds.

Wheels slammed against pavement, and instantly Pierce went to full throttle. If for some reason he missed the arresting cables, he would take off and try to land again. The mission could still be deemed a success for the contractor if he made it the second time—as long as wheels left runway before passing over the white lights at the north end of the box on this attempt.

But there was no reason to worry. Instantly Pierce was thrown forward against his harness. From his run-out he could tell it was the third arresting cable that had caught the plane's landing hook. Quickly he powered down.

Jack Finnerty, president of General Engineering & Aerospace, finally exhaled as he watched the A-100 jerk to a stop on the simulated carrier deck. For several moments he simply stared forward as the full impact of the successful flight washed away the gut-wrenching stress of the past two and a half years. It was almost over. There was just one more test for the plane to pass—a catapult takeoff—and then they could start full production. As soon as the A-100 had lifted off again, he would call the others to relay the good news.

Commander Pierce gave the thumbs-up sign to the deck monkey as the man trotted toward the A-100.

Just one more task to complete and the master would be pleased.


It was almost midnight when the woman slipped into the passenger seat of Phil Rhodes's car. She was jittery, constantly glancing out the window to check the darkened side street for anything suspicious.

"Relax," he said gently, trying to reassure her.

She hated his Brooklyn accent. "I can't relax. I don't ever want to be seen with you, and this is too public a place." She opened and closed the glove compartment several times, trying to work off nervous energy. "Why are we meeting?"

"I need the name of Senator Walker's informant at Area 51." Rhodes got to the point immediately.

The woman laughed aloud at the request. "Are you crazy?" She shook her head. "Forget it. I told you. No specific information. Nothing that can incriminate me."

"I gave you money, ten thousand dollars."

"All in cash that can't be traced," she retorted. "Don't get me wrong, I appreciated that money, because I had a need, but it won't get you the name of Walker's Nevada informant."

"I'll ask you one more time."

"And I'll tell you one more time," she replied quickly, her voice shaking in anger. "You aren't getting anything from me." She reached for the door handle. "I think it's time for me to leave. Maybe we ought to forget about this whole thing."

Before the woman could step out of the car, Rhodes reached across her body, slammed the door shut, and dropped a brown envelope on her lap.

Startled, she glanced down. "What's this?"

"Pictures." Carter Webb had been right, Rhodes thought to himself. Everyone was tempted at some point. Everyone had at least one skeleton in the closet. It had taken just forty-eight hours to find this woman's.

"Pictures?" Her fingers trembled as she touched the envelope. She had lived in fear of this moment for a long time, but over the last few years had convinced herself that the pictures were gone, never to resurface.

"Yes. You and another young woman engaged in several acts of perversion Senator Walker and the rest of the world may find interesting. There's bondage, bestiality, and a few sexual aids I'd never seen before. Something for everyone." Rhodes had never done anything like this before, and he felt a pang of guilt, but he kept going. "I've never seen pictures like that, and I thought I'd seen everything. You must have needed money then too."

"I did." She sobbed. "I had nothing. How did you find these?"

"I can find anything."

She wept softly, clutching the envelope of influence. As rain began to fall gently on the windshield, Rhodes's guilt suddenly evaporated. His goal was to take his relationship with Webb to the next level, and he was absolutely committed to that now. He wanted to be a real player. And if that involved blackmail, so be it. "I'll never show them to anyone," he lied. He no longer cared about her feelings. She was nothing, just a pawn.

"Sure you won't," she said sarcastically, biting her fingernails. How could she have given in to the sleazy man's request for photographs? How could money have been that important?

"I promise I won't show them to anyone. As long as you give me a name."

"Is that all I have to do?"

"Yes," he lied again. It was becoming easier each time. "Captain Paul Nichols."

Rhodes quickly committed the name to memory.

"Can I go now?" The woman wiped her nose and mouth with a tissue.

"I want anything of importance from Senator Walker's office. Anything that has to do with the A-100 project."

"This isn't going to end, is it?" she asked dejectedly.

"No." Rhodes looked away, then back at her. She was suddenly his disciple, and the power was intoxicating. It had been so easy, as Webb had said it would be. He had simply needed to find her moment of weakness and be willing to exploit it. "You can go now. I'll be in touch."

She opened the door and disappeared into the night.

# Chapter 11

"Hello," Jesse called out loudly as she turned the key and pushed open the front door. It was midmorning and the modest home lay in the heart of a quiet neighborhood, but her mother kept the door locked at all times now that she lived alone. "Where are you, Mom?"

"In the kitchen, sweetheart."

Jesse placed her pocketbook on the hall table and walked toward the kitchen. She had taken her birthday off from work even though she didn't feel much like celebrating. Neil Robinson's death had deeply saddened her. "Oh, excuse me." Jesse stopped short at the kitchen doorway. "I'm sorry if I'm interrupting." Father Francis McCord, the priest of Glyndon's Sacred Heart Church, sat at the kitchen table with Jesse's mother, Connie.

"Don't be silly, Jesse," Father McCord said as he rose from the chair. "Your mother and I were just chatting about her fine work at the church." He smiled down at Connie. "She's a tireless volunteer at Sacred Heart, and we all adore her. She's an inspiration to everyone."

Connie blushed at the priest's kind words.

"I really have to go," Father McCord said. "Thanks for tea, Connie, and I'll see you tomorrow at the charity fair."

"Good-bye, Father." Connie kissed the back of his wrinkled hand, then crossed herself twice.

"May God be with you," he murmured.

"And also with thee," she answered.

Father McCord walked across the tiled kitchen floor to Jesse. "It seems like forever since I've seen you. How have you been?"

"Fine, Father." She gazed at the stiff white collar standing out sharply against his black shirt and jacket. She had almost opened her soul to this man so many times over the years about that terrible night long ago. But each time, she had decided against confiding in him. Because of his close relationship with her mother, it would have put him in a terribly difficult position—priest or not. It was better for him not to know, so she had sought counsel elsewhere.

"Come by and see me sometime."

"I will, Father." But she knew she wouldn't.

"Well, good-bye. I'll see myself out." Father McCord nodded to Jesse and once more at Connie, then moved into the hallway.

Jesse watched him go, then walked to where her mother sat and wrapped her arms around Connie's thin frame. "How are you, Mom?"

"Fine, dear. Happy birthday, by the way. My youngest is twenty-nine years old. I can't believe it."

Jesse heard the front door close as Father McCord left. "You can't believe it? How about me? One more year and I'll be thirty," she moaned.

"Oh, you look wonderful. I don't want to hear any complaints. What I wouldn't give to be twenty-nine again."

Jesse pulled back from the embrace. Connie was small, with a friendly face and an independent personality. Even at sixty-eight she remained vibrant, working several days a week at the church. Still, Jesse worried about her being alone in the house. "So how is everything at Sacred Heart, Mom?" The church was her life now.

"Fine, fine. You know, you really should stop by and visit Father McCord. He asks about you all the time. He has always been there for our family. He was there for me when you were sixteen and your father died. And again when your stepfather passed away last spring. Father McCord visited and called me almost as much as you did." Connie smiled lovingly at Jesse. "I don't know what I would have done without either of you. Father McCord was my Rock of Gibraltar and you were my angel. You've always been around for me when I've needed you. Unlike your siblings," Connie muttered under her breath as she stood up and moved to the sink.

"They've been there for you too, Mom."

Connie picked up a dish and began rinsing it. "I know your brothers and sisters have lives of their own, but it would be nice to hear from them more often than just that obligatory once-a-month call."

"They have kids. You know how hard that is. You raised nine of us."

Connie put the dish down on the counter and picked up another from the sink. "You have a full-time job and you go to school at night. You find the time to come and see me," she sniffed.

Jesse sat down at the kitchen table and shook her head as she remembered the family crowded around it for dinner, remembered the wonderful times they had all enjoyed—even without much money. Wonderful times—until her father had died.

"How's Todd Colton these days?" Connie asked.

Todd Colton was an old high school friend of Jesse's. "Fine, I guess. I had lunch with him a few months ago. Why do you ask?"

"I always thought you two would make a nice couple. He's a good-looking boy, you're a nice-looking girl. You always seemed to get along so well together. You're both still single. I never understood why it didn't turn into more."

"We tried a long time ago, Mom." Jesse hesitated. "It just didn't work out. But we're still good friends even though we don't see each other much."

"I remember the way you used to look at Todd. You could find romance with him."

"Mom, please."

"He's even better-looking now than he was in high school," Connie teased.

"When did you see him?" Jesse couldn't avoid her curiosity.

"He stopped by the house the other day, just to say hello. He's such a nice person."

"Yes, he is." Jesse noticed paint peeling from the ceiling. "How is your money holding out, Mom?"

"Fine." Connie's tone went flat.

"Don't brush me off so fast," Jesse admonished gently. "Tell me the truth."

Connie rinsed the last dish in the sink, then trudged wearily to the table and sat down. "I have a little bit of money in the bank, and I have my monthly Social Security check and your father's pension."

Jesse looked up, a look of mild surprise on her face. She had asked her mother so many times about her money situation but had always gotten nowhere. Now she was finally getting answers. "How much is a little bit in the bank?"

"A couple of thousand dollars."

"That's all? Didn't Dad have any life insurance policies?"

"Yes, but that money went to pay for your step-father Joe's hospital bills. For his heart attacks. It turned out Joe didn't have the retiree medical benefits we thought he did."

Jesse felt the anger rise instantly at the mention of her stepfather's name. Joe Schuman had been good for nothing—except spending her father's money. "Mom, how could you use Dad's money on Joe?"

"Let's not get into that." Connie sighed.

Jesse fought the anger as it rose several more degrees. "What about the house? You've lived here for twenty-five years, so it must be paid for. Surely you could get some equity out of it if you needed to."

Connie put a hand on Jesse's arm. "It's funny how things like clothes and braces cost so much. It just seemed like your father and I were never able to get ahead. We were always taking out another mortgage. I can't tell you how many of those papers I signed."

"Didn't Joe leave *anything*?"

"No." Connie had always wanted Jesse and Joe to get along, but it hadn't happened. Now Joe was dead and the opportunity for reconciliation was gone forever. "I never understood why you wouldn't give Joe a chance. He was a good man, not the monster you made him out to be. I needed someone. It wasn't his fault your father died."

Jesse felt the knot in her stomach tighten, but forced herself to say nothing, to hold back the story she so wanted to relate. "How much is the Social Security check and Dad's pension?"

"Together they come to eight hundred dollars a month."

"Have you fixed the roof yet?"

"Not yet. That takes a backseat to food and utility bills. I'm trying not to touch what I have in the bank just in case there's an emergency." Connie's expression became grim. "I've always told you not to ask about this. It's kind of depressing when you stop to analyze it. But it isn't your problem."

The fall wardrobe would have to wait. Jesse rose from the chair, retrieved her purse from the hall, then sat back down at the kitchen table.

"What are you doing?" Connie asked suspiciously.

Without answering, Jesse withdrew two hundred-dollar bills from the purse and laid them on the table. "Here, Mom. It won't fix the roof, but it'll help."

"I can't take that, Jesse. You gave me money last month and I swore I wouldn't take any more."

"Just take it."

"But . . ."

"Take it, Mom," Jesse said firmly.

Slowly Connie's fingers crept across the wooden tabletop to the money. "You really are an angel."

The man blew thick smoke into the dimly lighted office. "Do you smoke, Commander Pierce?"

"No, sir."

"Would you care for something to drink?" He motioned toward a wet bar in one corner of the room. "I know you don't allow yourself alcohol, but there are soft drinks as well."

"Thank you, no sir."

The man watched the naval aviator for a few moments as he puffed on the Monte Cristo again. Commander Pierce wore civilian clothes, but his crew cut, steely eyes, and ramrod-straight posture still exuded a no-nonsense military veneer. "I appreciate your flying in so quickly from Nevada. I know it's a long way to come just for a discussion, but this wasn't something I felt we could talk about over the phone."

"Absolutely no problem. It's a short flight in the jets I pilot. And I had other business here in Washington, so it worked out well."

"Good." The man rubbed his lips for a moment before continuing. "We have a situation at Area 51."

"What kind of situation, sir?"

"A situation that requires the skill you and the other men of your unit possess. I have ascertained that someone at Area 51 is passing along highly sensitive information to Senator Malcolm Walker regarding the A-100 project. Information Walker plans to use in an attempt to derail the project."

The commander's top lip curled into a sneer.

"The Navy needs the A-100, Commander Pierce. We *all* need the A-100," the man emphasized.

"Yes, sir."

"We organized your unit for this exact situation. You know what to do."

"Of course."

The man smiled. "You are protecting your country, Commander Pierce. You are doing the right thing. Sometimes we can't always play by the rules in our effort to do the right thing."

"I understand, sir," Pierce answered resolutely. "What is the traitor's name?"

"Captain Paul Nichols. Do you know who he is?"

"Yes. We'll take care of him."

"Good." The man puffed on his cigar once more. The situation had been addressed and resolved that quickly.

Jesse nodded politely at the receptionist, then moved quickly out of the professional offices and into the hallway. There she leaned back against the wall, shut her eyes, and exhaled heavily. The unexpected encounter with Father McCord and the conversation with her mother had rekindled the memories. Thank God Becky had been able to meet on such short notice.

# Chapter 12

Middleburg, Virginia, located thirty miles west of downtown Washington, lay claim to some of the most beautiful and expensive real estate in the East. Handsome stone mansions were set behind miles of six-foot-high white post fences dotting the rolling hills and lush fields of the picturesque countryside.

Middleburg also lay claim to some of the most expensive Thoroughbred horses in the world. For many who lived in this moneyed enclave, breeding horses was a livelihood highlighted by the Triple Crown, the Grand National, or the sale of a particularly fine stallion to a wealthy Arab emir for an exorbitant amount of cash. These people resided on thousand-acre farms, owned many horses, drove old-model Volvo station wagons to town on errands and Rolls-Royces to the fall steeplechases, and waited breathlessly for the spring crop of foals. They never discussed money, never flaunted it, and were never without it. They were the old money.

Jack Finnerty's fifteen-acre farm lay in the middle of this moneyed expanse. At one time his six-bedroom colonial had been a guest house on the huge Auchincloss estate, which now bounded Finnerty's farm on three sides. Four years ago, Finnerty had purchased the property to mark his election as president of General Engineering & Aerospace, the huge defense conglomerate headquartered in the Washington suburb of Falls Church.

Through brilliant afternoon sunshine pouring down from a cloudless blue sky, David Mitchell eyed the Finnerty stable, blue and white racing colors flying from the weather vane. The stable was two hundred yards away from the house, across neatly manicured lawns. He shook his head. This place seemed almost surreal, it was so beautiful. But would he really want to deal with the snobbery and false pretenses of this life? He laughed. Who the hell was he kidding? It was exactly what he wanted, why he was willing to take these huge risks. This was financial security. All he had ever wanted.

David's expression turned sour. God, the waiting was killing him. The test flight was supposed to have taken place yesterday and Finnerty was to have called from Nevada to relay the good news. News that the A-100 was a monstrous success, and that it would only be a matter of time before GEA's stock price lifted off into nosebleed territory. Only a matter of time before David could walk into Art Mohler's office and drop a newspaper story concerning the A-100 and its powerful effect on GEA right down on Mohler's antique desk.

But Finnerty hadn't called from Nevada. Instead his secretary had called, inviting David to Finnerty's home for a face-to-face meeting. That couldn't be a good sign, could it? A face-to-face instead of a simple phone call. Maybe the test flight hadn't gone so well after all. Suddenly a tidal wave of doubt rushed over him.

"Good afternoon, Mitchell." Finnerty moved into the room from the study, arms crossed tightly over his chest.

It occurred to David that he had rarely seen Finnerty without his arms crossed. "Hello, Jack." He always addressed Finnerty by his first name even though Finnerty always used David's last. David assumed Finnerty's use of last names in conversation—even when addressing close associates—was a habit with its roots buried in his military days.

"Sorry to keep you waiting." Finnerty spoke in a precise, nasal voice tinged with the hint of a New England accent. He was a fair-skinned man with short red hair reflecting his Irish ancestry via Boston. A former Marine made good in the corporate world, he spoke in rapid bursts, supremely confident of his observations and analysis.

"It's all right." But David's tone was measured. He wanted Finnerty to understand that he was irritated at not being called from Nevada yesterday.

"How's Wall Street?" Finnerty took David's hand and gripped it tightly.

David withdrew his hand quickly. He hated the way the guy always tried to tear fingers off when he shook hands, as if it was some kind of macho game to see if he could bring pain to your face. "I've told you before, Jack, what I do isn't considered Wall Street. As a port-folio manager I buy what Wall Street sells."

Finnerty tilted his head to one side and smiled his I-don't-give-a-crap-and-didn't-really-expect-an-answer smile. "Buy side, sell side, who the hell cares? It's all money, and money is Wall Street to me." Finnerty hesitated. "I don't have time to worry about Manhattan smoke and mirrors. I build military equipment for the United States government." He set his jaw. "And I do a damn good job of it."

"The stock market thinks otherwise," David replied coolly, unimpressed with Finnerty's bluster. "The stock was at twenty-five when I persuaded my people at Sagamore to buy the new issue from GEA. Now it's down to twenty-one and a half as of this morning. You told me this was a sure thing, and so did that damn godfather you sent me to."

The pressure had to be eating Mitchell's guts out for him to cut to the chase so quickly, Finnerty surmised. "You know it's been a tough time for the defense industry, what with all the budget slicing and the end of the cold war."

David sensed a certain sadness in Finnerty's tone at the mention of the cold war's demise, but he wasn't interested in reminiscing with an ex-Marine about outfoxing the Soviet Union. "What happened in the desert yesterday, Jack?"

"Let's take a walk, Mitchell. It's never a good idea to speak about these things in an unsecured place. The walls have ears." Finnerty's fear of listening devices bordered on paranoia.

"You mean you don't have your entire farm swept by the CIA every day?" David asked. He was trying not to control his impatience, but it was becoming more difficult by the minute.

"Enough, Mitchell." The sudden edge in Finnerty's voice zipped through David like an electric shock. It was a tone he had never before heard from Finnerty, a tone laced with warning.

"Fine." David's stomach churned but he managed to maintain a calm demeanor.

Outside the large front door the two men turned right, then walked slowly over the neatly manicured grass toward the stable. "How did it go in the desert yesterday?" David could wait no longer.

They stopped beneath a huge oak tree. Finnerty turned toward David. His face was grim. "Mitchell, the landing went fine. But the catapult takeoff . . ." Finnerty paused a beat and looked down. ". . . was perfect." He was suddenly grinning, obviously enjoying the fact that he had toyed with the younger man's emotions. "The entire flight couldn't have gone any better if we'd scripted it. And the billion dollars from Sagamore was a key factor in the A-100's success. GEA couldn't have done it without that friendly up-front money to help build the prototypes." Finnerty put a hand on David's shoulder. "I'm sure you took some heat from your people as the stock went down, but rest assured, Sagamore is ultimately going to reap a huge profit from this transaction."

"The test flight was successful." David whispered the words as if he couldn't believe them. As if the weight of the world had been lifted from his shoulders after two and a half years.

"Yes."

"Really?" he asked again, still unconvinced.

"Yes. What's amazing is that in this day and age of leaks and moles we've been able to keep this project secret for two and a half years. The black program stayed black. It gives me faith. If someone had leaked information about the A-100, GEA's stock price would have bounced around."

David barely heard Finnerty's voice. Insufferable stress had turned to euphoria in the time it took to flip a light switch. But there was still one thing that bothered him. "Why didn't you call me from Nevada yesterday? You said you would."

Finnerty began walking toward the stable again. He had called the others immediately, but Mitchell would never know that. "I couldn't find a secure phone." It was a lame excuse, but it was something for Mitchell to hang on to.

"But I asked you to—"

"What difference does it make?" Finnerty cut David off abruptly. "You know now."

They reached the stable and stopped at the paddock gate. Finnerty checked the area to make certain none of the grooms were within earshot. "The plane easily fulfilled all prototype specifications. We can begin production immediately." He dropped his arms from his chest for a moment. "A hundred and fifty planes a year for the next seven years. Over a thousand in all, not to mention the maintenance agreement." Finnerty's voice was hushed. "When details of the contract become public, the investment community will go ballistic. The A-100 means an extra twenty to twenty-five billion dollars of revenue a *year* for GEA. Maybe more."

David nodded but said nothing. He was furious that Finnerty had put him through an extra day of agony. The bit about the lack of a secure phone line was bullshit and they both knew it.

"GEA's stock will skyrocket," Finnerty observed.

"The stock should be pushing a hundred dollars a share very quickly, based on my projections of GEA's incremental cash flow attributable to the A-100 project," David agreed. The price would now certainly blow past the fifty-dollar number Art Mohler had been so worried about. David raised an eyebrow. "It's going to make all those GEA stock options you and your management friends gave yourselves six months ago extremely valuable." He watched for Finnerty's reaction.

"That's none of your concern." Finnerty's eyes narrowed. "Don't forget, Mitchell, you've got your own personal GEA options too. The ones I was able to siphon off for you and put in a street name. If the stock goes to even fifty bucks a share, you're going to be worth ten million dollars more than you are right now. This will have been a very nice deal for you personally." A slight breeze blew dust up from the paddock, and Finnerty turned his head for a moment. "I've always wondered how the senior people at Sagamore would react if they knew one of the conditions you imposed on me, before you would consider investing in GEA, was that you personally receive options to buy stock." Finnerty crossed his arms over his chest again. "Of course, no one will ever know about that

little detail"—Finnerty glanced at Mitchell ominously—
"except me."

David cleared his throat nervously. He had negotiated the options as an insurance policy, as his own
bonus for taking this huge risk on behalf of Sagamore.

"I bet they'd also like to know about the million dollars you took out of that Sagamore holding company
two and half years ago as influence money for your
godfather downtown," Finnerty continued. It was
time to start hammering David Mitchell, time to start
making him realize that he'd fallen into a maze, one
from which there was no escape. "I'm sure you used
some creative bookkeeping to account for the payment."
This was why Finnerty hadn't called from Nevada, why
he had requested the face-to-face instead. So that he
could begin to tighten the screws. Mitchell had to realize
that he had unwittingly become their pawn. "What did
you call the payment to the man downtown, Mitchell, a
loan to a supplier?"

David swallowed hard. Loan to supplier. That was
exactly what he had called the payment. Finnerty's
accuracy was eerie.

"You're going to use profits from your GEA options
to repay the money you took out of the Sagamore
holding company, aren't you?"

David almost nodded, then caught himself.

"Because after all, you'll still have a ton of cash from
the options even after you personally repay the money.
*And* you'll have your job." Finnerty pressed his arms
tightly against his chest. "The FBI would probably like
to know about all this too."

"Why the hostility, Jack?" David asked, his voice low.

"I don't need you commenting about options my management team and I vote ourselves."

"I was just making an observation."

Finnerty didn't give a rat's ass if Mitchell cared about the options. This conversation wasn't about that at all. It was about an intricate initiation process. Just as in the Marines, you broke them down, then rebuilt them the way you wanted them. "Don't forget, Mitchell, I brought you into this game, and I can kick you out anytime I want. And I can make things very difficult for you."

David suddenly felt his blood burn. "And I couldn't do the same for you?" This was a bad idea, but he didn't want Finnerty thinking he could be manipulated so easily. "You give me away and my godfather downtown gets his too. The FBI would trace the payment from the holding company straight to him. I doubt he'd like you very much for that."

Finnerty smiled faintly. Mitchell was a strong one. Which was why they liked him. "You really think the FBI would find him at the end of that trail?"

David missed the implication. "I bet I could make enough noise to have production of the A-100 put on hold indefinitely. That would screw up your plans, wouldn't it, Jack? It might even push GEA into bankruptcy. GEA needed the A-100 to survive. Isn't that what you told me at the beginning of all this?"

Finnerty said nothing.

"Can you imagine if I really went to the FBI?" David kept going. "Christ, there would be investigations everywhere, from the White House to Capitol Hill. It would tear the entire secrecy veil off the black budget. There wouldn't be any way to keep a lid on it at that point. The press would devour the story. It would be bigger than Watergate and OJ combined. The country would be glued to the tube watching the hearings. I can see it now, Jack. I can see you sitting behind one of those hearing-room tables, facing a couple of rows of senators, sweating your ass off." David had suddenly realized that the ordeal wasn't over just because the A-100 had passed from prototype into production. It was just beginning, and it would follow him for the rest of his life.

"Be careful of what you think you know, David," Finnerty murmured quietly.

It was the first time David could remember Finnerty's addressing him by his first name, and he recoiled slightly in surprise.

"Things aren't always as they appear."

"What the hell does that mean, Jack?"

Finnerty pointed a finger at the younger man. "Figure it out for yourself. Despite this conversation, I think you're a savvy individual. But remember, there are a lot of savvy people in the world. Savvy people who've been around a lot longer than you."

David studied the intensity in the older man's eyes, trying to understand. Then the stretch limousine rolling up Finnerty's long driveway caught David's eye. "Expecting someone?" He motioned toward the vehicle.

Finnerty shook his head. "No, it's for you. I didn't want you to have to take a train all the way back to Baltimore."

"Mighty considerate of you."

"You're welcome," Finnerty said dryly, as they began walking back to the house.

The limousine pulled around the circle before the house and stopped in front of the stone walkway leading to the main door.

"Remember, Mitchell, you've got another two-million-dollar payment to make. A million when the contract was signed. Two million when full production started. That was the final deal. Production has started, and you need to make that second payment to your godfather, as you like to call him."

"I'll make the payment. Don't worry."

A small man hopped out of the driver's side and rushed to the back door to open it as the two men neared the limousine.

"Just wanted to make sure you . . ." Finnerty hesitated for a moment as he saw the driver. ". . . to make sure you were on the ball."

"Oh, yeah." David had noticed the strange look Finnerty had given the driver. "I'm on the ball." He slid into the backseat without shaking hands.

Minutes later the limousine turned left out of Finnerty's driveway and began heading away from the farm. What the hell had Finnerty meant by that comment about things not always being as they appeared? David glanced at the rearview mirror and into the eyes of the driver. "Got anything to drink in here?"

"Everything's in the cabinet under the television." The driver turned partially on the bench front seat and spoke loudly through the open partition.

"Thanks." David quickly filled a highball glass half full of scotch and ice, then took a long swallow. Normally he didn't care for scotch, but today it tasted good.

Farms flashed by outside the tinted glass as he reclined into the leather seat and took another swallow. How had Finnerty found him two and a half years ago? The question had always nagged at David, but he had never asked Finnerty, assuming there wouldn't be a straight answer.

"Where are we going?" The driver turned again on the seat.

"Baltimore," David answered listlessly.

"Are you another Sagamore person?"

"Excuse me?" David's eyes flashed back to the rearview mirror.

"I'm sorry, I thought maybe you were with the same firm as the other guy."

"What other guy?"

"A guy I gave a ride to late last night—early this morning, actually."

David leaned forward on the seat. "Do you remember his name?" He tried to ask the question casually, as if he weren't really interested in the answer.

"Uh, yeah. His name was Mohler. What a work-aholic. It was three in the morning and he was going back to the office."

David didn't hear the last few words. As far as he knew, Mohler had never met Jack Finnerty. Mohler had accompanied David on a due-diligence trip when Sagamore was originally considering the GEA investment two and a half years ago, but Finnerty hadn't attended any of the meetings that day. Mohler was certainly concerned about the GEA investment now, and might have contacted Finnerty on his own to ask questions about the company's financial stability. And it would be typical of a corporate executive, even the president, to respond to that call. After all, Sagamore had a $1 billion investment in GEA—a 30 percent ownership stake. But why would Mohler meet Finnerty at the farm? GEA headquarters was much closer to Baltimore. And why would they meet at three in the morning?

"Where in Baltimore are you going, sir?"

Finnerty had given the driver such an odd look, as if he had wanted to pull the man aside to say something, then thought better of it. He must have recognized the guy and worried that this might happen.

"Sir!"

"What?"

"Where exactly are you going?"

David hesitated, trying to remember. "The Stouffer Hotel, downtown Baltimore."

"Thanks."

Things were not always as they appeared. David tipped the glass nearly upside down, finished the scotch in one gulp, and poured another drink.

Elizabeth Gilman rose from her seat at the head table and moved gracefully toward the podium to the din of a standing ovation from the thousand guests crammed into the Stouffer Hotel's main ballroom. The Governor's Round Table—a group of the state's most prominent corporate executives, political leaders, and philanthropists—had just selected her as Maryland's woman of the year.

The governor met Elizabeth at the podium, shook her hand gently, whispered something in her ear, then held up his hands as a signal for quiet. Slowly the ovation died away as people sat down again.

"Ladies and gentlemen, I would just like to say a few words before I give you your woman of the year." Bulbs flashed as cameramen documented the event for tomorrow morning's *Baltimore Sun* papers. "Elizabeth." His deep voice reverberated throughout the huge room as he turned to face her. "You are a shining example for us all. You operate one of the largest and most successful investment funds in the country, and yet you constantly amaze us with the time and energy you devote to your charitable endeavors.

"Specifically, we must thank you again for the new wing at the Children's Hospital. But, ladies and gentlemen"—he turned back to face the crowd—"it isn't just the fact that she has made the funds available. She has also made her valuable time available to those children. Children who don't have families to help them through their ordeals. I have seen the tears of a little five-year-old girl as she lay alone on a sterile bed wondering what cancer was, why it had struck her and why she would have to endure another operation. I have seen those tears evaporate as this wonderful lady standing next to me sat on the bed for hours and gave that little girl hope. I can only say that her actions are an inspiration for us all. There is much to do, and we can make a difference. Ladies and gentlemen, Elizabeth Gilman."

The assembled throng rose again and thundered their approval. Elizabeth moved to the microphone as the governor retreated a few steps to cede her the entire spotlight. She gazed out over the auditorium, a picture of grace and humility. She motioned for the crowd to be seated, but her action only served to intensify their ovation.

David stood and clapped with the rest, but he was not looking up toward the podium, he was gazing over at the next table, watching Art Mohler applaud. Why had Mohler been at Jack Finnerty's farm? Why at three o'clock this morning? Why hadn't Mohler told him he was going to see Finnerty? Why hadn't Finnerty said something? The questions kept running through his mind.

He turned and focused on Elizabeth, who was still basking in the glow of the ovation. Somehow he was going to find the answers.

# Chapter 13

Todd Colton was only twenty-nine but had already purchased his tombstone and inscribed the epitaph— *Here lies a man who attacked life*—because, as he put it, the odds were damn good he wouldn't be around very long and he wanted it to read as it should, not as someone else *thought* it should. He was allergic to suits, short on commitment, and completely uninsurable.

On most weekends he raced motorcycles, parachuted from airplanes, and was an avid scuba diver. During the week he supported his hobbies with fees earned as a private investigator, generating a steady caseload from referrals by friends on Maryland's state police force. He had no pretensions, was generous to a fault and wore his heart on his sleeve.

Once in a while Todd gave himself a break from risking life and limb on weekends to pursue an even more dangerous pastime—the blackjack tables in Atlantic City.

The black bow-tied dealer stared at Todd. Dealers wanted people to play quickly, because the odds were always in the casino's favor. Therefore, the more hands played the better the chances for the house to come out way ahead. Todd sipped the bourbon and water while he studied his cards. He knew the dealer was irritated but he ignored the man's fingers tapping angrily on the green felt of the table. The bet was five hundred dollars and he was going to take as much time as necessary.

The dealer showed an ace on top of his down card. Todd had fifteen showing. The odds were excellent he wasn't going to beat the dealer with fifteen. But the odds were even better he'd go over twenty-one and bust if he took another card. Suddenly the bells of the slot machines in the background sounded like fingernails on a chalkboard.

"You want a hit, pal?" the dealer prodded.

Todd grimaced. "Yeah."

The dealer smiled and the other five players shook their heads. Bad idea.

Todd's eyes narrowed as the dealer slid the card quickly from the dispenser and flipped it over. His heart jumped a beat. Six of clubs. Twenty-one. He tilted his head and grinned triumphantly at the dealer. "I'm back," he announced loudly, then glanced up at the ceiling. "No stopping me now." The men who ran the casino were up there walking around on the floor above, staring down through one way glass to make certain no one was working on the inside with a dealer. "My luck just turned."

But Todd's luck hadn't turned. The six of clubs was just a momentary respite from a long losing streak. The next hand he bet a thousand dollars—everything he had—and went bust as the dealer flipped over a king of hearts on top of Todd's eight of hearts and five of spades. It was the dealer's turn to smile triumphantly.

"Too bad." An older man in a gray T-shirt and jeans, gambling away his monthly Social Security check, smacked his lips in disgust. "That dealer's just too hot."

"I'll be back." Todd grinned and slapped the old man on the back. "Save my place for me, will you, Charlie?"

"Sure." Charlie laughed. You had to admire the young man. He could smile in the face of anything. Charlie had seen this same scenario unfold a few weekends before. Todd gambled big, lost it fast, but smiled right through the disaster.

Todd moved away from the table and walked down a long, noisy corridor separating the blackjack and craps tables. He had to find Harry.

Harry the Horse sat in a small office on the fourth floor of the casino perusing racing forms. He was a huge man with a bald head and a tough Philadelphia accent. Todd tapped on the door.

"Hello, Mr. Colton," Harry said casually as he looked up from the papers. "Burn through that last five thousand yet?"

"As a matter of fact . . ." Todd hesitated. This was embarrassing. "I did."

"You just don't learn, do you?"

"I'm one hand away, Harry."

Harry had been a loan shark for years. He knew better. "Everybody always is."

"Can I have another five thousand?" Todd asked impatiently. He wanted to get back to the tables.

"Mr. Colton, you already owe us twenty-five thousand. We've advanced you fifteen against your car and ten unsecured. Do you really think borrowing another five is a good idea?"

"Come on, Harry. No sermons."

"You're gonna have to start paying us back soon."

"Okay."

"I'm not kidding."

"Sure." Harry had been saying that for months.

Harry pulled open a desk drawer, withdrew a stack of fresh one hundred dollar bills and counted out fifty, then counted them again. He arranged them into a neat pile and held them out for Todd. As Todd's hand came forward, Harry suddenly pulled his back. "I'm going to take five hundred as an interest payment on what you already owe us." Harry pulled five hundred-dollar bills from the stack in his hand and placed them down on his racing forms. "Only forty-five hundred dollars left but the loan is for five thousand. You sure you want it now?"

Todd took the money from Harry and grinned. "Absolutely. Hell, I'll probably be back up here in an hour to pay off my entire debt. I can feel lady luck on my arm already." Todd turned and trotted toward the elevators with his new cache stuffed into his shirt pocket.

Harry picked up the racing forms. That wasn't lady luck young Mr. Colton had felt take his arm. That was the devil.

Air Force Captain Paul Nichols watched the two F-22s take off side by side through the window of his office. The bright Nevada sun glistened off their sleek fuselages as they rose quickly from the desert. It was a beautiful sight. He watched until they were nothing but black specks against the azure sky, then stood up and moved out of the office and down the corridor toward the lavatory.

"Captain Nichols?"

The captain stopped halfway through the lavatory doorway. "Yes?" He glanced at the sergeant, then noticed the two MPs behind the man.

"Sir, I've been ordered to take you into custody immediately."

The captain began to protest, but quickly realized it would be pointless to do so.

After spending hours in a small windowless holding cell, the captain was blindfolded and clandestinely moved to the cargo bay of a C-130. Hands secured behind his back, he heard the familiar whine of propellers as they began to turn, then had to steady himself with his feet as the plane lurched forward and taxied away from the hangar.

"Can you hear me?" someone screamed in his ear over the din of the engines as the plane throttled up and began lumbering down the runway.

He nodded immediately, wanting to seem as cooperative as possible. He had heard rumors of the small detachments that protected black-budget secrecy, but never thought it possible that they actually existed. Now he wasn't so certain.

"You provided Senator Malcolm Walker with information regarding the A-100 black program, didn't you?" The same voice screamed at him again.

This time Captain Nichols didn't answer immediately. His head remained tilted forward at a thirty-five-degree angle—the natural posture for a blindfolded person.

The voice screamed the question once more.

Nichols nodded slowly. It was pointless to deny the charge. They probably had videotapes of him going through the files. Christ, how could he have been so stupid?

"On your feet, Captain!"

When he didn't react immediately, several pairs of hands pulled him to a standing position, then hustled him across the floor of the cargo bay. He turned his head in both directions quickly. "Hey, what the hell are you doing?" he yelled, but there was no response from his captors.

Suddenly he realized what was going to happen. He kicked and twisted his body frantically against their hold, but to no avail. They simply picked him up and carried him to the door.

"Think twice next time about being so free with information, you bastard!"

Air whipped about Nichols's face as the plane continued to climb. "Please don't do this!" he begged, screaming so loudly he tore a vocal cord.

For a few minutes they held him there, teetering on the brink of death, allowing the plane to reach the desired altitude. Then they pushed him out the door at ten thousand feet.

He tumbled over and over, struggling to free himself from the twine securing his wrists as he dropped sickeningly through the night sky. Commander Pierce remained close to Captain Nichols all the way down, watching his pitiful struggles remorselessly. Military men who would break the code they had sworn to uphold and who would jeopardize national security had to be dealt with severely. There was no alternative but swift, harsh retribution in matters such as these.

Captain Nichols realized he had precious little time left. He had jumped many times and had a sixth sense as to his altitude. He was probably five thousand feet up at most, probably closer to four or three. He was screaming through the air at terminal velocity, completely blind. One moment he would be alive, the next dead. But he wouldn't have any warning. He would never know what hit him. Maybe it was better that way. Suddenly he felt himself beginning to convulse. The end must be near.

Commander Pierce checked the altimeter one more time, then pointed the remote control at the falling body several hundred yards away, outlined by the flashing lights on the ultralight parachute they had forced over the captain's head during the struggle in the cargo hold. He pushed the button, then pulled the rip cord of his own chute.

Suddenly Captain Nichols felt the incredible G-forces strain his entire body as the parachute opened, responding to the electric pulse from Commander Pierce's remote. His body flipped almost upside down against the snap of the ropes, then settled comfortably beneath the parachute, and he floated gently to the desert floor.

For several moments he lay on the sand beneath the chute, sobbing, then felt the material being pulled from atop his body and sensed someone kneeling down next to him. Then he heard the voice.

"You will remain silent on this matter for the remainder of your life. You will be incarcerated for six months, at the end of which time you will be dishonorably discharged from the military. You will accept that punishment without question. Any attempt by you to interfere with that exact course of events and the parachute will not open next time. Do you understand that, Captain Nichols?" Commander Pierce spoke calmly.

Nichols lifted his head slowly, still blindfolded. "Yes," he moaned. Then his head fell back to the sand and he blacked out.

Two hours later, just as dawn was breaking over the Nevada desert, Captain Nichols was back on base, physically no worse for wear. But his nerves would never be the same.

Pierce watched with satisfaction as Nichols was hustled into the cell by the men of his rogue group. The commander's lips curled into a quick smile. Malcolm Walker's Area 51 informant had been neutralized.

# Chapter 14

Jesse watched Todd from across the table as he salted his french fries. He was tall and well built, with a strong, tanned face framed by long brown hair. It wasn't a face that would ever grace the cover of *Gentleman's Quarterly*, but he had something. Perhaps it was the sheer force of his outgoing personality, his caring nature, the crooked smile, or the way he looked at her with those eyes. God, those eyes. They actually changed color and could be steel blue or dark green depending on the day. She found herself gazing at them, thinking about the possibilities, then looked away quickly. It couldn't be. That had been Becky's consistent advice.

"It's good to see you, Jess." Todd never pronounced the last *e* of her name.

"It's good to see you too."

"Did your mom tell you I stopped by last week?"

Instantly Jesse thought back to her own visit with her mother, and how the chance meeting with Father McCord and the discussion of her mother's money problems had reminded her so vividly of her stepfather.

"Are you all right, Jess?" Perhaps it was only his imagination, but she seemed distracted.

She nodded quickly. "Yes. It was nice of you to check in on her."

"Well, I'm just a prince of a guy, aren't I?" He laughed.

"Yes, you are," she said quietly. "How's everything going for you?" She knew about his dangerous hobbies.

"Great. Well, a few weeks ago I was jumping from a friend's Cessna and my chute didn't open until a thousand feet. I landed in the top of a pine tree, twisted my ankle, and ran into a feisty woodpecker who wasn't very glad to see me. The ankle is still a little sore, but otherwise I'm fine." One side of his mouth rose noticeably higher than the other as he smiled. "What about you, Jess? How's life for you?"

She knew about his inability to make commitments too. Still, after all this time she was dangerously attracted to that smile, though of course she could never tell him that. He might try to spark what had lingered just below the surface for so long, and that could prove disastrous. It might break the delicate balance of her emotions and bring everything tumbling out into the open.

"Jess?"

He had been there for her that terrible night twelve years ago. It didn't seem fair that he had to be precluded from being with her because he had been the one to help, the one who had cradled her as she cried. But Becky had assured Jesse it had to be that way, that Todd could not be anything more than a casual friend. Not if Jesse wanted to keep the hostility under control.

Not if she wanted to keep it from her mother forever. Too much contact with the past and it would all come spilling out, Becky counseled over and over. And Todd was an intricate part of that past. Of that night.

Jesse grimaced. Becky would be upset to learn Jesse had come to Todd for help again and that there was a strong chance they would be seeing each other more than just infrequently now. But there seemed to be no other choice to Jesse. Once more, Todd was the one she had to turn to.

"Jess," Todd said loudly, "what's going on over there?"

She suddenly realized he was trying to get her attention. "What?"

"Where are you?"

"I'm sorry. I was thinking about something I have to do at work."

"I think you're just overwhelmed to see me again."

Jesse shook her head. She didn't want to give him an excuse to push. Or did she? Was that really why she had called him?

"Well, I guess we should get this over with." Todd reached down to his plate, picked up several french fries, and put them in his mouth, smiling as he chewed. "We go through it every time we get together. Which is not often enough, I might add. Of course, you'll get mad at me. But what the hell?"

"What are you talking about?"

"Can we start going out?" Todd's smile became wider as he saw her shake her head automatically. "See, I told you." He pointed at her. "I ask you the same thing every time we get together, and every time I ask, you say no."

"Todd, stop it."

"I think my problem is that you're dating those guys in suits and ties. You think they're the answer, but they aren't."

She looked away without responding.

"Enough of the boring bankers, Jess. You need somebody who doesn't sit behind a desk all day feeding irrelevant numbers into a computer."

"Todd, stop it!" Suddenly Jesse became aware that the other patrons were watching them curiously.

"What's wrong?" He was still smiling, enjoying flustering her.

"I called you because I need your help."

"And here I am, at your service, ready to leap tall buildings in a single bound."

"Be serious." Jesse folded her hands on the table in front of her plate. Perhaps it hadn't been such a good idea to call him after all.

"I'm sorry." He could see her irritation quickly turning to anger. "I just get a little crazy when I see you. You know that."

Jesse tried to hide her smile. He could always do this to her. She couldn't stay mad at him, no matter how hard she tried.

"Come on, Jess, who's your friend?" Todd smiled mischievously.

"Stop it." She felt her smile coming on again and didn't want to give him the satisfaction of seeing it.

"Who's your buddy?"

"Stop it."

"Who's your pal?"

She could fight it no longer. "You are." She put a hand to her face to cover her grin.

Todd laughed. "It would have been better if you had said you get a little crazy when you see me too, but I know you have a difficult time saying things like that."

"What do you mean?"

He pushed out his lower lip, as he always did when he was thinking deeply. "You're kind of uptight sometimes."

"I am not."

"Yes you are." He said it with such conviction there was no reason for her to protest any further. "But then you probably have a right to be."

He knew her so well. "I try not to be."

Todd picked up several more french fries. "You just need to spend more time with me. I'd loosen you up."

"I'm sure."

"What's that supposed to mean?" he asked quickly.

"Nothing."

Todd watched her for several seconds, tempted to push further. He had sensed an opening, a subtle signal from her that maybe she was finally ready to take a chance. But it was probably just his imagination. "What can I do for you?" His tone became businesslike for the first time since they had sat down. "I'd like to think you really did call just because you wanted to see me, but I have to believe there's another reason. You sounded a little jittery on the phone."

The words at the end of Robinson's memo flooded back to Jesse. *Trust no one.* But that was impossible. She couldn't follow up on Neil's memo completely by herself. She needed someone's help, and though Todd could be irresponsible and reckless at times, he was as trustworthy a human being as there was in the world.

"It might be dangerous," she said.

"Look at me—I'm shaking."

"I'm not kidding. It may involve some powerful people."

He nodded. Jesse wasn't prone to exaggeration, and he sensed this might be something more than just an active imagination. "Tell you what. Let's finish lunch, then take a walk."

"Okay."

They ate quickly, paid the lunch tab, and walked out of the diner. Five minutes later they were standing at the end of a long observation pier jutting out into Baltimore's harbor.

Todd leaned against the railing. "So, what's the deal?"

Jesse moved closer to him. A man seated on a bench twenty feet away seemed to be taking too keen an interest in their conversation, and she would take no chances that anyone other than Todd might hear this. "A few nights ago my boss, Neil Robinson, died of a heart attack in the lobby of the Grand Hyatt," she began quietly. "The next morning I received an E-mail message from him, sent on a delayed basis, asking for my help and citing a conspiracy he believed he had stumbled onto. He told me he had hidden a file at his river house, and I was to pick it up."

"Did you get it?"

"Yes."

"What was in it?"

Jesse looked at the man again, but he seemed to be paying no attention now. "Elbridge Coleman's personal and corporate tax returns for the last few years. And notes Neil had taken during a conversation with someone he doesn't identify. Apparently Neil had suspicions about Elbridge Coleman's election campaign."

Todd raised his eyebrows. A Senate election campaign. This might be interesting after all. "What kind of suspicions?"

"That Coleman is simply a front. That he's being funded by people in this country who want to get rid of the man currently holding the Senate seat Coleman is trying to win."

"You mean Malcolm Walker."

"Yes."

"Why would these people want to get rid of Senator Walker?"

"According to the notes, Neil believed the motive lies in the fact that Walker is an outspoken critic of the military. They want to get rid of him because he's waged war on the Defense Department since he was elected to the Senate six years ago."

"Waged war on the Defense Department. That's an interesting way to put it."

"Yes, I guess it is." Jesse smiled. "Anyway, he's been on a one-man crusade to hack the defense budget and has enjoyed some success during his first term. Neil wrote in his notes that he and his unnamed source believed Coleman was being funded by people friendly to the defense industry. People who would like to see the defense budget grow instead of shrink."

"Was Neil specific about who these people might be?"

"No."

"Was there anything else in the file?"

"No."

"That's it?" Todd was suddenly annoyed. "That's all you have? Just a few tax returns and your boss's notes?"

"Yes."

"Jess, I mean no disrespect to your boss, or to you for that matter, but I think he was just a little off his rocker." Todd held his thumb and forefinger so that there was a small space between them. "Look, people have suspicions all the time, but nine times out of ten, probably more, there isn't anything to them. Believe me, I see it constantly in my line of work. This is most likely one of those times. It's sad that he died, but you need to let him go."

"I would agree with you except . . ." Her voice faded.

"Except what?"

"Someone else came to Neil's house on the Severn the night I was there getting the file. I assume he was looking for the file as well. And this was not a friendly person."

"What do you mean?"

"The guy chased me through the woods to my car and shot out my windshield."

"My God, were you hurt?"

"Just some small cuts on my arms." She pulled up the sleeve of her blouse to show him the scabs.

"Do you think he saw your license plate?" Todd's skeptical tone disappeared.

"I don't think so. My headlights were in his eyes, and then I cut them as soon as I was past him."

"Did you report the incident to your superiors or the police?"

"No. I really didn't have anything concrete to tell them, and I figured someone might be able to trace me that way. If I filed a formal report, I mean."

He nodded. "Did you take your car into a shop to have the glass replaced?" Todd asked the questions rapidly.

"No. I didn't think that was a good idea either. I thought maybe someone could track me down that way too. Sara Adams, another woman in the branch, is giving me a ride to work. We live close to each other."

"I remember Sara. You introduced me to her last year when I came by your office."

"Oh, that's right."

"She's a pretty good friend of yours, isn't she?"

Jesse and Sara had known each other for six years now. "A very good friend."

"Well, it was smart not to have your car fixed. You probably would have paid with a credit card, and whoever was after you might have been able to trace you by checking glass repair shops. Tell you what—I'll rent you a car under my name until this is over."

"Thanks. That's really nice. I'll pay you back."

He waved a hand as if there was no need to worry about it. "How about the E-mail? Any way they could get to you because of that?"

"I talked to a person at the branch about it. He's in systems. I had erased the file from my computer, and when he searched the computer system, there was no record of Neil's sending the message to me. I don't know how Neil covered the trail, but he did. I never made a physical copy of the E-mail either, so there's no record on the printer log."

A seagull landed on the railing a few feet away. Todd watched it preen. "You don't think your boss actually died of a heart attack, do you?"

She hesitated. "It's strange. I found the young woman who waited on Neil that night at the Hyatt. He had a drink with another man. The waitress didn't remember much about the other man except that he didn't stick around when Neil had the attack. The paramedics asked if Neil was with anyone and she said yes, but then they couldn't find the guy. Don't you think that's odd?"

"Yes, I do. Did you check the date book in Neil's office? Maybe the person's name was in there."

"That's another curious thing. Someone took a lot of stuff out of Neil's office right after he died."

"Really? Like what?"

"His appointment book, the hard drive from his computer, disks, some files, and a few other things."

"Do you have any idea who it was?"

"No. Some workmen came and delivered a new desk around nine-thirty that morning. Neil's secretary thinks they took the things, because she found out later there was no requisition for a new desk and she noticed the things were missing from his office around ten, just after they'd left. Poor woman. She didn't even know Neil was dead at that point. She just thought he was late."

"Did she inform anyone that the items were missing?"

"She called the police and they came, but they don't have anything yet."

"And they probably never will."

The sound of a freighter horn rolled down the harbor as the huge ship cast off its moorings and tug-boats began pushing it toward open water.

"Anything else you can tell me?" Todd asked.

Jesse glanced down the harbor in the direction of the horn. She took a deep breath of salt air. "You'll probably just think I'm being paranoid."

"No, I won't. There are enough coincidences and unexplained events here to make me think you really should be careful."

"The other morning, the morning after I was chased, I had to pull an old file from our branch storage center. It was a file from a long time ago, so it wasn't on the central computer. Anyway, when I came back, I ran into this guy coming out of my office. I'd never seen him before."

"And?"

"He said he was looking for Sara. I asked her later if this guy had come by, but she didn't know what I was talking about. But the guy had a visitor's badge, so I figured they must have called Sara before letting him come up. They always do that before allowing visitors into the building. Security has been really tight ever since the Oklahoma City bombing."

"Did you talk to the security people at the front desk about this?"

Jesse nodded. "There was no record on the register of anyone signing in to visit Sara around that time."

"Someone seems to have excellent access to government buildings," Todd observed. "Was there a name on the guy's badge? The man who was coming out of your office."

"I don't remember."

"I know this sounds crazy, but do you think Sara could be involved?"

Jesse watched the seagull inch its way toward them. Sara had been asking so many questions lately, and she seemed flustered when pressed about the man who was supposedly visiting her. But the idea was ridiculous. "No."

"Was the guy doing anything in your office that would make you suspicious?"

"I don't know. We literally ran into each other in the doorway. I was going in, he was coming out."

"Do you think it was the person who chased you at the river house? Did you get a look at the guy that night?"

"Only for a second, in the headlights. He had a baseball cap pulled down over his face, so I didn't see much of his features, but I'm pretty sure he didn't have a beard. The guy in my office did."

Todd leaned farther back against the railing. "A beard's an easy disguise."

"Well, that certainly makes me feel better."

"I'm sorry," Todd said gently. "Look, if that was him in your office, he certainly had the opportunity to take action against you, and he didn't. And anyway, how could he have found you if he didn't see the license tag and you didn't take the car in to be fixed?"

She pushed her long blond hair behind her ears as she thought for a moment. "I don't know."

They stood in silence for a moment watching the commercial and pleasure craft crisscross the harbor.

"I like your hair that way."

"What?" Jesse looked into his eyes.

"I always remember you wearing your hair up. It looks great down like that. Are you wearing it like that all the time now?"

"Uh huh." She didn't want to tell him this was the first day she had let it down in a long time.

"By the way, happy birthday a day late. I have your present, but I forgot to bring it."

"Sure, sure." She nudged him playfully. "That's what you always used to say. And somehow the present never found its way to me."

"I'm serious. I have one for you."

"Oh, God!" She was suddenly alarmed.

"What's the matter?"

"I completely forgot. I've got a meeting at two o'clock." She checked her watch. "And it's already five after."

"So I'm making you forget time now." Todd gave her the crooked smile. "I think after all these years I'm finally making progress."

"Come on." She started walking quickly away.

A few minutes later they were almost back to the branch building. As they neared the main entrance, Jesse slowed down.

"Hello there," David called out. He pushed off from the long black limousine on which he had been leaning and moved toward them. As he came closer, he saw Jesse's surprise. "Oh, right." He snapped his fingers as if he'd forgotten something. "I told you I'd pick you up, but I guess I didn't tell you what kind of car to expect." David eyed Todd for a moment, then looked back at Jesse. "You look great today, Jesse. I like your hair that way."

Before she could protest, David had taken her hand and kissed her cheek. "Thanks," she murmured, glancing back at Todd.

David moved past Jesse. "David Mitchell." David extended his hand to Todd.

"Todd Colton."

As they shook, they exchanged curt nods.

"So." David turned back to Jesse as he let go of Todd's hand. "Ready for an afternoon at Sagamore?"

"Yes. But give me just a minute."

"Sure." David understood immediately and walked back to the limousine.

Todd whistled softly. "So, Jess, is this what you do in the afternoons now? Ride around in limousines? I guess bankers aren't so boring after all. No wonder we ran back here for your meeting."

"Stop it. David works for a money management firm in Towson called Sagamore. I met the woman who runs the firm at business school the other night and she asked me to come out and visit. It would be a great place to work after I graduate. That's all this is." She paused. "As if I have to explain anything to you."

"That may be all it is for you." Todd motioned toward David. "But that's not all it is for him."

"What are you talking about?"

"If there's one thing I can recognize, Jess, it's a bird dog on scent. That one's got yours so far up his nostrils it's driving him crazy."

"Quiet, will you?" She smiled at David, silently assuring him that she needed just a few more seconds, then turned back to Todd. "We met the other night for the first time. There's nothing going on." She grabbed his hand. "Hey, will you help me with what we talked about?"

Todd looked at her face for a moment without saying anything, as if trying to judge for himself whether or not there was anything going on with David. "Yes, but we'll have to talk about my fee at some point."

"Fee?"

"Sure," he said, smiling. "Some of us have to work for a living. Some of us can't afford limousines."

"Enough." Jesse held up her hands. "I'll call you later," she said over her shoulder, shaking her head as she slid onto the limousine's leather seat. So he was going to charge her a fee.

Todd watched the sleek black car move away from the curb. About the only kind of compensation he was going to require of Jesse Hayes was her time. And he was going to try to get as much of that from now on as he could.

"Ever been in a limousine before?" David asked from the seat facing hers.

"No," she said brusquely, still annoyed at Todd. The male ego was such a fragile thing. Of course, now that she thought about it, she had never seen Todd jealous before. Jesse smiled. Maybe a little jealousy wasn't such a bad thing.

"Hello." Elizabeth Gilman rose from the floral-patterned chair and moved out from behind the dark wood desk as soon as she noticed Jesse and David standing at her office door.

"Elizabeth, you remember Jesse Hayes." David played chief of staff for a moment.

"Of course." Elizabeth took Jesse's hand and guided her to the sitting area of the huge corner office. "Have you enjoyed the afternoon with us?"

"Very much." Jesse sat down on a comfortable couch as Elizabeth and David took chairs. "It was so nice of you to invite me here." She glanced out the windows at the impressive view, then at the beautiful antiques and paintings adorning the room. The office was a sharp contrast to the stark government gray of her cubbyhole downtown.

"Don't mention it. I like to do this with people I feel hold great potential. Your professor tipped me off about you before class, and as soon as I heard you discuss the markets, I knew he was right. I'm very much a first-impression kind of person, with stocks *and* people."

David laughed politely. "I don't know about that, Elizabeth. I've never met anyone who can remember so many facts about so many companies. You do a tremendous amount of research before you buy a stock, as your record shows."

"He's just saying that because I'm the managing partner." Elizabeth winked at Jesse.

It was Jesse's turn to laugh. "I'd agree except that he's right about your record. It's incredible."

Elizabeth gazed at Jesse for a moment without speaking. "I see so much of me in you."

Jesse glanced down at the floor, uncomfortable with the directness of her remark.

"I'm sorry. I shouldn't be so forward." Elizabeth shook her head as she recognized Jesse's sudden discomfort. "To be young again. What I wouldn't give. Oh, well. So who did you see today?"

"Frank Welles, Scott Miller, Ray Hume, and Art Mohler." Jesse ticked off the names.

"Good. I'm particularly glad you had the opportunity to see Art Mohler. He's a senior person here. He really runs the place these days. I'm more of a figurehead, you know."

"That's not true, Elizabeth," David interjected. "You are still very active."

"Not on the portfolio side," Elizabeth disagreed. "I concentrate more on bringing in new money." She smiled. "I don't want to manage the funds anymore. I might have a couple of bad years and that would spoil my record."

"Ms. Gilman." A young associate leaned into the room. "I'm sorry to disturb you, but the call from New York you were waiting for is on line three."

Elizabeth sighed. "I'm sorry, Jesse, but I have to take

this," she said, rising from the chair. "David is treating you to dinner, isn't he?"

Jesse glanced quickly at David. He had mentioned nothing about dinner. "Um, sure."

"Wonderful." Elizabeth took Jesse's hand. "I hope to see you again soon. I want you to think seriously about Sagamore as a career." Suddenly she brought a hand to her chest and coughed softly.

"Thank you. Are you all right?"

"Fine, but I really need to take this call."

Jesse and David moved quickly out of the office as Elizabeth answered the phone.

"You didn't say anything about dinner," Jesse said as they started down the hallway toward his office.

"I was afraid you'd say no. I knew you wouldn't say no to Elizabeth."

After picking up telephone messages from his secretary and making two short calls, David grabbed his briefcase off the credenza and led Jesse back to the reception area.

"Where are we going?" she asked as they waited for the elevator.

"Café Royal. It's a little French place downstairs in the lobby."

She had heard of Café Royal. It was one of the most popular new places in the Baltimore area—and one of the most expensive. "Very nice." The doors opened and they moved inside the car. "Can I ask you what might be a personal question?"

"You can ask anything. I may choose not to answer." He pushed the button for the lobby. "Especially in an elevator."

"There's no one in here but us."

"Doesn't matter. It's one of the first rules of business. Never talk about anything important in an elevator."

"Why did you lock your office door when we left?" She wasn't going to be put off by some silly insecurity.

"Did I?" he asked indifferently.

"Yes."

"Just force of habit I guess."

"Don't you think it's unusual to lock your office?"

David chuckled to himself. Elizabeth Gilman was right. This one was smart—and observant. "No. Don't you lock yours?"

"No, I don't even lock my file cabinet. I trust the people I work with."

"Maybe you shouldn't."

The elevator doors opened and they headed across the lobby toward Café Royal. The tables, covered with white linen and set with sterling silver and gleaming china, were spaced far apart, some in private nooks. The place was crowded but didn't seem so because of the spacing. The lighting was dim and a man played softly on a piano in a far corner of the room.

"This is kind of romantic," Jesse said as they neared the maître d' stand.

"Yes, the place has a wonderful atmosphere, doesn't it?" David smiled slyly.

Jesse tried to translate the smile. Was he simply playing the good corporate employee by entertaining someone the boss was interested in hiring? After all, Elizabeth had been the one to mention dinner. Or did he have another motive? For the first time she realized Todd might have been right about David.

"This way, please." The tuxedo-clad maître d' motioned for them to follow and led them to a small table off to one side of the room. "Madame."

The maître d' held the chair, and Jesse sat down. "Thank you."

The maître d' took David's briefcase to check it and was gone.

David sat down, picked up the wine list, and began to peruse it immediately.

"Limousines, offices with more priceless antiques than the Baltimore Museum of Art, and now dinner at one of the most expensive restaurants in Baltimore. What's a woman to think?"

"What can I say?" David didn't look up from the wine list. "Sagamore does things right." He said the words matter-of-factly, not as if he was trying to make an impression.

"David, how long have you been at Sagamore?"

He found the wine he was looking for. "Is red all right with you?" he asked, ignoring her question for the moment. "This Opus One is delicious."

She was impressed by him. There was no denying it. He was refined and articulate, obviously earned a great deal of money, and carried himself with an air of indifference she found alluring. He would go several minutes ignoring a question, but would always circle back to it at some point in the conversation without being prompted. She had noticed that habit several times today as he had accompanied her on the interviews with the other people at Sagamore. And then there was that glint in his eye she had noticed at the cocktail party. It was there, ever present. The bad-boy look, she and Sara called it. A look that was sometimes difficult to resist. "Yes, Opus One, that's a nice wine." Jesse moaned quietly to herself. God, now she was trying to act like a wine connoisseur to impress him. She so rarely drank wine she wouldn't know a zinfandel from a Beaujolais. But was she trying to impress the individual or the portfolio manager? Before he picked her up this afternoon she could have answered quickly and definitively. Now she wasn't certain.

"So you've had Opus One before?" David asked.

She hesitated, trying to decide how to handle this. It was either wade in deep now and possibly be embarrassed later, or admit she was no wine expert up front and give him a window into her less than privileged upbringing. Maybe this was her first etiquette test. "No, I haven't, but I like the sound of the name." She wasn't going to try to be someone she wasn't just to get a job.

David smiled. So she could work her way out of a tight conversational situation gracefully. He motioned to their waiter, who approached the table immediately. "A bottle of Opus One, please."

"Very good, sir." The waiter moved away.

David watched the man until he had disappeared through the kitchen doors. "I've been with Sagamore four years."

There it was, his ability to circle back to a question asked minutes before. "And you've had a good experience?" she asked.

A pained expression crossed his face. "That's a student question if I ever heard one."

"Well, I *am* a student." She was suddenly on the defensive.

"Ask me something specific, something difficult, something that will give you real information to help you make an informed decision if they offer you a job. You'll appreciate this opportunity later."

He had become abruptly businesslike, and the change in demeanor caught her off guard. "Fine. How much can someone make at Sagamore?" She would put him on the defensive. She was sure he wouldn't answer that question.

"Last year they paid me a bit over three hundred thousand dollars all in." He had no problem being open about his compensation. He was proud of how hard he worked and what they paid him. "My salary is one-fifty and Elizabeth gave me another one-fifty as bonus in January." He unfolded the linen napkin and laid it across his lap. "And I didn't even have a very good year compared to some of the others." He said the last few words as if he could not comprehend why they would still pay him so well. "Some people would say I was rich."

"I certainly would."

"That's all I ever wanted to be," David said softly. "Rich."

Three hundred thousand dollars. That certainly rivaled Wall Street. People always heard about the million-dollar Manhattan whiz kids, but Jesse knew the reality was that most people David's age working for investment banks in New York earned six figures, not seven.

"And there's the opportunity to make much more," he continued. "I know some of the portfolio managers regularly pull down seven figures."

"Have they all been at the firm longer than you?"

He nodded. "All more than five years."

"Well, I don't know much about pay scales at money management firms, but those numbers seem kind of high."

"They are. It's nosebleed territory, especially when you consider the fact that Sagamore is in Baltimore, where things are a lot cheaper than in New York. That's why no one ever resigns from Sagamore. The money is addicting. People are fired when their performance isn't acceptable, but no one quits."

"Are people fired often?"

He played with his knife for a moment, thinking. "Elizabeth would probably kill me if she knew I was saying this, but I will anyway. I told you to take advantage of the opportunity, and you've gotten to the heart of the matter." He put the knife down. "Typically you don't find out about this until you're inside the firm. I didn't." He laughed cynically. "The key is your first five years. No one ever actually says that, but everyone knows it. The pressure to perform is immense during that time, and if you don't, they fire you on your fifth anniversary. If you make it past that day, you're in the club. No one's ever been fired after making it past the fifth anniversary at Sagamore. Not that I know of, anyway."

Jesse shook her head. "God, that sounds incredibly stressful."

"It is, and the execution is almost a public event. People are obviously fired behind closed doors, but everyone at the firm is aware of impending five-year anniversaries. When the condemned is called in to meet with the executive committee, work stops and people joke about the lights dimming. You know, how the electric chair saps the juice."

Jesse nodded. "How many portfolio managers have been fired at their five-year anniversary since you've been at Sagamore?"

"Two. And one made it."

"Are you worried?"

David thought about the A-100 for a moment, about his deal with the godfather. "You always worry until you get past that fifth year."

"But you said you earned a hundred-and-fifty-thousand-dollar bonus last year. You must be doing fine. They wouldn't pay you that kind of money if they didn't like you."

David tapped his watch a moment before answering. It had stopped, and he made a mental note to get a new battery. "That's why it really hurts when you get fired. You become hooked on the money. They pay very well no matter what. Then they cut you loose if your performance is below par and you fall off a cliff."

"So you catch on with another firm," Jesse reasoned.

He shook his head quickly. "Senior people at the other big money management firms know Sagamore canned you, so they won't touch you either. And it wouldn't surprise me at all if Sagamore management actively puts out the word on people once they've been fired. That guy Art Mohler you met, the one Elizabeth said was such a great guy. He would do that. He's a bastard. She just doesn't see it. She's too nice." David reached into a linen-covered basket, withdrew a hot dinner roll, put it on his butter plate, then offered the basket to Jesse. "Of course, she still seems to be able to fire people if their results aren't what Sagamore requires. That's the thing about the firm. It's all about making money, nothing else. That's what you have to understand. Don't get me wrong—there's a huge upside to accepting an offer from Sagamore. But there's a huge downside too. If you don't perform, you lose your high-paying job and you can't get another one. Then you go flip burgers at McDonald's for a living."

Jesse took a roll from the basket and put it on her butter plate. "And if you can't handle that, you commit suicide, right?"

David's eyes flashed to hers as he put the bread basket back down on the table.

"Your wine, sir." The waiter leaned down to display the label.

"Fine, thank you."

They sat in silence as the waiter opened the bottle and put it down on the table to breathe. David picked up the cork, sniffed it, and nodded approvingly.

When the waiter had gone, David leaned close to Jesse. "What did you mean by that suicide crack?" He didn't take his time circling back to this question.

"I did a Lexis search this morning. I found news

articles about two portfolio managers at Sagamore who had committed suicide in the last few years."

Things weren't always as they appeared. Jack Finnerty's words. "Those two were older. They hadn't been fired," David assured her. "I told you, no one is fired after the fifth year." He picked up the wine bottle and poured the dark, rich liquid into her glass, then into his. "Cheers." He touched his glass to hers.

"Cheers." Jesse picked up her glass and drank, closing her eyes as she swallowed. It had been so long since she had let herself go, since she had forgotten about the pressures of work and school and simply enjoyed herself. Finally she opened her eyes. "Why have you told me all these things about Sagamore? As you said, I'm sure Elizabeth wouldn't appreciate it if she knew."

"Because I wish someone had told me before I joined. I probably would have accepted the offer anyway, because the money is incredible. But I would like to have known."

Three hundred thousand dollars a year, millions if you made it past year five. Jesse could hardly imagine what it would be like to earn that kind of a paycheck, hardly imagine the freedom and peace of mind that kind of money would provide—even with the performance pressures David had described. And from what he had said, the odds were one in three that you'd make it past year five. That didn't sound too bad. And Elizabeth seemed to like her. That ought to make the odds even better.

David pushed his glass against hers again. "And

I've told you these things"—he hesitated—"because I like you."

Todd had been right on target about David's intentions, Jesse realized now. She could see it in David's eyes, and under normal circumstances she would have been flattered. He was handsome, wealthy, and seemingly nice—quite a catch for someone. But any kind of romance with him was out of the question. It might put her opportunity to join Sagamore in jeopardy. Elizabeth probably wouldn't make an offer if she thought David and Jesse were involved. "To the start of a wonderful business relationship," she said firmly.

"Right," he answered, recognizing the meaning of her words. "To a business relationship." But his smile betrayed him.

# Chapter 15

Despite the steady rain he was enjoying his walk through Georgetown University's campus. The students had returned from their summer break, but at this late hour the grounds were empty, providing him a short respite from the constant crush of telephone calls received at the office and at home. He appreciated solitude immensely but was rarely able to find it these days. Life on the Hill was hectic. And the more senior one was, the more frenetic the pace.

Senator Webb tilted his wide green-and-white golf umbrella forward to hide his face as a lone couple approached from beneath the maple canopy swaying over the walkway in the gentle breeze. But there was no need to worry about recognition. They weren't looking around. They were huddled together, heads down beneath a small umbrella, trying to reach their dormitory as quickly as possible.

After the couple passed, Webb stopped for a moment and looked up at the trees in the eerie glow of a streetlamp. The tips of the leaves were just beginning to take on their fall colors. He inhaled deeply. The night held the slightest trace of a chill, and he smelled the faint scent of wood smoke from an impatient fireplace. Just one more six-year term after his certain victory in November. At the beginning of that term he would name his successor—as was his privilege—and train him in the ways of the Senate, specifically the Appropriations Committee. Then he would retire to his beloved Georgia and enjoy the spoils of war.

"Good evening, Senator," Phil Rhodes said quietly, as he approached from the same direction the couple had. Rhodes shook the senator's hand.

"Hello, Phil." Webb's tone was upbeat. The thought of going back to Georgia after his last term had suddenly boosted his spirits.

"Glad you're doing well tonight." Rhodes heard the amicable tone.

"Thank you." Webb checked up and down the path, but there was no one coming. "Why did you want to get together?"

Rhodes pushed his tongue against the inside of his cheek. The senator was in a good mood, and the odds were strong that this bit of information would spoil it.

"Come on, Phil. I told my wife I'd be home in thirty minutes." Webb was suddenly impatient. "Get on with it."

"Yes, sir." Rhodes pulled his umbrella down close to his head as the rain began to fall harder. "You remember I told you I had a mole in Malcolm Walker's office?"

"Of course."

"Well, she has relayed to me information I think you ought to hear. And I didn't want to say anything over the phone."

Webb nodded. Rhodes had turned out to be a strong source of information. "What is it?"

"Malcolm Walker is planning to hold a news conference in the next few days to blow the whistle on the black-budget project going on in Nevada." Rhodes's Brooklyn accent became more pronounced as he became nervous. This was really going to piss off the senator. "It's a plane known as the A-100. I'm assuming, given your position, you know about the project."

"Shit!" Webb kicked at a twig on the path. His pleasant walk had just been ruined.

Rhodes cringed. Sometimes it wasn't good to be the bearer of bad news, even if you had nothing to do with it and the information was valuable.

"That bastard. He ought to know when to keep his mouth shut. Christ, it's a top-secret project and he's got to be a bleeding heart. He just doesn't know how the game is played. I can't stand this new breed of do-gooders and their politically correct platforms. They don't know what it means to defend a nation. They've never had to fight a war." Webb looked at Rhodes menacingly. He was breathing hard. "The hell with Walker. It doesn't matter. The plane's already past the prototype stage. It's already gone to full production."

"I guess Walker lost his informant out at Area 51 and got scared that someone might put the clamp on him, so he's going public as soon as possible."

Webb nodded. Commander Pierce had done an excellent job of silencing Captain Nichols.

"Walker's going to try to whip up public sentiment against the project," Rhodes continued. "Apparently he's got numbers on how much the A-100 will cost taxpayers." Rhodes shook his head. "I must say, it's a huge contract. If Senator Walker doesn't railroad this thing, GEA shareholders will make out very well. I only wish one of my clients could have had a chance to bid on the plane a few years ago when it was offered, but I never heard a word about it. I've been here a long time. Usually I hear everything. GEA must have snapped up the contract very quietly." Rhodes flashed an accusatory look at Webb. He knew what had happened.

Webb saw the look but ignored it. "I could make things very uncomfortable for Senator Walker. Perhaps I should pay him a visit before the press conference."

"Walker would wonder how you found out." Rhodes was suddenly worried. He didn't want to be brought into this via the front page of the *Washington Post*. His clients wouldn't be happy about that.

Webb understood the lobbyist's concern immediately. "Don't worry, Phil. Your name will never be mentioned."

Relief ebbed through Rhodes's body. Senator Webb had proved to be a man of his word. Anonymity would be maintained. "There's one other thing you need to know." Rhodes was willing to talk more freely now that the senator had promised secrecy. "Another reason you *really* might want to consider taking action against him."

"What is that?"

"Apparently he has decided to go public with what he knows about the black budget in general. How it works, who is involved. He'll do it at the same news conference at which he plans to reveal the existence of the A-100." Rhodes sensed Webb's anger rising. "I thought you might want to know that."

"Prick!" Rage erupted violently inside Webb. Then, as quickly as it had exploded, it dissipated. This wasn't disaster at all, it was the opportunity they had been waiting for.

He turned to Rhodes. "Phil, there's a very large, very lucrative Army transport helicopter contract on the horizon. I think one of your clients will be very happy in the near future when he wins that contract, which means you've just earned yourself a nice fat fee tonight." Webb clasped the lobbyist's hand and pumped it hard.

Rhodes smiled at Webb curiously as they shook, uncertain of exactly what had just happened but ecstatic in the knowledge that he had just secured what sounded like a multibillion-dollar contract. "Thank you, Senator."

"No, thank you, Phil. Take care of yourself. I've got to go. I'll be in touch."

Rhodes spoke up quickly. "Senator, could I ask you a question before you go?"

Webb nodded.

"Why have you spent so long on Capitol Hill? I mean, you were an attorney before being senator, isn't that correct?"

Webb nodded again.

"It's just that you could have made so much more money in private practice, and without all the hassles of public life. Without every joker you've ever met looking for a handout. Why do you keep coming back to Washington?"

Webb peered at Rhodes. Rhodes could never know

the real truth about the money side. But the question was an interesting one, and its directness had taken him by surprise. "Power," he finally admitted. It was the first time he had ever answered that query to anyone—including himself.

"What do you mean?"

"The ability to manipulate people. To make them do whatever you want."

# Chapter 16

Voices rich in gospel song rose from the choir as the Reverend Elijah Pitts moved deliberately across the church's rostrum toward the raised pulpit. As he climbed the first of fifteen steps leading to the apex, the all-black congregation stood, raised their hands above their heads, and joined the choir.

When he reached the pulpit and stretched his arms out toward them, the celebration reached a frenzied crescendo. Men, women and children sang, clapped and swayed rhythmically to the piano so intensely that conversing with even the person immediately to the left or right would have been impossible. But it didn't matter. No one wanted to talk. They were there to see Elijah Pitts, supreme leader of the organization known as Liberation for African-Americans, and all eyes were upon him.

LFA had existed for only three years, but already numbered over half a million members. Its purpose was simple—to promote the advancement of Maryland's African-American population through nonviolent means. And in thirty-six short months, with the charismatic Reverend Pitts at the helm, LFA had become a force to be reckoned with.

Pitts raised his outstretched arms slowly and leaned back until he was facing heavenward. Bodies quivered and voices sang, until they could sing no louder. Only the reverend's bodyguards—twenty large young men dressed in dark suits, dark bow ties, white shirts, and dark glasses, positioned before the stage—did not join in the rapture. They stood perfectly still, hands crossed before them, faces expressionless.

Pitts brought his arms down and three hundred voices fell suddenly silent. "Brothers and sisters, I am honored to be here this evening." His voice was deep and mesmerizing. A woman in the front row screamed his name, then collapsed, but he took no notice as one of the bodyguards picked her up and carried her away. "Each time I see a congregation like yours, I am elated. I see that what was only a dream three years ago has become reality. Children, we are half a million strong now. We cannot be ignored. Our voices are being heard loud and clear in Annapolis and, more important, in Washington, D.C."

A great cheer arose from the throng.

The reverend motioned for quiet again. "When we founded this organization, people ignored us." His voice began to quake. "Rarely did I have my telephone calls returned. Rarely was I asked to join a panel or sit on a committee that was making decisions involving our people. Rarely was I asked for advice." He stopped orating for a moment, then began nodding. "Now we have the power."

Amens ascended from several in the crowd.

The reverend's expression became triumphant.

The cheers grew louder.

"Now we are so busy I must ask my assistants to attend functions for me. Now we always have our telephone calls answered immediately without having to await a call back."

People were jumping up and down, screaming his name. He had to yell to be heard even through the microphone. "And it is all because of people like you," he roared. "Congregations like yours all across this great state of Maryland. We are being heard! We are a force! We will prevail!"

The applause thundered up to him. He took one step back on the pulpit, bowed slowly, then descended the stairs as the choir broke into another gospel tune. At the bottom of the stairs he proceeded back across the stage, turned and waved to the screaming crowd as he reached the far side, then disappeared behind a purple curtain.

"Beautiful performance, Reverend." Derek Holmes, vice chairman of LFA, embraced Pitts as the reverend passed between the curtains. Holmes led the reverend through a gauntlet of bodyguards and well-wishers backstage to a small door at the side of the church, where a limousine waited.

Once inside the limousine, Pitts reclined on the bench seat. "When is the next meeting?" he asked Holmes, rubbing his eyes.

"Nine o'clock," Holmes replied. "We've got plenty of time—it's only eight-thirty now." The reverend had just finished his fourth engagement of the evening and there were still four more to attend. "Are you all right?" the younger man asked.

"Fine!" Pitts said loudly, sitting back up as the limousine pulled away from the church. "Absolutely fine. Just needed a few seconds' rest and now I'm ready to go."

Holmes was constantly amazed at the energy level Pitts—now sixty-one—could maintain. "Why don't you catch twenty minutes of sleep? I'll wake you up when we get to the next stop."

"Nonsense, that would be wasted time. Besides, there's something we need to discuss." Pitts watched the lights of downtown Baltimore flash by.

"Oh?"

"Yes. We need to talk about Malcolm Walker."

Holmes had anticipated that the topic would be Walker. Senator Walker had become an obsession with Elijah Pitts over the last few weeks. "What about him?"

The reverend stretched for a moment. "I told that congregation back there that we always have our phone calls returned nowadays, and that's true except in one case. That case is Malcolm Walker. He has continued to try to maintain his distance from us."

"But you know why," Holmes said. "He believes if he is linked too closely to LFA in the minds of white voters, they will turn against him in the November election. And he's probably right. The conservative media have successfully painted us as antiwhite, even though that tag couldn't be further from the truth. Whites make up seventy-six percent of Maryland's voting population, and Walker needs to keep the white vote he won six years ago to defeat Elbridge Coleman. It's just a numbers game. He can't win if he loses that white constituency."

The reverend was unsympathetic. "He is a United States senator. One of the most recognized black men in this country. He needs to give us respect, publicly."

Holmes said nothing. Pitts had broken into his sermon voice, and Holmes knew this was a subtle signal not to interrupt.

"Walker likes the title 'senator'—no, *cherishes* it," Pitts interrupted himself, "and all that goes with it. Derek, LFA has become a most powerful organization in Maryland, the state that gives him the title of senator. I could turn many of his voters against him, at least half a million, and take the title away. He is in a dead heat with Coleman right now. If he lost LFA, he would lose his seat. He must realize that I hold the power, not him. All I ask is that he give us the respect we are due."

Holmes was tired of this conversation. They had engaged in it one way or another every day for the last week. "Why do you want him in your pocket so badly?"

"Because of what he could do for us. Think of it."

"Reverend, we've done fine without him so—"

"He could take us to the next level," Pitts interrupted the younger man. "He could bring us into the major leagues. Perhaps help us go national. He should be doing all he can to help his people."

"I think he is, but he needs to win the election to keep doing that. That is how he can best serve us."

"He needs to recognize his power base, as do all politicians."

"Let Walker win in November," Holmes said gently, "then try to forge the relationship." It was his job to counsel, even if the reverend did not agree. That was what Pitts had said at the beginning of all this.

"I won't have a stick after the election, Derek. No leverage. He could ignore me at that point." Pitts pointed a finger at the younger man. "You worry me sometimes. You need to be more politically astute."

"I'm as politically astute as anyone," Holmes retorted. "I can't believe you said that. You told me to always voice my opinion, no matter what, as long as I was in your presence alone. That's what I'm doing."

Pitts looked at Holmes defiantly for several moments, then his expression softened. "I'm sorry, Derek. You've always been my strongest adviser. I appreciate that."

Holmes tried to swallow his resentment. "Why have you become so obsessed with Senator Walker?" There was still a trace of annoyance in his tone.

The reverend put his head back and closed his eyes.

"Reverend Pitts," Holmes persisted. "Why?"

"Have you reviewed our finances lately, Derek?" The reverend's tone was measured.

"No. I believe in division of labor. That isn't my area of expertise, so I stay away from it."

"We have a thousand dollars in the checking account. That's barely enough to pay for this limousine tonight."

Holmes's mouth fell open. "Just a thousand dollars? How is that possible?"

"It takes money to run this organization, Derek.

Lots of it. We're growing so fast that congregation donations aren't enough to sustain us. Someday they will be, but not yet."

"All the same, I don't see the connection between our need for cash and Malcolm Walker."

The reverend hoped he wasn't as transparent as he felt. "Our backers, the people who gave us seed money three years ago and who have kept us afloat since that time out of the generosity of their hearts and the courage of their convictions, have made it known to me that they want concessions from Walker now, while I can influence him. They have withheld their monetary support until I can forge that closer relationship with the good senator. They don't share your view that it should wait until after the election. They want it to happen before." Pitts paused for a moment. "We have to get that money soon, Derek. Very soon. I have a lot of people depending on me."

Derek Holmes was quiet as he analyzed what he had just heard. He had never met these angels the reverend constantly referred to, and as far as he knew, neither had anyone else at LFA other than Pitts. Now he wanted answers, because suddenly he realized the angels' motives might not be as pure as had so often been advertised. "Who are these people, Reverend Pitts?"

"It doesn't matter. What matters is that we get their money."

Holmes shook his head, trying to understand the reverend's consistent avoidance of the question. And then suddenly the awful truth became clear, and

Holmes turned away so the reverend wouldn't see the shock in his eyes.

But Pitts had seen Holmes's expression and sensed that the younger man had made the connection. "Derek," he said gently. "Sometimes we all have to compromise ourselves in the short run to attain our long-term goals. Compromise and contradiction are an inescapable reality of our existence. A part of life we can't avoid. We just do the best we can, and get on with it. That is what I do. That is what you must do."

# Chapter 17

The Corsica River was only ten miles long, but was broad and deep enough in its channel to allow even large sailboats access at low tide. The Corsica snaked its way west out of Maryland's Eastern Shore, emptying into the Chester River, which itself emptied into the Chesapeake Bay a few miles farther west. At its headwaters the Corsica was only a small stream, but like most rivers here, as it became tidal, it widened quickly until it stretched several hundred yards across in most places.

Jesse stood next to David on the sailboat's bridge as he carefully steered the thirty-seven-foot Dickerson through the choppy waters and the darkness, navigating by moonlight and a yellow running lamp at the bow. They had rented the exquisite craft—decked with teak and trimmed with mahogany—this morning at a Baltimore marina and had enjoyed a beautiful Saturday sailing the Chesapeake. Now they were headed to a place on the Corsica owned by a friend of David's to stay the night.

The original plan for the day had been to return to the marina by dark, but the weather and the wind had been perfect, and by late afternoon they had found themselves far down the bay—too far from the marina to make it back by dark. David had made a quick call to his friend on his cellular phone, and now they were navigating the Corsica, scanning the banks for the lights of the house.

David had been less than forthcoming about what to expect from his friend's home, but had promised running water and—because Jesse had made it clear that they would not be spending the night together— separate bedrooms. Jesse had been hesitant to accept another invitation to be with David so quickly, but it had turned out to be an excellent opportunity to learn more about Sagamore. And, she had to admit, she had enjoyed a wonderful time.

"A penny for your thoughts, Jesse," David said softly. "You've been awfully quiet for a while."

She pulled up the collar of the cardigan sweater draped over her shoulders. The air had turned cool since sunset. "I was just thinking."

"What about?"

"Sagamore and the fifth anniversary. The things you told me the other night at dinner. Things you told me today."

"Don't get too worked up about all that. I probably shouldn't have said anything, really." He flicked a mosquito from the back of his hand. "Look, it's a good place to work. They expect a lot because they pay a lot. It's just capitalism."

"No no, I'm glad you told me. It didn't scare me off." She put her hand on the boom to steady herself as the boat swayed from side to side with the chop of the river. "I don't get scared off easily."

"Good."

"It doesn't matter anyway," she murmured.

"What do you mean?"

"I probably won't get an offer."

"I wouldn't be so sure." David squinted through the darkness, trying to locate the next buoy upriver. He turned his face toward her for a moment to speak, his eyes still focused on the dark water ahead. "Red right returning, correct?"

"Aye." David had proved to be a good sailor. "Do you really think Sagamore will make me an offer when I finish business school?"

"I don't see why not."

"But based on what I saw during my visit, the firm is looking for blue bloods. Like you. I don't fit the profile. I didn't go to an Ivy League school. My family doesn't belong to a country club. I don't even know how to order wine. You saw that the other night."

So Jesse assumed he had led a privileged life. Well, he wasn't going to volunteer the truth. Not yet, anyway. "You don't have to be able to choose wines, just stocks. And Elizabeth thinks you can. As long as Elizabeth likes you, you're in."

"She's an incredible success story."

"That she is."

Jesse bent down to check the compass heading. "Tell me about yourself, David."

His pulse quickened. He didn't want to tell her about the Glen Owens row house, stickball in the street with a taped ball, shoplifting his lunches, and his mother's polyester pantsuit collection. He might become much less interesting to her if she knew. "What do you want to know?"

"Where you're from, where you went to school. All the normal stuff."

"Why? Is this a beauty contest?"

"No," she laughed, "it's the third degree." She straightened up from looking at the compass. "If I didn't trust you, I'd think you were hiding something."

"You've figured me out. I'm really a double agent from Berlin," he said in a bad German accent. "And being a portfolio manager is my cover. What's your deep dark secret?"

But she was unable to smile at the accent because of the question. "I told you everything this afternoon. I'm the youngest of nine children. We didn't have much when I was growing up. We weren't poor, but we always wore our clothes until there wasn't much left of them. My dad worked almost every day of his life to keep food on the table. Until he died when I was sixteen."

"I'm sorry."

"It's okay. He was a wonderful man, David. I still miss him."

"I'm sure." David thought of his own father for a second, buried in the trash-strewn Glen Owens graveyard.

"My mother's life was and still is the neighborhood Catholic church," Jesse continued. "She's always putting together a benefit, organizing a trip, or just cleaning up the place."

"That's nice."

"It's a large congregation. Father McCord can use all the help he can get, and she loves doing it. I don't know what she'd do without it." Jesse paused. "Sometimes it's hard for her to make ends meet, though. That's another reason I'd like to start making a good bit of money as soon as I graduate from business school. I want to use some of it to help her out."

"You and your mother must be very close."

Jesse nodded. "We are."

"Did your mother remarry after your father died?"

"No." She felt strange not telling David the truth, but she didn't want to think about Joe Schuman right now. Didn't want to have to go through it. She was enjoying herself too much to ruin the mood. "Hey, once again I'm the one doing all the talking."

"Mmm."

They fell silent in the serenity of the tranquil river. There were no other boats on the water at this hour and only a few lights glimmering from shore through the dense forest covering both banks. The only sounds were the lapping of water against the Dickerson's hull and the faint hum of the small motor—they had furled the sails at the mouth of the Corsica to avoid having to tack all the way up the narrow channel. Directly above them hung a full moon, ringed by a hazy halo.

"Beautiful out here, isn't it?" David observed. The moon was vivid in the black sky.

"I'll say."

To port, an osprey plunged into the water after a fish. Jesse cringed. Instantly she was back at Neil Robinson's river house, crashing through the woods with the predator in pursuit.

"Hey, are you all right?"

"I'm fine." She brought her hands to her chest. Her heart was racing.

"You sure?"

"I'm fine," she said again, this time more firmly.

"Okay. Look, will you take the wheel, Jesse? I appreciate your giving me the chance to play captain, but you're the one who really knows how to sail, and I'm having kind of a difficult time seeing the markers. I wouldn't want to run us aground. I doubt the marina would appreciate that."

"All right." She was still breathing hard.

David moved aside to let her steer. "When did you learn to manage a sailboat so well, anyway? Christ, at one point this afternoon you had us heeled over so far I was sure we were going to tip. But I have to admit, it was fun going that fast."

"A friend taught me," she said as she wrapped her fingers around the chrome wheel. Todd had taught her in the fall of their senior year in high school. They had explored the bay every weekend in a small sailboat he and a few friends had purchased, and she had become an expert. It was on one of those weekends that she had fallen in love for the first time.

"Would this friend happen to have been the guy you were with at the branch the other day when I picked you up to come to Sagamore?"

"You mean Todd?"

"If that's his name."

"Todd's a good person. You'd like him."

"I'm sure," David said dryly.

The river chart hung next to the wheel. "Hey, we're

running out of water here," she said, pointing at it. "Pretty soon the Corsica is going to be ten feet wide and three feet deep and we're going to be stuck in the mud. Where is this place, anyway?"

"I've only been to it once before, and that was by car."

"Oh, great. We're going to be sailing up and down the Corsica all night."

"Don't worry. The house shouldn't be hard to find."

"Why not?"

"There aren't many homes on this river, and . . ." David paused as they glided around a bend, then pointed across the water. "And my friend said he'd make certain to leave the lights on for us."

Her eyes opened wide. "There?"

"Uh huh."

A hundred yards away was a long pier, brilliantly outlined by lights, jutting out into the river. Moored to it were several powerboats and a seventy-five-foot Alden sailboat.

As Jesse steered the Dickerson toward the pier, the house lights came into view far up the hill. "My God, how big is that place?" she asked.

"Seven bedrooms, six baths," David answered. "You could play a football game in the basement."

"Whose house is it?"

"Martin Broadbent's. He's a member of Sagamore's executive committee. It's his summer home," David said, winking at Jesse. "As they say, it's good to be king."

As the Dickerson pulled alongside, David took the stern line in hand and jumped up onto the pier. He quickly pulled the sailboat to a stop, lashed the rope to a pylon cleat, then did the same with the bow line, making certain there was enough play in the ropes to allow the boat to rise and fall with tidal changes. Then he knelt down and lifted Jesse up onto the dock. For a moment they stood on the pier facing each other.

Finally, David lifted his hand and gently touched Jesse's cheek. "Thank you for a great day."

"Thank you."

Slowly, David leaned forward to kiss her.

She had enjoyed the day very much and knew for certain now that he was someone she could be quite interested in. But just as the kiss was becoming passionate, she broke away. She couldn't risk the opportunity at Sagamore. "We'd better get up to the house. It's late, and we shouldn't keep anyone awake just in case they're waiting up for us."

"Uh huh." David smiled to himself as she took his hand and began pulling him up the pier toward the house. He had seen that spark of interest in her eye. Just as he had seen it that night when they first met at the cocktail party.

"Good evening, Elijah."

Pitts hated these meetings. "Good evening." He was not a man who was comfortable exhibiting deference, but it was necessary in this case.

"I don't have much time, so I'll be brief."

"All right."

"I need a favor, Elijah."

Pitts cringed. The man always insisted on calling him by his first name, a subtle reminder of who wielded the power in this relationship. Everyone else addressed him as Reverend. "What is that?" he asked quietly.

"We've discussed this situation before."

"Malcolm Walker."

"That's right. Do I sense irritation, Elijah?"

"No." But his tone was unconvincing.

"You knew I would call in this favor sooner or later."

"Mmm."

"LFA is in desperate need of cash," the man pointed out. "I will inject more once you have completed this task."

The checking account was already overdrawn, and the next payroll checks had to be cut in a few days. Pitts needed money immediately or everything would be lost. The organization would die just as it was becoming real. Someday they wouldn't need this despicable patron, but for now he was their lifeline. "What do you want me to do?"

The store smelled richly of fine leather, but Roth took little notice as he approached the sales clerk standing behind the glass counter.

"Good evening, sir. May I help you?" The clerk's smile was sincere despite the late hour and a hectic day.

"I certainly hope you can," Roth said politely. He had waited until just before closing time to enter the store, and as he had hoped, it was deserted. "I need some information."

"What kind of information?" the clerk asked hesitantly.

Roth reached into his pocket and brought out the heavy badge. "I'm special detail to the Assistant Attorney General." His voice became serious as he quickly snapped the wallet shut. "I'm running an important investigation, and I need information on a glove I believe was purchased here. I need this information immediately."

"I'd better get the manager." The sales clerk had no interest in taking responsibility for this.

Fifteen minutes later, Roth exited the store with exactly what he had come for. Next stop would be the lab where the hair samples were being analyzed, although it didn't look like they'd even need that information now.

# Chapter 18

"Ms. Hayes?"

Looking at her tentatively from the office doorway was Rob Forester, a systems analyst who also ran investigative reports for the revenue agents. "Hi, Rob."

"I have that report you asked for."

"Well, come in here, silly." She motioned for him to enter as she rose from her seat. "Don't stand out there like a lost child."

The young man moved into her office. "It just looked as if you were thinking about something pretty hard. I didn't want to interrupt your work." He enjoyed any chance he had to run reports for Jesse. She treated him with respect, unlike most of the revenue agents, who thought their data requests were more important than edicts from God. "I didn't want to disturb you."

She had been lost in thought, but it had nothing to do with work. Saturday night she and David had stayed up until three o'clock, just talking as they sat together by themselves on the huge screened-in porch of the Broadbents' mammoth Corsica River home.

They had discussed everything from wines and sailing to Sagamore, Elizabeth Gilman, and Art Mohler. They had been together all day, but the conversation just seemed to keep going.

When the talk finally faded because they were both exhausted, David politely showed her to her room and shook her hand good night. He had been quite the gentleman, and somehow she had been disappointed he hadn't attempted another kiss. But that wasn't fair. She would have refused him again anyway.

"Ms. Hayes?"

Jesse snapped back from the daydream for the second time and stepped toward the young man to take the report. "I appreciate your help, Rob."

"If there's anything else I can do, just call me."

"I will."

"Okay." Rob hesitated at the door for a moment, hands jammed into his pockets, hoping she would make an immediate request. Finally he waved nervously and was gone.

Jesse smiled as she closed the office door and returned to her desk. Rob was nice, and it was flattering to have someone so smitten.

Last Friday she had obtained a list from the Federal Election Commission of everyone officially registered as employed by the Elbridge Coleman Senate campaign, along with their Social Security numbers. The report Rob had just completed took the Social Security number of each individual working for the Coleman campaign and generated a record of any other entities by which those people had been paid in the last two years. Employers were always required to withhold taxes on earnings and deposit those funds with the IRS, using Social Security numbers as identification, so generating the report had been simple once she had the numbers.

The objective of generating the report was to develop a profile of the Coleman campaign. Perhaps there would be something there that could lead her in the right direction. It was a long shot, but she had to start somewhere. She pulled the list of Coleman employees from a desk drawer, put it down next to Rob's report on the desk, and began to compare them.

Almost instantly the phone rang.

"Hello."

"Jess."

"Todd. How are you?"

"Fine, and you?"

"Fine." She sipped her coffee and continued matching the list of Coleman employees against Rob's report of wage withholdings.

"Tired?" Todd asked.

"No, why?" What was that about?

"No reason. Look, we need to talk about a couple of ideas I had regarding what we discussed the other day."

"But we haven't settled on your huge fee yet," she teased. "And you'll probably require a deposit, won't you?" Suddenly one of the employers on Rob's report caught her attention.

"Oh, come on, Jess. I was just kidding about that."

She focused on the name. That made no sense. Why would Coleman hire someone who had worked there?

"Jess, are you still on the line?"

It made no sense at all.

"Jess!"

"I'm here," she said, trying to figure it out.

"Let me tell you what I'm planning to do."

"No." Jesse's voice was suddenly ice-cold. "Not on the phone." The office could easily be bugged, she realized. "Tonight I want you to meet me at the place we used to go after the movies."

"You mean when we were in high school?" Todd laughed.

"Yes. Meet me there at seven o'clock."

"What's wrong?" He sensed strain in her voice.

"Nothing. Just be there." She hung up quickly, not giving him another chance to speak, then rose from her seat. There was one more thing she needed Rob to do.

As she opened her office door, she almost ran into Sara.

"Hi, Jesse."

"Hi." Instinctively Jesse slipped Rob's report behind her back.

"What are you working on?" Sara had noticed Jesse's maneuver. "Must be top secret." She leaned to the side and nodded down at the report.

"What, this?" Jesse brought the report back out from behind her back. "This is just an audit on some poor farmer out in Carroll County. I'm trying to find a way not to levy penalties or sic an investigative agent on him even though he hasn't paid income taxes in two years, but I do need one more thing before I can help him. So I'm off to records. Do you need anything?"

Sara shook her head.

"All right, see you in a little while." Jesse stepped past Sara. "Maybe we can have lunch together," she called back over her shoulder.

Sara watched carefully as Jesse moved down the hall. The records room was in the other direction.

Todd guided the white Corvette down the long gravel driveway toward his small farmhouse, proceeding cautiously to protect the car's underside against rocks kicked up by the tires. Finally he pulled the Corvette to a stop in front of the clapboard home.

It was a perfect bachelor place—rustic, quiet and remote. At one time the house had served as home to a tenant farmer managing the large estate for the owners who resided in the white-pillared manor house up on the hill. However, the tenant manager had died a year ago, and now the owners contracted their huge fields out to corporate farmers. But they had maintained the house and rented it to Todd.

The sound of another car moving over the driveway's crushed stones caught Todd's attention as he stepped out of the Corvette. The oncoming car was a sleek black Cadillac, large and expensive. However, the driver didn't show the same concern for his vehicle as Todd had. Instead he raced quickly down the tree-lined lane.

It was Harry the Horse, paying his weekly visit. Todd slammed the Corvette's door shut as the black car neared. In a strange way he enjoyed this game of chicken. Harry talked a good game but never followed through on his threats. He just loaned more money whenever Todd needed it.

Harry pulled his Cadillac behind the Corvette, blocking it in, then hopped from the car along with two other stocky men. He approached slowly while the other two leaned against the car's grille. "Hello, Todd." Harry's voice was gruff.

"Hi, Harry." Todd was nonchalant.

Harry moved directly to Todd until their faces were just inches apart. "We need a payment."

Todd grinned. "Sure, Harry."

Suddenly Harry launched a huge fist into Todd's stomach, instantly knocking the wind from his lungs. Todd slumped to his knees, clutching his belt.

"My boss is coming down on me about your loan. You owe us thirty thousand bucks. Fifteen on the car and fifteen from your unlucky weekends at the Atlantic City blackjack tables. We want at least five thousand of that before Monday and the balance by the end of the month. You got it?"

"Yeah." Todd gasped.

Harry nodded over his shoulder at his partners. They removed tire irons from beneath their long leather jackets and quickly smashed the Corvette's taillights and headlights. When they were finished, Harry grabbed Todd by his hair and pulled his head back. "I wanted you to have a little memento of our visit here today."

"Thanks," Todd muttered. Air was just beginning to seep back into his lungs.

"Anytime, my friend." Harry grinned. "Oh, just one more thing." Once again Harry slammed his fist into Todd's solar plexus. This time Todd collapsed and lay prone on the ground. "Remember, pal, five thousand by Monday, the rest by the end of the month. And the

interest rate has increased to twenty-five percent."
Harry laughed, then turned and walked to the car. As
he was about to get back into the Cadillac, he yelled at
Todd, "We know where your sister is too. Beautiful
little baby she's got."

Then three doors slammed shut, the motor revved,
wheels spun, and stones smashed against the Corvette
as the Cadillac fishtailed away. Todd tried to make it
to his knees, but collapsed onto the ground again.

Harry the Horse had made good on his threats for
the first time. It was no longer a game. It never really
had been, Todd realized now.

# Chapter 19

Unlike most fund management companies which invested exclusively in publicly traded corporations, Sagamore also purchased controlling interests in private firms where the executive committee could see an obvious opportunity to buy cheap, clean the company up, then sell it a few years later at a huge profit.

Doub Steel—a minimill operator that bought scrap steel and reprocessed it more cheaply than integrated manufacturers produced steel from raw materials—was one of those companies. A year after David had joined Sagamore, he had persuaded the executive committee to purchase an 80 percent interest in Doub for just over $70 million. Management was excellent, operations were efficient, products were strong, and the price seemed right.

But Doub's financial performance had gone south soon after Sagamore closed the transaction, and the executive committee had placed responsibility for turning the company around squarely on David's shoulders. Things had improved since the first year, but, as far as his portfolio was concerned, Doub was still his largest albatross—next to GEA.

Like most negatives David encountered in life, he had turned Doub into an opportunity. A week after inheriting the task of turning the company around, he had himself elected to Doub's board and was named chief financial officer by Sagamore's executive committee. Doub's controller performed day-to-day accounting, payroll and collection functions, and the executive committee had to approve any major financial moves, but as CFO David had wide latitude in between. This flexibility had enabled him to make the $1 million payment to the godfather in Washington two and a half years ago without being questioned. Just as Jack Finnerty had guessed, David had called the payment a loan to a slow-paying supplier, fooled the accountants, and set the GEA contract in motion.

Doub was headquartered just outside Frederick, Maryland, forty-five minutes west of Baltimore on Interstate 70 close to the Appalachian Trail. As David gazed out the window from the third-floor office of Doub's executive building, he could see mountains in the distance. The trees covering the mountains had broken into their fall glory, but he could hardly appreciate the beauty. His mind was on the payment he had to effect today.

A million dollars to the godfather in Washington had been manageable. Doub was a fairly large corporation, with almost $400 million a year in annual revenue. A million dollars could be hidden—not easily, but by being resourceful he had made it work. But now he had to send another $2 million to the man. This was the payment due upon commencement of production of the A-100.

This $2 million payment would be more difficult to hide for any length of time. The accountants would be back in six months and would probably want to confirm the debtor on this one with a written letter from the obligor.

David pulled his chair up to the desk. Just as Finnerty had suggested, the answer to the problem would be David's GEA options. GEA's stock price would start shooting up as soon as news of the A-100 program leaked, and he would execute enough of his options to repay the money he had sent out of Doub—the payment he had made two and a half years ago and the one he would make today. As long as the money was repaid by January 31, the end of Doub's fiscal year, there would be no questions from the independent accountants. The loop would be closed and they would have no reason to investigate.

It wasn't the optimal solution—GEA shares might have room to climb even higher in the short term when David exercised the options—so he'd be leaving money on the table. But he'd have his job at Sagamore secured for life, plus whatever options were left over after repaying Doub.

He picked up the phone and dialed the direct extension of his contact at the local bank. Finnerty had called twice this week urging David to make the payment, and he didn't want to irritate Finnerty too much. Finnerty could make cashing in the GEA options difficult. He could make lots of things difficult if he chose to. As he had so readily pointed out that day at his farm.

"Hello, Hagerstown National, this is Ida speaking," came the familiar voice.

"Ida, it's David Mitchell at Doub Steel."

"Hello, Mr. Mitchell. What can I do for you today?" the woman asked pleasantly.

Over the next twenty minutes, with four phone calls and a series of carefully directed wires originating at Hagerstown National, David transferred $2 million from the local Doub Steel account to a numbered account at National Bancorp in the Grand Caymans. It was a different number from the one he had been directed to use two and a half years ago, but once again Finnerty had provided him the information, so he hadn't questioned the change.

As David hung up the phone for the last time, he let his head fall to the desk. He had to keep reminding himself that no one was being hurt by all this, that he was personally going to repay the money he had wired out from the Doub account to the numbered account in the Caymans. At the end of the day everyone would be square. There was nothing wrong here.

He stood up. This wasn't the time to analyze the ethics of his behavior. He had to get to the controller quickly to explain the money movement as a loan to another slow-paying supplier and create the documentation to cover his tracks. He moved out of the office and headed downstairs.

David hesitated outside Rich Grainy's second-floor office and knocked, but there was no answer. This was good luck. He would be able to effect everything with no explanations.

He turned the knob and pushed, and the door gave

way. Grainy's office was small, furnished with just a metal desk and a few ratty chairs. They paid Grainy $43,000 a year to be controller. He had three children and two old American cars, vacationed just a week a year in Ocean City, New Jersey, because that was all he could afford, and yet he was happy. David surveyed the bleak space. Some people's expectations just weren't that high.

He moved quickly to the desk, sat down, and flipped on the computer—Grainy had a personal password, but David knew it and easily accessed the system. He would make the entry into the general ledger and create a separate debit account. Then he would create a borrowing note on Doub stationery and have a friend sign it. Afterward David would file the note in the company's official records. When he repaid the loan with money from the options, he'd cleanse any trace of the transaction from the records and the computer.

The official Doub stationery was stored in Grainy's lower right-hand desk drawer, and as David pulled out three sheets, he noticed an open envelope shoved behind the stationery box. He pulled it out, and inspected the return address. Third Huntington Bank. A representative from Third Huntington had called a few years ago trying to win local payroll business, but he had turned them down.

He glanced inside the envelope at the statement and canceled checks. This was odd. Grainy had no authority to open an account without first obtaining David's approval. That had been made clear to Grainy on several occasions.

David withdrew the statement from the envelope and noted the closing date—May 15, four months ago—then removed the canceled checks. There were only two, but blood began to pulse quickly through his system as he laid them down on the desk. Both checks were for $1 million, and both were payable to something called LFA. David had no idea who or what LFA was and at this point didn't care. What caused his pulse to throb so furiously was the signature on both checks—David J. Mitchell. It certainly looked an awful lot like his signature, but he had never signed these checks. He hadn't even known Doub Steel maintained an account at Third Huntington. He touched the signature with his finger, then stared at the M. It wasn't his M. But it was a damn good forgery.

David moved quickly to the small copier atop the credenza behind the metal desk. His hands shook as he lifted the top of the machine, made copies of both checks, then folded the copies and shoved them into his coat pocket. The questions raced through his mind as he closed the top of the copier, then moved back to the desk and put the canceled checks back into the envelope.

"Can I help you, Mr. Mitchell?" Rich Grainy stood in the doorway, looking at the opened bank envelope in David's hand.

David made a snap decision. It would be better to go on offense rather than try to explain this. He stood up slowly, then dropped the envelope onto the desk. "What's the meaning of this?" He pointed down at the envelope.

Grainy shifted from foot to foot nervously.

"Rich," David tried again, "what the hell is this?"

Still Grainy did not answer.

"Rich!" David slammed his fist down on the metal desktop. "Have you been stealing money from Doub? Should I call the police right now?"

"You might want to call Art Mohler first." Grainy's voice was barely audible, but there was no fear in it. "He set that account up, and said not to tell anyone about it. I've never looked in that envelope because I don't want to know what's there." He stopped for a moment. "I don't appreciate your accusing me of stealing. I've worked at Doub for twenty years. I'm an honest man."

But David didn't hear Grainy's rebuke. He was swimming in his own pool of resentment. First Mohler had visited Finnerty at the Middleburg farm without telling David. Now he had been here at Doub Steel without acknowledging that either. Worse, he had opened a secret account and was paying significant amounts of money to something called LFA *and* forging David's signature to do it.

Mohler was setting him up. There could be no doubt of that now. But why? And then an eerie sensation crawled up his spine, and he shook his head violently. No, that couldn't be possible.

# Chapter 20

"So why here?" Todd wanted to know. He touched his stomach gently. It was sore from the punishment Harry the Horse had inflicted.

"This was the only place I could think of that you'd recognize without my actually saying the name." Jesse slipped into the seat as he held it for her. "I don't feel comfortable talking on my office phone," she said quietly.

"You're serious?" he asked, sitting down in the seat across the table.

"Yes."

"Why?"

"Hi." The waitress interrupted their conversation. "What can I get for you?"

"Diet Coke," Jesse answered quickly without looking up.

"And I'll have a chocolate milk shake, please." Todd smiled pleasantly at the woman.

"Sure." The waitress ambled slowly away.

Todd put his elbows down on the table. "It's a great old place, don't you think? Hasn't changed at all since we used to come here in high school."

Jesse laughed. "It's changed a lot. The furniture is different. They used to serve pizza and burgers, now it's Mexican. And the name is different."

Todd smiled. "I was talking about the flavor of the place. Take a look." He nodded. "Boys in letter jackets still chasing girls in short skirts. Those things never change."

"I should tell the girls to watch out for those kinds of boys."

"Hey, I had one of those jackets."

"Exactly," she teased.

The waitress was back quickly with their drinks. She served them and then moved to a table of loud teenagers.

"So what did you do this weekend?" Todd picked up his chocolate shake and sucked on the straw.

"Studied." There was no need to get into the day of sailing with David.

"I called you at midnight on Saturday and got your answering machine."

She knew he would be hurt if he heard the truth, and she always avoided causing someone else pain if she could. "I was home, but I let the answering machine pick up. I was tired." She began tearing the paper napkin into small pieces.

"Nah, you're just like me that way. You can't let a phone ring without answering." He watched her fidget.

"I was home," she said firmly.

Todd put down the milk shake, and his expression became serious. "Jess, I've missed you."

"What?" She had heard him, but was trying to buy

time. Trying to figure out how to respond. He had taken her completely off guard.

"I've been thinking a lot about you. I guess I realized at lunch last week how much I'd like to see you more. I know how good it feels to see you tonight. You've been avoiding this for a long time, and I think I know why. But hasn't enough time passed?"

She didn't want to deal with this now.

"I'd really like for us to date again," he continued. "I want to take you to dinners and just hang out together. We'll take it slow, and I'll be very much a gentleman until you tell me it's okay. I won't assume anything. If too much comes back, we'll stop."

"I can't."

"It's that guy who picked you up in the limousine, isn't it?" Todd was suddenly angry.

"No."

"No?"

"No! I told you, I just met him last week. He works at Sagamore."

"Were you with him Saturday night?"

Jesse looked away quickly. She couldn't deny it.

"I knew it."

"It's not like that, Todd. We're just friends. We were just talking business."

"At midnight on Saturday?"

"Yes."

"He's a suit, Jess. He's boring."

For the first time she heard real emotion in his voice. "Let's talk about why I wanted you to meet me here," she said. Jesse suddenly needed to talk to Becky. Maybe she could still reach her tonight.

Todd held up his hands. "Is it that you're worried I can't make a commitment, that I'm not serious about anything? That I do these things on the weekend that are going to get me killed? I can change, Jess. Really."

"I don't want you to change," she said softly. "Please, let's talk about how we're going to find out if there's anything going on in the Elbridge Coleman campaign. I found something this morning I think is really important."

For a moment Todd said nothing, searching her face for the truth. "Okay." He smiled as best he could. "What did you find?"

Jesse reached across the table and touched his arm gently. "Are you all right?" This was so difficult.

"I'm fine. Don't you pity me. I hate pity. Come on, tell me what you have."

"Todd, are you sure you can do this with me now? Maybe we should forget it."

"Jess!" he said loudly, holding up one hand. "It's business. I can handle it if you can." He smiled broadly to reassure her. "Whether you agree to date me or not, we're still very good friends. If somebody is chasing you around shooting out your car windshield, I'm going to find him and make him wish he'd never been born."

He was so loyal. "Okay. Thanks."

"So what do you have?"

She took a sip of Diet Coke. "I wanted to get a profile of the people working for Elbridge Coleman, so last week I obtained a list of individuals working for his campaign from the Federal Election Commission. This morning I had a friend of mine in the systems group at the branch run a report for me. It listed any place from which any person working for the Coleman campaign had received wages in the last two years."

"How did you do that?"

"I got the Social Security numbers of the people working for Coleman. Then I gave those numbers to my friend and had him search through the IRS data bank for any employer that had made withholding deposits to us on behalf of those Social Security numbers."

"That's a little Big Brotherish, isn't it?" Todd asked.

"It's nothing compared to what some agents do."

"Tell me more about that."

"Maybe some other time." Being a revenue agent meant being able to get almost any kind of information on someone you wanted. It was tempting, and as in all walks of life, some individuals gave in to the temptation. "Anyway, I found something interesting."

"What?"

"One of the people currently working for Elbridge Coleman recently received two payments from an organization known as Liberation for African-Americans. And that person received the payments *while* he was working for Coleman."

"Isn't LFA that militant group headed by the Reverend Elijah Pitts?"

"The group is headed by Pitts, but it's far from militant. In fact, it's done some very good things for Baltimore's inner city. You know, youth programs, work education programs, that kind of thing. But I still can't understand why someone who had worked for LFA would also work for Elbridge Coleman. You have to admit that LFA and an establishment Republican like Elbridge Coleman are pretty much at opposite ends of the political spectrum."

Todd pushed out his lower lip. "I agree, but maybe the person is a secretary with no particular allegiance to a political party. Maybe the allegiance is simply to their children, who need to eat. Maybe it's just a case of someone picking up a little money on the side at one job and working full-time at the other."

"Good point," Jesse agreed, "and in the case of the Coleman campaign this individual is receiving regular payments, which would support your theory. The thing is, I can determine the annual salary of the person by reviewing the withholding payments and assuming a tax rate. The person is making almost a hundred thousand dollars a year at the Coleman campaign, if I've calculated correctly."

"Not a secretary."

"I doubt it."

"What about the money from LFA?" Todd asked.

"That's where it gets even more interesting. Judging by the withholding amount, the gross amount must have been almost two hundred thousand dollars."

"Jesus." Todd shook his head. "And you're sure this person was being paid by Coleman at the same time?"

"Yes."

"That is strange, especially given the amounts."

"Wait," Jesse said. "It gets better. A week after LFA made the withholding they came back to the IRS and claimed they had made a mistake. They claimed there had been a computer error in the payroll system. That the withholding payment should never have been made."

"Sounds like they were covering up a mistake."

"Exactly. So why would someone be working at both places?"

"Working for one and gathering information on the other," Todd offered. "That's what comes to mind first."

"Right. And it seems to me it would make more sense if the person was really working for LFA and trying to get information on Coleman." Jesse was talking quickly now. "Why would Coleman care about LFA?"

"Maybe he wants to know if LFA is going to hold demonstrations at his functions or something."

"That sounds weak to me. It's a lot for Coleman to risk for not much return."

"At least I'm trying."

"Sorry, I shouldn't have criticized you."

"It's okay." Todd picked up his milk shake and took another sip. "I don't know, counselor, you've stumped me. But why would LFA necessarily want to know what was going on at the Coleman campaign?"

"Maybe LFA would pass information on to Malcolm Walker. I think Senator Walker is close to LFA—at least, every time I see Pitts on television he's calling Walker a good friend. Maybe the person is ultimately spying for Walker, stealing strategies, that kind of thing. If the person is making a hundred thousand at the Coleman campaign, he or she is one of the top aides, because that's a lot of money for a campaign worker, even in a

United States Senate race. The person would have access to very sensitive information."

"So then this person alerts Walker as to Coleman's strategies, through LFA, so that Walker can have the jump on Coleman. And if they were ever caught, it would be LFA's ass and not Walker's."

"Right."

Todd shook his head. "Sorry to throw a monkey wrench in your theory, Jess, but I thought you told me the file you got from Neil Robinson's summer home indicated that the improprieties were at the *Coleman* campaign."

Jesse didn't answer for a moment. "I know. That kind of shoots everything down, doesn't it?" She was suddenly dejected. "So what do we do, private investigator?"

"There are only two real options," he answered quickly.

"And they are?"

"Try to get a look at personnel files at the Coleman headquarters and/or at LFA." Todd took the straw out of the milk shake, turned the large glass up, and finished what was left.

"Do you really think Coleman or LFA is going to just hand over personnel files to us?"

He smiled brazenly. "Of course not."

She caught her breath. "Are you talking about breaking into those places?"

Todd shook his head. "Not both. If I happen to get caught breaking in somewhere, I certainly don't want it to be at the headquarters of a man running for the United States Senate."

"So then it's LFA headquarters."

"In the dead of night, baby." Todd slammed his fist down hard on the table. For a moment the buzz of the restaurant went silent as people looked around at Todd and Jesse. Then slowly the sound level returned to normal. "Sorry about that." He winked as he pulled his head down like a turtle going into its shell. "I got a little carried away for a second."

"Are you sure you want to break into LFA?" She shook her head. He was like a bulldog once he got into something. Nothing stopped him.

"I don't have any other ideas. I told you I did this morning on the phone, but that thing kind of fizzled this afternoon."

"I just don't want you to get in any trouble."

"That's why you're going with me to LFA. You'll be able to talk us out of trouble if we get caught."

"I can't go with you!"

"You have to. I won't know what to look for. And I'm not going back if I don't get the right stuff the first time, that's for sure."

Jesse began to protest again, but she realized he was right. She nodded her head slowly. "All right."

Todd rubbed his hands together. Another opportunity to be with her. And it would be dangerous. She would be aroused. Maybe he could finally break down her resistance.

"You're certain?" The man could hardly contain himself.

"Absolutely," Roth replied. "I have a copy of a credit card receipt from last March when she purchased the gloves. And I have the lab telling me that the hair from the glove almost certainly belonged to a blond woman. There are only two women in the department with blond hair as long as the one from the glove."

"Kill her right away. But make it look like an accident."

"Yes, sir."

"And, Roth, get that file if you can. But make sure she doesn't see another morning."

Becky Saunders had been Jesse's psychotherapist for twelve years and never charged her a dime for the many visits, even though that flew in the face of professional canons. Becky had been on duty the day Jesse—an emotional wreck—had entered the hospital for the operation. The particulars of Jesse's case had been so disturbing to Becky that she had stayed in the recovery room for five hours after the procedure talking with Jesse about what had happened, assuring her that she needn't feel guilt, that it wasn't her fault. And they had developed a bond that had lasted ever since. Jesse did Becky's taxes every year, but it wasn't as if she did it in an attempt to compensate Becky for the visits. They were simply friends helping each other the best way they could.

Just like tonight. Becky had already seen six patients today, and it was past ten o'clock in the evening. But Jesse had called and asked for an appointment at the last minute. And Becky had agreed immediately.

Becky opened her second pack of cigarettes of the day, lighted one, and inhaled. "So Todd Colton is becoming a larger part of your life again."

"Yes."

"He asked if you two could start dating, is that right?"

"Yes," Jesse replied again. "I told him no."

"But you thought about saying yes, didn't you?"

"I did," Jesse admitted.

"Do you think that would be a good idea, to start dating him?"

"That's what I'm here to find out."

Becky took another puff from her cigarette. "You know what I think."

"Tell me again." Jesse had heard Becky's opinion so many times, but it was always therapy to listen.

A column of smoke rose from the cigarette tip and curled around Becky. "I'm going to go through the whole thing," she warned.

"I know."

Becky felt the beginnings of a headache, but ignored the dull throbbing over her eyes. "You'd been sailing with Todd since early in the morning." Her voice was raspy from years of smoking. "It's a beautiful day, you're having a great time together, and you both realize that you're crazy about each other. You go back to his parents' house that evening because they're away on a trip. You make love for the *first* time in your life."

"Yes."

"Afterward, Todd takes you home. He walks you to the door, kisses you good night, and leaves. You come inside. You're an hour past your curfew. Your stepfather, Joe, is waiting up, and he starts in on you as soon as you come through the door."

"Starts in on me," Jesse repeated sarcastically. "That's an understatement. He was *screaming* at me. God, I hated him."

"He's had bourbon. Normally he wouldn't have been drinking, but your mother is on an overnight retreat with one of her church groups. Joe follows you to your bedroom, still screaming at you."

Jesse felt the anger and resentment building, as it always did. But it helped her to go through this. It helped to be able to share the physical pain and mental anguish of those moments with someone who understood. Pain and anguish that twelve years had not healed. It helped to share all this with someone who didn't judge. Who wouldn't be devastated knowing. They had been over it so many times, but it was cathartic on every occasion—once she was past the attack.

"He pins you down on the bed, pulls your clothes off, and—"

"—rapes me." Jesse finished Becky's sentence, then let out a long slow breath. "He rapes me." She said it again. It was part of the therapy to say it—and repeat it. She hadn't even been able to say it once until five years after the attack. Now she could say it twice in a row, sometimes three times.

"So in the same night you've lost your virginity to Todd and been raped by your stepfather. You're a psychological mess, and the person in the world you're closest to, the one you've always turned to for everything, can never even find out. You won't let her help you this time."

"Can you imagine if I had confided in my mother or

told the police and filed charges? Can you imagine if my mother had found out? Found out that her husband had raped her daughter? And her entire congregation at Sacred Heart Church would have found out. She's a devout Catholic. It would have pushed her over the edge. She would have committed suicide. I couldn't tell her."

Becky allowed Jesse to finish, then moved on. "A month later you find out you're pregnant, and you don't know who the father is." Becky closed her eyes and shook her head. "I don't know how you kept it together. You were a very strong woman, even then."

Jesse felt tears coming and coughed a few times to help hold them back. "I didn't feel strong."

Becky saw the tears. "You still have such a violent reaction to all this. *That's* why I don't think it's a good idea for you to see Todd, or anyone you associate with the attack. I think you've still got ghosts inside that you and I haven't found yet. If you and Todd became involved, those ghosts might make an appearance. I'm not certain the results would be good."

"But the tests showed the baby wasn't Todd's." Jesse was pleading his case. "That it was Joe's. And Todd still took care of me. He took me to the hospital and paid for the abortion." Jesse let her head fall into her hands, and the tears suddenly spilled down onto her blouse. "I was going to go to an inner-city clinic, for God's sake. Todd wouldn't hear of it. He insisted I go to the hospital and have the operation done right. Who knows what would have happened to me at the clinic? A week after I was going to go there the government shut the place down because they lost a young woman on the table."

"Keep him at a distance, Jesse. He's got a lot of baggage too."

"He knew it was Joe's, and he still took care of me. And he's never said anything to anyone. He's just been there for me whenever I've needed him." Jesse wiped the tears from her face. "He was so wonderful to me during that time. He got me to you."

Becky watched Jesse carefully. There must be some terribly stressful outside forces putting pressure on her. She had suddenly become vulnerable again. "Is that it?"

"Is what it?"

"You just said he got you through all that. Do you feel you owe him? Is that the real problem?"

# Chapter 21

One by one they filed silently into the dimly lighted meeting room. It was unusual for them to reconvene so soon, but circumstances had dictated the meeting.

Senator Webb hesitated for a moment, allowing the others time to take their designated seats. "If we're all ready, I'd like to begin." His gravelly voice brought the meeting to order over the strains of Bach.

The members nodded in agreement as they pulled their chairs to the table.

"The first topic tonight will be the security leak I mentioned at the last meeting," Webb began. "As I told you then, someone had stolen a file from Neil Robinson's river place before we got to it. We believe the file contains incriminating information concerning the Senate race between Malcolm Walker and our associate Elbridge Coleman." He nodded in Coleman's direction. "Tonight I'm happy to inform you that we've identified the individual who took the file," he said triumphantly.

"Who was it?" Finnerty asked, arms crossed tightly across his chest, a worried expression on his face.

"A woman who works as a revenue agent in Baltimore. She reported to Mr. Robinson before his untimely demise."

"How did you identify her?" Admiral Cowen wanted to know.

Theodore "Ted" Cowen was the Chief of Naval Operations—the United States' most senior naval officer—and Webb suddenly wondered how the man had managed to achieve that position three years ago. Cowen was overweight, swarthy, and for such a senior official, constantly focused on unimportant details. But he had proved malleable on bigger issues, like the A-100, and able to influence the Secretary of the Navy and the Secretary of Defense at opportune times, so his minutia fixation could be overlooked.

"We recovered a glove we believed was worn by the individual when she took the file from Robinson's house," Webb explained. "We traced the glove to a store and then matched the list of people who had purchased those types of gloves from that store in the last six months to the names of the revenue agents. She was on both lists."

"Excellent." Cowen smiled. "It sounds as if we have a positive identification. No chance of mistaken identity."

"No chance," Webb assured him. Of course, there was always a chance of mistaken identity. All you could ever do was take the physical evidence you had gathered and make the best deduction possible. But if Cowen felt better hearing there was no chance of mistaken identity, so be it.

"Good." Cowen rubbed his large belly. "I just wouldn't want to have any innocent people involved."

Cowen was so damn self-righteous. It was all right with him to kill someone as long as you were certain it was that person who had committed the offense. A crime so horrible as usurping a simple file. But hold the train if it might be an innocent bystander. What a crock of shit that was, Webb thought to himself. It must be the military training, he guessed. Perfectly acceptable to eradicate *anything* interfering with a mission. Unacceptable to use force otherwise.

"I don't want this to be a loose end any longer than is absolutely necessary," Art Mohler said. "When will we address the problem?"

"Tonight," Webb answered quickly, watching Cowen grab a roll of his belly.

"Good." Mohler was relieved.

"Second issue on the agenda," Webb announced loudly. He wanted to waste no time. He was exhausted from a long day on the Hill. "The issue of Malcolm Walker . . . and not in the context of the election," he added.

The others looked up as they heard an ominous tone in Webb's voice.

"I have learned that Walker had an informant at Area 51," Webb continued. "The informant was passing information to Senator Walker concerning the A-100."

"What? Bullshit," Cowen growled through clenched teeth. "Area 51 is a secure base. One of the most secure in our system. The civilians working on projects there are carefully screened and strictly monitored. We've never had a problem."

"His informant wasn't a civilian, Admiral. It was an

Air Force captain." Webb looked down at a paper on the table. "His name is Paul Nichols. He was receiving payments in exchange for the information and of course had the added incentive of derailing a Navy project."

"You're kidding!" Cowen was suddenly alarmed.

"No, I'm not. Apparently Senator Walker was paying him big. As they say, money talks, bullshit walks. And what we pay our military is bullshit, so those with questionable moral character are easy targets. Anyway, I have taken care of the problem under black-budget authority. Captain Nichols has been incarcerated. He is no longer a problem and won't be for quite some time. I can hold him in jail for at least six months without trial." Webb withheld a smile as he imagined the captain's fall from ten thousand feet through the Nevada night with Commander Pierce by his side.

"Was Nichols able to pass anything important on to Walker?" Mohler removed his half-lens glasses, and put them down on the table. He was clearly worried.

"Apparently. A friend of mine tells me that Walker will be holding a news conference tomorrow to disclose the existence of the A-100."

"Jesus Christ!" Mohler brought his hands to his forehead.

"The purpose of the news conference will be two-fold," Webb continued. "First, Walker will be trying to derail production of the A-100 by hyping figures the government will spend on the program. As we all know, it is a large program, and he will play on the public relations problem we in the defense arena have. You know, six-hundred-dollar hammers, thousand-dollar toilet seats, and the like. All the ridiculous stories leaked to the press by the liberals in the last few years and swallowed hook, line, and sinker by this country's gullible public. Walker will compare the A-100 to these stories and try to have the plane's production put on hold."

"How do you have this information on Walker's plan?" Cowen was impressed.

"I have a mole in Walker's office." Webb moved on quickly. He didn't want Cowen focusing on that little detail. "The second and potentially more disturbing reason for the press conference is that Walker plans to lay open the black budget and the programs within the black budget in an attempt to bring it under greater public scrutiny. Apparently he has become privy to certain information he should not have through his informant at Area 51, and probably through other avenues as well." Webb's expression became defiant. "Malcolm Walker has decided to raise the level of his Defense Department war to a new and very dangerous level."

"That bastard!" thundered Admiral Cowen. "I need the A-100 program at least six months into production before word of its existence leaks out. It would be too easy for someone to shut it down now. I must have that fighter-bomber."

"Easy, Ted." Finnerty waved a hand at Cowen. "Keep your pants on."

Finnerty was as calm and composed as usual in the face of adversity, and it was reassuring, Webb thought to himself.

Art Mohler picked up his glasses from the table and put them back on. "It's obvious to me what's happened. Walker has realized he's in trouble as far as

November goes. He's seen the polls and knows he's on the bubble," Mohler analyzed. "Elbridge is pulling ahead, and Senator Walker can't stop the express. It's almost as if we've done too good a job with Elbridge. Walker's going to a scorched-earth strategy with the black budget because it's the only option he has left. He's going directly to the American people with black-budget details as a last-ditch effort to show them he's a true establishment fighter."

"But he can't just babble on about the black budget in front of the national press corps," Cowen argued. "I know it's no secret that there's a black budget, but people don't know the inner workings of it. They don't know the extent of it. We can't have some joker giving away national secrets on network television, for God's sake." Cowen turned toward Webb. "Senator, can't you invoke a gag order under the national security rule black budget allows? Then we could have people there to put the clamps on him when he opens his mouth."

"Wouldn't that look great?" Finnerty interjected. "The Defense Department gestapo marching up to the podium, locking a black senator in chains, and leading him away. Land of the free and home of the brave. Walker would have a fucking orgasm. The press would be all over him for the story. In thirty seconds we'd destroy everything we've been building for three years, Ted."

Cowen saw Finnerty was right. "But we've got to do *something*. We can't just let him go on national television and torpedo the A-100 and maybe the entire black-budget process." Cowen swallowed hard. "Think where that could lead. I mean, forget about the fact that we lose our wealth engine for a minute. There's the other side of the coin too. I'm sure there are a few people who would love to know what's been going on here in this room. What if someone really starts digging?" He looked at Webb pleadingly. Suddenly he was nervous. "We can't let that happen, can we, Senator?"

A slight smile inched across Webb's face. "I have a solution."

"What's that?" Finnerty had known Webb for years and recognized the smile. God bless him. He had an answer for everything.

"Jack, and the rest of you," he said, making eye contact with all of them, "I'd like to keep that to myself. Please indulge me."

The others nodded hesitantly. They trusted Webb implicitly, but Malcolm Walker had suddenly proved himself a formidable opponent.

"Good. Next on the list is movement in the GEA stock. It ticked up today a few points." Webb kept the meeting moving forward. "Art, what's going on?"

Mohler slowly pulled his chair closer to the table. He was still distracted by the news that Walker intended to lay open the black budget like some skewered pig. He wanted to push Webb on his solution but decided against it. "Uh, it is true that the common share price of General Engineering & Aerospace rose a few points in today's trading session. The stock closed today at twenty-seven, up three dollars a share from the beginning of the day and up five and a half from its fifty-two-week low. But I don't believe the activity is attributable to a leak about the A-100. Remember, the overall market has been up in the last week too. And all the defense stocks have gotten an additional shot in the arm on rumors that U.S. budget negotiators have reached a compromise on the size of the defense portion for next year. It's a smaller amount than last year, but still more than was anticipated."

"Art, have you calculated the effect the A-100 will have on GEA shares?" Cowen grabbed another roll of his belly. It was a nasty habit but he'd been doing it so many years he was no longer aware of it. "I know you analyzed that a while back, but I was wondering if you had looked at the situation lately."

The room fell silent. Suddenly there was no sound except the symphony playing softly in the background. It was the key question. They had all profited via this infrastructure before, but the GEA transaction was to be the mother lode.

"I really hate to put a specific figure on it at this point, because you will all hold me to it later," Mohler complained.

"But you will give us the figure."

Mohler looked up at Webb, recognizing the tone. There would be no further stalling. "My rough calculations indicate a stock price of almost one hundred dollars a share within a year."

"Does that take into account any incremental business GEA will pick up from the DOD as a result of successfully engineering and bringing to production as high-profile a program as the A-100?" Finnerty asked.

Mohler shook his head. "No."

"Bear with me," Cowen said slowly, leaning over

the table. "I know we've been through this before, but I want to make sure I've got this straight."

Finnerty suppressed a grin. Admiral Cowen was still new to the game. They had brought him into the circle three years ago, specifically for the A-100 because of the size and scope of the project. Webb could appropriate the money from the black budget, but they had needed someone actually at the Pentagon to approve the contract quickly and quietly within DOD. To his credit, Cowen had immediately recognized the enormous potential inherent in the partnership of a private investment firm and a black-budget insider. After a few stock tips from Webb and Mohler, Cowen had become a disciple. Then they had made him a member. Now he was just as greedy as the rest of them.

"Sagamore invested a billion dollars in GEA common stock, right, Art?" Cowen asked.

"Yes," Mohler answered. "And we paid twenty-five dollars a share."

"So if the stock goes to a hundred the way you said it would—"

"The way I said it *might*," Mohler corrected.

"Sorry, might."

"Yes."

"It means—"

"It means," Mohler interrupted the admiral again, "that Sagamore would net almost three billion dollars on the billion-dollar investment."

"How much of that is ours?" Webb demanded.

Mohler paused. This would raise their expectations to a stratospheric level—something he didn't want to do—but he didn't have the nerve to ignore, or even dance around, a question from Webb. For some reason the man scared him. Perhaps it was his relationship with Gordon Roth, or his ability to lock up an Air Force captain and throw away the key for six months. "Scared" wasn't the word. The word was "petrified." "Sagamore earns a two percent fee on any profits," he said. "On three billion dollars that would be sixty million. Half of that remains at Sagamore, half comes to this group."

Cowen began to laugh. He was going to be a millionaire and the envy of every other branch of the service with the most advanced stealth fighter-bomber in the world—as long as Malcolm Walker could be neutralized. "Ain't that some shit," he said to no one in particular.

Mohler's posture stiffened at the obscenity. He hated Cowen's brash manner. But Cowen had come through on the A-100 project with flying colors. Webb had assured them, against some resistance, that Cowen and the Navy were the best choices for the project that would make them millions, and he had been right, as always.

"It's a helluva profit. But we've all worked hard and we deserve it." Webb gestured at Mohler. "You are certain you can suck that money out of Sagamore without raising too many eyebrows?"

"Yes."

Finnerty changed the subject. "How's Mitchell doing, Art?"

"All right. Yesterday he made the two-million-dollar transfer to the Grand Caymans account you gave him from one of Doub Steel's local banks." Mohler smiled. "He's very predictable."

"Does he have suspicions?"

"They always have suspicions."

"The next topic," Webb interrupted forcefully, "will be the election." He pointed down at Coleman. "Give us an update, Elbridge."

Coleman cleared his throat. He hadn't spoken since the meeting had started. "There isn't much new to report. We continue to run strong, especially in the western part of the state and on the Eastern Shore. Senator Walker has a lock on inner-city Baltimore. There really isn't anything we can do about that. The battle will be won or lost in the Baltimore and Washington suburbs."

"Won or lost?" Mohler was suddenly annoyed. "Does that imply that the election is still in doubt? I thought the trend was positive. Last I heard we had gained nine points in the last six weeks."

"The trend *is* positive." Coleman shot back. "I'm very confident. I just don't want to underestimate Malcolm Walker. He is a resilient man, as we've discussed this evening."

Admiral Cowen tapped the table for attention. "I don't know about the rest of you, but I like what we've got going here. I've heard tonight that we stand to make an incredible profit on GEA, and that's great, but we need to keep this thing in place. Not only because of the profit potential, but also for patriotic reasons. I don't want to sound too much like a military zealot, but we must maintain the integrity of the black budget. We can't allow the liberals to lay it open. That would make it impossible to develop weapons in secret. That could compromise national security." He turned to Webb. "Senator, it sounds like Malcolm Walker is going to try to drop a bomb tomorrow. I hope you have effective countermeasures planned, because we're going to need them."

All eyes turned to Webb.

Webb's expression was steely. "Don't worry. After tomorrow Malcolm Walker may never call another press conference in his life. He'll certainly wish he hadn't called this one."

# Chapter 22

Hot water coursed down Jesse's body, gently massaging and relaxing her tired muscles. A nice hot shower felt so good at the end of a long day. It would put her right to sleep.

Steam rose slowly from the shower floor, enveloping her, and she closed her eyes, concentrating on the tiny droplets pounding her skin. It was hypnotic, and her mind drifted back to the restaurant earlier this evening—and Todd. He had been devastated at her rejection. She had seen it in his face instantly, and his reaction had tugged at her heart. But Becky strongly agreed that Jesse had given the right answer. That Jesse still wasn't ready to date him.

Jesse turned off the shower and squeezed water from her long hair, twisting it into a ponytail on one side of her neck. She lifted a large, thick towel from a hook on the wall as she stepped over the side of the tub and dried herself thoroughly. Finished, she tossed the towel onto the sink and moved quickly into the small apartment's single bedroom.

The formal dress hung from the top of the closet door by an embroidered hanger, and Jesse stopped for a moment to admire it again. The dress, delivered today to the apartment complex management office, was a gift from Elizabeth Gilman. Also in the beautifully wrapped dress box had been an envelope containing an invitation to a black-tie affair Elizabeth was hosting for the governor. Jesse moved to the dress slowly and touched the material. Silk. It must have cost a fortune. It was, of course, totally improper for her to accept it. Government employees had to adhere to strict regulations with respect to gifts. She gazed at it. Well, maybe she'd wear it to the governor's affair, *then* send it back.

Jesse moved away from the dress, and as she did, she glimpsed her reflection in the full-length mirror standing in the far corner. She put her hands on her hips and pivoted her body to both sides quickly, scrutinizing herself. Slender shoulders, thin waist, long toned legs, and a behind that filled out the seat of a pair of jeans perfectly, even if she did say so herself. Jesse turned to face the mirror. She wouldn't mind having larger breasts, but then didn't almost every woman feel that way?

The Persian cat rubbed against her ankles. As Jesse bent down to scratch its chin, the doorbell rang. Instinctively she covered her body with her hands and arms. Who could that be at this hour? Again the bell rang. She hurried to the bed, picked up her ankle-length terry-cloth robe, and slipped into it as she walked quickly toward the hallway.

In the middle of the darkened living room she stopped. It was five minutes after midnight. Why would anyone come to her apartment now? She took one more step toward the door and stopped again. *Be careful.* Neil Robinson's words. Had the man who had chased her at Neil's house finally found her? But why would he bother to ring the bell? That could give her time to climb down the fire escape. Of course, maybe that was what he wanted. Someone else could be waiting at the bottom of the fire escape. It was darker in the back. A better place to finish what he had started the other night.

Jesse moved slowly over the thick carpet to the door and pressed her eye to the peephole. But she could see nothing. It was too dark. She could illuminate the outside light, but then her caller would know she was at the door. The man had been willing to shoot out a car windshield. He might think nothing of firing through a door. For several seconds she stood in the apartment foyer, frozen, uncertain of her next move.

Finally she shook her head. There was just no reason to take chances at this point. Over the last few days she had convinced herself that the man was no longer searching for her. But that was silly, actually stupid, she realized. No one fired at another person with the intent to kill and then gave up the pursuit so quickly. It would be irrational to think that. It was time to call the police.

"Jesse." The voice quietly called her name. "Jesse!" Louder this time.

"David?"

"Yes! Hey, can I come in?"

Instantly she flipped on the outside light, pulled the chain across the lock, turned the deadbolt, and tugged the door open. He stood before her, still dressed in a suit and tie. "What are you doing here?" she asked.

"Well, that's a helluva greeting."

"Get in here." She reached out and grabbed his forearm, laughing a relieved laugh as she pulled him into the apartment.

From behind his back David produced the sweater Jesse had worn Saturday night on the sailboat. "You left this in my car."

"And you decided to bring it to me now?"

"Well, I was working late, and your place is on the way home for me."

"No it isn't."

"When I take the long way home it is."

She smiled. He was quite charming sometimes, she had to admit. "I never should have let you pick me up to go sailing," she teased. "I never should have let you see where I live. God, you're probably a stalker."

"No, German secret agent, remember?"

"Oh, right." She pulled the robe more tightly around herself. "So why did you really come by?"

"Elizabeth is going to ask you to meet a few more people at Sagamore. If those interviews go well, she's going to make you an offer right away. You'd join after finishing school. All of that's off the record, but that's the deal."

Jesse brought her hands to her mouth. "You're kidding."

"No, I'm not. I found out late this afternoon. But she's going to ask you to meet these people very soon. Several of them are going out of town for a while, and I guess she wants you committed to Sagamore now."

Why, David couldn't understand. Jesse was bright, but there would be lots of other candidates to choose from. "Anyway, I thought you might want me to go over these people's backgrounds. Some of them are kind of quirky, and it'll help to know a little bit about them before you meet them. I realize it's late, but it sounded as if Elizabeth was going to ask you back pretty fast. Maybe even tomorrow. I'd do this in the morning, but I've already got a breakfast meeting and it may go quite some time."

"It was so nice of you to do this for me." Without thinking, she kissed him on the cheek.

"I just thought it might help."

"Absolutely." She held up a finger. "Give me just one minute, can you? I'm going to put some clothes on."

"Do you have to?"

"I'll be right back," she said, laughing as she moved back down the hallway toward her bedroom. "Make yourself comfortable. There's beer in the refrigerator."

David watched her disappear into the bedroom, then walked into the kitchen and opened the refrigerator. He scanned its contents, pulled out a Michelob, and set it down on the counter. As he was about to twist off the top, he noticed a dark brown folder lying on the counter next to the stove. In the upper left-hand corner of the folder was a white label marked simply "Elbridge Coleman." David twisted the cap off the beer, took a long sip, leaned back against the sink, and stared at the file.

Jesse took off the robe, dropped it on the bed, then quickly pulled on a pair of jeans and a sweatshirt. A few more interviews. If they went well, she'd be offered a job at Sagamore. At Sagamore Investment Management Group, one of the most prominent firms in the money management business. Sara wasn't going to believe it. Jesse could hardly believe it herself.

She sat down at the dressing table, picked up her hair dryer and flicked it on. Instantly the appliance's loud hum drowned out everything else. And then her heart skipped a beat. The file. It was on the kitchen counter.

She threw the hair dryer to the floor and ran for the living room. As she turned the corner of the hall, David was coming from the kitchen, beer in hand. "Hi."

"Hi yourself," he said, then took a swallow from the bottle. "Are you okay? You look a little unsettled."

"I'm fine." Suddenly she realized she hadn't exhaled in what seemed like forever. She let air out through her mouth slowly, trying not to make her alarm obvious.

His eyes moved down her body as he put the bottle on a table and sat down in a chair. "You look great."

"Thanks." Her pulse was racing.

"You sure you're okay?" David took another sip of beer.

"I'm fine, really. Let me get something to drink too. I'll be right back." She walked through the kitchen's swinging door, then to the counter next to the stove. The file from Neil's house was still there and didn't appear to have been touched. But there was no way to know if David had gone through it. If he had looked inside, he would have made certain to put the file back exactly as he found it.

"What are you doing in there?" David called.

"Just getting a beer. Be out in a minute."

"Okay."

Jesse hid the file in a cabinet next to a box of cereal, then pulled a beer from the refrigerator and headed back into the living room.

David smiled at her as she sat down on the couch opposite his chair. "I have a confession to make, Jesse."

"What's that?" Fear ripped through her. Was this going to be about the file? What would she say?

"Elizabeth really is going to ask you to interview with some more people," he said. "That's on the level. But, well, I came by for another reason too."

"And that is?"

David hesitated. "I was hoping we might have dinner again sometime soon."

Jesse placed her beer down on the coffee table, then pulled her knees to her chest without answering.

David sensed her discomfort immediately. "Are you worried that if we go out, Elizabeth might disapprove? That she might not make you an offer because of it?"

He had read her mind. "That thought had occurred to me."

"What if the situation was different? What if you weren't interviewing for a job with us? Would you go out with me then?"

Jesse nodded. "Yes."

"What if I told you that Elizabeth wouldn't mind us going out at all? That she's actually said to me that we'd make a nice couple? Would you feel different about it then?" David picked up a business card lying next to the phone and tapped it on the tabletop carelessly.

Jesse thought about his question for a moment. "I guess it would be okay then." She focused on the business card David was now gazing at. "Don't take this wrong, but I'd like to hear it from her."

David didn't answer. He was still staring at the card.

"Did you hear me?"

The card indicated that the woman had a Ph.D. in psychology. "Who's Rebecca Saunders?"

"A friend," Jesse said quietly. She wanted to grab the card from him, but she knew that was out of the question. David was too smart for that. He would recognize her anxiety immediately.

"A friend?" There were numbers scratched all over the card—obviously appointment times.

"Yes."

"Hey, Jess!" The loud banging on the front door startled both of them. "Jess, open up!"

"My God." Jesse jumped up from the couch. "What is this tonight, Grand Central Station?"

The banging persisted. "Jess, come on! Open the door!"

She recognized Todd's voice. "What is he doing here?" She hurried to the door and opened it.

"Hey, gorgeous." Todd was clearly excited.

"Hi." Her voice was cool. This was going to be a terribly awkward situation.

"Don't be so happy to see me, Jess. I know it's late, but I think you're really going to be . . ." Over Jesse's shoulder Todd saw David coming toward the door.

"Oh, Jesus." The enthusiasm drained from his voice. "I'm sorry."

Jesse brought a hand to her face and shook her head. "It's all right."

"I'd better get going." David moved to Jesse and kissed her cheek. "If Elizabeth calls you, call me right away. Tell my secretary to pull me out of my meeting if you have to. I'll give you the lowdown on the people you're seeing." He and Todd exchanged the same curt nods they had outside the IRS building, then Todd stepped aside and David passed through the doorway.

"Thanks, David," she called after him.

He waved without looking back as he descended the apartment complex steps.

Jesse turned around and moved back into the apartment. Suddenly she was exhausted.

"I really am sorry, Jess."

"It's okay."

"Looks like I got here just in time," Todd murmured to himself.

"What?"

"Nothing. Hey, I won't keep you. It's just that I found out something pretty interesting about Elbridge Coleman, and I wanted to tell you right away." He pulled out a notepad from his back pocket.

"You couldn't call me?" Suddenly she was worried. He was coming on way too strong. Becky was right.

"I thought you said you were worried about talking on the phone."

She looked up. That was true. "I did," she said apologetically. Instantly she felt guilty for questioning him. For thinking that Becky had been right about him. "What did you find out?"

He shut the door and moved several steps into the apartment. "I have a broker friend who's been nice enough to lose me a decent amount of money over the last two years. He feels kind of bad about it, so I asked him for a favor." Genuine excitement filled Todd's voice. "He was only too happy to oblige."

"And?"

"That file you got from Robinson's house mentioned something about investigating the initial public offering of Coleman Technology. That was one of the reasons he had pulled the corporate tax returns. Robinson mentions in his notes that the price for the stock seemed very high. I asked my broker friend to check it out. He works for Legg Mason here in Baltimore. Legg Mason wasn't part of the syndicate selling the shares, but he has friends at other firms that were."

Jesse nodded. "Go on."

Todd flipped several pages in the notepad, studied them for a moment, then began. "It turns out the offering was handled by only a few small brokerage houses. None of the big bulge-bracket firms like Morgan or Merrill Lynch were involved, just some small-time players, bucket shops, in places like Seattle and San Antonio.

"My friend confirmed for me that the price *was* very high for a company involved in the defense industry, especially in light of the list of investment banks selling the shares. They just weren't very powerful firms. They didn't have the breadth of investors a

Morgan or a Merrill would have, so they shouldn't have been able to command such a high price."

"That's interesting." Jesse nodded. "But I don't think it's enough to nail Elbridge Coleman for something other than getting a good deal."

"It gets better. My friend at Legg Mason had a conversation with a broker at one of the firms handling the Coleman underwriting, a firm by the name of"— Todd checked the notepad once more—"Zarb & Co. It's in Phoenix. Apparently even the brokers at Zarb thought it was a strange deal. The shares had already been presold before they got their hands on them. Essentially all they had to do was write tickets for names a senior person at Zarb had given them. Usually the brokers have to call everyone from their blue-haired great-aunts to the President of the United States to sell shares. This deal was already done when they got the shares."

"Orchestrated, in other words," Jesse said.

Todd nodded. "And the buyers of Coleman shares were midsize industrial companies, not mutual funds or retail investors that typically dominate the buy side of the IPO market."

"Can your friend get information on any of these firms that purchased Coleman shares in the IPO?"

"I'm way ahead of you, Jess. The guy at Zarb did a little more digging. At least three of the small companies that bought shares of Coleman were all themselves owned by a common holding company. He's getting more information on the holding company. You know, who actually owns it. Sometimes with these corporate shells it takes time to figure all that out."

Jesse knew that as well as anyone. People were constantly trying to fool the IRS with all kinds of convoluted ownership structures. "Pending that information, your theory is that one corporate entity might have been responsible for purchasing all Coleman Technology shares in the company's initial public offering, but tried to mask what was really going on by spreading the shares around its portfolio companies."

Tod nodded. "Exactly."

This was excellent information. Something that could be confirmed and might give them a concrete trail to follow. "And why would someone do that?" She was thinking out loud.

"It would be a convenient way to fund a candidate's campaign without making it obvious who the money people were."

That was her idea as well, but she had wanted to see if Todd would come to the same conclusion without prompting. She glanced down at the table next to the chair in which David had been sitting. Her eyes narrowed. Becky's card was gone.

David climbed into the back of the limousine next to Elizabeth Gilman as the driver shut the door. He had walked all the way to the other side of the apartment complex because Elizabeth didn't want the limousine parked where Jesse might see it.

"What happened?" she asked. "You weren't in there very long."

He was barely able to make out her profile in the

darkness. "A friend of hers came by out of the blue. It wasn't going to happen."

"What friend?"

"Some guy named Todd Colton. She claims he's just a friend, but I don't know."

"Todd Colton," she whispered. "Todd Colton." She said the name again, committing it to memory.

David closed his eyes and relaxed. He was coming to find there was a great deal more to Elizabeth Gilman than the refined grande dame exterior she portrayed.

"Did you find anything while you were in her apartment?" she asked.

David hesitated. The file on the kitchen counter had accused candidate Elbridge Coleman of conspiring with a group of corporate angels to manipulate his election, of working with a conservative faction focused on controlling the defense industry and beating down people like Malcolm Walker. David's godfather in Washington would be a likely candidate for that faction. So would Jack Finnerty, he thought to himself. And the potential link to GEA, Sagamore, and himself had crackled through his brain like lightning as he stood in the kitchen staring at the papers.

Then David had heard Jesse's hair dryer turn off and realized he had to put the file back. The frenzied look in her eye as she came running from the bedroom told him she was afraid he had seen it. "No, Elizabeth, I didn't find anything." Information such as the file was best kept to himself until it could be used as a bargaining chip. "Nothing out of the ordinary, anyway."

"All right, but I want you to search her apartment again thoroughly. And I want you to get closer to her. I want you two in constant contact." Elizabeth needed to know where Jesse was at all times now.

"I don't understand, Elizabeth." David's voice was flat. "Why is that so important?"

She couldn't tell him the truth. "I'm thinking of making her a job offer now, contingent upon her graduation from business school, of course. I don't want the investment banks to have a chance at her, so I'm going to preempt them."

"I don't understand why you're going after Jesse so hard. There will be lots of candidates to choose from. Candidates from Ivy League business schools with much more experience than Jesse Hayes."

"I can recognize raw talent immediately." She turned toward him. "That's why I run Sagamore," she said coldly, "and you are a portfolio manager just hoping to celebrate your fifth anniversary with the firm."

But even as the whip snapped, David felt her fingers on the back of his hand.

"David, in four years we've never had a chance to really get to know each other." Her voice softened, and she pulled his hand to her lap. "I think we should have that opportunity tonight." She saw the strange look come to his face. The words had quickly achieved her goal. To distract him.

David bowed forward in the seat and rubbed his forehead. The promise of millions and all that money could buy. Of financial security. All he had ever wanted. To be rich. But was it really worth all this?

Gordon Roth watched from behind a minivan as the man on the porch said good night to the young woman, then turned and made his way down the stairs. The apartment's outside light flipped off and for a moment the man was obscured by darkness, but at the bottom of the stairs Roth picked up his shape again as he walked out into the parking lot and slipped into his car.

As the red taillights of the man's car disappeared around the corner, Roth moved from his hiding place, walked quickly to the back of the complex, and scaled the fire escape to the third floor. There he crouched down next to the bedroom window and slowly leaned forward. Through the curtains he watched the woman disrobe and slip under the covers. Then the light went out and he could see nothing more.

For two hours he waited. Finally, when he was certain the woman was asleep, he pulled the black ski mask over his head and raised the unlocked window— a window he had unlocked this afternoon in preparation for tonight. In just seconds he had stolen across the room, straddled her with his knees on her elbows, and clamped a hand down over her mouth. For a moment she struggled, but despite his average size he was immensely strong and her efforts were useless.

When she lay still, Roth bent down until his mouth was only inches from her ear. "I'll take my hand from your mouth, but if you scream, I'll kill you," he whispered. With his free hand he removed a long, serrated hunting knife from his belt and pressed it against her cheek. "Do you understand?"

She nodded frantically, her eyes wide open.

Quickly Roth removed two long pieces of cord from

his belt and secured her wrists to the bedposts, then ripped the covers back and did the same to her ankles.

She gazed up at him, on the verge of tears. "Please don't hurt me," she begged.

"I need information. If you cooperate, you'll be fine." He pushed the razor-sharp knife point against the soft skin of her neck.

Instinctively she moved her neck as far away from him as possible, but he followed and pushed the knife in until a tiny drop of blood oozed onto the tip. "You're hurting me." Her voice was loud.

Instantly he clamped a hand over her mouth again. "I told you not to make a sound," he hissed. "One more time and you're dead." He took the hand away slowly.

"I'm sorry," she murmured.

He bent down until his mouth actually touched her earlobe. "Where is the file?"

"What file?" she sobbed.

He tried again several times, but to no avail. Clearly she wasn't going to cooperate easily. He pulled a rag from his coat and shoved it into her mouth roughly. "I'll be back."

For half an hour, starting with the bedroom, he tore the apartment to shreds, but found no file. Grim-faced, he returned to the bedroom, knelt over her again, and removed the gag. "Where is the file?" he asked firmly.

"I don't know about any file," she insisted. "I swear to you."

"Did you give it to the man who was here tonight?"

"I told you," she sobbed pathetically, "I don't know about a file. Please let me go."

"This is going to get very bad unless you cooperate right now. It would be so much easier if you'd just tell me."

"I don't know about any file!"

Roth jammed the gag back in her mouth, and for an hour he tortured her. He left no marks on her body but devastated her psychologically with the threat of the huge knife. Still she gave away nothing. Finally he pulled a pillow over her face and meted mercy. When she had gone limp, he untied her wrists and ankles, picked up her body and moved to the window. She had died in her bed of asphyxiation. But the world would think her death had been the result of a fiery car crash.

# Chapter 23

"Good morning, Malcolm." Monique Howard was Walker's chief of staff. She was tall with long dark hair, a pretty face, and a slender frame. She had been with Walker since his campaign for the state senate and often accompanied him to formal government affairs, because the senator's hectic schedule allowed him little time to date. As they were both unmarried, rumors of a physical involvement abounded. And if he had made it obvious that he was interested, Monique knew she would have agreed, because she was extremely attracted to his sharp features, quick wit, and natural charm. But in their ten years together, he had always been a perfect gentleman. So like most Washington gossip, the talk was just that—talk.

"Monique, how are you this morning?" Walker's voice boomed out over his huge desk, cluttered with papers and empty Styrofoam coffee cups.

He was naturally disorganized. He had tried to convince Monique for years that he kept the desk a mess on purpose because it helped him to think in a more liberated fashion. That the mess represented free thought. But she knew the truth. He just didn't like cleaning up. So it was she who reorganized the desk once every two weeks to keep him from being buried by the paper mountain.

Monique eyed Walker suspiciously. "Why are you in such a good mood today?" He had been outwardly discouraged lately by Coleman's strong showing in the polls.

"Today we begin the comeback." He stood up quickly and moved to the large office doorway, acknowledging the four young interns working in the outer office with a quick nod before shutting the door. Then he began pacing, as he always did when he was excited. "Today we grab the spotlight back from Elbridge Coleman." Walker smacked his lips as if savoring a delicious meal.

"Oh, right, the news conference." Monique was not as excited about the day's possibilities as Walker.

He continued to pace. "Yes, the news conference." He heard the skepticism in her voice. "Why do you say it like that?"

Monique smoothed her pleated knee-length skirt. "Let's go over your remarks," she said, sidestepping his question for the moment.

Walker paused at the window of his first-floor suite in the Russell Senate Office Building to collect his thoughts. From this spot he had a wonderful view of the Capitol. Only senior senators were allowed office space in the Capitol itself. The rest of them walked or took the short train ride through the underground corridor connecting the two structures to attend sessions. "First, I will disclose the existence of the A-100 stealth fighter-bomber," he began. "I will detail the A-100's immense cost to the American people, probably a hundred fifty billion dollars over seven years when everything is said and done. And the fact that it represents an extraordinary waste of taxpayer money in this day and age of United States military dominance. I will, of course, point out that the funds could be used more effectively in a number of social programs, citing several specific examples.

"Second, I will discuss the black budget in general and how the A-100 contract was awarded under its veil. I will call for a full Senate investigation of the contract process, both in Congress and at the Pentagon, with the objective of shutting down the old-boy network." He pushed out his chin defiantly. "There. What do you think of that?" he asked, turning away from the window.

He would be taking a huge gamble following this strategy, Monique knew. "What exactly do you intend to say about the black budget?"

"What I know."

"Tell me again what that is."

Once more Walker began pacing. "That a select number of senior senators, possibly as many as three, probably two, but maybe just one, can, on their own authority, without accountability to anyone, secretly appropriate up to ten percent of the defense budget each year and spend it on new weapons development. That no one has the ability to question the allocation of these funds by the black budgeteers. Not Congress, not the Office of Management and Budget, not the General Accounting Office, not even the President, for crying out loud. That deals with defense firms can be cut under the protection of the program without any objections being raised." Walker noticed that his chief of staff seemed to be more interested in her skirt than his remarks. "Monique?"

She'd been rubbing a spot on the skirt. "Yes?" The spot was an irritating reminder that she'd eaten a fruit-filled Danish for breakfast and spilled a good bit of it on herself.

He didn't appreciate the indifference she consistently showed for his fight against the Defense Department. "People need to know about the black budget, Monique. They need to understand that this system has been in place for years. That black programs are costing taxpayers a great deal of money, at least thirty billion a year, and that tremendous opportunities exist for fraud and at the very least, incredible conflicts of interest. It's a system that has never been audited and never will be unless someone takes a stand. I've been fighting government waste in the DOD ever since coming to the Hill. I'm the logical choice to lead this battle." He sat down behind the desk, picked up a tennis ball lying in an unused ashtray, leaned back in the leather chair, and tossed the ball toward the ceiling. "And the press conference will generate a lot of great publicity for us right when we need it the most."

"How do you know the black budget actually exists?" The spot wasn't coming out. And she'd just picked up the skirt from the dry cleaner.

"Come on." He was annoyed. "We all know it does."

"Specifically, how do you know? The press will ask

if you really choose to let loose with all this. You'd better have an answer prepared."

"Okay, okay. How about an example? The B-10 bomber was a black-budget program. And what do they estimate each one of those nasty little buzzards cost the American people?" Walker asked rhetorically. "A billion two, that's how much. Of course, the real price was probably twice that high, and you know people got wealthy off the books. You know development money found its way into secret coffers."

"What proof are you going to offer?"

"The fact that no one will account for the money. Talk to a Pentagon accountant and there's the fear of God in the expression below the green eyeshade. Talk to OMB or GAO and their eyes just glaze over."

"You need more," Monique said decisively.

"Look, if you hang around the halls of Congress for six years, you hear things. Whispers about how the DOD budget game is really played. How the contracts are awarded. You never hear anything concrete, never anything anyone will own up to, but you know what you know."

"Maybe there's a good reason no one will own up to it," Monique offered ominously, still scraping at the spot on her skirt with her long fingernails.

"Hey, we promised each other we'd never be scared off by these people." Walker sensed her apprehension, and it irked him. She was a strong-willed woman, and he had never seen her this way before. "Are you getting soft on me?"

"No!" Her eyes flashed to his. "But sometimes it's

better just to let the lions take their pound of flesh and not bother them."

"I can't believe I'm hearing this." Walker threw the tennis ball toward the ceiling again. When it came back down he bobbled it. It fell to the floor and rolled across the thick red carpet toward a far corner of the office. "Did someone get to you?" he demanded.

"Of course not."

"Be honest. Did someone approach you?"

"No, dammit, I'm just trying to protect you."

"Then what's your problem?"

"Malcolm, let's suppose you're right. Let's suppose there is a huge fund within the Defense Department budget that one or two senators personally control. That there is a conspiracy involving a small cadre of senior Pentagon officials and defense industry top management. Do you really think you're going to persuade Congress to investigate what's going on? If the fund is there, it's there because senior legislators think it ought to be there. You're going to ask the very same people who think the fund ought to exist and who would then be profiting from it to investigate it. To investigate themselves, in other words. It isn't going to happen, and you're going to be ostracized in the process." She gave up on the spot and resigned herself to another trip to the dry cleaner. "I know you're disappointed in me, but my advice is to fight them on a project level. Expose the A-100, but leave it at that. Play the game by the rules. You'll make points with voters and you'll stay alive."

"Oh, please." He waved a hand at her. "You're being a little melodramatic."

"Am I?" She wasn't so certain.

"Yes."

"Stay away from the black budget, Malcolm. It's not that I'm scared. I just don't think it's a good move politically to focus on it. I'm your chief of staff. You pay me to give you advice. That's what I'm giving."

"How about the fact that there's an Air Force captain sitting in a cell at Area 51 who hasn't been charged with anything?" Walker asked. "Taken into custody and left to rot. Doesn't it bother you that they can do that?"

"Of course it does. But doesn't it bother you that he hasn't said a word? That he hasn't accused anyone of anything? That he's so scared he's willing to sit in an eight-by-ten room and play tic-tac-toe on cinder-block walls rather than fight to get home to his children? I'd say they've gotten to him. If you don't draw that conclusion from his silence, you're blind." She paused. "Doesn't it bother you that his Washington contact, Senator Malcolm Walker, hasn't tried to get him out?"

Walker banged the desk loudly with his hand. "That's not fair! Captain Nichols came to me. I told him there wasn't anything I could do if they got to him. He knew the risks."

"You've got to help him anyway."

Walker rose from the chair and began pacing again. "I know," he said, emitting a long, guilty sigh. "And I will. Just let me lay open the black budget first. Then I really will be able to help him."

"But I don't think anyone on Capitol Hill is going to start an investigation on the basis of what you've told me," she reiterated.

"What do you want me to do, Monique?" His voice

suddenly reflected the strain of the last few months. "If I don't try something drastic, Elbridge Coleman is going to roll over me in November. That's obvious from the trend in the polls. I need a splash. Something that will take the spotlight away from him and put it on me. Otherwise I'm gone. It won't matter if I'm politically ostracized or not, because I won't be around. Look at the numbers." He stopped pacing and jammed his hands in his pants pockets. "There's an ABC poll coming out tomorrow that has Coleman *five* points ahead of me now."

"How did you find that out?" she asked quickly. Usually she was able to screen those calls.

"Peter Jennings, for Christ's sake. He called me directly for a comment."

"I'm sorry, Malcolm."

"It's all right." He rubbed his forehead for a moment. "There's one more thing I haven't told you." He picked up a paperweight from the desktop, then put it back down. "I have a piece of physical evidence."

"What? Really?"

"Yes. It's small, but it would probably be enough to at least start a Senate investigation."

"What is it?" She was suddenly excited. "I mean, if you have something like that, maybe it would be enough."

Walker sat back down in his chair and pulled open a desk drawer. He removed a manila envelope and tossed it toward her.

She grabbed the envelope from where it had landed atop several unread *Washington Posts*, pulled out the single piece of paper from inside, and read it quickly.

Her eyes widened. "This is a handwritten memo from Chief of Naval Operations Ted Cowen to Senator Webb requesting an appropriation from the black budget for the A-100! I mean it actually says the words 'black budget.' And it's clearly addressed to Senator Webb."

It was like a gift from God. And just when he had needed it most. "Can you believe it?" Walker asked. "From what I understand, nothing important like that is ever written down when it comes to the black budget. I guess it just goes to show how the Navy's been ignored over the past few years. Admiral Cowen must not have been aware of black-budget protocol."

"Is that definitely Admiral Cowen's signature at the bottom of the memo?"

"Yes. No doubt of it. I had an expert examine the handwriting."

"But how did you get this?" She could barely contain her excitement.

Once more Walker thought about Captain Nichols sitting alone in the cell. He would get the man out if he had to call in every favor he had. "From a file at Area 51. It was the last piece of physical evidence Captain Nichols was able to smuggle out before he was silenced."

At precisely one in the afternoon, Senator Malcolm Walker moved through the wide doorway into the Central Hearing Facility of the Hart Building. The large room was packed, mostly with members of the press. Several reporters nodded or patted Senator Walker on the back as he approached the dais. He had always enjoyed an amicable relationship with reporters—even ones sympathetic to the conservative side who detailed his investment portfolio and school résumé. It was never a good idea to irritate the press, no matter what. Walker had learned this lesson at the outset of his political career.

He tapped the microphone a few times and smiled at several familiar faces in the crowd. "Good afternoon, ladies and gentlemen." He turned his head slightly, tilted it down, and stared directly into the CNN camera. "Thank you for coming today. What I am going to tell you will—"

"Senator Walker!" A deep voice rose from somewhere in the back of the huge room, interrupting Walker's delivery.

Walker shaded his eyes against the bright lights, trying to identify the speaker.

The Reverend Elijah Pitts began moving toward the podium, flanked by two large young bodyguards. "Senator Walker, for some time we at LFA have been attempting to initiate a dialogue with your office."

Walker turned quickly to an aide. "How the hell did they get in here?"

The aide shrugged nervously, aware that his job was suddenly in jeopardy.

"Senator!" The reverend used his sermonic voice, wavering his tone for effect.

Walker spun back around to face Pitts, who had now made his way to within a few feet of the podium through a rapidly parting sea of reporters.

"I have repeatedly tried to contact you, but you have ignored my calls. You and I have many things we need to discuss about the black community." He pointed a long finger at Walker. "Why are you ignoring our organization? Why do you ignore Liberation for African-Americans? Have you forgotten your people, Senator?" The last words reverberated dramatically throughout the room.

Walker whipped back toward the aide. "Where the hell are the Capitol Police? They should be here to take this guy away."

"I don't know where they are, sir," the young man stammered.

"Where's Monique?"

The aide shrugged.

"Dammit." Walker glanced into the CNN camera, then quickly away. He could feel the opportunity to disclose the A-100 and the black budget slipping away. "As I was saying—" he attempted to begin again.

"Answer me!" the reverend roared above the growing hum of the crowd.

"Yeah, answer him," a reporter for *The New Republic* piped up. "Why won't you recognize LFA?"

Camera bulbs began to pop, and Walker felt perspiration forming on his forehead. Suddenly the lights seemed hellishly hot. Never let them see you sweat, he thought. "I am of course happy to meet with the reverend at some point down the road to begin mapping out ways for us to work together." He turned his head to the side so he wasn't speaking directly into the mass of microphones.

"Will you invite me onto your stage as a sign of brotherhood? Will you invite me up there today? Right now?" the reverend yelled.

Walker gave the CNN camera one more forlorn look. The tape of this news conference was going to be broadcast on the evening news over and over in every home in America. He swallowed hard. If he displayed overt unity with LFA, he could easily lose a substantial block of white voters. On the other hand, if he didn't embrace Pitts now, he might lose his core black constituency. Not that they would vote for Elbridge Coleman, they just wouldn't vote at all. Which would be just as devastating. Suddenly there was no way out, and Malcolm Walker felt the floor beneath his feet thinning to tightrope width.

"Ask me to join you on the dais, Senator Walker. Show me you respect our people." Pitts launched a deadly arrow at the stage.

And it might as well have been real. Walker felt pain, as if an arrow had actually seared into his chest. Slowly he nodded, then smiled a broad, political smile. "Join me on the stage, Reverend Pitts." It was the only option. He couldn't turn his back on LFA in such a public forum and expect to hold together his black support. He would simply have to engage in damage control later and hope for the best.

Pitts stepped up onto the podium, where he took Walker's wrist and raised his arm in triumph. For several minutes they stood together, arms held high together as hundreds of cameras clicked.

Senator Webb watched from the doorway as Walker's campaign disintegrated. Doub Steel's secret support of LFA had suddenly earned a destructive dividend, as had Webb's control of the Capitol Police. His ability to direct the building's guards to permit the good reverend into this room had allowed a stake to be driven right through the heart of what remained of Walker's campaign. Webb smiled as he turned away and headed for his office in the Capitol.

# Chapter 24

"You are a very beautiful woman. It's been a pleasure meeting you tonight."

The cozy, candlelit table was tucked into a corner of the tasteful Four Seasons private suite. "I don't feel very beautiful," Monique said softly.

Senator Webb slid his hand slowly across the linen tablecloth and patted her delicate fingers. "Well, you are. You're one of the most exquisite women I've ever seen," he said in an exaggerated Georgia drawl, watching her hair shimmer in the candlelight. "Phil Rhodes told me you were very attractive, but I had no idea. I'm very glad he arranged this meeting." Webb picked up a sterling silver pot. "Would you care for any more coffee? Any dessert? I'd hate to think dinner was over."

If this interlude could have been over before it began, that wouldn't have been soon enough for Monique. "No thanks," she said politely, trying to act as if she were enjoying herself.

Webb could see that the lies and deceit were taking their toll on Monique, but that was all right. It would only serve to make her more vulnerable, more malleable. There was no escape from this, and he could see in her eyes that she had already realized that. "Rhodes mentioned that you might have something for me."

Monique hesitated a moment, then reached down to her purse leaning against one leg of the table, and pulled out an envelope. "Here."

Webb calmly took the envelope, extracted the single sheet of paper from within, and perused the handwriting quickly. "Is this the original?"

"Yes."

"Are there any copies?"

"No. That's the only record of Admiral Cowen communicating to you about the black budget."

"How did Senator Walker obtain this?"

"How do you think?"

"Captain Paul Nichols?"

"Yes." The young pilot was sitting alone in the bowels of Area 51. She had given him away to Rhodes, and for what? A few extra dollars and the chance to save herself the embarrassment of having her pictures exposed to the world. She brought her hands to her face. Captain Nichols had two children and a wife who had no idea what had happened to him.

"Thank you, Monique." Webb slid the envelope and its precious contents into his suit jacket. "I will make certain there is a bonus in your account tomorrow."

"Keep your damn money." Monique stood up and threw her napkin on the table, disgusted with herself and the temptations to which she had so easily yielded. "I'm leaving." She turned to go.

"Stop right where you are." Webb's voice turned unfriendly. "You're not going anywhere."

"What?"

Webb sipped his coffee. "You can leave when I say you can leave. And not before." He placed the cup down and smiled. He couldn't wait to get his hands on those perfectly tapered legs. "Take your clothes off."

It was her worst nightmare. "You're out of your mind."

"Mmm." Webb took off his suit jacket as he stood. "Maybe." For a split second his mind wandered to the other members of the inner circle; to his detachment of young military disciples at Area 51—led by Commander Pierce—who had instilled the fear of God and the devil in Captain Nichols; to his beautiful home on the lake in Georgia; and to his massive Swiss bank account. He had built an incredible life by doing just as he was doing now. Manipulating. Cornering people until they had no choice but to obey. Maybe he was a little insane. But no one could argue with his success. His focus snapped back to the woman. "Take your clothes off now. Don't make me say it again."

She held out her hands, palms up toward him. "You're crazy. I'm out of here."

"You go anywhere near that door and first thing tomorrow morning Malcolm Walker will be informed that you stole this memorandum and delivered it to unfriendly factions. He'll be informed that you gave Captain Nichols's name to Phil Rhodes as your boss's contact at Area 51. And that you have accepted money in exchange for both the Cowen note and the information regarding the Air Force pilot. Finally, he will receive the pictures I believe were taken of you with a certain blond woman. Pictures Phil Rhodes and I have enjoyed reviewing several times already." His eyes roamed her body again. "Oh, yes. The *Post*, the *New York Times* and *Penthouse* will also receive those photographs." Webb smiled evilly. "Now, if you want to leave, you may." He gestured toward the door.

Monique's eyes filled with tears. The trap was closing in around her. "You wouldn't."

Webb laughed. "How long have you been in Washington, Monique? Almost six years, right? And you haven't learned how the game is played yet? No wonder Senator Walker is lagging behind Elbridge Coleman in the polls. His damn chief of staff doesn't understand the rules." He moved behind Monique and rubbed her shoulders, then slowly began undoing the buttons down the back of her dress. "You know I wouldn't hesitate to relay all of the information to Senator Walker and the press. And it's not as if Phil Rhodes or I have done anything wrong. The axe will fall on your neck, not ours."

"Please don't," she begged as he undid the last button.

But Webb paid no attention to the entreaty, sliding the dress off her arms and down her body until gravity pulled it to the floor. "God, you are beautiful." Quickly he unhooked the bra and stripped it from her chest, then pulled the lace panties down her legs until they too fell to the floor. "Come with me." He took her wrist roughly and led her to the king-size bed. "Kneel down on the floor and lean over the bed."

Monique obeyed dutifully. She had no doubt Webb would follow through on his threats, and she could not have Malcolm finding out what she had done. That was the bottom line. So now she would pay for her moment of weakness.

"Good girl." Webb stripped off his clothes quickly and knelt behind her. God, it was an aphrodisiac to have this much power over someone. To have someone respond to your every command exactly. It was all about the money to a point, and then when you had enough, money became pointless and power became the only thing. The power to make people do what they didn't want to do. The power to force them to please you. He couldn't remember being so aroused before in his life.

He had never used his position on the Hill to curry female favors. He didn't want anything out there anyone could use against him. But now he was in his last term, and it no longer mattered as much.

As he entered Monique he suddenly knew there would be many more times. It was like the laboratory rat exposed and instantly addicted to liquid cocaine, his mentor had explained to Webb long ago during Webb's first term. You'll know it's dangerous, but once you give in to the temptation you'll need it as much as the air you breathe or the food you eat. And the mentor hadn't meant simply the physical act of sex. It was the power and domination that made it so exhilarating. There could be no substitute for power. Nothing else that could make you feel so alive. Nothing that could make the blood pound so ferociously.

# Chapter 25

First Maryland Trust's nineteenth-floor lobby was sparsely decorated and the furniture worn and out of date. This was a back-office floor of the state's largest bank, an operations area not often graced by high-powered visitors, so the bank's executives did not spend generously on accouterments here.

"May I get you anything while you wait?" The receptionist smacked gum as he talked.

"No thanks," David answered. It was funny how people always spent money to impress people they didn't know, he thought to himself as he stretched in the uncomfortable chair. Lobbies outside the offices of the professional staff were probably decorated with expensive antiques and tasteful paintings. But the back-office people—the backbone of the entity—who kept money flowing in and out on a daily basis were greeted every morning by peeling gray wallpaper, metal furniture, and a receptionist who smacked gum. There was a lesson to be learned here, but he was too tired to think about it.

"How's the weather out there this afternoon?"

Great. A chatty receptionist. "Hot and humid." He

kept the response brief, hoping the man would get the message.

"It's really August weather for Baltimore. Usually by this time in September we don't get days like this."

"Uh huh."

"David!"

Johnny Antolini was coming through the swinging door leading to the back offices. David rose from the chair and met Johnny in front of the receptionist's desk.

"How the hell are you, David?" Johnny asked as he pumped David's hand.

"Good." Johnny had been David's best friend in high school, and though they had drifted apart as their careers diverged, they had managed to maintain at least sporadic contact. "You saved me," David said quietly, motioning toward the receptionist.

"Oh, you mean Chuckie?" Johnny asked loudly, pointing a thumb at the young man, who was still smacking his gum loudly.

David brought a finger to his lips subtly.

But Johnny was not to be deterred. He turned toward the gum smacker quickly. "Yo, Chuckie. You can't be harassing our guests here. We don't get too many of them anyway. Leave them alone, will you? Don't talk so much."

Chuckie looked up unhappily as David cringed. Johnny hadn't changed at all. He was still as direct as ever.

"Just kidding you, Chuckie boy." Johnny reached over the desk and slapped the young man hard on the back. "Come on, David, let's go." Johnny pushed through the door to the back offices and led David through a maze of desks to one in the middle of the floor. "Have a seat, buddy." He pointed at a chair beside the metal desk.

Several other employees sat very close to Johnny's space. He and Johnny would enjoy little privacy here, David saw. "Could we use a conference room?"

Johnny laughed. He moved to an older woman sitting at the desk next to his and put a large hand on her shoulder. "We've got no secrets here."

"I'm serious."

Johnny detected a tiny trace of fear in David's expression, and the thought crossed Johnny's mind that perhaps he shouldn't have been so eager to help his old friend after all. "Okay." He led David through the maze once again to a small room at the side of the central space and closed the door when they were both inside. "This better?"

"Much."

"Well, have a seat."

"Thanks." David sat down in a spindly chair. Its cushion was worn to the metal on one side.

"So how are things at the finger-food firm of Sagamore Investment Management, or whatever the hell it's called?"

"Good. Well, okay."

"What's the problem, David?" Johnny became serious. He had sensed that there was something wrong with his old friend even as they had shaken hands in the lobby. He wasn't going to kid around anymore.

"I'm not exactly sure." A strange look came to David's face. "I need your help to figure that out."

Johnny folded his hands on the veneer table. "Always at your service, Señor Mitchell. Always here to help."

That was true. Johnny had pulled David out of more than a few scrapes in high school. David hesitated. This was difficult.

"Come on, out with it." Johnny checked his watch. "No offense, rich boy, but it's almost five o'clock. You might burn the midnight oil out at that blue-blood firm of yours, but those of us who toil in the funds transfer area of First Maryland Trust leave exactly at five when we arrive at nine in the morning. Especially when we have a softball game at six."

David held up a hand. "Okay, I get the message. Look, I need you to track down an account for me."

"Be more specific."

David hesitated again.

Johnny raised an eyebrow. He had known David too long to miss the signs. "There must be something very wrong."

"Why do you say that?"

"You're having a real hard time getting this out. And you look like dogshit. Should I go on?" Johnny asked.

"No." By actually asking for help, David would be verbalizing his suspicions for the first time, and they would suddenly become more real as a result. He was about to take all of this to a new level. All he could hope for was that he was wrong. "Johnny, I need to know the name on an account. All I have is the account number."

"And let me guess," Johnny said. "The account is located in Switzerland or the Caymans."

"Yeah."

"Those places don't give up information like that easily. For good reasons. You know that."

"I know. I just thought you might be able to help."

"Are you in trouble, David?"

If his suspicions were correct, he was in a great deal of trouble. "I hope not."

Jesse waved as David entered the bar. She noticed several women interrupt conversations to give him the once-over as he pushed through the crowd. He *was* attractive, and she suddenly realized that she had been thinking about him more than a few times a day now.

"Hello there." David bent down and kissed her cheek gently as he reached her bar stool. "How are you?"

A kiss on the cheek had become their customary greeting and good-bye, and she liked it. "Great. How about you?"

"Fine." Bodies were stacked four deep waiting to be served at the bar. "Why don't we get out of this traffic jam?"

"Okay."

He took her hand and led her through the crowd to an open table at the back of the establishment. "This is much better." He held her chair, then took off his suit coat, draped it over the back of his chair, and sat down. "What do you want?"

"Now there's a loaded question." She smiled and eyed him up and down seductively, before she burst out laughing.

"I meant to drink." He laughed, dropping heavily into his seat, as if it had been a very difficult day. "But I liked the look I just got."

"Don't read too much into it," she cautioned.

"You know, you're starting to intrigue me."

"What are you talking about?"

"I think you're this innocent, naive woman and then I see you do something like that." He leaned over the table toward her, placing his elbows on the table. "It makes me wonder."

"Oh, please." She shoved one elbow out from under him playfully.

"So what do you want?"

"Diet Coke is fine."

He gave her a disappointed look. "Have a beer with me, Jesse."

"I can't. I have school tonight."

"Do you have an exam or something?"

"No, just class."

"Have just one beer then."

She smiled. "You're terrible."

"The devil. Haven't you figured that out yet?"

Jesse ignored him. "I really shouldn't, but okay, I'll have a beer. Just one, though." She held up her forefinger.

"Good." Satisfied with his small victory, David turned and motioned to the waitress for the two beers. "How was your day?" he asked.

"Fine. One strange thing happened, or I guess didn't happen."

"What do you mean?"

"A woman I work with, Sara Adams, didn't show up at the branch today."

"Why is that strange?"

"We're pretty good friends. She usually tells me if she's taking a day off and who she's going to be with if she does. I do the same with her. It's kind of a buddy system."

"Did you call her at home?"

"Yes, but there wasn't any answer." Jesse was more worried than she was letting on, but there was no reason to bother David with Sara's unexplained absence. He looked worn out. "It's probably nothing. How was your day? You look a little tired."

"Fine."

They sat in silence for a moment. Finally she could no longer contain her curiousity. "So tell me about yourself."

"What?"

"I want to know about you. Every time I ask, you give some short answer, then turn the focus of the conversation back on me. I have to admit it's nice to find someone who does that, who doesn't want to talk just about himself, but now I want some answers about you."

David shrugged. "There isn't much to know."

"Tell me anyway. Tell me about where you grew up, your family, the schools you attended. All the normal stuff."

"Sounds like an interrogation."

The waitress served the beers. As she walked away, Jesse slid her hand across the table and touched David's arm gently. "I'm serious. Talk to me. You never do. It occurred to me that we spent all day together last Saturday on the sailboat and I really don't know anything about you."

"Cheers." He tapped his glass to hers and drank.

She shook her head. "No. That's another diversion. I'm putting my foot down. Talk to me. I won't take a sip until you start talking."

"Okay." But still he remained silent.

This was getting ridiculous. "Let's try something easy. Where did you go to college? Wait, let me guess. Princeton, Harvard, Yale?"

There would be no more dodging the issue. That was clear. "Cecil County Community College," he said quietly.

"You just aren't going to give me a straight answer, are you?"

He had anticipated this. She was going to be very disappointed. Her image of him was about to shatter. "That's as straight as it gets. I'm not kidding."

He was telling her the truth, she suddenly realized. "You're serious."

He nodded.

"But you said you went to an Ivy League school."

"No, you said that, Jesse. I just didn't bother to correct you."

"Where did you grow up?"

David pulled a pack of cigarettes from his pocket. "Right here in the city. In Glen Owens, the Hell's Kitchen of Baltimore. You're from this area. You know what Glen Owens is like. It was the same way when I was growing up." He dropped the pack on the table and pushed it toward her. "Want one?"

"No thanks. I didn't know you smoked."

"Do you mind? I'll stop if it bothers you."

"No, it's fine. My dad smoked. I don't mind."

A woman at the bar had been watching David's every move, and he finally acknowledged her interest with a subtle smile. Might as well, he thought to himself. The prospects of seeing Jesse on a social basis had just dimmed considerably. "So now you know. I'm just a poor boy with no heritage."

"Is that why you wouldn't tell me about yourself?"

"We're all supposed to be the Third or named Rockefeller out at Sagamore. And except for me, we are. I'm the black sheep of the group. I figured if you knew, you might not be interested."

"You must not think much of me."

"Well, I've been dropping pretty big hints about how I'd like to see you socially, and you haven't accepted. I assumed that if you knew about my background, that would be just another reason not to go out with me."

"You know why I'm uncomfortable about going out with you." Jesse had seen the look David had given the woman at the bar, and to her surprise she had felt a twinge of jealousy. "I don't want Elizabeth to get the wrong idea."

"I understand. By the way, did she call you?"

"Yes. I'm coming out to Sagamore Thursday evening for final interviews. She gave me the list of people I'm seeing, and I would like to talk about them with you at some point."

"I told you, I'd be happy to do that."

"Thanks." Jesse gave the woman at the bar a curt

hands-off glare. "But let's do that later. I want to talk more about you. I'm just curious. How do you get from Cecil County Community College to Sagamore? No offense, but I can't imagine Sagamore recruits heavily at Cecil."

David laughed loudly, suddenly relieved to have finally told her. "Well, I got an operations job at a bank in town after Cecil Community College through a friend of mine. I talked my way into the executive training program there, then talked my way into the University of Virginia business school, then talked my way into Sagamore."

"You must have been a good talker."

"I had to be. I was wearing polyester and leather until a couple of guys in the bank training program took me out and introduced me to wool and cotton." He still had one of those polyester suits hanging in his closet as a reminder of where he had come from. As a reminder that every day he had to work harder than the rest because he had started at the back of the pack. "That little shopping spree was one of the most embarrassing experiences of my life, and one of the most valuable."

"David, you must have done very well at Virginia for Sagamore to take an interest. I mean, it's a great school, but it isn't Ivy League."

"I did okay. But the reason Sagamore was interested in me was that they wanted a token. Somebody they could point to and say, 'Hey, we take people from different backgrounds.' "

Jesse could see his resentment even though he tried to hide it.

He inhaled from the cigarette. "I'm reminded of where I've come from every day I'm at Sagamore."

"Is it really that bad?"

"Life is simply a menu of trade-offs," he said, taking another puff. "I liked the money they were offering. I knew none of those people would ever be my friends, but I didn't care." He looked straight into her eyes. "Now they're doing it to you. Presenting you with the same choice. And remember, Elizabeth won't be at Sagamore forever. She'll be gone and you'll have to deal with the rest of them."

"So if you don't like it, why don't you leave? Get another job?"

"I told you at dinner. It isn't that easy." His expression darkened.

"You mean because Mohler will blackball you within the investment community if you don't make it past the fifth year? I'm sure you could get another job. Look, he can't call everyone in the world."

David shook his head. "It runs deeper than that."

"What do you mean?"

He had said it without even thinking. Suddenly he regretted being so open and pulled back. Being loose with his thoughts might get him in trouble. "Let me take you to dinner. I know a great place down in Little Italy."

"I told you, I have to go to school, and . . ."

"And you think Elizabeth would get the wrong idea if she found out," David finished the thought.

Jesse said nothing. Meeting for a beer after work was one thing, but a second dinner would be different.

David reached into his coat pocket. "Here."

"What's this?" Jesse took the envelope from him.

"Just read it."

Curious, she pulled out the letter and began reading. It was a hand-scrawled note from Elizabeth, thanking Jesse for her interest in Sagamore. After Elizabeth's signature was a P.S. It read: "David is a wonderful man, but he works too hard. Perhaps you could help him with his problem and show him what it means to relax a bit." Jesse glanced up at David as she finished the letter. "You probably put Elizabeth up to this," she said, smiling.

That was the strange thing. He hadn't asked Elizabeth to write that. She wanted him around Jesse as much as possible, but when he had pressed her as to why, Elizabeth simply explained again that she didn't want anyone else preempting a Sagamore offer. It was a ridiculous explanation, but she wouldn't elaborate. And Elizabeth was the managing partner, so he couldn't press too hard. "No, I didn't."

Jesse sensed he was telling the truth. So Elizabeth had no problem with them seeing each other. Jesse felt the spark run from her fingertips to the rest of her body. A spark she suddenly wanted to explore.

"So, how about dinner?" he asked again. "You can miss one little class. It won't kill you."

"I'd like to, but I can't tonight."

"How about when you get out of class?" He conceded dinner.

She was already very nervous about tonight. God, what if they were caught breaking into LFA? "I can't. Really."

"Why not?"

"We, um, there's a study group I have to attend after class." That was a plausible story. "It's going to run very late. How about tomorrow night?"

"Okay." Finally. Progress. He leaned forward over the table. "Tell me something about yourself, Jesse."

"What are you talking about?" The question had taken her off guard.

"I told you all about me. Now it's your turn. Tell me something about Jesse Hayes I don't know."

"I'm exactly five feet six inches tall."

"I'm not kidding. Something dark. Something no one else knows." He smiled strangely for a second. "Is there anything like that to know about you?"

What did he mean by that? Did it have anything to do with Becky's card? The card she was certain he had taken. Was he fishing for information about that? "If there was anything, why would I tell you?"

"Because you like me. Because you feel comfortable around me. Because I'm trustworthy."

Was he? She still wasn't certain about that yet. "Something deep and dark, huh?"

"Yes."

"Okay. I'm a double agent from Berlin too."

David smiled. But he had seen the momentary sadness. There was something here, and the answer probably lay with Rebecca Saunders. If Jesse wouldn't tell him, there were other ways to find out. And Elizabeth had said she wanted to know everything.

The elevator doors opened onto the fifteenth floor of the Hughes Building. David stepped through them and moved into Sagamore's deserted reception area toward the large mahogany double doors leading to the inner offices. He swiped his magnetic identification card through the security system, then checked his watch. Almost midnight. The security system would now give management a record of his late-hour visit to the firm, but that was all right. He had come here late on many occasions to finish research, so no suspicions should be aroused.

The lock clicked open after a five-second delay. David walked into the inner offices and made a quick check of the entire floor. There was no one else working. The place was empty tonight.

Sagamore's incredible investment record. The fact that the firm's performance *always* outpaced the Dow Jones index. It just didn't add up. There were a few down years with all portfolios. Everyone experienced them. The probability of an investment management firm such as Sagamore maintaining the kind of performance it had for so long was small. No, closer to infinitesimal, he thought to himself as he flipped on his office light. At least not without an edge. Like the edge they had with the GEA play. The thoughts had been nagging at him since joining the firm four years ago, but he had never followed up on his suspicions. Now he was finally going to at least try to get some answers.

David threw his suit coat down on his desk and headed for what the portfolio managers called the hall of records—a room filled with rows of files detailing every stock trade anyone at Sagamore had ever made. A room kept under tight security. He stopped outside the door to the large room. It was only a hunch, but Jack Finnerty's words had kept haunting him. Things weren't always what they appeared. Perhaps the answer lay behind this door.

The lock pad protecting the hall of records beeped as David keyed in a long sequence of numbers. Only the executive committee and one administrative assistant had the code. But he had seen a string of numbers on a piece of paper atop the administrative assistant's desk one day during his first month at Sagamore and memorized them as he flirted with her. Then he had hurried back to his desk, written the numbers down, stayed late that night, and inputted the code after everyone had left. It had worked perfectly, but as he stood in the doorway that night, he had decided not to enter. Someone might come back, and he didn't want to be caught there. And he had really just wanted to see if the code worked.

He had gone to such lengths to acquire the code because he felt that if someone was trying so hard to keep something from you, it was probably worth having and someday would prove valuable. Tonight he was going to find out if he was right.

To check a record of a past trade, portfolio managers had to submit a written request for the file to the administrative assistant. It might take hours for the woman to retrieve it from the hall of records, and no copies were ever made.

Management claimed to have implemented the cumbersome system for two reasons. First, in keeping with Sagamore's high standards, they wanted meticulous records of all activity maintained on-site, not just at the broker shops that executed the trades. Brokers were known to be lax in their attention to detail, and Sagamore did not want to be unable to provide trade records if the SEC requested them.

The second reason the executive committee gave for the security surrounding the hall of records was that it did not want portfolio managers inspecting the investments made by other Sagamore portfolio managers. It wanted diversity and original thought within the firm. It was really a tacit admission that the firm didn't trust its own employees, but that admission was not greeted as resentfully as it might have been in other industries. People in the financial world were conditioned not to be trusted.

The small light atop the keypad flashed from red to green, and the lock snapped open. David pulled the handle up and pushed. The door swung open, and he switched on the overhead lights. It was as if he had suddenly gone back in time. Rows of file cabinets stretched back to the wall, filled with trade records arranged by company in alphabetical order. He almost laughed aloud. A single laptop computer could easily have stored all the information in this entire room of file cabinets. However, the executive committee had considered the computer option and rejected it. The members of the committee were older and less familiar with computers, and therefore less trusting of a computer's security. They worried that the information might be too easily accessible to too many people. They were *too* worried, David thought to himself. There was something in here they didn't want people to see.

For the next two hours David systematically reviewed several specific files he believed might fit the pattern. Each time he identified the pattern he was searching for, he pulled the buy order—a yellow piece of paper on which was the name of the company in whose shares Sagamore was investing, the number of shares purchased, the date purchased, the brokerage house with which the trade was executed, and the portfolio manager who had ordered the trade—and walked down the hall to the office equipment station and made a photocopy. Then he quickly returned to the hall of records, replaced the original in its file, and moved on to the next trade.

When he closed the last file, he had accumulated forty-two trades that could potentially confirm his suspicions. He placed the copied pages in a small box, carried it out of the hall of records, carefully relocked the door, and headed to his office.

It was after two a.m. and he was fighting sleep. He had been awake since six yesterday morning, and the three beers he had consumed after Jesse left for school were working against him as well—of course, they had also given him the courage to do this. He considered fixing coffee in the firm's executive kitchen but decided against it. It would take too much time, and he wanted to get out of here as soon as possible.

The Bloomberg machine on the credenza behind his desk beeped to life as he flipped the power switch. Bloomberg was a worldwide financial news network that provided real-time prices on stocks, bonds, and currencies in any market around the globe. It also provided historical stock price information as well as significant news on the subject company.

David entered his password into the machine, then reached for the first trade record from the top of the box. For another two hours he researched price fluctuations of the specific stocks around the dates Sagamore had invested in them and searched for any news stories about the subject companies for those dates as well.

Finally, after he finished researching the forty-second trade, he took a deep breath and rubbed his eyes. So that was how they had done it. Elizabeth Gilman and Art Mohler weren't geniuses after all. They were simply master manipulators with connections to die for. No wonder they shunned publicity like the plague. They didn't want the SEC observing these same patterns.

David rose from the desk chair, put the trade records and the price and news histories he had printed from the Bloomberg machine into the box, then put the box into a sports bag he had brought from the trunk of his car. In seconds he was back out into the reception area, sports bag over his shoulder, waiting for the elevator.

As David waited, he leaned back against the wall next to the elevator bank and shut his eyes. It was after four in the morning and he was almost out on his feet. But the research had proved invaluable, and now he was glad Jesse hadn't been able to go out tonight.

He shook his head and opened his eyes. What they were doing at Sagamore should have been obvious to him long ago. He should have figured it out as soon as they set him up with the GEA investment. However, the money and the pressure to perform had blinded him. But now what was he going to do with the information? As Finnerty had pointed out last week in Middleburg, David had bribed a senior government official and committed fraud at Doub Steel. If he went to the authorities, things could get messy. And a district attorney might not necessarily find what was in the box to be proof positive of what was going on.

The bell chimed and a red arrow over the far doors illuminated. David moved slowly to the doors as they opened. As he turned into the elevator he bumped into a man coming out. David stepped back, staring at the long sandy blond hair, beard, and mustache. Instantly he recognized this man as one who had been in Art Mohler's office several times over the past few months. But for what?

"Hello," the man said. He reached down to the car's control panel and turned off the power.

David took another step back. After ten at night the elevators would not leave the lobby unless you punched in a specific code. Clearly the man knew the code for this floor. But what was he doing here at this hour? "Can I help you?" he asked.

Gordon Roth didn't respond immediately. He glared at David for several moments, then glanced down at the sports bag hanging from David's shoulder. "Maybe. What's in the bag?"

"Jimmy Hoffa's remains." David put his hand down on top of the bag as if to protect it.

"Very funny." The .44 Magnum hung from Roth's

shoulder holster inside his windbreaker. He pressed it against his chest with his arm. "What's in the bag?" His tone turned unfriendly.

"None of your business. Who are you, anyway?" David demanded.

"I work for Mr. Mohler."

"Doing what?"

"That's none of *your* business."

"Okay. Then it sounds like we're even. I'm leaving." David stepped toward the car, but Roth blocked his path.

"Let me see the bag." Roth's voice was ice-cold. He moved toward David as if to grab the strap from his shoulder, but David stepped back again.

"Hey, easy." In the faint light David spied the gun protruding from inside the man's windbreaker. He swallowed. This was no time to be a hero. "If you want to see it, I have no problem with that." Slowly David dropped the bag to the carpet, knelt down, and unzipped it. "Here, take a look."

Roth pulled a flashlight from his pants pocket, flicked it on, bent over, and glanced inside the bag. It contained three tennis rackets, several cans of balls, and tennis clothes and shoes. Beneath the athletic equipment was the box with the copies of the trades and the Bloomberg information David had spent the last four hours compiling.

Blood pounded through David's veins. What the hell was he going to say if the man saw the box, opened it, and found the copies?

"Why did you bring all of this stuff up to the office?" Roth wanted to know.

"One of the other portfolio managers wanted to see that Wilson racket. He was thinking of buying the same model." David's heart skipped a beat as the man reached into the bag and touched the racket.

But the man looked no farther. "What were you doing here tonight?" Roth stood up. "It's after four in the morning."

Relief coursed through David. "I was doing some research on a company I'm thinking about putting Sagamore into. It's a time-sensitive project. There are rumors in the market that the company is about to be taken over, and I want to get in before the price goes up." The man seemed satisfied with the explanation. "Wall Street never rests, and if you want to play on it, you have to live by its rules. Which sometimes means you work at odd hours." David zipped the bag shut again, slung it over his shoulder, and rose, hoping the man wouldn't notice the unnatural sag in the bottom. "But I'm not certain why I have to tell you all this."

"Because I asked," Roth hissed.

"I see. Well, I'm going home to get some sleep. It's been wonderful chatting with you." David moved for the elevator, but still Roth would not allow him to pass.

Finally, Roth moved to the side. David walked deliberately into the car, trying not to seem too eager to leave, pressed the button for the lobby, and watched as the long hair and beard disappeared behind the closing doors. As the car began to descend, his shoulders sagged heavily.

For a long time Roth stood in the reception area not moving. David Mitchell hadn't seemed nervous, but the tests they had administered before offering him employment at Sagamore had indicated that he was extremely strong psychologically. Which was, of course, why they liked him, why they wanted him. Roth turned and slowly began moving toward the double doors. He would report this incident to Mohler in the morning.

Thirty minutes later, David staggered through his apartment door, threw the sports bag on the sofa, and walked to his bedroom. He was about to undress when he noticed the light on the answering machine flashing. He walked wearily to the night table, sat down on the edge of the bed, and pushed the message button.

"David, it's Johnny. I've got the information you wanted on those two accounts. It certainly wasn't difficult to find." Johnny's voice became sharper. "And hey, if this was some kind of joke, I don't appreciate it. The name on both those accounts is yours. David J. Mitchell. There isn't any money in the accounts now—in fact, in both cases there hasn't been much activity. Just one deposit and one withdrawal." Johnny's voice paused for a moment, then laughter crackled from the machine's speaker. "But they were pretty large deposits. The first was for one million, the second for two million. I knew you were getting paid well out there at Sagamore, but I had no idea it was that kind of money. Anyway, give me a call tomorrow. It was good to see you." The voice paused once more. "I hope you're all right. Bye."

The machine clicked off. For several minutes David

sat on the bed, staring into the darkness. He had taken the account numbers from Finnerty and sent the money out to the Caymans, supposedly to his god-father, Senator Webb, the man who had arranged for the A-100 contract to be awarded to GEA under cover of the black budget. Supposedly in exchange for three million dollars—one at contract signing and two when production began. But the money hadn't gone to Webb at all. David had unwittingly sent it to himself. Now it was gone. They had swept the accounts clean so that on the off chance David did discover what they had done, he wouldn't be able to return the money to Doub Steel. The whole thing had been a setup after all.

David fell slowly back onto the mattress. They could nail him on fraud and embezzlement charges—three million dollars' worth. Because undoubtedly that three million was sitting in another account some-where in the world. Another account they had set up with his name on it, but that he wouldn't be able to find. At the appropriate time they could present docu-mentation showing that David had spirited the money away and that it was still sitting in an account waiting for him.

They were guilty too—of many things. But there was no way David could approach the authorities. He couldn't prove anything. They could, or at least the courts would believe them even though it was a frame. He was the only person who would lose by bringing the law into the equation now. It was perfect. Finnerty was right. They were very smart people who played to win.

David put his hands behind his head and gazed up at the ceiling fan rotating slowly above him in the predawn light. And then it blurred before him as he made the connection. He rose quickly from the bed and ran for the door.

# Chapter 26

"This way," Todd whispered as he turned left down the darkened alley.

Jesse followed him closely as he moved cautiously along the eight-foot chain-link fence topped by razor-sharp barbed wire. Ten minutes before, they had left Jesse's rental car on a lonely side street—so as not to attract the attention of private security personnel—and now they were moving covertly through the shadows of the city's warehouse district. "How much farther?" she whispered back.

"It's not far now."

"Good." It was almost one in the morning and she was exhausted after a full day of work and class until ten.

Suddenly Todd grabbed her wrist and pulled her toward a building on the other side of the alley. "Come on!"

"What's wrong?" Then she saw the security vehicle coming toward them, spotlight flashing.

"Just come on!"

Broken glass crackled under their feet as they

sprinted across the pavement to a large doorway recessed several feet into the structure.

"Press yourself against the wall," Todd ordered. "And look away from the alley."

Jesse obeyed instantly, forcing herself against the rough brick as though she were trying to squeeze into one of the cracks in the mortar.

The private security car rolled slowly up the alley, spotlight flickering from side to side. Jesse heard radio static and the purr of the engine as the vehicle moved slowly over the broken glass. She squeezed herself more tightly against the brick. This was insane. They were going to be stopped before even getting to the LFA building. And how were they going to explain themselves? Two people hiding in a warehouse doorway at one in the morning, dressed in black.

She held her breath and closed her eyes as the car moved around the corner of the doorway. This was it. In the next instant she was going to sense the brilliant spotlight bathing the doorway and hear a terse voice coming through a speaker in the security vehicle's grille instructing her to kneel down with her hands behind her back.

But the car didn't stop. It glided past their hiding place, reached the small side street from which she and Todd had turned into the alley only moments before, turned left and roared away into the night.

Todd let out a long breath. "That was close."

"I'll say." Jesse brushed crumbled mortar from her cheek as she relaxed.

"They were a little early tonight."

"What do you mean?" she asked.

"I've been down here checking the place out. They had a pretty set schedule for their rounds. They were ahead of their normal time this evening."

"Earning your fee, huh?" She tried to laugh, but her voice cracked as she spoke. She took several quick breaths to calm her racing heart.

"You bet," Todd replied, scanning the alley for any further trouble. "Come on. Time's wasting." He began jogging down the alley.

She took a deep breath and ran after him.

They followed a twisting course through the maze of side streets and alleys crisscrossing Baltimore's warehouse district. Most of the huge buildings they passed were in reasonable condition—obviously in current use. However, some stood like lonely ghost ships, their windows smashed out and their walls crumbling. During the day, when there was commercial activity, this area was as safe as any in the city. But in the gloom of early morning it seemed eerie and foreboding as they pressed on toward their target.

Finally, Todd slowed to a walk. "There." He pointed at a building across the street as he bent over to catch his breath.

At one time the building had been a warehouse. LFA had converted the wide-open two-story space into offices by erecting partitions. There was a small door in the middle of the wall facing the street, but otherwise the building's front was an uninterrupted wall of bricks.

"I wouldn't have a clue this was LFA." Jesse passed a hand over her forehead to wipe away the perspiration. "There are no signs in front, nothing to tell anyone this is it."

"And for good reason," Todd said. "If you were running a militant outfit I doubt you'd want to advertise your headquarters either."

"It's not a militant outfit," Jesse said forcefully.

"I know." Todd laughed, holding up his hands. "I just like razzing you."

"So how are we going to get in, Einstein?" Jesse asked. LFA's headquarters looked impenetrable.

"Follow me."

They jogged around the side of the building to the unused loading bays at the rear of the structure. It was pitch black here and they had to feel their way along the wall. Finally Todd stopped, pulled a small flashlight from his pocket, and pointed it ahead and up until he located the fire escape. Then they moved forward again until they were directly beneath the ladder. Todd stretched high up in the air to reach the bottom rung. He pulled hard and with a loud screech brought the ladder down. With Jesse close behind, Todd scaled the ladder to the first landing.

"Now comes the hard part," he said over his shoulder.

"Why do you say that?" she asked, pulling herself up onto the landing next to him.

He flicked on the light again and flashed it out over the railing along the brick wall. "We have to go out there." Stretching out below was a huge empty Dumpster. "We need to walk along the rim of the Dumpster to get to that window." He flashed the light up to a small window five feet above the top of the Dumpster. "It's a bathroom window. I came down here this afternoon to volunteer my services to LFA. After I finished filling out the application, I asked to use the bathroom. I opened the lock while I was in there."

"You volunteered for LFA?" Jesse almost laughed aloud.

"They seemed a little surprised too." Todd smiled. "I'm probably the only white guy ever to apply for work here, but as the receptionist said, LFA is an equal opportunity employer. So she gave me an application."

"What about this window here?" Jesse nodded at the window next to the landing.

"I tried it this afternoon. It's nailed shut. I guess the fire inspector hasn't bothered to visit LFA lately."

"Okay, let's go." She stepped carefully over the railing onto the upper rim of the Dumpster, which ran parallel to the building.

"Hey, what are you doing?"

"Going to the window," she said as she balanced herself precariously on the thin edge of the huge trash container.

"I'll go first, Jess."

But she was already several feet out onto the Dumpster, sliding her feet carefully along the inch-wide metal frame toward the window, balancing herself by holding her hands flat against the side of the building two feet away. "Just keep the light on the frame in front of me." It was like walking the train tracks near her house in Glyndon as a little girl, she thought to herself as she kept inching forward. Except that a train rail was at most six inches off the ground. Here the drop would be ten feet.

Finally she reached the window. She placed her palms beneath the wooden frame of the lower panes and pushed. Instantly the window rose up. In one deft motion she grasped the bottom of the window frame, pushed off the Dumpster, and pulled herself into the building. She picked herself up quickly from the floor and leaned back out the window. "Come on," she beckoned. "It's not hard at all."

"Uh huh." Todd stepped gingerly over the fire escape railing onto the Dumpster. He had never liked heights. Not even ten feet.

"Hurry!" Jesse was growing impatient.

"Easy!" He had thought she would be the hesitant one.

Slowly Todd made his way out onto the Dumpster rim until he reached the window. He handed Jesse the flashlight, then grabbed the bottom of the window frame and pulled. But as he pushed off, his foot slipped and for a moment he hung by his fingers, unable to regain his balance on the Dumpster's rim. Jesse grabbed him roughly by the shirt as he slowly pulled himself up. Seconds later they fell in a heap together on the tile floor.

"That was graceful, Mr. Private Investigator," Jesse groaned.

"Yeah, well, I missed Dumpster-climbing class in PI

school, all right?" He was annoyed. "I assume we need to go to the executive offices," he said, rising to one knee.

"I think that's the best place to start."

They moved out of the bathroom and into a narrow hallway paneled with cheap veneer. The carpet was worn and the air was dusty and heavy with the scent of furniture polish. They came to a locked wooden door, but Todd negotiated it easily with a pick set. It popped open and they were in.

"Not a very secure building," Jesse observed.

"It's a goddamn renovated warehouse, Jess. What do you expect, laser beams and heat sensors? They've probably put this whole organization together on a wing and a prayer. They aren't going to spend very much on security because there isn't anything to protect."

She could tell by his sharp tone that he was still embarrassed by his clumsy entry into the building. "We're here, aren't we?"

"Yeah," he grumbled, rubbing a knee. "Unfortunately."

She ignored his complaint and moved to the file cabinets against the wall. They too were locked. "Can that pick set handle file cabinets as well?"

"Sure." Todd moved to the first one and popped it quickly, then moved on to the next.

Jesse pulled a tiny flashlight from her jeans pocket, opened the cabinet's top drawer, and began her search. To avoid leaving fingerprints, she and Todd wore clear latex gloves he had purchased at a local hardware store that afternoon. As she pulled out the first file with her gloved hand, she was reminded of the leather glove she had lost at Neil's river house the night she'd been chased. She had borrowed the gloves from Sara's desk drawer that night after everyone had left the branch. She didn't have any at the office—after all, it was the end of summer—and didn't want to waste time going to the store. But Sara was a pack rat and seemed to keep one of everything at the office no matter the season.

"What now?" Todd had opened all five cabinets.

"Start looking for personnel files. When you find them, let me know."

"Right."

For several minutes Jesse combed the files, culling through invoices, copies of correspondence, and internal memoranda. And then her eyes caught something—a file marked "Funding/Doub Steel."

"Hey, here we go," Todd murmured. "Employee records."

"Good." Jesse held up her hand. "Hold on a second, I'll be right there." Her pulse jumped as she looked at the name on the file again. Doub Steel. It sounded so familiar. Where had she heard the name before?

She opened the thin file and held the flashlight over the pages. Suddenly she brought a hand to her mouth. The page was a copy of both sides of a million-dollar check—a check signed by David J. Mitchell. She would recognize that distinctive M anywhere. She had seen it as he signed the check at Café Royal and at the marina when he had signed for the sailboat. "Oh my God." Doub Steel. Now she remembered. David had mentioned the company as one of his primary investments when they had been out in the sailboat that night on the Corsica River. She leaned against the cabinets for support.

"What's the matter, Jess?"

"I'll tell you later." She closed the file quickly and placed it on a small table next to the cabinet. "Where are the employee records?" Her voice was shaking.

"Right here. Come on, Jess, what's the—"

"Nothing!" She cut him off as she moved to the next set of files.

"What do you want me to do?" he asked.

Jesse pulled a small piece of paper from her shirt pocket. Scrawled on it was the Social Security number she had matched to the list of LFA employees and the list of Elbridge Coleman campaign workers. "Just make certain no one surprises us."

"Okay."

Carefully she read through each file, checking the Social Security number of each. Finally she came to a file without a number, a file on which the number had been whited out. She touched the dried fluid gently, then glanced to the upper left and the employee picture. For a moment she gazed at it. The face was so familiar. Then it hit her, and another icy chill raced up her back. It was the man who had been coming out of her office at the branch last week looking for Sara. This man had short hair and no beard or mustache, but as Todd had pointed out, disguises were easy to manufacture. She glanced at the name. Gordon Smith.

This was what she had come for. And she had stumbled onto the check from Doub Steel. It was time to get out. "Let's go, Todd."

"Sounds good to me."

Jesse put the Smith file under her arm, closed and locked the file cabinets, picked up the Doub file from the table, and headed back toward the hallway. In seconds she was hanging from the bathroom window, feeling for the rim of the Dumpster with her tennis shoes. Her nerves were on fire. As on the night she entered Robinson's river home, something was telling her to get the hell out of here. That danger was close. Finally her feet touched the metal of the trash container.

Through the window Todd handed Jesse the two thin files, and she began to move quickly toward the fire escape. But in her haste to get back to the landing her foot slipped, and a short scream escaped her lips. For a moment she hung in the air, arms reaching for anything to grab. But as she began to fall backward into the metal Dumpster, she felt Todd's strong hand wrap around her wrist like a vise, and she regained her balance. Carefully she made her way back to the fire escape.

In a moment Todd was there too. She placed a hand on his shoulder as he stepped onto the landing. "Thanks," she murmured.

"No problem," he whispered. "Maybe we should have just tried to find a door on the first floor."

"No," she whispered back. "There would be alarms on the doors."

"So what? We would have been gone before anyone could have gotten here."

"I don't want anyone to know there was a break-in."

Jesse handed the two files to Todd as she began to climb down the ladder. "Drop them to me when I get to the ground."

"Right."

She descended the ladder agilely, jumping the last several feet to the pavement.

"Hold it right there!" a voice barked as a brilliant light suddenly illuminated the entire area beneath the fire escape.

Instinctively she put her hands before her face. She had been caught. Fear surged through her as she pictured the headlines: REVENUE AGENT NABBED IN LFA BURGLARY. That could not happen.

She turned to run, but the private security officers anticipated her move and were on her instantly, wrestling her to the ground, pulling her hands behind her back.

"Look what we got here." One of the men pointed the brilliant light directly into her eyes as he rested with his knee in the small of her back.

"Not your typical warehouse district thief," the other laughed, pulling handcuffs from his belt. "You're awfully pretty, ma'am, but we treat everybody the same down here. Cuff 'em and turn 'em in."

Jesse closed her eyes and turned her face from the light. This was the nightmare scenario. The one she had so worried about.

"Yup, we—" But as the second man began to cuff Jesse, two gunshots tore through the still of the night, stifling his words.

The two men tumbled away, scrambling for cover

behind the Dumpster. Almost immediately two more gunshots exploded into the darkness, followed instantly by the sound of shattering glass as the slugs hit the security vehicle's windshield.

Jesse jumped to her feet and began to sprint. She knew exactly what had happened. The security officers hadn't seen Todd, and now he was creating a diversion—and she was going to take advantage of it.

Two more shots rang out. She heard the men yelling at each other, and then she was around the corner of the building and their screams faded. But she kept running.

Finally, as she neared the rental car, Jesse slowed to a trot, then stopped and bent over, gasping for air. She knew it was not a good idea to stay with a vehicle that looked so out of place in this area of town at this time of night. The car was an obvious inspection target for the police, who would be crawling all over this neighborhood in a matter of minutes—police carrying a detailed description of her. She began to move unsteadily back into the shadows, uncertain what to do. She couldn't leave Todd here, but she couldn't stay either. Then she heard the sirens.

"Come on!"

Jesse felt a sudden tap on her shoulder, screamed, and whipped about. Todd had already raced past her and reached the car.

"Come on!" he yelled again. "Let's get the hell out of here! We don't have much time!" He was pounding on the car's roof.

She darted to the car, shoved the key in the door,

unlocked it, and jumped in. "Do you have the files?" she yelled as he fell into the passenger seat beside her.

"Right here." He held them out.

"Beautiful." She grabbed the folders and thrust them beneath the driver's seat, then guided the key into the ignition and turned it. The engine revved loudly as she pressed the accelerator to the floor. "Hold on."

A half hour later, Jesse whipped the car into a spot in her apartment complex, turned off the engine and the lights, reclined against the headrest and closed her eyes. She had been so certain that one of the several police cruisers they had passed on the way home was going to turn around suddenly and give chase. But none had. Now she was glad they had brought her plain rental car instead of Todd's flashy Corvette.

"You're a helluva driver." Todd laughed.

"My brothers taught me." Todd had really come through for her tonight, she suddenly realized. "I can't tell you how much I appreciate your help."

"No sweat."

Jesse reached up and pulled out the large pin keeping her hair up in a bun. It fell to her shoulders as she shook her head from side to side.

Todd nodded approvingly. "Much better."

"Thanks." Suddenly she remembered the gunshots breaking the quiet of the night as she had lain prone on the asphalt about to be handcuffed. "I didn't know you carry a gun, Todd."

"All the time." He reached beneath his shirt and withdrew a snub-nosed .38 caliber revolver. "Say hello to Mary. She's all out of bullets right now, but she did a nice job tonight."

Jesse eyed the gun. "Yes, she did."

Todd replaced the revolver in the shoulder holster, then pulled a paper from his pants pocket. "I almost forgot about this."

"What is it?"

"Remember we talked about a broker friend of mine who checked out the Coleman Technology initial public offering for me? About how three of the companies that invested in the deal all had the same parent company?"

"Yes."

"The guy did a little more research."

"And?"

"Every company that invested in the Coleman Technology IPO is ultimately controlled by Sagamore Investment Management. Can you believe it? Looks like you were exactly right. The Coleman offering was manipulated by a small group of senior brokers at some very out-of-the-way investment banks, on orders from Sagamore." He rubbed his stomach for a moment. It was still sore from Harry's fist. "But I can't tell you why they did it."

Jesse could. Elbridge Coleman had funded his campaign—and the massive advertising blitz accompanying it—with money from the public offering. With money from Sagamore, it seemed safe to assume now.

"Didn't you go out to Sagamore the other day, Jess?"

And there was that huge check from Doub Steel to

LFA. Signed by David. Her eyesight blurred. And there was a man who had been paid by both Coleman and the LFA. Gordon Smith, if that was his real name. This was getting crazy.

"Jess?"

She glanced at him. For a moment she thought about confiding in him, telling him what she suspected. But then he'd probably go after David immediately. And she didn't want that. Not yet, anyway. "I've got to go, Todd. I'll walk you to your car." She turned and pulled the door handle.

"But . . ."

"Come on," she insisted, shutting the door.

"All right." Todd jumped from the car.

"Where's your Corvette?"

"Over there."

She spotted the white Corvette parked directly beneath one of the large overhead lights and began walking toward it.

"Hey, wait." But he did not catch up to her until they had reached the Corvette. "What's your rush?"

"I've got to get some sleep. I'm exhausted." In the light she suddenly noticed the damage to the front and back of the Corvette. "What happened?"

"Vandals got to it the other night while I was food shopping," he lied. "I guess some people just get jealous when they see a nice car."

"I'm sorry."

"It's all right. It'll be as good as new soon."

An odd expression crossed her face. "When did *you*

start food shopping? I thought you ate out every night."

"Did I say food shopping? I was picking up beer."

"Uh huh. Can you drive it like this?"

He nodded. "I replaced the bulbs. It's fine. I'll get the body repaired at some point."

"You and I aren't having much luck with cars lately." She smiled.

"That's the truth." Suddenly the impulse struck him. "Jess, why don't you spend the night with me out at the farmhouse?"

"What?" She glanced at him quickly.

"Come with me to the house. It's nice out there."

She shook her head.

"You'll feel safer out there tonight. With me. Besides, I need to tell you some things."

"Todd, please." This was something she couldn't handle right now.

He moved closer and touched her cheek with his fingers. "I'm not kidding." He hesitated, looked down at the pavement and then back up at her. "I really care about you."

She touched his hand with hers. "I care about you too, it's just that . . ."

"Come to the house with me then. I don't mean we're going to sleep together, just talk, like we used to." He took her cheeks gently in his large hands. "Take tomorrow off. God, think about what we've been through tonight. You deserve a day off."

"I'd love to, I really would. It's just that I've got things to do."

"Is it that guy, David Mitchell?" Todd was suddenly angry. "Are you going to see him now?"

"Of course not." Jesse felt Todd's grip tighten as she tried to pull away. "Todd!"

"Kiss me, Jess." He slid his hands down her back and pulled her body to his roughly.

"Todd, what are you doing?" She tried to push him away, but it was useless. He was much too strong.

"Kiss me." He brought one hand to the back of her head, leaned forward, and pressed his lips to hers.

"Please stop! Please!" Finally she broke free from his grasp and stepped back, wiping her lips with the back of her hand.

Todd stared at her intently for a moment, then slowly lowered his eyes to the pavement and shook his head. "Jess, I'm sorry. I don't know what got into me," he said softly. "You know I'm not like that."

"I know." She went to touch his arm, then held back. The strength he had used to hold her head had shocked her. She had not broken free from him, she now realized, he had chosen to let her go. "I know," she said again. "Hey, I appreciate what you did for me tonight."

He nodded dejectedly. "Yeah, sure."

"It's okay. Don't worry about it."

He nodded again, then pulled the keys from his pocket, unlocked the door and slipped behind the wheel. "I've got to go."

"Todd, don't leave like this."

But he wasn't listening. He threw the Corvette into reverse, pulled out of the space and raced away.

As Jesse watched the sleek white car speed through the parking lot, she touched her cheeks. God, that had been strange. He had never acted that way before. So why now? Perhaps Becky would have an explanation.

Jesse checked her watch in the glow from the parking lot light. Almost three o'clock. She turned and hurried back toward her rental car. There was something else she had to do before she could get some sleep.

As always, the stuffed animals lay neatly arranged on the top bunk, smiling at her from the pillows. Jesse gazed at them sadly from the doorway. Her mother kept the room exactly as it had been the day she left the house for good. She glanced down at the lower bunk, then at the single bed on the other side of the small room. She and her two sisters had grown up here. One day they had been adolescents arguing about boys, the next they had all gone off to lead their own lives. At least it seemed that way.

"Jesse?"

"Yes, Mom."

"Oh my God, you scared me to death. I'm so glad it's you."

Jesse turned away from the room toward the voice. Connie stood in the dark hallway clad in a long cotton robe. "Hi, Mom. I'm sorry. I didn't mean to frighten you."

"It's all right, but it's almost four in the morning, sweetheart. I love when you visit me, but why now?"

Jesse moved the bag behind her back, then dropped it gently to the floor, hoping her mother wouldn't notice. The bag contained Neil Robinson's file from the river house, Gordon Smith's personnel file and the Doub Steel file from LFA, the broker data from Todd linking Sagamore's money to Elbridge Coleman's campaign, and the W-2 information matching Gordon Smith's Social Security numbers at LFA and the Coleman campaign. It contained everything she had accumulated so far since receiving Neil Robinson's E-mail from the grave. "I needed to pick something up," she offered lamely.

"And drop something off, I see." Connie nodded down at the floor.

"Uh huh." Jesse offered nothing more. "Mom, go back to bed."

"Can't we talk for a while? You know how much I love it when you come by." Connie hesitated. "You're the only one that really does."

"I'll come out this weekend, I promise." Jesse took her mother's hand and led her back to her bedroom. She helped Connie into the bed, then pulled the covers up to her chin. "I love you, Mom." She sat down on the edge of the bed and stroked her mother's hair for a moment. "I have something for you," Jesse whispered.

"What?" Connie asked softly, already drifting back to sleep.

Jesse reached in her pocket and pulled out fifty dollars. "Just something I'm leaving in the night table." She opened the drawer and dropped the crumpled bills inside. "I'll call to remind you it's there."

But Connie didn't hear. Her breathing had become regular and she had fallen into a deep sleep.

Jesse smiled, kissed her mother's forehead, then moved quietly back to her old bedroom. She picked up the bag containing the information, opened the closet door, and placed the bag on the top shelf between stacks of jigsaw puzzles and board games. The information would be safe here.

# Chapter 27

Jesse pushed open her apartment door and trudged wearily into the living room. Her eyelids felt so heavy, as if someone were slowly sewing them shut. She had pinched the top of her thigh all the way home from her mother's, until it was black and blue, to stay awake and had still almost run off the road several times. It was now after six and she had to be awake again by six-thirty at the latest to be at work by eight. She sighed. Maybe Todd was right. Maybe she should just take the day off.

She had almost reached the bedroom when she touched her palm to her head and turned back toward the kitchen. The cat hadn't been fed since yesterday morning and had to be starving by now.

The shadow outlined by morning light streaming through the living-room window curtains seemed surreal at first. The shape registered in Jesse's brain, but for a split second she did not allow herself to accept its existence. Only when it moved did her heart rise to her throat and her hands to her neck. She attempted to scream, but no sound escaped her lips but a strange choking noise, as if the form's fingers were already wrapped tightly about her neck.

Instinctively she turned away from the shadow and bolted toward the bedroom. Suddenly the room was brightly illuminated as the form flipped the light switch.

"Jesse!"

She recognized the voice instantly, caught herself on the corner of the wall with her hand and spun around. "David! What are you doing here? How did you get in?"

David held up a set of keys, then tossed them onto the sofa. "I found them in one of your kitchen drawers the other night when you were back in the bedroom."

God, had he seen the file after all? Was that why he was here? Had he come back for it? Had she interrupted a burglary? The questions spun through her mind. And all the time she kept thinking about his signature on the Doub check she had found in the LFA file cabinet. "What were you doing going through my kitchen?"

"You told me to get a beer. I did. The cap got stuck and wouldn't twist off, so I was looking for a bottle opener. Was that something I shouldn't have done?"

"No." She *had* told him to get a beer that night. "But you had no right to take the keys."

"Why the hostility, Jesse?" He took a step toward her.

She moved back, maintaining the distance between them. She could not be certain of his intentions now. Sagamore was somehow entangled in the Elbridge Coleman campaign and LFA. The people there could no longer be trusted, and David Mitchell was one of those people. "I don't appreciate people taking my keys without my permission. Can you understand that?"

"You should be more careful," he said ominously.

"What do you mean?"

"Just what I said."

David was exhausted. She could see it in his eyes. He too had been up all night. "Why are you here?"

He hesitated for a moment. "To help you," he murmured quietly, his voice suddenly subdued.

"What do you mean?"

It was foolish to play games at this point. "Look, I'm going to be honest with you."

"That would be nice."

He ignored her cynical tone. "I saw the file in your kitchen the other night."

"What file?"

"Don't play games."

For the first time Jesse heard a chilling, almost menacing tone in David's voice. "You mean the file concerning Elbridge Coleman's campaign."

"Of course I do," he shot back.

Jesse quickly analyzed the possibility of fleeing. There was no way to make it to the front door. David would block her escape easily. "So you saw the file. So what? My boss had an active imagination."

"I told you, Jesse, I'm here to help." He had seen her gauging the odds of escape. "If you want to leave, go ahead. I'm not going to stop you." He stepped to the side of the room. "I care about you very much. I'm here to help. You have to believe that. You have to trust me."

She wanted to believe his words. She wanted to trust him. But there was something strange in his eyes now, a desperation she hadn't seen before, a desperation that might mean he was actually telling the truth—or that he might be willing to do almost anything to extricate himself from a nasty situation.

"Just give me a minute to explain. If you don't believe what you hear, then leave. I promise I won't stop you."

"All right."

"Good. Jesse, the truth is that Sagamore Investment Management Group isn't what it appears to be. We aren't better than anyone else at investing. We're playing an insider's game. That's how we've been able to generate such incredible returns for so long. We play with a stacked deck."

Her eyes widened.

"I've had suspicions for a long time, but I wasn't able to prove them," David continued. "Tonight I did, at least to myself. What I have wouldn't be enough to convict anyone in a court of law, but a ten-year-old would see the patterns in the stock trading and know what the senior people at Sagamore are doing."

He was offering up his information without requiring anything in return from her. That was a good sign. "What do you mean?" she asked.

"Sagamore plays on the inside with defense stocks. We buy stocks in other industries too, but we focus on defense. There are lots of companies that deal with the Department of Defense in some way, so there is a wide array of stocks we can buy. The DOD budget is almost three hundred billion a year. That's a lot of money for anyone to spend, so it involves many different firms. We buy the stocks ahead of good news, like the awarding of a huge DOD contract, and sell ahead of bad news."

"You shouldn't tell me this. I'm an agent of the federal government," Jesse said quietly. "I have a responsibility to alert my superiors."

"You aren't going to tell anyone and you know it."

"What are you talking about?"

"I don't have any real proof. If you told your superiors what I'm telling you, they'd start an investigation, which Sagamore would quickly hear about. It would take weeks or even months to get the investigation going. By that time people at Sagamore would have had time to erase any proof that they were trading on the inside."

He was right. "But how could Sagamore trade that way on a consistent basis? For so long? The firm has posted incredible results for years."

"Because Sagamore has a contact in the Senate. A very powerful contact. A man who not only alerts our executive committee of impending news regarding defense companies ahead of time but can actually award massive amounts of the DOD budget to specific companies secretly, on his own authority. A man who controls the black budget. I'm sure he's paid very well by Sagamore for what he does. Probably through numbered offshore accounts." David shook his head, remembering the shadowy meeting with Senator Webb two and a half years ago. A meeting in which he had naively believed he had bribed the senator, but in which, in fact, they had effectively sucked David into the conspiracy. It all made so much sense now. "Imagine what that means."

It didn't take much to imagine. "Give me an example," she said evenly. "An example of how Sagamore trades on the inside."

"A plane called the A-100," he answered. "It's a new fighter-bomber being developed by General Engineering & Aerospace for the Navy. The plane has been secretly under development for the last two and a half years. Its existence will be announced very soon. The contract will total a hundred and fifty billion dollars over seven years. It will make GEA's stock price at least five times what it is now. Two and a half years ago, just before the A-100 contract was awarded to GEA, Sagamore purchased a billion dollars' worth of GEA stock. You can check the SEC filings. The investment is a matter of public record. The timing of the contract and the investment is no coincidence, Jesse. I promise you."

"Which senator controls the black budget and works with Sagamore?" She was riveted.

"It doesn't matter."

"It *does* matter." She suddenly realized why Sagamore would want to manipulate the contest between Elbridge Coleman and Malcolm Walker. Coleman was going to be the next in line—the next man to control the black budget so Sagamore could keep trading on the inside well into the twenty-first century. "Who is it?"

"I'm not going to tell you, Jesse. Frankly, I think it's better that you not know."

"Do *you* know who it is?"

He nodded hesitantly.

"But how could Sagamore keep it secret? If this has been going on for years, as you say, why hasn't anyone ever come forward?"

Simple, he thought to himself. The almighty dollar. "Jesse, the average annual compensation for portfolio managers who have been with the firm more than five years is over two million dollars. Why would anyone come forward? And it isn't like Sagamore is such a huge place. There aren't that many people who have to keep the secret. People are screened carefully before they're given a job offer."

"Money wouldn't keep everyone quiet. The guilt would get to someone."

"Don't bet on it." David knew better. "Besides, there's something else."

"What?"

"As portfolio manager, by the time you realize what's going on, you've broken about twenty laws pertaining to the securities business. From insider trading to embezzlement, fraud, and bribery. You name it, you've done it. And the most insidious part is that you don't even realize what you've done until it's too late."

That sounded like a guilty man rationalizing. "But someone would cut a deal with the authorities. Immunity for information."

"Why, Jesse? Why would someone voluntarily go to the SEC to cut a deal? You tell me what's easier—playing the game at Sagamore and earning at least two million a year, or feeding the federal government information, feeling good about yourself for a little while, then living the rest of your life in the poorhouse because you've been blackballed by the industry. And you would be, too. No one would hire you. And once the government is finished with you, do you think it's going to take care of you? Not to the tune of two million a year, anyway."

"So, have you?" she asked evenly.

"Have I what?"

"Have you broken twenty laws pertaining to the securities business?"

David ignored her. "We can talk more later, but we need to get you out of here, Jesse. *Right now*."

She was frightened by the intensity of his voice and the fear she saw in his eyes. "What do you mean?"

"I think you're in danger."

"Why?"

"Because of that file in your kitchen. I went through it quickly the other night. I believe everything in it is true, Jesse. Whoever wrote it was either being fed information by an inside source or was a genius. I'm certain the senior people at Sagamore are attempting to manipulate the election. It only makes good sense. Their Senate contact, the one who controls the black budget, is getting old. If they don't do anything to address that problem, once he's gone they'll be left without their lifeline, without their ability to outperform the market every year. So they need a younger man, someone who can ultimately replace their contact. But they want the young man to be in the Senate concurrently with their contact so an orderly transition can be orchestrated." David paused. "And I'm sure they want Malcolm Walker gone too. In the worst way possible. So they get two for the price of one in this election."

It was just as she had surmised. "My God," she whispered.

"Yes. It's incredible. What's most frightening of all is that the man in the Senate controlling the black budget has to be working with someone in the Pentagon. The senator can appropriate, but he needs help with contracts. He needs someone senior in the Pentagon as well."

Jesse's mouth ran dry. What had seemed unimaginable only a few days ago—just Neil's active imagination—was suddenly becoming a conspiracy of immense proportions.

"But the most important thing right now is to get you out of here," David urged again, taking a step toward her.

She saw the move but didn't step back this time. "The only person at Sagamore who knows about that file is you. Why would I be in danger?"

"Do you think it's just coincidence that you became such good friends with Elizabeth Gilman so fast?" He had to persuade Jesse to trust him completely.

"Obviously you don't."

David shook his head. "No, I don't." He saw the disappointment in her expression. "I don't want you to take that the wrong way. You're a bright woman and you could certainly hold your own as a portfolio manager at Sagamore. But I've been around Elizabeth more than four years. If nothing else, she's a businesswoman. She has a wonderful way with people, but the bottom line is she doesn't allow emotion to cloud her judgment when it comes to Sagamore. She knows there will be a great many applicants from which to choose, applicants with much more experience in the business than you have. It just doesn't make sense for her to latch on to you the way she has. It's a hunch, I'll admit. But I'm sure I'm right."

"Do you know for a fact that she's involved in all of this?"

"For Christ's sake, Jesse, she's Sagamore's managing partner." David was suddenly irritated. "The pattern of insider trading I traced goes back years. She knows. Don't kid yourself."

"Is there anything you aren't telling me?"

"What do you mean?"

"You've told me you have a hunch they know about the file, but you haven't told me for certain they know. Do they know?"

A wry smile came to his face. "Are you asking me if I told them?"

"Did you?"

"Jesse, down deep I'm an honest person. I've made some mistakes, but it's time that I own up to those mistakes and atone for them. I'm not going to be part of the game anymore. I'm not going to let them get away with this." He paused and looked into her eyes. "And I care about you. I wouldn't do that to you."

It was a wonderful speech, but she wasn't going to give him the benefit of the doubt so fast. "You just told me the average portfolio manager who has been at Sagamore five years earns two million dollars annually. You said it was easier to play the game and earn the money. I imagine telling them about that file would get you the two million pretty quickly."

"If I had told them about the file, why would I be here telling you all this?" He shook his head. "Besides they wouldn't have sent me back, they would have sent a professional. You'd be dead by now. If you erect the infrastructure they have and take the risks they have, you play for keeps. Killing an IRS agent to maintain secrecy of the conspiracy isn't something you even think twice about. You just do it."

Slowly Jesse brought her hands to her face. Sara. The lost glove at the river house. Had they been trying to trace her and found Sara instead? "No," she said aloud. She was letting her imagination run away with her. Sara had simply gone AWOL for twenty-four hours and would show up today.

"No, what?" David asked curiously.

"Nothing." But somehow she knew something awful had happened to Sara. "What about a check from Doub Steel to LFA, signed by you?" She had to ask the question.

"Check?" David asked hoarsely, clearly taken off guard.

"Yes," she said evenly. "I have a copy of a check made out to the organization known as Liberation for African-Americans. It's a Doub Steel check and it's signed by David J. Mitchell. You told me that afternoon we were sailing that Doub Steel was one of your portfolio companies."

"I know what I told you," he answered, suddenly upset. "How did you get a copy of that check?"

"You don't want to tell me which senator runs the

black budget. I'm not going to tell you how I got the check. But I have it, the file you saw, and a good deal of other pertinent and damning information stored in a safe place."

"Jesse, that isn't my signature on the Doub check. It's a forgery. You've got to believe me."

"I saw your signature that night at the restaurant and at the marina when you paid for the sailboat. I'm no expert, but you have a distinct signature. The one on the Doub check looks a lot like yours."

"I'll admit that. I was as shocked as I'm sure you were when you first saw it." His pulse was racing. How in the hell could she possibly have stumbled onto the check? Sagamore would only use it against him if he tried to expose what was going on. That was clear. But there was no telling what Jesse would do with it. "They set me up."

"I'm really supposed to believe that?" She saw the desperation in his eyes again. Its intensity was screaming truth. And if he was here to do her bodily harm, wouldn't he have done it already? Why would he bother talking this long?

"You have to believe me," he said through gritted teeth. "Look, I want to take these people down—"

"So do I," she cut in angrily. "I think they killed Neil Robinson. A man I cared very much about. Not to mention the fact that they're trying to manipulate an election and they've broken more laws than you and I could imagine."

"I want to help you, Jesse. Please believe that."

"Everything I've heard you say is based on assump-

tions. If you want to help me, tell me what you know."
She turned away from him.

He couldn't tell her about his meeting with Webb
so long ago. Couldn't explain how he knew so much
about the A-100 and the GEA contract, couldn't
explain his relationship with Jack Finnerty, couldn't
explain that they had framed him with the offshore
accounts. And couldn't tell her what he believed were
the true motivations behind Elizabeth Gilman's odd
behavior. He needed Jesse to trust him, but telling her
everything would make him too vulnerable.

"Give me just a little more time. There's more information I can get," he said. He saw her anger. "You
have to trust me," he said earnestly.

This was where it got tricky. "Trust you? You could
be setting me up." Suddenly she felt his hands gently
massaging her shoulders. "My God, you steal my keys
and let yourself into my apartment. You admit to
going through a personal file of mine. You won't tell
me how you know about Sagamore's contact in the
Senate, or who it is. You admit to SEC violations."

"I never admitted to SEC violations," he corrected her.

"You didn't have to. I can draw that conclusion for
myself." She felt his arms coming around her waist.
"David, stop." But suddenly she didn't want him to
stop. Suddenly she realized how truly scared she was,
and his strong arms felt wonderful and comforting
around her. "Stop," she said. But there was no conviction this time.

"No, I won't." Slowly David turned her so she was
facing him. He gazed deeply into her eyes. "I'm going
to take care of you. But I need your help too. We're

going to beat these bastards. But we have to depend on each other."

It was so dangerous to trust him—to trust anyone, for that matter. But he could be so convincing. And wasn't he right? If he had told them about the file, they wouldn't have sent *him* back.

"All right," she said softly.

Through the early-morning light Jesse followed David's BMW in her rental car. As she focused on his taillights, she felt her attraction to him growing stronger. It was crazy, but she couldn't help herself.

"We're going to beat these bastards." He had said the words with such intensity. But that tiny seed of doubt was still there as well, as much as she tried to convince herself it shouldn't be. Two million dollars was a lot to throw away. He could be setting her up so easily. There was a manipulative side to David Mitchell. She couldn't deny that. But how strong was that side? That was the question. When she had looked into his eyes in the apartment, she had seen sincerity. Or perhaps he was simply an actor giving the performance of a lifetime. But why would he be protecting her now? Why would he have told her to get out of the apartment?

They pulled up in front of the Towson Sheraton Hotel. David jumped from the BMW, jogged back to her car, and opened the door, holding her hand as she stepped out.

"That's very gallant of you," she said.

"Thank you." He kissed her on the cheek. "I really am going to take care of you." She was trusting him now. Against the odds, he had persuaded her to do so. But then he had always been able to do that when he really needed to. It was a God-given talent. Something about his eyes, a woman of his past had murmured. "Let's go inside, Jesse. I'm going to get you a room, then I have to go. But I'll be in touch." He took her by the arm. "I think it would be a good idea if you didn't go to work today."

Jesse nodded. She would follow his orders to the letter now.

"And don't call anyone from the room. They might have caller ID. If you have to use the phone, go to the mall next door. But don't stay away from your room too long. That might be dangerous."

She nodded again.

David reached into the backseat of her car for the bag she had packed hastily at the apartment, started toward the door, then stopped. "Jesse, I need to know where that Elbridge Coleman file is. And the other things you said you had as well."

She had agreed to help him. She trusted him now, didn't she?

He took her hand in his. "What if, God forbid, they find you? I'd be the only one left who could stop them. It sounds like that file would help a great deal." He hesitated. "Will you tell me?"

Todd Colton watched as Jesse said something into David's ear, then kissed him deeply. He had watched them leave her apartment fifteen minutes ago. He had watched Jesse disappear into her mother's house sometime before dawn this morning, only to reappear minutes later. He had never really left her after tearing out of the parking lot in his Corvette. Instead, he had followed her everywhere she had gone. And now, as he watched them enter the Sheraton arm in arm, his anger rose to a level he had never experienced. Jesse had lied to him about her feelings for David Mitchell. She cared about Mitchell deeply.

That was the real reason she had spurned his advances, had pulled away from his attempt to kiss her in the parking lot. Her feelings for Mitchell. How could she do this to him when he had always been there for her?

"You wanted to see me?" Monique stepped into Malcolm Walker's office warily.

Walker sat in his office chair, head back, hands covering his face. "Come in." His voice was hushed.

She coughed nervously, then moved across the thick carpet to the chair in front of his desk and sat down. He must know by now that the communiqué between Cowen and Webb was gone. Her lip curled involuntarily at the thought of Webb. The bastard had kept her at the Four Seasons until four this morning, taking her over and over.

"What's the matter?" Walker asked.

"What do you mean?"

"You look like you just bit into a lemon. And you look exhausted too."

She felt as if his eyes were searching her for clues. "I'll be fine," she answered. "I think I ate something for breakfast that isn't agreeing with me."

"Maybe you should go home."

"I'll be fine, Malcolm." She hated herself. She

had been with Malcolm for ten years, and now she had given Webb the note from Cowen to keep the pictures with the blond woman off tabloid front pages. She had ruined Malcolm's chance to nail the black budgeteers and probably his chances for reelection as well just to save herself. "Why did you want to see me?"

"Have you turned on your television this morning?"

Monique shook her head.

"The tape of yesterday's abortion of a press conference is playing everywhere. It's the lead story on all the local newscasts and many of the network broadcasts as well. Was it really that important? Do they really have to show it that much?"

"It's the conservative machine flexing its muscles." Sometimes there was no way to fight the system. It was frustrating as hell, but you just had to learn to accept it.

"You think the local stations are being paid to play it, don't you?"

"It wouldn't surprise me at all if there was something going on." Her voice was a monotone murmur. She wanted to tell him what she had done. She owed it to him. But there was no way to pull the trigger. And what would it accomplish, anyway? She had already handed over the Cowen note. Malcolm would know that she was a turncoat, and her body would be splashed all over every sleazy magazine, wrapped around an equally sleazy blond. "They'll do anything to destroy you, Malcolm. You surprised them last time and won before they could do anything. They're out to get you this time."

Walker gazed at Monique strangely. She had never been so forthright. "Morty Andrews over at CNN called me first thing this morning. They conducted a poll last night, after the tape had started playing on all the newscasts."

"And?"

"Coleman's lead is twelve points now. I've solidified my position within the black community, but the white vote is abandoning me." It was over, he knew. There would be no coming back from this.

"As if you needed to solidify your position with the African-American population. Great. Because you showed unity with LFA yesterday your approval rating in the black community went from ninety-five to ninety-six percent. Big deal."

"That's what I don't get." Walker put his head in his hands. "Elijah Pitts must have known this would happen. Why would he want me to lose?"

David pulled the extra set of keys he had made out of his pocket as he climbed the steps to Jesse's apartment. What she didn't know wouldn't hurt her. He glanced around to make certain no one was watching, then guided the key into the lock, turned the knob, and pushed.

For a moment he could not comprehend the full extent of the damage, and then it hit him. It was as if a tornado had ripped directly through the middle of the living room. Chairs and sofas were overturned and shredded, their insides spilled all over the carpet. Pictures had been torn from the walls and lay shattered on the floor. In places the carpet had been slashed and pulled from the plywood. And in the corner, Jesse's cat lay dead, gutted and disemboweled.

David stepped back against the outside railing, suddenly shaking. There was no reason to search inside. They had certainly found anything of interest. Without shutting the door, he headed back down the stairs and ran to his BMW.

Gordon Roth bent over, rolled up his pant leg, and replaced the hunting knife in the leather sheath affixed to his calf. He pulled the living-room curtain back slightly and checked the parking lot one more time but saw no one. Too late, as he hid behind the bedroom door poised to kill whoever had entered the apartment, he had realized that the person had run at the sight of the mess without closing the door.

# Chapter 28

"I call the meeting to order," Webb growled, glancing down the table at the other members. "It's so nice to see you, Ms. Gilman," he said sarcastically.

"I'm sorry for not being here last time," she said apologetically. "I had Sagamore business."

"Don't make it a—"

"I think congratulations are in order," Finnerty spoke up.

The others looked up, surprised by the interruption.

"I trust you all either saw or heard about our friend Mr. Walker's press conference yesterday," Finnerty continued. "I believe we owe a rather large debt of gratitude to Senator Webb for his incredible foresight in setting up LFA. We fortuitously destroyed a career yesterday, and we have the senator to thank."

The other members snapped their fingers in agreement.

"Thank you." Webb acknowledged the praise quickly. "But we have serious business to attend to, and we need to get started." He nodded subtly to Finnerty as a gesture of thanks. "I must report to you that we have received several pieces of bad news in the past twenty-four hours."

The room fell still as the mood turned suddenly apprehensive.

"I told you at the last meeting we were going to take care of our security leak." Webb's voice was dead calm. "Gordon Roth disposed of a young woman named Sara Adams. She was a revenue agent in the Baltimore IRS office. Gordon believed, based on strong evidence, that Ms. Adams was the individual who had stolen the file from Neil Robinson's house on the Severn River. Ms. Adams, as it turns out, was not the individual responsible for that act." It didn't bother him that the wrong person was dead. The tragedy lay in the fact that the real target, the one who could potentially damage them, was still running around out there.

"Oh, God!" Cowen brought his hands to his face.

"These things happen, Admiral Cowen." Webb was clearly annoyed at Cowen's show of emotion. "We just have to accept that and move on. It's all part of war, as you ought to know."

Cowen's mouth set into a grim straight line.

"It seems the person we were looking for," Webb continued, "is really a woman named Jesse Hayes."

Art Mohler turned instantly toward Elizabeth, but she ignored his glare.

Webb noted Mohler's look but said nothing. "Ms. Hayes is also a revenue agent in the Baltimore branch of the IRS. In fact, she and Ms. Adams were friends, which may account for Gordon Roth's regrettable error."

"Are you sure this time?" Cowen blurted out. "Are you absolutely certain this Hayes woman is the right person? Christ, are we going to kill this one too? When does it all stop?"

"I'm positive this time," Webb snarled. "Listen, Admiral, I don't need you questioning my orders. You certainly don't mind the benefits of being included in this circle. Just as with any other endeavor, if you are willing to enjoy the spoils, you have to bear the losses as well."

"Maybe we should take things slower, Senator Webb," Cowen said forcefully. "Maybe we shouldn't be so quick to pull the trigger. That's one thing you learn in the military. To take your time."

"Maybe you'd like to tell us how you were taking your time near Fort Myer last Saturday night at three in the morning."

Cowen's face turned instantly to stone. He picked a spot on the far wall and concentrated on it. How could Webb possibly know about the young man he had met in the woods near the Iwo Jima Memorial?

"I didn't think so," Webb snarled.

The others shifted uncomfortably in their seats. They had never seen an exchange like that in this room. And they had never seen Webb so visibly agitated.

"How did you find out the perpetrator was Jesse Hayes?" Finnerty asked. "How do you know she's the one and not Sara Adams?"

"Last night there was a break-in at LFA. Two files were stolen." Webb slammed his palm on the table in disgust. "One contained a copy of a check to LFA written out of a Doub Steel account. One of the checks Art had cut using Mitchell's signature."

"What?" Art Mohler leaned over the table. "You've got to be kidding me. That could lead somebody right back to Sagamore. Right back to me."

"Precisely." Webb was angry now. "Why the hell Pitts had his people make copies of that stuff and keep it in such a vulnerable place I'll never know. The other piece of information taken was a personnel file concerning one Gordon Smith."

"Gordon Smith?" Mohler was perplexed. "Is that another name for Gordon Roth?"

"Very good, genius." Webb held up his hands and closed his eyes. "I'm sorry, Art. I don't mean to snap at you. Incompetence just irritates the hell out of me. I thought Pitts was at least a *little* savvy. I didn't think he'd leave sensitive information just lying around like that."

"I don't understand," Cowen interjected.

"We were using LFA to fund some of Roth's activities," Finnerty cut in. He had helped Webb arrange the details with LFA. "It seemed better to do it from there than from Sagamore or GEA."

"Why not out of Doub?" Admiral Cowen asked.

"We were already using that company to fund LFA and frame David Mitchell," Finnerty explained. "We didn't want to do too many things with it."

"So what does Jesse Hayes have to do with the break-in at LFA?" Mohler wanted to know.

"Jesse Hayes was the one who got into LFA last night and took the files," Webb answered. "We had an eyewitness. A security guard who matched her face to a picture. Jesse Hayes had to be the one who was at the Severn River house. The coincidence is too great."

"Why couldn't she and the Adams woman have been working together?" Mohler asked.

Webb glanced at Finnerty quickly.

Finnerty took his time explaining this one. "Gordon Roth is an expert at, shall we say, drawing information out of people."

"You mean he's an expert at torturing people," Elizabeth said disgustedly.

"Enough, Elizabeth," Webb reprimanded.

"Sara Adams wasn't involved," Finnerty confirmed. "She didn't know anything. If she had, she would have told Roth. Believe me."

Elizabeth turned away.

"We have to find Jesse Hayes," Mohler said. "Immediately."

"Exactly." Webb glanced at Finnerty. "Gordon Roth is already working to that end. Unfortunately, the woman hasn't been easy to track down. She hasn't been at her apartment since this morning and did not report to work today. Apparently she took a vacation day."

"We'll get her tonight," Finnerty assured the rest of the members. "When she comes back to her apartment."

"If she comes back," Mohler said, turning toward Elizabeth. "Can't you help us, Elizabeth? You've been all over that woman for some time."

Webb's eyes flashed to Elizabeth's.

Elizabeth saw Webb's curiosity turn to suspicion instantly. She swallowed hard and nodded at the senator respectfully. "Carter, quite coincidentally I have been recruiting Jesse Hayes for employment at Sagamore."

Webb raised an eyebrow.

"I can leave her a message at her office. She's supposed to be coming out to Sagamore for interviews, so she wouldn't think it suspicious to receive my call. She's extremely responsible. I'm sure even though she's taken a vacation day she'll be calling in for messages. I'll have her call me and try to arrange a meeting."

Webb stared at Elizabeth for thirty seconds without speaking. Finally he nodded. "Call her."

"As soon as we're done here," Elizabeth assured him.

Webb watched her a moment longer, then finally moved on to the next topic. "Elbridge isn't here because he's out at some event. His campaign against Malcolm Walker is progressing better than we could ever have expected. He will win in a landslide. GEA's stock is rising and will bring us incredible wealth as production of the A-100 begins. Everything is progressing as planned or better." He paused. "We just have to find Jesse Hayes." He ground his teeth for a moment. "That's all I have. Meeting adjourned." He glanced down the table. "Can I see you for a second, Art?"

As Elizabeth began to walk from the room she saw Mohler sit down next to Webb. The two men began whispering in tones too low for her to hear. She hesitated at the door, then turned back and moved toward them. Webb touched Mohler on the arm as he noticed Elizabeth nearing them, and they cut off their discussion.

"Yes?" Webb looked up at Elizabeth from his seat.

"I just thought of another way you might find Jesse Hayes."

# Chapter 29

"Hello."

"Helga?"

"Yes."

"Helga, it's Jesse."

"Hello, dear." Helga's heavy accent crackled through the static of the mall pay phone. "What can I do for you?"

"I'm calling in to get my messages before you go home for the evening." Jesse pressed her ear to the phone. The mall was crowded with noisy teenagers buying jeans or a CD on their way home from school.

"There's only been one more message since you called last. It's from a woman named Elizabeth Gilman. Something about interviews and a job offer. She wanted you to call her whenever you got this message. She said it was urgent and it didn't matter what time you called. Honestly, she seemed agitated. She gave me three numbers. Office, home, and car."

Why would Elizabeth be agitated? What could possibly be so urgent? David had warned her that Elizabeth's ultimate loyalty would always be to Sagamore. But how could Elizabeth's phone call be related to the file? How could she possibly know Jesse had it? Unless David had told her. A shiver tore through her. She had decided to trust him. Now once again she wasn't sure that was such a good decision.

Then another thought raced through Jesse's mind. There was clearly a connection between LFA and Sagamore through Doub Steel. The senior people at Sagamore would know there had been a break-in at LFA by now, and perhaps they had figured out that Jesse was the perpetrator. The security guards at LFA could easily identify her. They had pointed the flashlight directly into her face. Perhaps Elizabeth was luring her in so they could reclaim the evidence Jesse had taken from the files at LFA. David wouldn't have been involved at all in that scenario—as long as he had been telling the truth about his signature on the Doub Steel check being a forgery.

"Jesse." Helga was becoming impatient. "Do you want those numbers for Elizabeth Gilman?"

"Sorry, Helga." Jesse suddenly realized she hadn't answered the first time. "I already have them."

"Okay. Is there anything else?"

"Did Sara ever call in?"

"No. She must have taken off again today. People are worried, though. She was supposed to visit her parents last night but didn't make it. She hasn't called them either."

Something was definitely wrong. Sara would never miss a dinner date with her parents and not call. "Did you talk to her parents?"

"Yes, first thing this morning."

"And you've heard nothing since?"

"No."

Jesse clutched the phone tightly. "Okay. Thanks for your help, Helga."

"Will you be in tomorrow, Jesse?"

"I'm not sure yet."

"Is something wrong?"

"No."

"I don't mean to be rude, but, dear, you sound a little strange. As if something's bothering you."

"I'm fine," Jesse said firmly.

"All right. Well, call me in the morning if you won't be coming to work."

"I will. Can I ask you to do one more favor for me?"

"Of course."

"In my Rolodex is the number for Sara's parents. Can you get that?"

"Hold on a minute." A few seconds later Helga was back. "Here it is, dear."

Jesse jotted down the number quickly. "Thanks. I'll talk to you later." She accessed a new dial tone, then quickly punched out the numbers Helga had just given her.

"Hello." It was Sara's mother. Her voice was barely audible.

Jesse knew instantly that something was very wrong. "Mrs. Adams, it's Jesse."

"Oh, Jesse. I'm . . ." But Sara's mother could go no further. She broke down into terrible sobs.

"Jesse?"

"Yes." Jesse's voice shook.

"It's Bill Adams."

"Hello, Mr. Adams."

Sara's father could barely speak either. "They found Sara." He coughed. "She had a terrible car accident. Apparently she was going very fast and lost control. The car exploded. Her body was . . . burned beyond recognition. They had to use dental records . . ." He couldn't go on.

"I'm sorry, Mr. Adams." Jesse turned so that her face was pressed into the corner formed by the pay phone and the wall. Tears began streaming down her cheeks. "I'm so sorry." The car accident was a sham. Jesse shivered. The man who had chased her at Neil Robinson's river house had never stopped searching. He had been out there hunting the entire time. He had simply killed the wrong person.

"Jesse, I need to go. I'm sorry to be so short with you but I . . ."

"I understand." Jesse heard Sara's mother sobbing in the background.

"Good-bye."

"Bye." Jesse hung up the receiver slowly. David believed the conspiracy reached senior levels in the Senate and at the Pentagon. And people with that kind of power would go to any length to conceal their crimes. As he had said, those lengths would certainly include murdering an IRS revenue agent.

Guilt suddenly overcame her. They meant to kill me, Jesse thought to herself, and Sara suffered the consequences. She wiped her eyes and face with the back of her hand as a sob racked her body. The glove. Her pursuer must have found it and traced it to Sara.

Jesse began looking for a tissue in her purse, then froze. The man who had been coming out of her office that day asking for Sara. The picture of the man in the LFA personnel file. The eyes matched perfectly. She had been that close to death.

Now Elizabeth was trying desperately to reach Jesse, supposedly about a job offer. Why would Elizabeth be so specific about the purpose of the call? Especially when she was leaving the message at Jesse's current job. No one did that. Jesse leaned against the pay phone. Maybe they had realized their mistake by now. That they had gone after the wrong person. She hated to admit it, but David was right. Elizabeth's interest in bringing her to Sagamore was *too* coincidental.

Jesse pulled out another quarter, pushed it into the slot, began to punch out a number, then stopped abruptly. Was she out of her mind? Mitchell had said it himself. It was easier to play the game and earn two million a year. But he had moved her to the hotel, hadn't he? And then it hit her. Perhaps he was using her as a hostage without her even knowing. That check to LFA could represent his own fraud. Money he was moving for himself. Perhaps he was keeping himself out of a deadly situation by keeping her away from them.

The quarter fell through the pay phone as Jesse pushed down the receiver button before finishing the number sequence. She picked it up, reinserted it into the slot at the top, and punched out a different number. The line began to ring. "Answer! Come on!" Suddenly, she was petrified.

"Hello."

"Todd!"

"Jess?"

"Yes." He had tried to kiss her against her will in the parking lot and it had unnerved her. But it had to have been just a momentary lapse of judgment on his part. Perhaps he had gotten caught up in the moment with their escape from LFA. Todd was still the only one she could really trust at this point, and she needed someone desperately.

"Where are you?"

"In the Towson Mall. Todd, I'm scared."

"What's wrong?"

"I think I'm in a lot of trouble. I need to see you."

"When?"

"As soon as you can get here."

"Jess, I'm sorry again about what happened in the parking lot," he said sheepishly. "That was unforgivable."

"It's okay."

"Thanks. Look, I'll be right . . ." Through the farmhouse window, Todd noticed the sleek black Cadillac moving quickly down the long gravel driveway between the line of maple trees. "I'll meet you at the bar in the Friday's Restaurant in the west end of the mall. But give me a couple of hours."

"A couple of hours? Can't you make it any faster than that?"

"I'll try. Just be at the bar."

"All right."

"See you then." Todd slammed down the receiver, raced to the bureau, picked up the .38, shoved it into his shoulder holster, and moved back to the window. It was Harry the Horse. There was no mistaking that car. How the hell had he ever gotten himself mixed up with these people? It had seemed so innocent at the beginning. Just a small gambling debt he could take his time repaying, Harry had said. Now he owed them thirty thousand dollars, and if he didn't come up with the cash soon, they were going to make an unfriendly visit to his sister and her baby.

Harry pulled his Cadillac behind Todd's Corvette, effectively blocking its escape route—just as he had done the last time. He switched off the ignition, stepped from the vehicle and stretched, as if this were nothing more than a casual visit. A large accomplice stepped out of the passenger side, and they shared a laugh about the Corvette's damaged fenders as Todd emerged from the farmhouse front door.

"Hello, Todd," Harry yelled across the front yard. "Wonderful day, isn't it?"

"Uh huh." Todd moved cautiously down the three steps leading from the small landing outside the front door to the ground.

"I'm here for my money, Todd." Harry wasted no time.

"I thought I had more time."

Harry stroked his neck. "The payment plan's time frame has changed."

Harry's gorilla-size associate chuckled to himself.

"Why are you doing this to me, Harry?" Todd stopped twenty feet away from them. He felt the gun resting in the holster next to his chest. He would have no problem using it to defend himself against anyone but Mafia people. He might be fortunate enough to kill both of these goons, but then he'd be on the run for the rest of his life. The Mafia never stopped looking for outsiders who killed their comrades. "I'm good for the money."

Harry began to walk slowly toward Todd. "You know I like you, Todd, I really do," he said insincerely. "It's my bosses that are the problem. They've never met you. They don't know what a peach of a guy you are. I've been trying to tell them, but they just won't listen." Harry stopped five feet in front of Todd. "Ain't I been telling them, Anthony?" Harry called over his shoulder to the gorilla.

"Yeah, boss." Anthony smiled as he moved out from behind the black car and began ambling toward them. "You've been trying, but they just won't listen."

"There, you see?" Harry glanced back at Todd. "I've been pleading your case, but it hasn't helped. So do you have the money, Todd?"

"I'm . . . I'm getting it." He should have run out the back door into the woods when he first saw them coming down the driveway.

"Oh, yeah? From where?"

Todd eyed Anthony, now standing shoulder to shoulder with Harry. "My parents put some money away for me in a trust account. It's just a matter of getting all the paperwork executed so I can get to it."

"Oh, God." Harry made another face, as if he had just suffered a sharp pain.

"What's the matter?" Todd kept an eye on Anthony's right hand as it slid down toward his belt. Todd would pull the .38 if he had to. If it was the only option. He checked the driveway for any sign of someone Harry might have dropped off to serve as lookout, but saw nothing.

" 'Executed' is such a nasty word. I hope it won't apply in your case."

"Don't pull that intimidation crap on me, Harry."

"Crap?" It was as if Todd had suddenly flipped a switch deep within Harry. "Crap?" he screamed this time.

"Easy, Harry." Todd held up his hands.

Harry wasn't listening anymore. Veins bulged in his neck as he lunged toward Todd, hands outstretched. But Harry the Horse had collected his last payment.

The slug entered Harry's skull directly in the middle of his massive forehead, creating a neat hole in the pallid skin before tearing out the back of his head and ricocheting off the top of the Cadillac. Harry's eyes crossed instantly, as if he were trying to actually see the puncture wound while he staggered like a drunken man in front of Todd. Then the blood poured down his face and he crumpled to the ground.

Anthony reached for his weapon, but his fingers never touched metal. A second slug zipped through the air, smacking his broad chest with a sickening thud. He grabbed his shirt with both hands, ripping at the material, gasping for breath. A third shot cracked into the late afternoon, passing through Anthony's hand before tearing out a lung. He dropped into a heap next to Harry.

Todd fell to the ground and rolled behind the Corvette, pulling the .38 from his holster as he took cover. Behind the car he lay as flat and still as possible, pointing the revolver in the general direction from which he believed the three shots had come. Then a

man stepped calmly from behind a corner of the farmhouse and began walking toward the Cadillac, rifle at
his side. Todd trained the gun on the figure.

"Put the gun down," the man said as he moved past
Todd to where the two Mafia men lay. The man knelt
down next to Harry and felt for a pulse, but there was
none to find. He moved to Anthony, and found the
same result.

Todd kept the gun trained on the man. "Who the
hell are you?" he screamed. "What are you doing
here?"

"I'll explain later," the man growled as he grabbed
Anthony under the arms. "Are you going to lie there
with your mouth open, or are you going to get off
your ass and help me put these guys in the trunk?"

Slowly Todd rose from the ground, shaking. The
man could have easily killed him too. But he hadn't.
"Who—"

"I told you. I'll explain," he yelled. "First we need to
clean this place up."

"Jesse, I'm sorry I took so long." Todd moved to
where Jesse sat at the bar. It was after eleven o'clock.
Almost six hours had elapsed since she had called him.

"Are you okay?" She stood up and hugged him
tightly. It felt so good to be wrapped in his strong
arms. He was someone she could absolutely count on,
she had concluded over the last few hours as she sat at
the bar waiting. David's situation was much more
complicated. He had other loyalties. There was no
question of Todd's. "The bartender gave me your message about being late."

"Can I get you something?" Todd's arrival was obviously a disappointment to the bartender.

Todd saw the bartender's disappointment. Men were drawn to Jesse so fast. It had always been like that, and suddenly Todd felt the jealousy rising again, the same emotion he had felt watching her kiss David this morning in front of the hotel. He glanced cautiously around the restaurant, wondering once more—as he had since she had called this afternoon—why she had called him and not David. The jealousy burned hotter as the vision of their kiss became more vivid. "Coors Light, please."

The bartender put a glass under the tap and began to draw the beer.

Jesse sat back down, took Todd by the hand, and pulled him onto the seat next to her. "Thanks so much for coming."

"It's not a problem at all." He checked the restaurant once more, then shook his head. "Listen, I really want to apologize for the way I acted in the parking lot. I don't know what I was thinking. It was inexcusable."

"Don't worry about it," she said reassuringly. "The whole thing's forgotten."

The bartender placed Todd's beer down, then moved away.

"I was just a little overcome. We hadn't spent so much time together in a while, and I guess I'd forgotten how great it was to be with you."

"I told you, it's okay."

Todd smiled and took a sip of beer. "Thanks." He gazed at her lips. Mitchell had kissed her there this morning. "So what's wrong? You sounded really upset on the phone."

First Neil, now Sara, Jesse thought to herself. And it was supposed to be me. "Sara's dead." A lump came to her throat as she thought of Sara.

"Your friend Sara from the office?"

"Yes. Her car ran off the road and burned."

"That's terrible. I'm sorry."

"I don't think it was an accident, Todd."

"What do you mean?"

"I think she was murdered by the people Neil Robinson suspected of manipulating the Elbridge Coleman campaign. By the people who murdered Neil. They must have believed Sara was the one who took the file from Neil's house on the Severn." Jesse squeezed his hand. "I'm really scared."

Only forty-five minutes ago, Todd and the stranger had pushed the black Cadillac, with the bodies of Harry and his sidekick locked in the trunk, down a steep embankment into the deep waters of a lonely cove of the Loch Raven Reservoir. For a few agonizing minutes the sedan had floated, tilted forward by the weight of the engine. Then it had finally slipped below the surface with its human cargo. He only prayed to God the stranger hadn't been able to follow him here.

"We'll be out of here in no time," Jesse called over her shoulder to Todd as they climbed the darkened steps to her apartment. "I need to get the cat. I can't leave him here like this with no food or water."

Todd did not respond. He was concerned that the man who had killed the mobsters might be here.

Jesse inserted the apartment key into the lock, pushed the door open and flipped the light on. "Oh, my God." First she saw the destruction, and then the cat, dead in the corner. She turned around and buried her face in Todd's shirt. "Get me out of here, Todd! Get me out of here!"

# Chapter 30

As the stretch limousine cruised down Interstate 95 toward Washington, D.C., David gazed through the tinted glass into the darkness. He hadn't slept in a day and a half and should have been exhausted. But four cups of coffee and nervous energy were keeping him wide awake. Their destination hadn't been made clear, and suddenly he realized he shouldn't have so willingly honored Mohler's request to enter the limousine waiting outside Sagamore's Towson offices. However, there wasn't much he could do about it now.

Jesse hadn't been in her room at the Sheraton Hotel all day. He had called once an hour but never reached her. Perhaps despite all his efforts to conceal her they had found her anyway and she had met with the same fate as Neil Robinson. Perhaps he was headed toward that same end at this very moment.

Mohler sat on the other side of the limousine. "Where are we headed, Art?" David asked him.

"I told you," Mohler said quietly, "I've got a meeting with the CEO of a small computer software company. They've got what I understand is a revolutionary product but don't have the money to develop it. This could turn out to be a nice investment opportunity for Sagamore. You have experience in this area. I want you there. I'm a member of the executive committee. End of discussion."

"You scheduled a meeting with a CEO at eleven-thirty at night?" David asked suspiciously.

"They need money fast. There are other investment firms knocking on the company's door. What can I say? We work when we have to. You know that."

"Can you show me some financial information on the company so I can be prepared for the meeting?" David gestured toward Mohler's briefcase lying on the seat.

"I don't have anything yet. It's a private company and the CEO is stingy about divulging any information without a face-to-face meeting first. You know how these entrepreneurs are. They think everyone's out to steal their idea."

Mohler was doing an excellent job of avoiding the questions. David suddenly had a very bad feeling about this little excursion, as Mohler had called it in Baltimore.

Fifteen minutes later the limousine turned off Interstate 95 at the Laurel, Maryland, exit several miles northeast of the Capital Beltway.

"I thought you said the meeting was in downtown D.C."

"Relax, David." But Mohler's voice was not at all reassuring.

How stupid could he have been? There could easily have been a hidden camera in the hall of records last night taping his actions, David suddenly realized. If so, they would be well aware that he had made copies of the trading records.

As the limousine rolled to a stop at the end of the exit ramp, David gently tugged at the door handle but it was locked. Subtly he pushed the lock button on the door's console, but there was no sound. The dominant controls were up front with the driver and the ones in the back had been disengaged. There would be no leaving the vehicle until Mohler allowed him to.

The driver turned onto a lonely road. David squinted through the window but saw nothing except the vague outline of trees and fields in the night as the limousine cruised through the farmland outside Washington. It was too damn dark out here. Too remote.

David's eyes flashed to the bar tucked into the side of the limousine. In a rack on top of the small wooden counter there were several large bottles that could be smashed and used as weapons. They wouldn't be very effective against guns, but at least they were something. One always had to have a plan. Even if it wasn't a very good one.

But then David looked back out the window and his fears slowly subsided as the landscape became dotted with house lights. Then there was a strip mall and then a Marriott Hotel. By the time the limousine had turned in to the hotel and pulled up in front of the main entrance, his pulse had returned to normal.

"Here we are." Mohler grabbed his briefcase as the limousine's locks popped up. "Let's go, David."

They stepped out of the limousine and moved through the Marriott's lobby to the elevator. It rose quickly to the fifteenth floor, where they exited, turned right, and walked down a long hallway. Finally Mohler stopped in front of a door and knocked hard three times, then pushed. The door swung slowly open, and he moved into the suite.

David stood in the hallway. Would they risk trying anything here? Wouldn't they have taken him someplace less public if they intended to cause him harm?

Mohler leaned back out of the room. "Come on."

As David moved hesitantly into the foyer, the strong scent of cigar smoke came to his nostrils. He waited for Mohler to close the door, then followed him around the corner into the large living room. Seated there were Senator Webb and Jack Finnerty.

"Good evening, David," Finnerty said calmly. "Have a seat." He smiled politely, gesturing toward a wing chair on the opposite side of the coffee table from where he and Webb reclined.

David stood next to Mohler at the foyer's edge and watched as Webb inhaled from the cigar. Two and a half years ago he had come before this man to bribe him. He had believed the millions he would siphon out of Doub Steel would influence Webb to award GEA the huge A-100 contract out of the black budget. And that Sagamore would make billions when GEA's stock surged. Then he could keep his high-paying job and profit personally from the GEA options he had so cleverly negotiated for himself. He had believed that with guile, moxie, and guts he had brilliantly engineered a transaction that would be the answer to all his problems and make him wealthy beyond his wildest dreams. But those had been the beliefs and presumptions of a pathetic neophyte, David now knew. They were all in league together, and they had craftily led him down the garden path. They were the masters. He was just a babe in the woods.

Mohler tapped David on the back and smiled warmly. "Have a seat, young man." He placed his briefcase on a table and took a seat at one end of a long sofa.

Still David stood in the foyer entrance, staring at the three men who had so easily manipulated his life for the last two and a half years. "You three must have enjoyed some long laughs at my expense over the last few years," he finally said.

For the first time Webb removed the cigar from his mouth. He placed it in an ashtray on the coffee table. "We don't find humor in any of this," he replied curtly. "In fact, there is nothing we take more seriously. Now sit down."

David finally obeyed. "So what is this little gathering all about?"

"Information and explanations," Webb answered. "The time has come to let you in on a few things."

"Such as?"

"The GEA transaction was a setup. We had you execute the dirty work in case anything went wrong. So there was no way to link us to any aspect of the transaction."

Finnerty crossed his arms, and Mohler removed his half-lens glasses. The discussion would clearly be a dialogue between Webb and David.

"And so that I was trapped," David uttered, almost to himself. "The money I believed was going to you as compensation for your influence on awarding the

A-100 contract to GEA actually went to an account in my name. I know that now."

Webb smiled. "Yes, that's true."

"So you could set me up on fraud charges in case I ever became a problem. In case I ever considered cutting a deal with the authorities. There would be no evidence of your wrongdoing, but clear evidence of me sending three million dollars from Doub Steel to myself and covering the transfer by creating phony documentation for the accountants. The authorities would nail me, but they wouldn't see any connection between Sagamore and you, Senator Webb, because, in fact, there wasn't any." David shook his head. "And you handed me the cash to pay the money back by giving me the GEA options." Now that David thought about it, Finnerty had actually been the one who first brought up the possibility of the options.

"Very good, David. All things we planned to inform you of tonight, but I see that we don't have to worry about that."

"You would never allow yourself to be so easily connected to bribery."

"Of course not."

"And that money I sent myself has all been swept away from those accounts so I could never reverse the transaction if I did find out about it. It's probably all waiting for me in some Swiss account. But I'd never be able to find it."

"The authorities could be made aware of it quickly."

"I'm sure." David had never been madder at himself. "God, I should have known what was really going on that night I came to see you."

"Don't be too hard on yourself." Webb was enjoying himself. "You were eager to make a deal. Eager to save your job."

"I should have figured out that you would never just let me send you money that way. And I should have known that you were looking for a much bigger payday than the three million dollars we finally agreed to." David glanced up at the senator. "Your payoff is a piece of the Sagamore action, isn't it? A big piece. Probably the biggest."

"Of course." Webb picked up the cigar again. "Why shouldn't I have the biggest share? I approached Elizabeth Gilman fifteen years ago when her little investment fund wasn't as successful as it is today. In fact, it was going down the drain. I saved her. I set up this whole infrastructure and risked losing everything. I ought to have the biggest piece."

David watched Finnerty and Mohler nod like puppets.

"So, let's say the GEA transaction nets Sagamore a three-billion-dollar profit. If Sagamore keeps two percent for itself, which I believe is the agreement the executive committee strikes with investors"—David paused for a moment and glanced at Mohler, who nodded in agreement—"that's sixty million dollars. Senator Webb, let's say you take twenty million of that." David laughed cynically. "Twenty million sure beats the hell out of a senator's salary."

"It certainly does," Webb said quietly.

"And there's probably no way to track funds out of Sagamore. Taxes are probably paid on gains through some kind of sharing agreement, then money is distributed through some intricate network running through Europe, Southeast Asia, and South America. A network erected by experts. A network no one could ever figure out."

"You seem to have it all figured out."

"So why am I here tonight?" David asked. "Why the intrigue of the limousine ride just to tell me that I sent myself the money out of Doub Steel? Something I already knew anyway."

"Several reasons, David."

They were being awfully friendly tonight. He hadn't heard his last name once. "What reasons?"

"Art." Webb motioned to Mohler.

"Yes." Mohler cleared his throat. "David, Sagamore Investment Management Group has recorded tremendous investment results for years. We've done so, as you've probably surmised, through our relationship with Carter Webb. We use his access to information to our advantage, and as you accurately stated, he shares in our success. Just as with you tonight, we have explained all of this to each of the small number of managers who have made it to their fifth anniversary with Sagamore. We were just as open in explaining all of this to them as we've been with you, because just as with you, we had them in a very tight corner."

Mohler paused so they could gauge David's reaction, then continued. "Your test was GEA, admittedly the largest project we have ever embarked on at Sagamore. But the portfolio managers who were invited before you into what is a rather exclusive society had their own baggage—the same kind of fraud or embezzlement trail you have, which could land them in jail, just as it could you," Mohler said sternly, pausing for just a second to allow the truth to sink in. "You see, it isn't your performance in the first five years at Saga-more that concerns us. It isn't the fact that you've been in the bottom half of the monthly rankings that we really care about. I know that's what all you people who haven't been initiated believe. What we really care about is whether you're willing to take on the responsibility of that inside trade, in your case GEA, and excuse it. Whether you're willing to take a cue from Jack Finnerty to approach Senator Webb, then enter into the investment and lock yourself in to us by sending him the money out of a Sagamore subsidiary. Whether you're willing to protect Sagamore's execu-tive committee, Senator Webb, Jack Finnerty, the other portfolio managers and the rest of our group."

"Because if I'm willing to do that, I've effectively committed myself to a life of crime," David murmured.

"To us," Webb corrected. He turned to Finnerty. "David's heard enough bad news, Jack. Tell him the good stuff."

Finnerty smiled. "David, we've never had a problem at Sagamore after making all this clear to a portfolio manager. In fifteen years no one has ever turned on us. There are two reasons for that. First, as Art said, we have the stick. We have you nailed on fraud. But we also recognize the need for an incentive." Finnerty's smile broadened. "If you agree to secrecy, which I trust you will because there's really no other logical option, you will receive a one-time cash payment of two million dollars."

David looked at Finnerty incredulously. "Two million?" His voice was almost inaudible.

"That's right. And you can count on at least that much in salary and bonus every year. Probably much more. Would you say that's accurate, Art?" Finnerty leaned forward and glanced past Webb to Mohler.

"Yes."

Two million dollars. A nervous smile David couldn't control played across his face. He really was going to be rich.

"You should feel honored, David," Webb said. "GEA is the largest transaction we've ever executed. And we chose you to execute it for us. You scored very well on the psychological tests we asked you to take before we made you the offer. Higher than anyone else ever has at Sagamore. You'll have a long and prosperous career at the firm, I guarantee you. We've got a lot planned for you. I can even envision you on the executive committee someday."

"You people play a mean game of poker." David turned to Mohler. "I was convinced you really wanted me to sell GEA that day you were in my office screaming about how it was the worst investment Sagamore had ever made."

"If you had tried to sell it, I would have intervened." The men shared a loud laugh.

"I was also sure you didn't like me."

"I didn't," Mohler admitted, his laughter fading. "But these gentlemen convinced me I should feel otherwise. Now I'm glad they did."

"Why isn't Elizabeth here? After all, she founded the firm."

"Usually she is," Finnerty responded quickly. "But . . . um . . ."

"But she had other business to attend to." Webb finished Finnerty's sentence, but offered no further explanation.

"I've got another year before my fifth anniversary," David pointed out. "Why are you doing this now?"

"Sometimes it isn't necessary to wait until the end of the fifth year. Sometimes we feel there is more to be gained by allowing the individual insight into our group before that time. This is one of those occasions." Webb inhaled from the cigar once more, then snuffed it out in the ashtray. A thick smoke column rose before him. "On your fifth anniversary, Art will call you in before the executive committee and officially knight you for appearance sake, but you'll already know what's going on."

"I see." David brushed a piece of lint from his suit pant. A $2 million one-time payment. Huge annual salaries and bonuses. That kind of money would mean a lifetime of large houses in exclusive neighborhoods, private schools for children, and the best vacations money could buy. The alternative was prison. "How do I officially accept your generous offer?"

"Look us in the eye and tell us you accept," Webb answered immediately.

For a few moments there was no sound in the room. Finally David smiled graciously. "Of course, I accept."

"Remember, someone will always be watching," Webb warned. "We've never had to resort to this, but we wouldn't hesitate to dispose of someone who would make trouble, who would try to destroy what we have built at Sagamore."

"Is that what happened to the men who supposedly committed suicide?" David asked. "The one who jumped from the Bay Bridge and the one who sucked down carbon monoxide in his garage? Were they . . . disposed of?"

"No. Those were real suicides. I told you we've never had to resort to that. Perhaps those men were driven to suicide by what they were hiding. Maybe they just weren't mentally strong enough. I really don't know and I really don't care. The only thing I do care about is that those two events brought unwanted attention to Sagamore. Which is why we implemented the psychological testing to rectify that potential problem." Webb tapped the arm of the chair. "I'm happy to tell you, David, you have no chance of killing yourself."

"Great," he whispered to himself.

"David, the bottom line is that you can look forward to an extremely prosperous life." Webb crossed one leg slowly over the other. "There is one more thing."

"What's that?"

"It's come to our attention that you know a woman named Jesse Hayes."

David tried not to allow the recognition of Jesse's name to register on his face.

"Elizabeth Gilman relayed this information."

Still David said nothing.

"Is what she said accurate? Do you know Jesse Hayes?"

"Yes," David said quietly. It would have been stupid

to deny their relationship. Webb obviously knew about it or he wouldn't have said anything.

"David, we need to find her. Quickly."

"Why?"

"She's taken something of ours and we want it back."

"Are you talking about the copy of the canceled check from LFA?" David knew he had just dropped a bomb.

The three men looked up together. "How the hell do you know about that?" Webb asked.

"She told me. I've made her believe she can trust me." They were clearly impressed. "Elizabeth Gilman was a guest lecturer at the Maryland Business School and met Jesse Hayes there. Afterward, Elizabeth asked me to get to know Jesse. Elizabeth thought Jesse might be a good candidate for Sagamore, as a portfolio manager. So I did get to know her. And I found out that for some reason Jesse was investigating Elbridge Coleman's political campaign. I think it had to do with tax violations or something. Anyway, it led her to LFA, and she found the check from Doub Steel." David's expression became grim. "I believe she said I was the signatory on the check, but I didn't write it." He watched the three men carefully. "I couldn't figure out why someone at Doub would be sending checks to LFA or would use my name to do it. I was going to say something, but I didn't know who to tell. So I just kept quiet."

"You did the right thing." Webb nodded approvingly. "Can you contact her for us?"

"Her number's probably in the phone book."

"She hasn't returned to her apartment since early this morning. As I said, we need to reach her as quickly as possible."

"So that you can retrieve the information?" David asked.

"Yes."

"And dispose of her?"

Webb suddenly wondered if David Mitchell might not be just as good a poker player as they were. "That may be necessary."

"I wouldn't do that," David warned.

"Why not?" Webb asked suspiciously.

"I can't understand why Elizabeth was so adamant about me getting to know Jesse Hayes so well, but as I said, I did as she asked. After all, as far as I knew then, Elizabeth was my ultimate superior." David noticed a subtle glance between Webb and Finnerty. "So I made Jesse believe I cared about her, and I think I did a pretty good job, because she confided to me she was involved in something she was frightened about. Even when she found the copy of the Doub Steel check made out to LFA with my signature, I was able to convince her that I hadn't written it, that there had to be some sort of conspiracy going on and that I was just as confused as she was. Which, frankly, I was. But I also wanted to keep track of her for selfish reasons at that point because of the check copy. I had to find out what was going on, so I convinced her that we should work together to figure out what was happening. Fortunately, she bought everything I told her and agreed."

They were hanging on his every word now. "Anyway, Jesse told me she believed someone was manipulating the Elbridge Coleman campaign," David continued, glancing at Webb. "She didn't tell me exactly what she had, but she said she had put together a great deal of information which in the aggregate would nail someone. She also told me she had hidden the information, and that if anything happens to her, there is another person who has instructions to take the material to federal authorities. So you can't just find her and dispose of her. That won't work. You'll still be vulnerable."

"Why hasn't she gone to anyone yet?" Webb asked.

"I told her she couldn't be certain of who to trust, and that if the information she had wasn't compelling enough, wasn't enough to convince someone to investigate right away, she would pay the price. I scared her, but I had to. Even though I didn't write it, I couldn't have her giving the copy of the Doub Steel check to her superiors with my name at the bottom. That would have been very bad for me. It would have caused them to go through Doub's books with a fine-tooth comb, and someone would have discovered that I'd sent the other money out as well. I would have gone to jail. I'm sorry, but that isn't in David Mitchell's future."

"If what you say is true, you've acted with great foresight, David," Webb said. "And I appreciate your advice about dealing with her fate delicately. But the question still stands. Can you contact her? Do you know where she is?"

"I want to ask another question first."

"Go ahead," Webb growled, growing impatient.

"Was Jesse Hayes correct in her investigation of

the Coleman campaign? Is someone attempting to manipulate his election?"

The young man was smart, perhaps too smart. He knew exactly what was going on, but he wanted confirmation. He wanted to hear the words. "Yes, she was correct." Webb leaned forward in his chair. "David, what we have put in place here, Sagamore's coordination with the black budget, is much too valuable to let wither away once I'm gone. I'm pragmatic enough to realize I won't be around forever, and we need to make certain it keeps going. You will benefit from our hard work on Coleman's campaign." His jaw was clenched. "*Now*, can you find Jesse Hayes for us?"

David rifled through Rebecca Saunders's files. Hager, Halston, Hayes. He yanked the thick file from the cabinet, set it down on the table and opened it. As he leafed quickly through the pages his expression did not change despite what he was reading. Raped by her stepfather at age seventeen. Rage, guilt, fear. An abortion. But where? Clinic or hospital? Jesse would have been nothing but a number at a clinic. But there might be a name on her file at a hospital.

And then he saw it, scrawled in script on the edge of a typewritten page. The answer. Edgewood General.

David replaced the papers in the envelope, closed the file, put it tightly under his arm, and headed toward the door.

It helped to know people—and to have a face women were attracted to. "Thanks, honey," the young man said sweetly as the nurse handed him the bag.

Inside was confirmation that Jesse Hayes had visited Edgewood General at age seventeen and had an abortion performed. Something she was still guilt-ridden over. Information they could use against her.

"I shouldn't have done this." The nurse shook her head.

"Don't worry. No one at Edgewood General will ever know it was you," he assured her. "I promise. Here." The young man slipped the letter-size envelope into the nurse's hand. Inside was $1,000.

The nurse snatched it from the young man's hand, checked the contents, and walked away into the night.

# Chapter 31

David sipped black coffee from the Styrofoam cup in his left hand as he held the receiver and punched in the number with his right. It was six in the morning, but time of day was of little concern to him now. If she wasn't awake yet, she soon would be.

"Sheraton North," the operator answered loudly.

"I'm trying to reach Jesse Hayes. She's in room ten-eleven."

"One moment please," the woman said enthusiastically.

David groaned. Anyone who was that chipper at six in the morning didn't have a life, or had been completely brainwashed during corporate training. Finally the line began to ring.

"Hello," a groggy male voice answered.

David pulled the receiver away from his ear for a second. What the hell was going on? "Is Jesse Hayes there?" he asked hesitantly.

"There's no one here by that name."

"Sorry." David hung up quickly and hit the phone's automatic redial button.

"Sheraton North." The same obnoxiously chipper voice greeted him.

"Yeah, I just called. I'm trying to reach Jesse Hayes. I believe she's in room ten-eleven. Could you check that?"

"Just a minute."

He heard the tapping of fingertips against a keyboard, then the woman's voice was back on the line.

"She is a guest here, but not in room ten-eleven. I'll connect you now."

"Operator!"

"Yes?"

"Could you tell me which room she's in?"

"I'm sorry, I can't do that. We aren't allowed."

"She's my fiancée," he lied. "And it's my credit card paying for the room. The name is David Mitchell. You can check it out. I can give you the Visa number. I think I'm entitled to the information."

"I'm sorry, sir. It's corporate policy not to give out room numbers over the phone or at the front desk no matter what," the woman answered firmly. "Would you like me to ring her room?"

"Yes," he said quietly, accepting that this woman wasn't going to violate protocol.

There was a single ring and then an answer.

"Hello."

"Jesse?"

"Yes."

"It's David."

"What do you want?" she asked coolly.

"What the hell is your problem?" David sensed the chill instantly.

"My friend Sara Adams, the one I told you about at the bar the other day, is dead."

He heard the accusatory tone. "I'm sorry."

"You know whoever killed her meant to kill me."

"Is that why you switched rooms? In case they figured out their mistake?"

"Yes."

"Because you knew the operator wouldn't divulge room numbers?"

"Yes."

"But I'm the only one who knew which room you were in?"

"Yes," she said evenly.

For the moment he ignored the implication. "When you switched rooms, why didn't you use an alias if you wanted to keep people away?"

"I was worried the front desk would give me trouble if I changed names when it was your card paying for the room. And of course I don't want to use my card."

"You have to have faith in me, Jesse," he said, interrupting the flow of conversation, subtly acknowledging the distrust so evident in her tone. "I'm trying to help you. You must believe that."

"They killed Sara. You work for them. They can make you rich. You said it yourself. All you ever wanted was to be rich. Why should I trust you?"

"I don't care about money now. I want to do what's right. I want to protect you."

"Does protecting me include moving me out of my apartment so you could destroy it searching for information? I told you none of the information I have is there."

"What are you talking about?"

"My apartment was ripped apart. I went there last night." She listened carefully to his breathing for any clue to the truth.

He knew what she was thinking. "I didn't have anything to do with your apartment being ripped apart. You must realize that." He had to think, fast. He had to win her confidence back. "You told me the Neil Robinson file wasn't there when I dropped you off at the Sheraton. Why would I rip your apartment apart?"

"Simple. You didn't believe me."

"I want to take care of you, Jesse." Again, rather than respond to her words, he tried to play on her emotions.

"I can take care of myself," she answered icily.

Todd groaned as he came out of his sleep. Jesse glanced over at the couch and covered the phone's mouthpiece.

"Who the hell is that?" David asked quickly.

Todd rubbed his eyes, then looked up at Jesse.

She held a finger to her lips. "It's Todd Colton. I felt I needed protection last night, so I asked him to stay here with me."

David banged his desk hard with an open palm. "Don't trust that guy, Jesse. Get away from him. I'm not kidding."

She heard the smack of his hand hitting the desk. "I told you, I'll make my own decisions from now on."

David pressed the receiver to his ear tightly. "Jesse, they have something on you." He had to tell her now. It was the last chance.

"Something on me?" Her voice suddenly wavered. "What do you mean?"

"I don't want to talk about it on the phone. I have to show you in person. I'm telling you, it's definitely something you don't want them to use against you."

Her hand began to shake. "What is it?" But she already had an idea. It could only be one thing.

"Meet me."

"So someone can shoot me?"

"That's not going to happen," he said soothingly. "I have their assurances. You name the place. It can be as public as you want. You can bring Todd if that makes you feel better. I've told them you possess incriminating information, but that it is safely stored and that there are instructions with a friend to go to the authorities if anything happens to you. I've told them that the information you have would put them behind bars for the rest of their lives. They believed me. They are willing to work out a deal. Perhaps with a large cash payment. This can all work out for the best, Jesse. We can all be safe. I urge you as strongly as I can to consider this option. They believed me, now *you* have to believe me."

The bastard. He had been working with them the entire time.

Todd sat up on the couch as he saw the sadness in Jesse's eyes.

"Name the place, Jesse." David was insistent.

She felt the emotion hurtling to the surface but choked it back. There was no time for emotion. "The

Mercantile Bank branch on York Road just north of the fairgrounds," she uttered despondently.

"When?"

"Ten o'clock."

"Good. You're doing the right thing, Jesse."

Slowly she put the phone down without answering.

"What's wrong, Jess?" Todd sat down on the bed next to her and gently took her hand.

"Nothing. Everything. Just hug me, Todd, please."

At ten-fifteen, Jesse and Todd sprinted across York Road, dodging heavy traffic, to the Mercantile Bank branch. They had been watching the building for thirty minutes but had seen nothing to make them wary. Each car that had rolled into the small parking lot had exited, and now the lot was empty. There seemed no reason to be suspicious.

They entered through the glass doors at the front of the building and moved quickly to a counter on one side of the lobby. A guard stood amiably in one corner of the room next to a large fern, hands behind his back. Jesse glanced at the guard, then at the two unoccupied tellers.

"Are you okay?" Todd asked.

"Yes," she answered without taking her eyes off the door. "You have your gun, right?"

It was the third time she'd asked. "Right here." He touched his chest.

"Jesse."

She recognized the voice and whirled around. David stood in a doorway next to the guard.

"Would you come with me, please?" He motioned her toward him.

Jesse heard the glass door swing open and turned quickly back toward the front of the building. A man with long sandy blond hair and a beard and mustache entered the building. She recognized him immediately and grabbed Todd's hand. "That's the guy who was in my office that day," she whispered.

"Jesse, come on," David called.

"Do you want to get out of here, Jess?" Todd watched Gordon Roth carefully.

"I don't know." Her nerves were on fire.

"Is everything all right here, folks?" The guard moved out away from the corner.

"Everything's fine, sir." David walked confidently to where Jesse and Todd were. "Hello, Todd." David's tone was flat, neither friendly nor unfriendly.

Todd stared at Mitchell. Jesse had cared about him for a short time. But she had seen the error of her ways. Todd had made certain of that.

David turned to Jesse. She was like a cat on a hot tin roof searching for a way down. But there wasn't any. "Jesse, I saw the way you looked at the man who just walked in. He does work for them. I'm not going to deny that. But he's here to watch over me, not you. He's here to make certain I don't take off with what I'm going to show you." Though she was doing an admirable job of hiding her emotions she had to be frantic inside. And who could blame her? "Jesse, you and I are going back into a private room I've arranged for. The guy isn't coming back there with us. Todd can watch him while we're there."

"You're crazy." Who knew what David would try? He had to be desperate at this point.

"There's nothing I could do to you back there." He had read her expression. "I know you have lots of questions. Just come back to the room with me and I'll answer them."

"Jess, if you want to leave, say the word." Todd's eyes flashed quickly from Roth to Mitchell.

"It's all right." She had come this far. And she needed to know what David had. "I'll come with you, David, but Todd's going to watch that guy. If anything at all out of the ordinary happens, he's going to have the guard call the police immediately." She paused. "Todd, if David comes out of there alone, start yelling." She said the words loudly, so David could hear them.

"I will."

David nodded. "Fine. Now come on." He retraced his steps to the doorway and moved into the hallway beyond.

Jesse followed a few feet behind, hesitating at each corner of the hallway, expecting an attack at every turn. But finally they were in a small room together alone, a room normally for people who wanted to be left alone with their safety deposit boxes.

David closed the door. "Have a seat." He pointed to a chair positioned before a small table. "Don't worry, Jesse. Nothing is going to happen." He dropped the information from Edgewood General on the table. "Go ahead. Read it."

Slowly she sat down at the table and reached for the

envelope. She scanned it for just a few seconds, then pushed it away. "I can't believe you." Her voice was barely audible. "You saw Becky's card. You took it from my apartment that night. You went to her office and took my file, didn't you?"

David said nothing.

"The name of the hospital. The fact that my stepfather was the one who attacked me. Becky knew all that. It would have all been in the file." Jesse was suddenly on the verge of tears again. "And after you saw Becky's file, you went to the hospital and got this." She pointed at the envelope on the table.

"No. I didn't get this information."

"Don't lie to me!"

"I'm not. I wouldn't. Look, they know your stepfather was the one who attacked you. They know it was his child. And they will tell all of this to your mother, everything, if you choose to go to the authorities." He shook his head. "They will go so far as to tell your mother that it wasn't rape. That it was consensual. They know how dedicated your mother is to the Catholic Church. They know what it would do to her if she found out."

"You bastard!"

"Listen to me, Jesse. It doesn't matter what you think of me now. What matters is that they have this information and they intend to use it."

She put her head in her hands, suddenly overwhelmed.

"Jesse, there's something else I'm supposed to relay to you."

"What?" She could barely speak.

"They want you to have the proper incentive."

"What does that mean?"

"It means they want to buy your silence as well as intimidate you. They find that to be an extremely successful strategy. It means a cash payment of two million dollars and lifetime employment at Sagamore."

"Are you really so naive? I would never have thought that possible."

"What are you talking about?"

"They'll never stop trying to get their hands on what I have. On the copy of that check from Doub to the LFA. On Neil Robinson's information. On everything else. And when they find all of it, and ultimately they will, I'm dead. It's that simple."

"But Jesse, if you try to expose them, they'll show all of that information to your mother. And they'll publicize it so that everyone in that congregation she values so much will see it too. It will absolutely destroy her. You know it will. Then they'll kill you anyway. That's the reality. The alternative is working with them and finding yourself in a very nice position financially. And your mother no wiser to what your stepfather did. They are willing to deal. And they do believe that money can buy silence."

"I suppose you know that from experience."

"Jesse, I—"

"How could you do this to me?" she screamed. The chair tumbled backward crashing to the floor as she stood.

They could read people so well. David realized

that now. They were master manipulators. He hadn't thought that the threat of her mother's learning about the abortion would affect Jesse so deeply, but now, as the tears streamed down her face, he could see he had been dead wrong. She was disintegrating in front of him.

"I thought we were going to go to the authorities together." She tried to regain her composure for a moment, wiping the tears from her face, but then her shoulders heaved as another tremor racked her body. "I thought we were going to put them away with what we both knew. I so completely misjudged you, David. I can't believe you gave them the information about my abortion. About the fact that my stepfather . . ." But she couldn't finish. The image of her mother's face flashed through Jesse's mind. The horrified expression. The humiliation.

"I didn't tell them anything about what happened to you," he murmured quietly.

"Stop lying to me," she shrieked.

"I'm not lying." His face was grim. "Your friend Todd told them. He's the one who got them the file from the hospital. They've taken care of a rather large problem he had."

"What are you talking about?"

"He owed the mob some money."

Jesse shook her head slowly. That was preposterous. "God, you're pathological." She could no longer believe anything David Mitchell said.

"I should have told you all this before." David passed a hand through his hair and exhaled heavily.

"The evening I was in your apartment and Todd interrupted us, Elizabeth was waiting for me. She wanted me to search your place that night, but I never had a chance because of Todd. She told me it was all routine to investigate someone she planned to make an offer to. That they were just being careful. I knew it was crap, but I was trying to protect my job. When I got into the limousine, she asked me why I had come out so fast. That's when I told her about Todd. That's how they found him. Todd has to have been the one who set you up, because it wasn't me. You said you've known him since high school. You must have told him about what happened to you. About the attack, I mean. Todd's responsible for all this."

Todd wasn't capable of something so terrible, Jesse thought to herself. David was. It was as simple as that. "I know you're lying, David."

"No, I'm not." He looked straight into her eyes. "Look, if I could steal this information from them and be certain they wouldn't kill me too, I'd go to the authorities with you. I swear it. But we're better off agreeing to what they've proposed."

"You bastard! You gave me away to save yourself. I hate you." She lunged at him.

But he was too strong for her. He caught her arms and held them against her body as she struggled. Finally, she gave up and he let her go. She raced to a corner of the room and stood there, her back to him, wondering how she would get through this. And then she heard his voice. It was devoid of emotion.

"Don't screw with them, Jesse. They're more powerful than you can imagine. You have until eleven o'clock tomorrow morning to respond to their generous offer. I suggest you reply in the affirmative."

# Chapter 32

He stole silently down the hallway toward the small master bedroom, and hesitated for a moment in the darkness outside the door as he withdrew the ether-soaked rag from his pocket. Then he moved into the bedroom purposefully, pushed the rag against Connie Hayes's sleeping face, and stared down into her petrified eyes through the stocking mesh pulled tightly over his head as she struggled in vain against his strong hold.

It was over quickly. When he was certain she had lapsed into unconsciousness, he removed the rag, put it back in his pocket and began a systematic search of the house.

An hour later, he was rewarded for his determination when the flashlight's gleam fell on the IRS bag between the stacks of board games and jigsaw puzzles. He pulled it down, unzipped it, and shined the light inside. Pay dirt.

Quickly he removed the pile of papers and transferred them to another bag, then put the IRS bag back where it had been. This discovery was going to make him a rich man. He smiled widely, then looked out the window. First light was just seeping across the horizon.

"We've got it." Mohler slammed down the conference-room phone triumphantly. "Apparently there was quite a pile of stuff. Quite a bit of information. The Doub check to LFA. Information about how we rigged the Coleman Technology IPO through Sagamore, and about how we were trying to manipulate Coleman's election. Things we definitely would not have wanted out in the open. But now it's in our hands. Jesse Hayes has nothing left to bargain with."

Finnerty heaved a sigh of relief. "Thank God." He turned to his right. "It's over, huh, Carter?"

Webb rubbed his forehead, then glanced at his watch. Seven-thirty in the morning. "When will we receive the material?" The war wasn't over yet. He knew that as well as he knew the halls of Congress. It wasn't even close to celebration time. Only after he held in his own hands what had been taken from Connie Hayes's home, and Gordon Roth had assured him that Jesse Hayes was dead, would he relax.

"He said he'd arrange a meeting after he spoke with the Hayes woman." Mohler had convinced himself during the night that it was over, that everything they had built was going to unravel. Now Sagamore seemed safe again.

"He was quite helpful," Finnerty commented. He turned to his left. "You were right on the button about him, Elizabeth. Good job."

"Thank you." She held a hand to her mouth and coughed twice.

"Are you all right?" Finnerty was suddenly concerned. "You look a little pale."

"I'm fine," she said softly. "Just a bit tired. It's been a long night."

Webb watched her for a moment, then reached inside his suit coat for a cigar. She was hiding something. He had been reading faces too long, and hers was telling a story. He sliced off the cigar tip with his sterling silver cutter and turned to Finnerty. "You can reach Roth at any time, right?"

Finnerty nodded. "Yes. On his cellular."

"As soon as we hear back, I want him on Jesse Hayes. I want her taken care of as soon as possible."

"Right, Carter."

They had moved from the Sheraton to the Towson Motor Inn just to be safe. And fortunately, by means of a small bribe, they'd been able to persuade the man at the front desk to take cash and not a credit card so they couldn't be traced. Jesse reached for the phone. It was nine-fifty and the deadline would expire in a little over an hour. As the line began to ring at the other end, she glanced at the door. Where the hell was Todd? He had been on the couch when she'd fallen asleep last night, but gone this morning when she awakened at six. She wanted to talk to him before she made the call, but she couldn't wait for the last second. She'd kept the whole ugly affair to herself this long. She couldn't let them destroy her mother and her after so much pain.

"Hello," David answered on the second ring.

"It's Jesse."

"Jesse, I have to see you right away."

He was speaking so softly she could barely hear him. "What are you talking about? I'm calling because the deadline is only an hour away. I'm going to accept what they've proposed. What you've proposed. I don't know what choice I have. It would devastate my mother to know everything, and for all her friends to know. It would devastate me too, for God's sake. I couldn't handle it. I'll accept their proposal and learn to live with it. But you can tell them to go to hell with their two-million-dollar bribe."

"Shut up, will you? And forget the deadline."

"*What?*"

"I can't talk too long right now, but don't worry about the deadline. I've bought you some extra time." He was breathing hard into the mouthpiece.

"Do you want the world to find out what happened to me? Is that what it is?"

"Stop questioning my loyalty, dammit," he said angrily. "Here's what you're going to do. Are you familiar with the Worthington Valley?"

"Of course."

"How about the Stenersen Farm Store?"

"You mean the little country shop out on Falls Road?"

"Yes. It's at the intersection of Shawan and Falls."

"I know."

"Meet me there in two hours."

"David, tell me what this is about," she begged.

"I can't. Just be there. And for Christ's sake, don't go outside of wherever you are until you come to meet me. Don't leave that room until then. When you do leave, be very careful. They're probably everywhere." He paused for a second. "And come alone. You can't trust Todd. I mean that."

"David!" But he was gone. Jesse's hand shook wildly as she pressed down the receiver button to access a new dial tone. She punched his office number again, but this time the phone rang four times until his voice mail message answered.

"I got the number!" Finnerty frantically jotted down the telephone number from the caller ID liquid crystal display. It sat on one corner of the huge conference-room table, connected to the phone in David's office. "We'll have the exact location of the call's origin in ten minutes."

"Make it five." Webb drew on the cigar. "There's no way David could know about us hooking this thing up to his phone, is there, Jack?"

Finnerty shook his head.

The knock on the conference-room door was loud, startling Webb, Finnerty, and Mohler.

"See who it is." Webb ordered Mohler to the door.

When Mohler reached the door, he opened it just a crack. "Oh, hello. Come in."

"Thanks." David moved into the doorway. "She called." He directed his words at Webb. It was an indication that he now considered Webb his leader.

"Excuse me." Elizabeth squeezed past David and left the room.

"Certainly, Elizabeth." He stepped farther into the room to let her out.

Once in the hallway, Elizabeth moved quickly away

from the conference room toward her office, murmuring the numbers she had seen on Finnerty's notepad over and over. Everything had spun out of control so quickly, faster than she could ever have anticipated. She had given Webb and Mohler information at the end of the last sanctum meeting out of a survival instinct. She had seen them talking and been afraid they were discussing her. Afraid that they had found out about her treason, and were planning her untimely demise. So she had told them about how she had pushed David into getting close to Jesse because of her suspicion that Jesse was somehow involved. And about a man named Todd Colton. They had promised no harm would come to Jesse, but now they were going back on that promise.

Elizabeth moved into her office, closed the door, picked up the phone, and quickly dialed the memorized number. She had to do this. Otherwise Jesse wouldn't be in the land of the living much longer. Then there would be no living with herself.

"Hello."

"Jesse, it's Elizabeth Gilman." She did not await a reply. "Get out of wherever you are. They know where you are."

Jesse raced for the door. David. He had set her up again. Don't leave the room, he had said. Of course. So she would be a sitting target. She threw open the door. "Oh, God!" Someone was standing in the motel doorway. Instinctively she covered her face.

"What's wrong?" He saw her animal fear instantly. The fear of one being hunted.

"Todd!" Jesse clutched her chest, then fell into his arms. "I'm so glad it's you." She caught her breath. "They're coming. We've got to get out of here." She grabbed him by the wrist, pulling him away from the door and out into the parking lot toward her rental car.

"Where are we going?"

"I've got to get something from my mother's house. It's time to end this once and for all."

"What the hell are you talking about?" He stopped her as they reached the line of cars.

"Elizabeth Gilman just called me. She's the woman who recruited me at Sagamore."

"I remember."

"She said they're coming. That somehow they found me here at the motel. We've got to get out of here. Come on!"

"All right. I'll follow you in my car."

"No." She shook her head. "That Corvette would stand out like a beacon. We're both going in my car."

"Okay. But let me get something from the Corvette first. Bring the rental around."

Jesse turned and sprinted to the rental, started it, backed out of the spot, and whipped it quickly behind the Corvette. Todd hopped in and threw the overnight bag he had retrieved from the Corvette into the backseat. As the passenger door slammed shut, Jesse gunned the engine, and they squealed out onto York Road and sped north.

Minutes later, Gordon Roth guided his car into the space Jesse's rental had vacated, jumped from the car and ran to the door number they had specified. He burst in, but was back out in a second.

From the summit of a small hillside overlooking the motel, Jesse watched the assassin through Todd's binoculars. Elizabeth had saved her life. Slowly Jesse allowed the binoculars to drop from her eyes.

"Can you see anything?" Todd stood next to her, squinting down at the motel.

"Yes," she said quietly. "We just made it. That guy who came into the Mercantile Bank branch when I met David is down there right now."

"David set you up, didn't he?"

Jesse nodded.

"I knew he was no good that day I met him outside your office," Todd muttered. "Mr. Limousine," he sneered.

"Come on. Let's go." Jesse handed Todd the binoculars and started back to the car.

Gordon Roth stood before the open motel-room door, scanning the parking lot. Jesse Hayes was gone, obviously tipped off just in time. Suddenly his eyes spotted a familiar sight—the battered white Corvette owned by Todd Colton, the same car he had seen at the farmhouse yesterday when he had killed the two mobsters and temporarily saved Todd's life.

# Chapter 33

"Mom! Mom, wake up!"

Connie's eyes fluttered open. She looked up at Jesse for a moment, then moaned loudly.

"What's wrong?" Jesse knelt down on the bed and held a hand to her mother's forehead. "Are you sick?"

"Oh, God. I feel like I'm going to throw up." Connie sat up and put a hand over her mouth. "The last thing I remember, someone was holding something to my face. The fumes were horrible. I passed out."

"What?"

"Yes." Connie glanced at the doorway. "Todd, could I have a drink of water?"

"Sure." He disappeared around the corner.

"Are you all right, Mom?"

"Other than my stomach, I'm fine." She smiled weakly. "I'm a tough old bird."

Todd returned quickly with the water and handed Connie the glass.

"Thanks, dear."

"Sure, Mrs. Schuman."

This on top of everything else, Jesse thought to herself. "It must have been a robbery. I didn't notice anything missing when we came in, but I wasn't looking, either. We'll have to . . ." Suddenly she stood up and raced from the room.

"Jess, what's the matter?" Todd called after her.

"I'll be right back!" Jesse sprinted down the hallway to her old room and yanked open the closet door. A wave of relief spread through her body when she saw the IRS bag exactly where she had left it. She reached up with both hands and pulled the bag down. Her fears were back instantly. The bag was much too light. She unzipped it and peered inside. Everything was gone. Whoever had attacked her mother had been here for one thing. The information in the bag.

Slowly she walked back to her mother's room.

"What's wrong, Jesse? You look like you just lost your best friend."

"It feels like I did, Mom." Suddenly she noticed that her mother was alone. "Where's Todd?"

"He said he was going downstairs."

There was only one option left, Jesse realized. And it wasn't a very good one. "Mom, I have to go. I'll stay until the ambulance gets here to take you to the hospital."

"I'm not going to any hospital."

"Yes you are. There'll be no argument." Jesse turned and headed out of the room and down the stairs, then walked quietly through the first-floor hallway to the kitchen. She stood in the kitchen doorway for a moment watching Todd as he talked on the phone with his hand cupped over the mouthpiece.

Todd saw her, said a quick good-bye to the person at the other end of the line, and hung up. "Is your mother feeling better?"

"I think so." She stared at him, considering whether to ask who he had called. "As soon as the ambulance gets here, we've got to get to the Stenersen Farm Store over in the Worthington Valley." She had told Todd about David's instruction to meet him there as she and Todd drove to her mother's. She had said she wouldn't go near the place. But now the information in the IRS bag was gone and everything had changed.

"What the hell's going on?" Webb barked into the phone.

"I went to the Towson Motor Inn, to the room Finnerty said the call had come from, but they were gone," Roth yelled, clutching the cellular phone in one hand and the steering wheel in the other as he guided the car up Interstate 83 north from Baltimore. "It looked like they cleared out of there pretty fast. I swear to you, Carter, I was at the motel within four minutes of Finnerty's call."

"I'm sure you were." He pounded his fist on the table. This damned Hayes woman was always one step ahead. His eyes narrowed. And there was probably a good reason for that, he suddenly realized. "Where are you headed now?"

"To the Worthington Valley." Roth smiled as he whipped past two cars as though they were standing still. "I've got good news. Our boy called me. Jesse Hayes is going to be out at a little store in the valley."

Roth checked his watch. "And in about twenty minutes she's going to be dead."

The Worthington Valley lay thirty miles north of Baltimore. Its rolling grasslands were home to Thoroughbred horse farms and sprawling apple and peach orchards. The Stenersen Farm Store sat nestled in the midst of the beautiful valley in a grove of huge oak trees at the intersection of Shawan and Falls roads. Shawan Road ran east and west, through the length of the valley, while Falls snaked out of the forest covering the valley's south side. It was the primary thoroughfare for city dwellers visiting the picturesque area on weekends.

For generations the Stenersen family had owned thousands of acres of the valley, their property stretching out in all directions from the intersection's four corners. The main house, a huge stone mansion, overlooked the intersection from high atop a hill to the northeast. From this vantage point the family could look out over its expansive orchards and the store at the bottom of the hill. On weekends the small clapboard store would be mobbed, but on a weekday there were typically only a few shoppers, which was the case today.

"Do you know what kind of car David drives?" Todd asked as Jesse guided the rental into the store's gravel parking lot.

"Yes, a black BMW. It's right over there." She motioned at the sleek car, gleaming in the brilliant noon sun, parked directly in front of the store.

"He certainly isn't trying to hide the fact that he's

here. But I don't see him." Todd scanned the lot as Jesse backed the vehicle in between two other cars parked against a tall rail fence behind which several horses grazed. "We've got to be careful. This could be a trap, Jess."

"But as you said, he's made the car obvious. He's not trying to hide his presence."

"Don't be fooled. Remember, he told them you were at the Towson Motor Inn just an hour ago. He sent that guy to kill you."

A gentle breeze swept Jesse's hair across her face as she stepped out of the car. Tall oaks spread their limbs over the store like a canopy. Their leaves were just beginning to take on a hint of fall luster. Behind a stone fence to the right of the store was an apple orchard, the trees laden with fruit almost ready to be harvested. And to the left of the store the lush pasture rolled away from the fence up a hill to the mansion atop the rise.

Jesse removed her sunglasses and peered into the darkness of the orchard grove again. Something in there had caught her eye, but as she looked again she saw nothing. It was just her imagination working overtime, she told herself.

"Jess."

She turned to Todd. "What?"

"There he is." Todd pointed to the store's front doorway. David calmly walked out through it with a brown paper bag in his arms.

David waved as he saw them. He placed the bag on the BMW's hood and jogged toward them. Twenty feet away, he stopped, sensing that he wasn't welcome to come closer as Todd stepped forward. "Hi, Jesse," he said.

"Hello," she answered coldly.

David glanced warily at Todd, then back at her. "Jesse, I need to talk to you alone, without him. Come with me to my car. I've got something to show you."

"Don't do it, Jess," Todd said quickly. "You know he works for them. He's on their side. It's a trap."

"You don't know what the hell you're talking about," David snapped. "I know about you, pal."

"You don't know anything."

Todd made a move toward David, but Jesse caught him by the arm. "Why can't you bring whatever it is here, David?"

"I need to talk to you alone. Come on, Jesse." David was insistent. "It's important."

She began to answer, then out of the corner of her eye noticed a figure walking slowly toward them from the store, little more than fifty feet away now, a large bag obscuring the figure's face and upper body.

David turned his head, following Jesse's gaze. From where he stood he could partially see the face behind the bag. Instantly, he took a step back.

Slowly the figure came closer, and then suddenly Jesse recognized the limp. She had watched that limp after the man had almost run into her that day coming out of her office at the branch, supposedly on his way to Sara's office. Jesse knew exactly who this was. She didn't need to see the face.

She tried to point and scream, but the scene suddenly became surreal, and she seemed caught in a nightmare, her actions slowed by some unseen force and her voice muted. She became acutely aware of every movement, because Todd, David and the approaching figure all seemed to be going in slow motion.

As a primal scream finally tumbled from her mouth, the bag fell away from the man's face to the ground, spilling its contents of fruit. David brought his hands up before him, turned and fell to the ground. Todd lunged against the car next to the rental as the man brought a handgun up and fired. The slug smacked the rail fence behind them as Jesse threw herself to the ground, and suddenly everything accelerated to real time.

Jesse scrambled on her hands and knees toward the fence, then jumped to her feet and began running, hunched over at the waist, in the tight space between the cars and the rail fence. Horses in the pasture behind the fence bolted in different directions at the crack of another gunshot, and an instant later one of the Thoroughbreds stumbled to the ground, the victim of a stray bullet. It kicked savagely for a moment, then lay still.

Jesse sprinted wildly on, racing past the last parked car, then past the storefront and behind David's BMW to the low stone fence in front of the apple orchard. She threw herself over it, vaguely aware of several more pops from the gun, and landed on her hands, arms and chest.

And then Todd was next to her, prone on the ground. He had followed her down the line of cars to the fence and tumbled over it just a second after her.

Jesse was on her feet again instantly, crouched behind

the stones. They couldn't stay here. The man would be on them in no time. She grabbed Todd's arm as he reached inside his shirt and into the shoulder holster for his .38. "Come on, Todd!"

"One shot," he snarled, rising up behind the rocks as he withdrew the gun. "Just one shot."

"No!" She tried to pull him back down, but it was too late.

The slug tore through the right side of Todd's chest before he could even aim, spraying blood on Jesse's blouse and jeans. The powerful impact threw Todd backward, and the .38 flew from his grasp into a thick clump of bushes. For a moment Jesse considered going after it. But what if she couldn't find it? The assassin would be over the fence and she'd be defenseless—and dead.

Todd struggled to his knees, holding his right side with his left hand as blood poured down his shirt. "Go, Jess! Get out of here!" he yelled.

"No!" She raced to him, grabbed his left wrist, and began pulling him back into the thick grove of trees. "I'm not leaving you."

"I can't run." He coughed, spitting blood.

"Come on!" she screamed, grabbing and pulling at his thick wrist until he made it to his feet and began stumbling into the dense underbrush after her.

She ran frantically through the low hanging branches, leading Todd deeper into the orchard, hoping to lose the assassin she knew was tracking quickly behind them. Todd tripped over a downed branch as he struggled to follow her, falling heavily on his side, screaming as he went down, giving away their position.

Jesse stopped, turned and pulled him to his feet again.

"I can't keep going, Jess," he gasped, collapsing back to one knee. "Save yourself."

"You're going to make it." His face was already ashen from the loss of blood and she had no confidence he would survive, but she had to keep helping him on. She couldn't leave him here. He would be killed.

"I can't go any farther."

Jesse saw the blood covering his shirt and fingers. He wasn't going to make it much further. She looked around quickly. Down the grove she spotted a particularly full tree. Its branches were so thick the tree's trunk was completely obscured. "Come on. We don't have to go far. Just a few feet."

He moaned as she helped him to his feet once more and led him through the tall weeds to the tree. She looked up and down the grove quickly, saw no one, and pulled several of the low hanging branches aside. "Get in there," she ordered.

Todd stumbled through the branches and fell onto the bare ground beneath the tree. Jesse darted in behind him, and from inside the canopy pulled the thick branches together again to hide any sign of their presence. Then she helped him crawl to the trunk, where they sat, backs against the tree, listening for any sound, trying not to breathe heavily and give away their presence.

For several minutes there was only silence, except for the gentle rustle of leaves as an early-afternoon breeze drifted through the huge orchard. Then someone sprinted past the tree, footsteps pounding heavily on soft earth. Jesse followed the sounds as they passed, trying desperately to see who it was, but she could discern nothing except the flash of a shirt through the leaves. And the sound of the footsteps faded until she and Todd were left with nothing but the rustling of leaves again.

She turned toward Todd. He sat with his head back against the trunk, perspiration pouring down his face. Every few seconds his face would contort as the pain from the wound tore through his body.

"We've got to get you to a hospital," she whispered.

He let his chin fall to his chest. "I don't know if I can even get up, much less make it back to the car."

"You can't stay here."

"The people at the store must have seen what happened. They will have called the police. That guy can't—"

Suddenly she thrust a hand over his mouth and put a finger to her lips. He nodded slowly and she pulled her hand away.

For a moment Jesse saw nothing, and then, through the leaves, she caught quick glimpses of someone moving slowly around the perimeter of the branches. A piece of a white shirt through one tiny aperture, a boot through another opening in the leaves close to the ground. Jesse held her breath as the figure moved. It was death and she knew it. And then she lost sight of the figure. There was no longer any movement or sound. But still she held her breath, unable to believe they had escaped a second brush with the assassin.

Thirty seconds passed before she finally let out a

long breath. Instantly the branches parted and Gordon Roth's face, arms, then chest appeared between the leaves. Instinctively Jesse backed up against the trunk. She tried to look away but couldn't. Her eyes were drawn to his hideous smile and for what seemed like forever they stared at each other. Then slowly he raised the gun, aimed and pulled the trigger. As he fired she turned away, closed her eyes and threw her hands before her face, expecting to feel excruciating pain.

Jesse heard the gun explode but felt nothing. The bullet had missed her, slamming into the tree trunk directly above her head, shattering the wood and showering her with splinters. Jesse opened her eyes. Amazingly, Roth was no longer before her, no longer peering at her through the branches. He was gone. Then she heard a frantic physical struggle going on just beyond the branches, and then several gunshots in rapid succession. The bullets zipped angrily through the leaves around them, and she flattened herself against the bare earth.

But this was stupid. They couldn't stay here. Jesse grabbed Todd, helped him to his feet, and pulled him through the thick branches on the opposite side of the tree from where Roth had appeared. She and Todd crashed through the foliage together, headfirst, and fell heavily to the ground, but they were up again instantly, running wildly after two more pops of the gun. They ran past tree after tree, uncertain which way they had come or which way they were going, trying only to put distance between themselves and the assassin.

Suddenly they were at the stone fence again, hurtling it, and then they were sprinting across the gravel toward the rental car. Jesse threw herself into the driver's seat, jammed the key into the ignition and revved the motor as Todd fell onto the passenger seat. But he could not close the door, so weak was his right side, and she had to reach across the seat and slam the door shut for him.

At that moment Gordon Roth leaped the stone fence and ran for the rental car.

"Jesus, there he is!" Todd pointed with his left hand, barely able to gasp the warning. "I don't see a gun, though."

Jesse punched the accelerator, and the rental car skidded across the gravel toward the main road. As tires met blacktop, Roth closed the distance to the car and lunged for Jesse's open window. He grabbed the door with one hand and a fistful of her hair with the other. His weight pulling at her hair slammed her cheek down against the doorframe and pain shot through her face, but she managed to keep her foot on the accelerator. The rental swerved out of control back toward the parking lot, scraping several large stones placed next to the road as barriers. Finally Roth fell away as the rocks tore gaping holes in his clothes and flesh.

"Dammit!" Todd yelled.

"What?" she screamed, jerking the steering wheel to the right to avoid a car bearing down on them. Todd had turned around and was looking into the backseat. "What is it?"

Todd turned back so he was facing forward. He shook his head, then suddenly grabbed his chest and doubled over. "Nothing, Jess. Just get me to a hospital," he groaned. "I think I'm gonna—"

But he didn't finish. The loss of blood and the intense pain finally overwhelmed him, and he slipped into unconsciousness and slumped against the door.

# Chapter 34

Jesse sat next to the bed, head forward, holding Todd's limp hand against her cheek, caressing his fingers. The assassin's bullet had grazed the right lung, causing significant internal bleeding, and the emergency room doctors had decided to operate immediately.

"Jesse!"

Jesse swung around in the chair. David Mitchell stood in the doorway. Instantly she was on her feet. "I swear to God, David, I'll scream. There'll be fifty doctors and nurses in here in two seconds."

"I'm not going to hurt you." He raised his arms above his head in a non-threatening posture and remained at the door. "I promise."

"How did you find me?"

"Simple. Greater Baltimore Medical Center is the closest hospital to the Worthington Valley. I knew you'd bring Todd here. I'm from Baltimore, remember? I checked the emergency room register when I got here, and, sure enough, Todd Colton's name was on it." David glanced at Todd. "I saw him get shot. How is he?"

"He's going into surgery in a few minutes." Her

eyes narrowed. "David, you played me for such a fool. And it's my own fault. I let you. I believed somehow that you couldn't do all this to me. That down deep you cared. That you weren't responsible. I let my emotions get in the way, and because of that, I walked right into that trap out in the Worthington Valley." She shook her head. "Is this another trap, David? Is that trigger-happy friend of yours standing outside? Is he going to appear behind you in the doorway in a second, take aim and finish Todd and me once and for all?"

"No," David said quietly. "Jesse, I've got a lot to tell you and not much time to do it in."

"What do you mean by that?" She touched her cheek and winced. It was swollen and sore from when Roth had grabbed her hair and pulled her face down against the car door.

"It won't be long before that guy who shot Todd gets here."

"Oh, right, you'll be giving him a call, I suppose. You two probably split up to check all the hospitals in the area more efficiently. Let me help you. There are pay phones just down the hall." She sat back down in the chair.

"Jesse, listen to me!" David took a step toward her, then stopped as he saw her recoil. He gritted his teeth in frustration. "All gunshot wounds received by emergency rooms have to be reported immediately to the police." His voice was low and even. "They'll be here soon." This was it. She had to listen to him now or it would be all over. "Jesse, I had my initiation."

"What are you talking about?"

"I'm officially a member of the club now. The other night, Webb, Mohler and another man named Jack Finnerty confirmed everything for me. About how Webb feeds information to Sagamore. About how Coleman is the heir apparent to Webb in the Senate and how they've been influencing that election. They told me everything." David paused. "And they gave me two million dollars." He shook his head. The after-tax amount was already in his account.

"I knew you could be bought." She continued caressing Todd's fingers. "That's why you've helped them track me down, and why you haven't gone to the authorities yet. Because they made you rich. And that's the most important thing in the world to you."

"You're wrong, Jesse. Look, I could go to jail for stealing a significant amount of money from Doub Steel. I didn't do it. It was a setup. But I'd have a hard time proving that."

"Sure you didn't do it."

"I'm not kidding!" David yelled.

"Why are you telling me all this?"

"Because I need you to understand how difficult a position I'm in. Because I need your help."

Jesse gently placed Todd's limp hand down on the bed and turned in her chair toward David. "You're incredible, David Mitchell." She could barely speak. "To save yourself, you gave them information about me that is terribly personal. Something I've kept inside of me since I was seventeen. Something that is going to tear my mother and me apart when she hears about it. And now you want my help." Jesse clenched her hands together to keep them from shaking.

"I have all the information about the abortion, Jesse."

Her eyes flashed to his.

"Everything. I have the file from Rebecca Saunders's office and the information from Edgewood General. It's in my car. It's safe. That's why I called you this morning. To tell you I had it all. Mohler left it in his desk. That's why I wanted you to meet me out at the store. To give it to you. No one is ever going to find out about the attack or the abortion."

Jesse's mouth fell slowly open. "But the assassin."

David shook his head. "I don't know how they found you. I didn't—"

"They found me because you told them where I was." She cut him off abruptly.

"You're wrong, Jesse. I wasn't working with them. I never have been. I've made them believe that to help you. I've never put you in danger. I've put myself in danger to save you. Why do you think the guy missed when you and Todd were under that tree? Christ, I almost got myself killed trying to take that gun away from him."

"That was *you*?" She stood up again.

"Who the hell did you think it was?"

"But what happened?"

"I saw him lean into that tree and I knew he was going after you. So I slammed into him and we struggled. We both had our hands on the gun, but I had mine on the trigger. I kept pulling it to unload the clip. When it was empty, I got away from him and started running."

"That's why he didn't have his gun when I was in the car getting Todd out of there."

David nodded.

"But you led them to Becky Saunders and to Edgewood General." Her voice was suddenly harsh again.

"No. I got the information from Becky's office. But that was to protect you. I'll admit, I wanted to know why you were seeking professional help. But I didn't get it to use against you."

"Then why did you get the information from the hospital?"

"That wasn't me, Jesse."

"It was me," Todd gasped.

Jesse turned back toward Todd, horrified.

"I'm so sorry, Jess." It was difficult for Todd to speak.

"Todd? No!"

"I owed some bad people a lot of money," he whispered. "Money I couldn't come up with. They took care of the situation for me. They were willing to protect me from the people I owed the money to. But if I didn't cooperate they were going to turn me over to them." Todd attempted to sit up but couldn't. "They told me they just wanted information in return for their protection. Information they could use against you. And all the stuff you'd compiled. So I gave them what they wanted. I was desperate. And no one was supposed to get hurt." He closed his eyes tightly. "Then that guy started shooting out at the store. Shooting at me. They lied to me." He shook his head.

"I can't believe it. How did you get everything?"

"I bribed a nurse at the hospital." His voice became

almost inaudible. "I took all the stuff from the bag in the closet at your mother's house too. I knew it was there because I followed you to your mother's after we broke into LFA. After I left you in the parking lot at your apartment."

"So *you* have all the information that was in the closet." Jesse was incredulous.

"I did," Todd admitted. "It was in the bag in the back of your rental when we got to the country store. But someone took it as we were getting out of there. I guess the guy who shot at us at the store got it somehow."

"You attacked my mother?" Jesse's voice began to shake.

"I didn't attack her, I—"

"You could have frightened her to death, literally. And you did all this to me? After all we've been through? As long as we've known each other?" She was so angry she could barely get the words out. "And I risked my life for you." She reached toward Todd.

But David was on her instantly, wrestling her away from the bed.

"Let me go," she screamed.

"No! Forget him. You've got to get out of here. I'm telling you. You've got to call the police. You need their protection."

"Why? It doesn't matter. I don't have anything left that will prove what they've done. The cops will laugh at me."

David pulled Jesse to the door. "Look down."

She glanced at him, puzzled, then followed his finger, which was pointing down at the floor. At her feet lay the bag she had seen Todd throw into the back of the rental at the Towson Motor Inn—the bag she now realized contained the information she had hidden at her mother's house. "But how?"

"I snagged it from your car when you and Todd ran for the woods. Elizabeth told me Todd had informed them he was going to get it last night. I didn't figure Todd would let it out of his sight, but I took a quick look in the back of the car anyway as you all were running for the woods. Sure enough, it was there."

Jesse threw her arms around David's shoulders and hugged him tightly. "I was so wrong about you, David. Can you forgive me?"

"With the right kind of convincing," he said slyly, wrapping his arms around her.

"Excuse me." A doctor stood in the hallway. "We need to get Mr. Colton to surgery right now."

"Sorry, doctor." Jesse pulled David out of the doorway so the medical team could pass. "What do we do now?"

"Go to the authorities."

Jesse shook her head. "What are we going to say? That Carter Webb, one of the most respected and influential men in this country, is at the center of a multimillion-dollar insider trading and fraud scandal? The police and the FBI would just laugh at us."

David pointed at the bag on the floor. "But we have the information you put together."

"It will take time for the authorities to confirm all of that. Days, maybe even weeks. In the meantime, we could be killed."

"They'll give us protection."

Jesse rolled her eyes. "You think Webb couldn't still get to us? Would you really feel safe?"

David's expression became grim. "I guess not. We really can't trust anyone, can we?"

Suddenly Jesse snapped her fingers. "I know who to go to!"

"Who?"

"Come on!" she yelled as she headed down the long corridor.

David picked up the bag full of information and ran after her. He caught up with Jesse at the door to the outside. "Where are we going?"

"Washington."

"Let's take my car," he yelled, as they jogged into the parking lot.

"Fine."

"It's over there." He pointed at the black BMW.

As they reached the car, David slowed down. "Damnit."

"What's wrong?"

"The trunk's been popped." He walked to the back of the BMW and pulled the trunk up. "The information from Becky's office and Edgewood General is gone," he said dejectedly, looking inside.

"What!" Jesse was instantly suspicious again. "Don't do this to me, David," she pleaded, glancing around the lot for signs of trouble.

"Stop it, Jesse." He knew what she was thinking. "Didn't you hear what Todd said back there?" David jerked his thumb over his shoulder at the hospital. "He took the information from Edgewood and stole the information on Webb and the rest of them from your mother's house. You've got to trust me once and for all." David ran his finger over a stain on the car. "Blood," he murmured to himself.

"What?" She was nervous as hell.

"You said something about the assassin not having his gun when you were getting away from the farm store. What did you mean?"

"When I was driving away, the guy ran out of the orchard and tried to stop me. He actually reached inside the car and grabbed my hair. I gunned the car and he fell away. Fortunately, he didn't have his gun."

David nodded. "He must have gotten hurt. That's what this blood is." David pointed at the trunk. "I guess he went through my car after you got away."

"Then why didn't he get the other information?" she asked warily. "What's in the bag you're carrying on your shouler?"

"Because when I took it out of the back of your rental car I didn't have time to get to my car *and* keep track of you. Things were happening pretty fast if you'll remember." He was irritated. She was still questioning him. "So I threw it over the fence into the field and came back for it when I was certain Roth was gone."

Jesse glanced around. "Maybe he took the Edgewood file just now." She nodded at the trunk.

"Not a chance. I made certain I wasn't followed here."

They were silent for a few seconds.

Finally Jesse shook her head. "So after all this, Webb

and Mohler still have the information about my abortion and my mother is going to find out about it anyway."

"Maybe not."

"What do you mean?"

"Get in. I have an idea."

# Chapter 35

Johnny Antolini handed Jesse the glass of water. "Here you go."

"Thanks." She was thirsty and drank the entire glass quickly.

"Do you want more?"

"No thanks."

"Johnny, can you call your people and see if the money is in yet?" David asked impatiently. "The other party is supposed to be sending the money right away."

"Relax." Johnny was starting to get annoyed. He'd done everything David had requested—set up an account at First Maryland Trust for Jesse Hayes without her having to come to the bank to present identification; instructed his people in funds transfer to check the account every five minutes for incoming wires; then left work, met them at his apartment and allowed them to use it as a place to hole up—without asking any questions. He'd done all of that and David was still giving orders. "They'll call when it comes in."

"We need to know the minute it comes in," David urged.

"Easy." Jesse reached over and put a hand on his knee. "Johnny's already done so much." She inhaled deeply. "I still don't understand why we had to get them to send the money."

"Because—" But David didn't finish.

"I don't want to hear anymore," Johnny interrupted. He stood up and headed toward the kitchen of the small apartment.

When Johnny had disappeared around the corner, David took Jesse's hands in his. "Because money is what they understand. You agreed to lifetime employment at Sagamore for two million dollars and the Edgewood file. They agreed to give you those things in exchange for the information you have on them. Adhere strictly to the terms of what's been negotiated. If you showed up before the money had cleared, they'd be suspicious."

As David finished speaking, the phone rang. They heard Johnny answer the call but could not discern specific words.

Moments later he appeared from the kitchen. "The money's in," he said softly.

Todd opened his eyes as the anesthesia finally began to wear away. They had surgically repaired the lung and though he would be months in convalescence, in time he would fully recover. He groaned as he became aware of the nausea and pain.

"Stop your fussing, you big baby." The nurse smiled down at him.

He managed a thin smile. "Hey, that's easy for you to say. You aren't the one with a hole in your lung."

"Yes, I suppose that's true." The nurse glanced over at the old man on the bed adjacent to Todd's. He had just come from throat cancer surgery and would be unconscious for hours.

Quickly she bent down, removed the small .22 caliber pistol from the black bag she had surreptitiously carried into the room, screwed the silencer on the barrel, wrapped a thick towel around the silencer, rose up, aimed carefully at Todd's head and fired three shots into him at point-blank range.

He was dead instantly.

"That's for Harry the Horse," she murmured, dropping the gun back into the bag, zipping it closed, and walking calmly from the room.

# Chapter 36

"I'm frightened." Jesse gripped David's right hand tightly as the BMW rolled up the long driveway of Jack Finnerty's Middleburg farm.

"You have every right to be." David slowed the car down as he guided it around the circle in front of the house. "We both do."

"Don't say that," Jesse implored. She glanced at the huge house and the stables. "God, this place is incredible."

"This is what having money is all about," David sighed. "If you can believe it, this mansion is just a guest house for that place over there." He pointed to a sprawling estate set on a ridge a half mile away. "Finnerty told me his place is over two hundred years old. And that the main house up there on the hill is almost three hundred." During the drive from Washington, David had explained Finnerty's role in the conspiracy. "Here we are." David pulled the BMW to a stop in front of the brick path leading to the home's front entrance.

For several moments they sat in the car, staring at the huge house in silence. Finally, Jesse reached for the door handle. "Time to go," she said with determination. "I want my Edgewood file back."

"Right." David opened his door and slid out from behind the steering wheel. "Remember, Jesse," he whispered over the roof of the car as she stepped out of the passenger side. "As soon as you have that Edgewood stuff, get down."

"Don't worry. I'll be so flat against the floor they'll have to pry me off with a spatula when it's over."

"Good." As David came around the back of the BMW, he motioned subtly at the trunk now tied shut with a piece of twine. Gordon Roth had broken the latch yesterday at the farm store when he'd popped the trunk to find the Edgewood file, hence the twine.

Jesse hadn't noticed David gesture at the trunk. She hadn't seen Gordon Roth standing behind a corner of the stable either.

"Ready?" David asked as he reached her.

"No," she answered honestly. "But I guess that doesn't matter."

"I guess not." He smiled at her reassuringly. "It'll be all right."

Cautiously they walked up the brick path toward the white double doors.

When they had moved inside the house, Roth broke from his hiding place and sprinted toward the BMW. Mitchell had indicated he would leave the information Jesse Hayes had put together in the trunk, convincing her that they shouldn't take it into the house until she had the Edgewood file. Roth smiled as he ran across the neatly manicured lawn. Once he had the information, he was to come directly into the house, per

Webb's orders. There he would kill Jesse Hayes and dispose of her body deep in the Shenandoah Mountains. And life at Sagamore would return to normal.

"Hello, Miss Hayes," Senator Webb said calmly as she and David moved into the large living room. Webb stood directly before the huge stone fireplace which dominated the north wall of the room. "It's such a pleasure to finally meet the woman who's caused me so much aggravation over the last few weeks," he said sarcastically.

Jesse said nothing.

Art Mohler stood to Webb's left and a crisp looking man with red hair Jesse guessed was Finnerty took his place at Webb's right.

Webb turned to Mohler. " Where is Elizabeth?"

"I don't know. She was just here a minute ago."

"Find her. Now."

"Okay." Mohler walked from the living room obediently.

Webb glanced at David. "Do you have the information?"

"It's out in the trunk of my car." He hesitated for a moment. "As we discussed."

Jesse's eyes flashed to David's. "What!"

Roth whipped the knife from his belt and slashed the twine holding down the trunk. Just a few more seconds and they would be home free. He yanked the trunk up.

The FBI agent rose to his knees as the trunk came up. Swiftly he brought the Glock 17 pistol straight up into Roth's face. "Don't move a fucking muscle, my friend."

For a second Roth froze, unable to believe. The agent's face blurred as Roth's blood pressure sky-rocketed and his brain locked. But almost instantly his head cleared and he remembered the deal he had made with himself at the beginning of all this. Never be taken alive. He lunged for the agent.

But the agent had his own deal. Never hesitate. And he unloaded the gun's cartridge into Roth's chest.

Roth staggered to the side of the BMW, keeled over and fell to the driveway, dead.

"Can I have my file from the hospital?" Jesse asked for the second time.

"It's right there on the mantel." Webb motioned over his shoulder. "You can have it—"

"I can't find Elizabeth," Mohler interrupted as he trotted back into the living room. "I've looked everywhere."

Webb's eyes narrowed. Something was wrong. He glanced out the window on the far side of the room and caught a fleeting glimpse of someone in a navy blue windbreaker darting behind a tree. "Jack! Red!" It was a code word Webb and Finnerty had hoped they would never be forced to use.

Instantly, Finnerty pulled a .38 from beneath his suit jacket, leveled it at Mohler and fired. Mohler dropped like a stone, blood pouring from the bullet hole in his temple.

Next Finnerty turned the gun on David and fired.

The bullet ripped through David's left shoulder, sending him cartwheeling back over a couch. He struggled quickly to his feet and staggered into the large formal dining room.

Webb heard screams from outside as FBI agents burst from their hiding places and ran toward the house, reacting instantly to the sound of shots fired. "Forget Mitchell," Webb yelled at Finnerty who was heading toward the dining room to finish off David. "Get the Hayes woman and let's get out of here!"

Finnerty turned and grabbed Jesse roughly by the back of the neck. "Come on!" he snarled, pushing her ahead of them toward the kitchen, then to the large walk-in pantry. When they were all three inside the pantry, Finnerty slammed the door shut, turned to a row of shelves on one wall and pushed.

To Jesse's amazement, the shelves gave way, opening onto a stairway.

Finnerty motioned with the .38 for her to go down the steps. "Don't worry. It's very safe. It's part of the old Underground Railroad used during the Civil War to smuggle slaves out of the South." Finnerty smiled. "And I've maintained it very well." As he kept the .38 pointed at Jesse, he grabbed a flashlight from one of the pantry shelves and handed it to Webb.

Webb flicked on the light, illuminating the steps and the tunnel at the bottom which was easily big enough for them to stand up in. "Go!" Webb yelled at Jesse.

She stumbled down the stairs and into the tunnel, followed by Webb and then Finnerty who closed the false wall behind them. "They'll never find us, Carter."

"I hope to God not."

The three of them moved quickly ahead, guided by the flashlight.

"Where does this come out, Jack?" Webb asked.

"Near an old logging road in the middle of the woods about a half mile from here," Finnerty answered. "I've got a jeep waiting."

Webb laughed to himself. For a moment he had actually felt panic. But how could he have doubted Finnerty? The man was more reliable than Old Faithful. Webb glanced at Jesse as they hurried ahead. "You just had to go to the authorities, didn't you?" he sneered. "Couldn't leave well enough alone, could you?"

She said nothing, her mind focused on when she would make her break. They weren't going to just let her go. That was obvious. They were going to kill her. She swallowed. They might shoot her down here or take her with them for protection until they were miles away. Then shoot her. But she wasn't going down without a fight.

"Did you really think you could beat us?" Webb laughed.

"I—"

"Stop where you are! Put the gun down, Jack!" Elizabeth Gilman stood before them in the tunnel holding a small revolver. The barrel shook wildly even as she clasped the handle tightly with both palms. "Put the gun down!" she screamed again. "I'll shoot you where you stand. I swear to God." Tears streamed down her cheeks.

"Easy, Elizabeth," Webb said gently. "Put the gun down, Jack."

Finnerty allowed the .38 to fall to the dirt floor.

"How did you get in here?" Webb asked icily.

"I overheard you and Jack talking about it one night when we were all here. I saw you go to the pantry and I followed. When you weren't in there, I suspected one of the walls was false. I tried it later that night after you two had come back." She glanced around the tunnel. "I was right."

"You're the one who went to Neil Robinson." Webb's gaze turned steely. "You're the one who had Robinson start looking into the Elbridge Coleman campaign. Aren't you, Elizabeth?"

She nodded. "I couldn't take it anymore, Carter," she whispered hoarsely. "I couldn't take what we were doing. The lies. The deceit. What that Gordon Roth did for us. It was sick." She paused. "And I couldn't take being beholden to you any longer either."

Jesse's eyes widened.

"Why now?" Finnerty asked, teeth clenched.

"Because she's dying," Webb answered, a thin smile coming to his face. "She's only got a few months to live. Lung cancer, isn't it, Elizabeth?"

"Yes. How did you know?"

"I had Roth break into your doctor's office the other night and check your records. I finally realized why you haven't been able to shake that cough. Funny how imminent death has a way of purging the soul," Webb growled. "And it all sounds so heroic. You giving us up. But you took the coward's way out. You only gave Robinson enough to get him started. You knew it would take him time to figure everything out.

That way you wouldn't be around when everything blew up."

"Do you blame me?" There was no remorse in her voice.

"But we found out about Robinson," Webb continued. "And then this one got involved." He pointed at Jesse. "And everything spun out of control, didn't it?"

"Yes," she answered softly.

"You had to take care of her."

"Yes."

"You're the one who called her yesterday when we had her nailed at the motel."

"Yes."

Webb shook his head. "You've enjoyed the success I brought Sagamore. The money, the awards. You're a hypocrite, Elizabeth. A goddamn hypocrite!"

"Get over here with me, Jesse," Elizabeth directed, ignoring Webb's invective.

Jesse darted away from Finnerty and Webb to Elizabeth.

"We're getting out of—"

But before Elizabeth could finish, Webb flicked off the flashlight and the tunnel turned pitch black.

Simultaneously, FBI agents poured through every exterior door of Finnerty's house, systematically fanning out through the massive structure. When the lead agent signaled that the mansion had been secured, Senator Walker moved quickly up the brick path escorted by five agents. In the living room he found Art Mohler dead on the floor and David Mitchell sprawled on the couch, blood staining his blue shirt and smearing the manila folder on his lap. "What the hell happened?" Walker demanded of the lead agent.

"I—"

"Webb saw someone outside," Mitchell interrupted, his voice barely audible. He gazed at the lead agent. "Where's Jesse? And Webb and Finnerty?"

The agent shook his head. "I don't know. They aren't in the house."

"What?" David asked angrily. "How could they just walk out of here with her? Didn't you guys have the place surrounded?"

"No one came out of the house," the agent assured David. "And they aren't inside. We've searched everywhere. We're getting the dogs brought in, but that will take a few minutes."

"Dammit!" Walker yelled. "I knew we shouldn't have done it this way." He picked up a picture from a table beside the couch and smashed it in the fireplace. He pointed a finger at David. "When you and Jesse came to me yesterday and suggested this I knew it was wrong. I knew we should have just let the FBI round these people up."

"No," David said quietly. "Jesse wanted this back." He nodded at the hospital folder in his lap. "She was afraid it would get lost in the chaos."

"No folder can be important enough to lead to all this," Walker said, grim faced.

"I didn't think so either," David said. "But I was wrong. It meant everything to her."

"Mr. Mitchell, I suggest we get you to a hospital." The agent pointed toward David's bloody shoulder.

He shook his head. "I'm not going anywhere until I know where Jesse is."

Instinctively, Jesse flung herself to the tunnel's dirt floor as Elizabeth fired in the direction of Webb and Finnerty. She heard a scream from one of the men and then several thunderous reports and flashes of light from Finnerty's .38. Elizabeth went down, a hole in her heart.

Jesse jumped to her feet and moved into the darkness, feeling her way along the wall as best she could, going as fast as she dared. Behind her she heard groans and someone getting to their feet. Then another shot, and another. The bullets hissed past, caroming off the walls, echoing evilly in the blackness. How many shots in total from the .38 now? Five or six?

And then there was a tiny ray of feeble light ahead. She moved faster. The other end of the tunnel. Suddenly her shin struck a wooden step and she screamed in pain. But there was no time to worry about the pain. She could hear someone running toward her.

She scampered up the stairway toward the thin stream of light, came to a set of small double doors and burst through them, tumbling onto the thick cover of leaves on the forest floor. The footsteps were coming up the stairs fast. She scrambled to her feet and raced toward the jeep twenty feet away.

"Stop or I'll shoot!" Webb yelled, standing on the top step, holding Finnerty's .38 with both hands.

Jesse stopped still, five feet from the jeep. "Dammit," she whispered to herself.

"Get your hands up!" Webb screamed. Perhaps

Jesse had gotten Elizabeth's gun, Webb suddenly realized as he moved toward her.

She turned slowly around, hands in the air.

Webb stopped a few feet away, gasping for breath. He glanced at the jeep. "I was thinking of having you drive." His eyes narrowed. "But that would be stupid. Never put someone else in control." He brought the .38 up and pointed it at her chest.

Jesse realized Webb was going to fire. That this was it. She lunged at him and watched in horror as his finger depressed the trigger and the hammer released. But there was only a click. No blast from the barrel. The gun was empty.

And then she was on him, adrenaline coursing through her body like floodwater through a dam. She knocked him to the ground, smashed the gun from his hand and fell on top of him, pinning his face to the leaves. But he was a large man, still in good shape despite his age, and he tossed Jesse away like a rag doll. He struggled to his feet and staggered toward the jeep.

Jesse stuck her leg in Webb's path and tripped him. And she was on him again, just trying to keep him pinned to the ground. Suddenly she heard the dogs on scent, barking and baying as they tore through the tunnel leading the agents to Webb.

Webb heard the pack too. He moaned as he threw Jesse off one more time, but she grabbed at his legs as he tried to stand and pulled him to the ground once more. Now he was breathing hard, laboring against fatigue. He kicked her in the cheek and crawled over the leaves to the jeep, pulling himself up, struggling with the door handle.

The German shepherds poured out of the tunnel entrance like lava erupting from a volcano. The agents screamed commands as they too emerged from the blackness and in no time the dogs were on Webb, pulling him from behind the jeep's steering wheel, ripping and tearing at his arms and legs. He screamed for mercy. And then it was over.

# Epilogue

David placed both hands on the banister and watched the turquoise water roll gently up to meet the white sand time after time beneath the late afternoon sun. The view from his tenth floor room overlooking the Caribbean was breathtaking. "Carter Webb won't be awarding black-budget contracts anytime soon."

"I guess not," Jesse said softly as she gazed out over the placid sea.

Webb, Coleman, Rhodes and Pierce had all received long prison sentences for their roles in the conspiracy. Ted Cowen had hanged himself in his cell before the government had a chance to try him. And Finnerty had died in the tunnel—as had Elizabeth.

Jesse shook her head. "You really threw me for a loop at Finnerty's house."

"What do you mean?" David asked.

"When Webb mentioned how you had called him about leaving the file in the trunk of the BMW."

"Oh."

"I swear, David, for a second I thought—"

"I just wanted to make sure Webb thought I was working for him."

"It scared me to death."

They stared at the ocean in silence for a few moments.

"How's your mother?" David put his hand on Jesse's, caressing her fingers lightly.

Jesse's face brightened. "Great. Senator Walker found a very nice assisted-care living facility for her in Baltimore County. She moved in last week."

"That was fast. The admissions process to get into those places can be pretty drawn out sometimes."

Jesse tried to hide a smile. "I think maybe he used his influence a little."

"Aha," David said, forcing a solemn look to his face. "The truth will out." He broke into a smile. "The senator probably used his influence to find a government program to pay for it all too."

"No comment."

David shook his head and laughed out loud. "Well, after all, Walker owes you his political career so it makes sense that he would help you as much as he could. He certainly wouldn't have won reelection without you."

"I guess that's true." She took David's hand in hers. "Not without you either."

"I helped. You did the hard part."

Jesse squeezed David's hand and laughed.

"What?" A puzzled expression crossed David's face. "What is it?"

"I was on the phone with Senator Walker before I came to your room."

"And?"

"He wants me to think about running for state

senator from Maryland in the next election. He said he would support me one hundred percent. Help me with the campaign and all. He thinks I have a future in politics. Someone at a political consulting firm told him I came across well on television during the hearings and the trials." She laughed. "Can you imagine? Me in politics?"

"Yes I can. You'd be great. You'd be a breath of fresh air."

She turned toward him. "I don't know." She saw he was serious and was suddenly embarrassed. "Senator Walker told me that GEA wil be delivering the first fifty A-100s to the Navy this week." She changed the subject. "He was disappointed."

David nodded. "I'm sure."

They lapsed into silence again, lost in their own thoughts.

"So what about you, David?" Jesse finally spoke up. "What are you going to do now that it's all over?"

"I don't know." David glanced at the horizon. "I won freedom in return for my testimony, but I doubt too many places will hire me now. Of course, I did get to keep my two million." He looked at her slyly.

"What?" She let his hand go.

David nodded. "I told you Sagamore paid me two million dollars immediately after my little initiation. I got to keep that as part of the deal. Of course, it only comes to about a million after taxes."

Jesse brought both hands to her mouth, then poked him playfully in the ribs. "You jerk. And I was worried about you. And you made me pay for my own room down here." She went to jab him again.

But he intercepted her wrist and pulled her arms around him, then put a finger beneath her chin as he pulled her close. "Well, you'd have a million too if you hadn't been so honest and turned over your Sagamore money to the Feds."

"I couldn't keep it. It wouldn't have been right."

David gazed at her. He had asked her to stay with him, but she'd refused, opting for her own room instead. The two days they had spent in the island paradise so far had been very romantic, but he was still saying goodnight to her outside her room. "I was always intending to pay for your room, anyway."

"I see." She gazed back at him for a few moments, then brought her hands to his cheeks and kissed him deeply. Finally, she pulled back. "Tell you what. Take me to a nice dinner tonight. Then maybe we'll stop by the front desk afterward. And I'll check out." She smiled provocatively. "That is, as long as you know of another place I can stay."

# Prologue

## *November, 1963*

Her real name was Mary Thomas, which she knew wasn't a tag likely to attract the eye of a fast-track Hollywood producer with only time in his day for a cursory scan of a casting sheet. So now she went by Andrea Sage.

A Manhattan native, Andrea fled New York City after completing her studies at Columbia University, intent upon escaping a tyrannical father obsessed with the idea of her following his footsteps onto Wall Street. She had no desire to commit herself to a lifetime of dealing stocks and bonds just days after finishing college. So the morning after graduation, she slipped out of her parents' Upper East Side penthouse, emptied the trust account her grandparents had set up for her on her tenth birthday, caught a taxi to La Guardia Airport, and flew to Los Angeles in search of stardom on the silver screen. Andrea was young, beautiful, and at the tender age of twenty-one, ready to conquer the world.

Six months had elapsed since her freedom ride to

the West Coast aboard the Pan Am jet and things hadn't progressed as quickly as she had anticipated. Because of her beauty, she'd landed a few bit parts in several low-budget films; however, the roles were nothing to write home about—and she still hadn't. Her mother had no idea where her only child had gone and Andrea was beginning to feel guilty about not at least calling to say she was safe.

An unusually cool and rainy autumn quickly transformed Los Angeles from sunny sanctuary to a depressing land of exile. So on a whim, to try to forget about the looming inevitability of crawling back to Manhattan to face her triumphant father, Andrea took a few days' vacation from her waitressing job at the Beverly Hills Bistro and bought a plane ticket to Texas. The trip would serve as a much needed respite from her cramped studio apartment overlooking the back of a Chinese restaurant, a chance to explore another area of the country, and an opportunity to see this man who had so captivated the public's attention.

Andrea squinted through the lens of the Bell & Howell movie camera she had purchased yesterday, practicing with it before the event began. She stood near a small tree, a few feet away from a reflecting pool retaining wall, and aimed to the right of the crowd milling about in front of the tall building on the other side of the intersection. Then she panned to the left and followed the pavement as it snaked away toward the triple underpass at the far end of the plaza. This would be the motorcade's route.

As she gazed at the underpass, Andrea sensed a buzz ripple through the onlookers. She glanced to her right, and through the crowd, saw flashes of the motorcade approaching. Once more she aimed up Elm

Street at the people standing in front of the building across the intersection. This time the movie camera shook slightly. She took a deep breath to calm an inexplicable uneasiness, then began filming as the sleek dark blue, open-top limousine made a slow sweeping turn to the left off Houston Street and cruised into her field of vision. She focused on the man in the back of the vehicle, marveling at his overpowering charisma, obvious even through the lens. As the limousine coasted past her, she began to move alongside it, able to shoot extraordinarily clear footage of the man because she was so close to him as he waved from the open vehicle. For some reason the Secret Service had been lax about security along the route that day.

Moments later Andrea heard a loud pop, like a firecracker exploding somewhere in the plaza, followed quickly by a second one. Concurrent with the second pop, the man in the back of the limousine hunched forward, his elbows up and out and hands to his neck. Still filming, Andrea continued to half walk, half run along Elm Street. She was vaguely aware of moving past a little girl wearing a red skirt and white sweater, who had run past her only moments before. She also sensed a sudden panic in the crowd, as the understanding that something terrible was unfolding began to set in. At the sound of the third shot, people began to take cover and Andrea stopped moving.

Then the fourth shot came. More of a blast this time, it was definitely louder and closer. Instantly the man's head snapped back toward Andrea and a fine red mist sprayed the air, forming a crimson halo around the glossy limousine. The man's body slumped to the left, his brain exposed and bloody.

At once people were screaming and running in all

directions, but Andrea wasn't sucked into the flood of panic. She calmly kept filming, detached from the horrible events rapidly unfolding around her as if the lens somehow protected her. As Andrea watched, the man's wife climbed out onto the limousine's trunk and reached for a piece of her husband's head, which had been torn away by the killing shot. But she was quickly pushed back into her seat by a Secret Service agent as the vehicle sped away toward Parkland Hospital. Andrea followed the limousine until it was gone, then refocused on the spot where the vehicle had been at the moment the red mist sprayed in the air. Behind that spot people were sprinting toward a grassy area and a fence beyond.

Suddenly everything went dark. Andrea panned up, and for a moment the entire lens was consumed by an angry face. Then two large hands tore the camera from her grasp and pushed her roughly to the ground.

A sharp pain shot up her back. "You have no right to treat me that way!" she screamed, gazing up at her attacker.

"I have every right," the man snarled. "Now get out of here."

"Give me my movie camera!" she insisted.

"I said, get out of here!"

Andrea jumped to her feet and made a grab for the camera, but the man easily repelled her with a thick forearm to the chest and she tumbled to the ground once more.

"I'll give you one last chance," he yelled viciously. "Leave or I'll arrest you."

One look directly into the man's steely gray eyes and Andrea's confident sense of surreal detachment evaporated, replaced by the make-your-skin-crawl, get-the-hell-out-of-here sensation that she had stumbled upon a hornets' nest. She realized it would be pointless to protest any longer, so she turned and scrambled over the grass on her hands and knees, then staggered to her feet and sprinted wildly away through the chaos. When she finally dared look back over her shoulder, the man who had brutally confiscated her movie camera—and the film of President Kennedy's assassination—was gone.

# Chapter 1

*November, 1998*

Trading floors at New York City's largest and most powerful brokerage houses can be intimidating environments. The cavernous rooms are often raucous, typically devoid of warm and nurturing decor and always staffed by aggressive, impatient opportunists buying and selling massive amounts of stocks, bonds, and other financial securities with house money. These opportunists sit side by side at long narrow desks resembling lunch counters. In front of them are the two primary tools of their business—phone banks and computer screens constantly relaying market information. Traders base their split-second investment decisions on this information as well as the tips they receive over their many phone lines. Sometimes they remain within their capital limits—predetermined management-imposed dollar amounts they may commit to transactions—and sometimes they don't. Caffeine is a trader's only dependable ally, while ulcers and the fortieth birthday are mortal enemies. On these floors tempers flare constantly, physical confrontations occur more frequently than most would admit, stress is constant, and privacy is nonexistent. It is a godawful career, except for one thing. Traders can make more money in a year than many people can in a lifetime.

Cole Egan scrutinized his three computer screens for any hint of what was going on at the Federal Reserve's Open Market Committee meeting in Washington; however, the markets were dead calm. But that would change in a heartbeat and all hell would break loose if the Fed officials suddenly exited the meeting and made what—up until yesterday—Cole had considered an unexpected announcement. An announcement that could send his huge government securities portfolio plummeting into a death spiral.

Every six weeks the chairman and district governors of the world's most powerful central bank convened behind the tightly shut doors of an ornate Washington conference room to determine the general course of interest rates in the United States. At the conclusion of most meetings, the Fed took no action and interest rates continued to fluctuate with supply and demand as traders bought and sold bonds and money market instruments for their clients and firms. But if the Fed announced new targets, interest rates spiked or fell to those levels almost instantly. The Fed was that powerful.

In front of Cole lay two keyboards. With them he could access Reuters, Bloomberg, and the Internet—all the real-time information services a nineties trader required. However, nothing in those databases could give him what he really needed right now, which was a listening device planted inside the Federal Reserve conference room. But as far as he knew, no one had that.

Cole gazed out the trading floor window at the skyscraper across Fifth Avenue. He didn't allow others to see it, but the waiting was killing him. Yesterday, lower-level Fed officials had sent subtle signals to the market that the committee might raise interest rates to head off a sudden spurt of inflation. For the last month Cole had been betting that the Fed wouldn't raise interest rates at this meeting and had structured his portfolio accordingly. If the Fed raised rates even slightly, his portfolio could lose millions of dollars in seconds because he would be stuck holding securities earning a rate of return which was less than what the market was offering. And there was no chance to get out at this point because the market had already moved against him in anticipation of the Fed announcement. If he sold now, he'd be selling at a huge loss.

Cole took a deep breath. If the announcement he was dreading came and his portfolio tanked badly, senior executives sitting in plush offices on the top floor of Gilchrist's world headquarters building would hit the roof, right before they sprinted down to the trading floor to rip his heart out. There would be no compassion from them, only punishment. Cole shut his eyes tightly. Even with the chaos constantly swirling around him, trading could be a lonely business sometimes.

Gilchrist & Company was a powerful brokerage house, rivaling other preeminent firms such as Goldman Sachs, Morgan Stanley, and Merrill Lynch in its ability to raise capital for corporations and governments around the world. It also rivaled those firms in its ability to trade stocks and bonds for its own account and earn billions of dollars each year in profits. To ensure its proprietary trading success, Gilchrist hired only the best and brightest individuals, constantly snatching top-performing people away from other Wall Street firms or cherry-picking the cream of the crop from the nation's most revered business schools. Compensation packages for those lucky few were lucrative—millions each year if you were successful—but there was a catch. You had to consistently make money for the firm, and lots of it. One losing year was tolerable—barely. Two in a row and you consumed your morning coffee and bagel at the unemployment office.

During his first three years on Gilchrist's trading floor, Cole had enjoyed reasonable success buying and selling government securities with the firm's capital. He had hit no home runs during that time, but had smacked plenty of singles and doubles—trading floors are rife with sports analogies—which was code for strong but not outstanding performances. As a result, he'd been paid solid, though not earth-shattering, year-end bonuses. Cole's January bonus checks were made out for several hundred thousand dollars. Not close to the tens of millions the home-run hitters earned, but he was happy nonetheless. After all, six-figure checks were nothing to sneeze at. Particularly for a guy from the blue-collar side of a small, upper-Midwest town on a lake.

Unfortunately, Cole's performance had taken a turn for the worse. Last year he hadn't been able to buy a hit and had lost twenty million dollars of the firm's money. Now he was approaching the end of an even worse year. He was on the bubble and everyone on the trading floor knew it.

"How you doing there, sport?" Lewis Gebauer asked smugly, ogling a young woman wearing a short, tight skirt, who was walking past him.

"Fine, Lewis," Cole replied curtly, glancing quickly at Gebauer, then back at the computer screens.

Gebauer was grossly overweight, almost bald, sported pallid skin after years of not seeing the sun, and wore ties and shirts permanently stained by the fat-laden foods he consumed in huge quantities. Despite his offensive physical appearance, he had deluded himself into believing that he was quite a ladies man and kept a close eye on any woman who visited the trading floor. He was insufferably obnoxious and universally disliked, but he traded government bonds with startling success. In the last five years he had earned over three hundred million dollars for Gilchrist & Company, buying and selling the U.S. Government's thirty-year debt obligation. As thanks for his performance and to make certain he wasn't lured away by a competitor, Gilchrist senior executives had bonused him sixty of that three hundred million. Gebauer lived in an opulent stone mansion in Connecticut with his third wife, a twenty-six-year-old platinum blonde he'd met at a bar in Manhattan and married two days later, and to whom he wasn't faithful. She hardly cared about his infidelity with a long line of paid escorts because she had only married him for the ultimate payday, which would come either through his death or their divorce.

Cole had been forced to sit next to Gebauer since his first day on the trading floor and had grown to detest the man just as everyone else did.

"I'm doing fine, Lewis," Cole repeated.

"Really?" Gebauer asked sarcastically, gumming an unlit Cuban cigar from a box he had smuggled into New York through Kennedy Airport after a trip to Paris. "That's not what I hear." Gebauer enjoyed kicking people when they were down. It was entertainment for him.

Cole recognized that Gebauer was bored with the afternoon lull and was simply trying to start an argument in order to make the time pass more quickly. In these situations it was sometimes effective to launch a preemptive strike. "I'm surprised you can hear anything with all of that protein sprouting from your ears."

Two traders on the other side of the desk snickered loudly at the ear-hair crack. Cole was fast with a comeback, and not someone you dueled carelessly.

"I hear you've got a big fat mortgage on that Upper West Side penthouse condominium you bought two years ago," Gebauer sneered, adding specifics to his verbal attack. He had no intention of backing down. "And I hear you haven't gotten a bonus since George Bush was president," he exaggerated. "Thanks to that, you're way behind on your Mount Everest-size mortgage." Gebauer's pulse quickened as he recounted the information recently conveyed to him by the man with an ugly scar cutting through his left cheek.

Cole tried hard to focus on the computer screens and ignore Gebauer, but the numbers in front of him blurred as the question raced through his mind: How the hell was Gebauer aware of the bonus and the mortgage? Only Gilchrist's top executives knew he'd been shut out of the bonus pool last year, and he hadn't told anyone on the trading floor he even owned an apartment, much less a penthouse with a huge mortgage. He stole another glance at Gebauer. Several times over the last few days, papers on Cole's desk seemed to have been rearranged when he returned to the trading floor after procuring one of the six Diet Cokes he drank daily. Surely, he realized, Gebauer must be responsible.

"Young blood with the sabre tongue isn't talking much now," Gebauer crowed.

One of the traders on the other side of the desk stood up and stretched casually, using the opportunity to glance over the computer monitors and phone banks at Cole to judge for himself whether Gebauer's mortgage missile was on target—trading floors thrive on gossip—but there was no way to tell for certain. Cole's face remained impassive.

"And I hear your honey has the same problem I do, lover boy," Gebauer continued, full of confidence now that Cole had gone silent. "I hear she likes girls, if you get my drift," he said, smiling lewdly.

Cole's right hand slowly contracted into a fist. He could send Gebauer into next week with one right to the jaw and probably earn a standing ovation from everyone on the floor. He swiveled in his seat, as if to take a swing, just as one of his ten phone lines began blinking. He stared at the blinking light for a few moments before finally unclenching his hand.

Forget Gebauer, he told himself. The guy isn't worth it. Besides, he'll be dead of a heart attack soon. Cole punched the blinking line instead of Gebauer and grabbed the receiver. If there really was a God, that heart attack would take place right here on the trading floor so he could watch it. "Hello."

"Who is this?" The voice was cold.

"Cole Egan," he answered, forcing himself to be cordial. Gilchrist senior executives sometimes buzzed the trading floor just to see how quickly calls were being answered.

"What is your middle name, Mr. Egan?"

Cole was instantly annoyed by what he considered a ludicrous question. "Who the hell wants to know?" In the background he heard someone shout a warning about an imminent announcement by the Federal Reserve and pressed his palm over the ear not covered by the phone to drown out the growing din. "Who are you?"

"Tell me your middle name," the voice insisted.

The noise level on the floor rose to a dull roar as a senior Fed official appeared on the many television monitors positioned around the Gilchrist trading floor. Cole hesitated, torn between the chaos erupting around him and something in the voice at the other end of the line.

"Your middle name," the voice demanded.

"Sage," Cole snapped, impatient to cut off the caller. Like any good trader he sensed a tempest bearing down on his portfolio and knew he should be directing his full attention to that right now, not the call. "What's it to you?"

"I'm an acquaintance of your father."

The Fed announcement burst like water through a cracking dam and bedlam exploded as traders shouted orders simultaneously over multiple phones, desperately attempting to take advantage of, or protect themselves from, the interest rate increase suddenly imposed by the central bank. However, Cole heard none of it. He had blocked out everything except the icy voice that had mentioned his father.

"I have bad news for you," the voice continued. There was no sympathy in the tone. "Your father is dead."

The news hit Cole like an avalanche, but he gave no indication of that to the individual at the other end of the line. "I can't say I'm overcome with grief," he offered defiantly. He had only seen his father a few times in his life, having been raised by an aunt and uncle after his mother's death. He had believed all his life that his father never wanted him.

"I don't care whether you grieve or not," the voice retorted indifferently. "My job was to deliver this message for the agency, and to deliver an envelope to you which is now out front at the reception desk. Goodbye, Mr. Egan." The line went dead.

"Hey, Egan!" one of the traders on the other side of the desk yelled. "There's a guy from Merrill Lynch on line two. He says he wants to buy some of your five-year paper. He says you're probably ready to sell it at this point."

"And Nicki's on line three!" another trader hollered.

For a moment Cole didn't respond. He shouldn't leave the desk right now, not seconds after the Fed announcement, but he had to. The envelope out front probably involved his father, and anything having to do with his father took precedence over anything else.

"Tell both of them I'll call back!" Cole yelled over his shoulder, as he dropped the receiver on the desk and sprinted through the chaos toward the reception area outside the wooden doors at the far end of the room. He dodged a young assistant obediently bringing coffee to the junk bond traders, raced the last few yards to the doors, burst into the reception area, and stopped short. There were always visitors milling about here and he scanned every face carefully, trying to memorize distinctive features of each one. Finally, he moved toward the reception desk and the noise from the trading floor subsided as the door swung shut behind him.

"Hi, Cole." Anita Petrocelli smiled cheerfully at him

from behind the large desk. She was a young Queens native whose infatuation with Cole was almost as obvious as the dark mole above her upper lip. He was tall and broad with rugged features—a strong nose, strong chin, and sculpted cheeks. His wavy, jet-black hair contrasted starkly with his neatly pressed, white cotton dress shirt and matched his onyx cufflinks perfectly. His hair was long on top, but short on the sides and in the back—not the more conservative style worn by most of the men who prowled Gilchrist's trading floor. His dimpled smile was alluring and mysterious, as if he was hiding something. The three tiny holes in his left earlobe provided a tiny window into a rebellious adolescence. And his large, steel-gray eyes, surrounded by long thick lashes, were the sexiest she had ever seen.

He had taken her to lunch several times, just to be friendly, and through their conversations in the more relaxed atmosphere away from work, she had come to know of his total abhorrence of conformity simply for conformity's sake, and his love of being different simply to be different. She had also come to know of his considerable appetite for risk. He was constantly wagering on something during lunch—how many minutes until the entree would be served, which patrons would be the first to leave, or who in the entire restaurant would next use their napkin. The stakes didn't really matter, and he never took her money if he won the bet. He simply loved to take a risk. She found this devil-may-care attitude electrifying, as did other women at Gilchrist, she knew. He was quite a package.

For Anita, the best thing about Cole was that he had made it to his twenty-ninth birthday single. There were rumors that he had a steady girlfriend, but no proof, and without a gold band on his left hand's ring finger, she considered him her primary target. Maybe even if he wore a ring, she admitted, slightly ashamed of herself. She had made no secret of her attraction to him; however, he had always told her she was too good for him. She understood this response as his way of letting her down gently, but she continued to flirt with him anyway because she believed that if you kept hammering long enough, the wall might finally crumble.

"What can I do for you, Cole?" she asked in her sexiest voice, batting her eyes playfully.

"Is there anything out here with my name on it?"

"Yeah, me." She placed her elbows on the desktop, rested her chin on the back of her hands, and batted her eyes again. "I went down to Greenwich Village and had your initials tattooed on a very private part of my anatomy last—"

"I'm not kidding around, Anita," Cole interrupted.

"Boy, you're serious this afternoon." Her smile disappeared as she scanned the desk quickly. Usually he gave her that dimpled smile she adored and a compliment on her hair or her outfit. "Oh, yeah, here's something." She handed him a large brown envelope with his name neatly typed across the front.

"Who gave this to you?" Cole wanted to know.

Anita shrugged. "I don't know. A messenger must have left it on my desk while I was using the restroom. I didn't notice it was here until you said something."

Cole turned abruptly and headed toward a small conference room off to the side of the reception area before she had finished speaking. She pushed out her lower lip, pouting. Usually he was so polite.

Cole moved inside the conference room, closed the

door, ripped open the envelope, and poured out its contents—a typed note, an official-looking document, and a small key that clattered onto the tabletop. He picked up the key, shoved it into his pocket, then read the note. It made two requests. First, he was to take out an obituary in the *New York Times* marking his father's death. Second, he was to proceed immediately to the Chase Bank branch a few blocks down Fifth Avenue from the Gilchrist building and retrieve the contents of a safe-deposit box the key would open.

Cole picked up the official-looking document that had been inside the envelope. It was a death certificate with his father's name on it. Jim Egan had appeared unannounced at Gilchrist's reception desk six months ago. It was the first time Cole had seen his father since high school graduation. The elder Egan had taken Cole to lunch—a sandwich, chips, and a Coke at a delicatessen on 47th Street. The conversation at the deli had been full of uncomfortable pauses and there were no great revelations as to the elder Egan's nearly lifelong absence. After lunch, the encounter had culminated with a strange, forced handshake in front of the Gilchrist building. Cole had offered a tour of the trading floor, but his father had adamantly refused, then taken off down Fifth Avenue without another word, disappearing into the lunch crowd hurrying over the sidewalk.

Cole stared at the death certificate. Christ, if he had just known that would be the last time they would ever see each other, he might have pushed harder for answers to the questions plaguing him for so long. And he might have said something to his father that mattered.